Praise for F

The Century trilogy

'The master storyteller Ken Follett knits together British, American, German and Russian points of view from the start to the end of the First World War into a fascinating and remarkably fertile tapestry of society and politics'   *The Times*

'Few works set out with such a grand concept as Ken Follett's new Century trilogy, but part one suggests that the series will be one of the literary masterpieces of our time . . . while grand events and themes are at the core of the novel, it is the richness of the characters and the intertwining of their often disparate stories that steal the show'   *Sunday Times*

'An extraordinary achievement'   A. N. Wilson, *Reader's Digest*

'This is hi-octane storytelling all the more powerful because the story it tells is, mostly, true. Follett's command of the vast forces he unleashes is as impressive as the battle strategies of his generals, and in many cases more so . . . overall Follett is masterly in conveying so much drama and historical information so vividly'   *Scotsman*

'Follett has managed to write an accessible and fascinating page-turner that leaves the reader wanting more, at the same time as staying true to history'   *Sunday Business Post*

'He's pulled it off again with *Fall of Giants*: it's classic Follett with the brewing cataclysm of war given a human angle'

Sunday Express

'An epic saga on a grand scale. Spiked with romance and intrigue . . . This involving historical saga is the perfect read for long winter evenings'   *Choice Magazine*

'The Follett trilogy's big start will have fans yearning for more . . . A powerful drama that rattles along at top speed. It's pacy, absorbing and packed with historical detail'   *Daily Express*

'This extraordinary novel spans a tumultuous time with effortless grace and style, making you laugh and cry with each turn of history, as you see the personal within the global. Follett is a master of storytelling'   *Waterstone's Books Quarterly*

'Follett's imagination falls on the First World War and the Russian Revolution in this kaleidoscope of a book . . . Follett travels a passionate path, marked by danger, romance and treachery. Like all great novels, the story leaves unforgettable memories'   *Oxford Times*

The Pillars of the Earth

'A historical saga of such breadth and density ... Follett succeeds brilliantly in combining hugeness and detail to create a novel imbued with the rawness, violence and blind faith of the era' *Sunday Express*

'A highly enjoyable tale ... this book evokes its period brilliantly' *Sunday Times*

'Enormous and brilliant ... this mammoth tale seems to touch all human emotion – love and hate, loyalty and treachery, hope and despair. See for yourself. This is truly a novel to get lost in' *Cosmopolitan*

World Without End

'Where Follett excels is in telling a yarn. There is sufficient intrigue here, enough turns within double-twists, to hold readers through all the 91 chapters ... you won't be able to put it down' *Independent*

'This is a huge book in every way, sweeping and yet detailed, a powerful story packed with superbly drawn characters and which brilliantly evokes the period that saw the devastating Black Death plague and the birth of modern medicine' *Choice Magazine*

'Follett's storytelling skills keep you compulsively turning the pages to the satisfactory ending of good triumphant over evil' *Daily Mail*

'Perfect for long, rainy autumn days, immersed as it is in an incredibly detailed medieval city and the lives within . . . You live and breathe the characters from their childhood and, in some cases, share the secrets they're all so desperately hiding'
Daily Express

'Follett takes you to a time long past and does so with brio and razor-sharp storytelling skills. He has crafted an epic tale in which you will willingly lose yourself for quite a spell'
Scotland on Sunday

'*World Without End* won't disappoint if you like a hefty plot'
Observer

TRIPLE

Ken Follett was twenty-seven when he wrote *Eye of the Needle*, an award-winning thriller that became an international bestseller. After writing several more successful thrillers he surprised everyone with *The Pillars of the Earth*, about the building of a cathedral in the Middle Ages, which continues to captivate millions of readers all over the world. The long-awaited sequel, *World Without End*, was a number one bestseller in the United States, Great Britain, Germany, Italy, Spain and France. His most recent novels are *Fall of Giants* and *Winter of the World*, in the epic Century trilogy.

Also by Ken Follett

The Modigliani Scandal

Paper Money

Eye of the Needle

The Key to Rebecca

The Man From St Petersburg

On Wings of Eagles

Lie Down with Lions

The Pillars of the Earth

Night Over Water

A Dangerous Fortune

A Place Called Freedom

The Third Twin

The Hammer of Eden

Code to Zero

Jackdaws

Hornet Flight

Whiteout

World Without End

Fall of Giants

Winter of the World

KEN FOLLETT

TRIPLE

PAN BOOKS

First published in Great Britain 1979 by Macdonald General Books

This edition published 2013 by Pan Books
an imprint of Pan Macmillan, a division of Macmillan Publishers Limited
Pan Macmillan, 20 New Wharf Road, London N1 9RR
Basingstoke and Oxford
Associated companies throughout the world
www.panmacmillan.com

ISBN 978-1-4472-2159-3

5 7 9 8 6

A CIP catalogue record for this book is available from the British Library.

Typeset by SetSystems Ltd, Saffron Walden, Essex
Printed and bound by CPI Group (UK) Ltd, Croydon, CR0 4YY

Visit **www.panmacmillan.com** to read more about all our books
and to buy them. You will also find features, author interviews and
news of any author events, and you can sign up for e-newsletters
so that you're always first to hear about our new releases.

It must be appreciated that the only difficult part of making a fission bomb of some sort is the preparation of a supply of fissionable material of adequate purity; the design of the bomb itself is relatively easy . . .

— *Encyclopedia Americana*

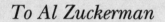
To Al Zuckerman

TRIPLE

PROLOGUE

THERE WAS a time, just once, when they were all together.

They met many years ago, when they were young, before all *this* happened; but the meeting cast shadows far across the decades.

It was the first Sunday in November, 1947, to be exact; and each of them met all the others – indeed, for a few minutes they were all in one room. Some of them immediately forgot the faces they saw and the names they heard spoken in formal introductions. Some of them actually forgot the whole day; and when it became so important, twenty-one years later, they had to pretend to remember; to stare at blurred photographs and murmur 'Ah, yes, of course,' in a knowing way.

This early meeting is a coincidence, but not a very startling one. They were mostly young and able; they were destined to have power, to take decisions, and to make changes, each in their different ways, in their different countries; and those people often meet in their youth at places like Oxford University. Furthermore, when all this happened, those who were not involved initially were sucked into it just because they had met the others at Oxford.

However, it did not seem like an historic meeting at the time. It was just another sherry party in a place where there were too many sherry parties (and, undergraduates would add, not enough sherry). It was an uneventful occasion. Well, almost.

Al Cortone knocked and waited in the hall for a dead man to open the door.

The suspicion that his friend was dead had grown to a conviction in the past three years. First, Cortone had heard that Nat Dickstein had been taken prisoner. Towards the end of the war, stories began to circulate about what was happening to Jews in the Nazi camps. Then, at the end, the grim truth came out.

On the other side of the door, a ghost scraped a chair on the floor and padded across the room.

Cortone felt suddenly nervous. What if Dickstein were disabled, deformed? Suppose he had become unhinged? Cortone had never known how to deal with cripples or crazy men. He and Dickstein had become very close, just for a few days back in 1943; but what was Dickstein like now?

The door opened, and Cortone said, 'Hi, Nat.'

Dickstein stared at him, then his face split in a wide grin and he came out with one of his ridiculous Cockney phrases: 'Gawd, stone the crows!'

Cortone grinned back, relieved. They shook hands, and slapped each other on the back, and let rip some soldierly language just for the hell of it; then they went inside.

4

Dickstein's home was one high-ceilinged room of an old house in a run-down part of the city. There was a single bed, neatly made up in army fashion; a heavy old wardrobe of dark wood with a matching dresser; and a table piled with books in front of a small window. Cortone thought the room looked bare. If he had to live here he would put some personal stuff all around to make the place look like his own: photographs of his family, souvenirs of Niagara and Miami Beach, his high school football trophy.

Dickstein said, 'What I want to know is, how did you find me?'

'I'll tell you, it wasn't easy.' Cortone took off his uniform jacket and laid it on the narrow bed. 'It took me most of yesterday.' He eyed the only easy chair in the room. Both arms tilted sideways at odd angles, a spring poked through the faded chrysanthemums of the fabric, and one missing foot had been replaced with a copy of Plato's *Theaetetus*. 'Can human beings sit on that?'

'Not above the rank of sergeant. But—'

'They aren't human anyway.'

They both laughed: it was an old joke. Dickstein brought a bentwood chair from the table and straddled it. He looked his friend up and down for a moment and said, 'You're getting fat.'

Cortone patted the slight swell of his stomach. 'We live well in Frankfurt – you really missed out, getting demobilized.' He leaned forward and lowered his voice, as if what he was saying was somewhat confidential. 'I have made a *fortune*. Jewellery, china, antiques all bought for cigarettes and soap. The Germans are starving. And –best of all – the girls will do anything for a Tootsie Roll.' He sat back, waiting for a laugh, but Dickstein just stared at him straight-faced. Disconcerted, Cortone changed the subject. 'One thing you ain't, is fat.'

At first he had been so relieved to see Dickstein still in one piece and grinning the same grin that he had not looked at him closely. Now he realized that his friend was worse than thin: he looked wasted. Nat Dickstein had always been short and slight, but now he seemed all bones. The dead-white skin, and the large brown eyes behind the plastic-rimmed spectacles, accentuated the effect. Between the top of his sock and the cuff of his trouser-leg a few inches of pale shin showed like matchwood. Four years ago Dickstein had been brown, stringy, as hard as the leather soles of his British Army boots. When Cortone talked about his English buddy, as he often did, he would say, 'The toughest, meanest bastard fighting soldier that ever saved my goddamn life, and I ain't shittin' you.'

'Fat? No,' Dickstein said. 'This country is still on iron rations, mate. But we manage.'

'You've known worse.'

Dickstein smiled. 'And eaten it.'

'You got took prisoner.'

'At La Molina.'

'How the hell did they tie you down?'

'Easy.' Dickstein shrugged. 'A bullet broke my leg and I passed out. When I came round I was in a German truck.'

Cortone looked at Dickstein's legs. 'It mended okay?'

'I was lucky. There was a medic in my truck on the POW train – he set the bone.'

Cortone nodded. 'And then the camp...' He thought maybe he should not ask, but he wanted to know.

Dickstein looked away. 'It was all right until they found out I'm Jewish. Do you want a cup of tea? I can't afford whisky.'

'No.' Cortone wished he had kept his mouth shut. 'Anyway, I don't drink whisky in the morning anymore. Life doesn't seem as short as it used to.'

Dickstein's eyes swivelled back toward Cortone. 'They decided to find out how many times they could break a leg in the same place and mend it again.'

'Jesus.' Cortone's voice was a whisper.

'That was the best part,' Dickstein said in a flat monotone. He looked away again.

Cortone said, 'Bastards.' He could not think of anything else to say. There was a strange expression on Dickstein's face; something Cortone had not seen before, something – he realized after a moment – that was very like fear. It was odd. After all, it was over now, wasn't it? 'Well, hell, at least we won, didn't we?' He punched Dickstein's shoulder.

Dickstein grinned. 'We did. Now, what are you doing in England? And how did you find me?'

'I managed to get a stopover in London on my way back to Buffalo. I went to the War Office ...' Cortone hesitated. He had gone to the War Office to find out how and when Dickstein died. 'They gave me an address in Stepney,' he continued. 'When I got there,

there was only one house left standing in the whole street. In this house, underneath an inch of dust, I find this old man.'

'Tommy Coster.'

'Right. Well, after I drink nineteen cups of weak tea and listen to the story of his life, he sends me to another house around the corner, where I find your mother, drink more weak tea and hear the story of her life. By the time I get your address it's too late to catch the last train to Oxford, so I wait until the morning, and here I am. I only have a few hours – my ship sails tomorrow.'

'You've got your discharge?'

'In three weeks, two days and ninety-four minutes.'

'What are you going to do, back home?'

'Run the family business. I've discovered, in the last couple of years, that I am a terrific businessman.'

'What business is your family in? You never told me.'

'Trucking,' Cortone said shortly. 'And you? What is this with Oxford University, for Christ's sake? What are you studying?'

'Hebrew Literature.'

'You're kidding.'

'I could write Hebrew before I went to school, didn't I ever tell you? My grandfather was a real scholar. He lived in one smelly room over a pie shop in the Mile End Road. I went there every Saturday and Sunday, since before I can remember. I never complained – I loved it. Anyway, what else would I study?'

Cortone shrugged. 'I don't know, atomic physics maybe, or business management. Why study at all?'

'To become happy, clever and rich.'

Cortone shook his head. 'Weird as ever. Lots of girls here?'

'Very few. Besides, I'm busy.'

He thought Dickstein was blushing. 'Liar. You're in love, you fool. I can tell. Who is she?'

'Well, to be honest . . .' Dickstein was embarrassed. 'She's out of reach. A professor's wife. Exotic, intelligent, the most beautiful woman I've ever seen.'

Cortone made a dubious face. 'It's not promising, Nat.'

'I know, but still . . .' Dickstein stood up. 'You'll see what I mean.'

'I get to meet her?'

'Professor Ashford is giving a sherry party. I'm invited. I was just leaving when you got here.' Dickstein put on his jacket.

'A sherry party in Oxford,' Cortone said. 'Wait till they hear about this in Buffalo!'

It was a cold, bright morning. Pale sunshine washed the cream-coloured stone of the city's old buildings. They walked in comfortable silence, hands in pockets, shoulders hunched against the biting November wind which whistled through the streets. Cortone kept muttering, 'Dreaming spires. Fuck.'

There were very few people about, but after they had walked a mile or so Dickstein pointed across the road to a tall man with a college scarf wound around his neck. 'There's the Russian,' he said. He called, 'Hey, Rostov!'

9

The Russian looked up, waved, and crossed to their side of the street. He had an army haircut, and was too long and thin for his mass-produced suit. Cortone was beginning to think everyone was thin in this country.

Dickstein said, 'Rostov's at Balliol, same college as me. David Rostov, meet Alan Cortone. Al and I were together in Italy for a while. Going to Ashford's house, Rostov?'

The Russian nodded solemnly. 'Anything for a free drink.'

Cortone said, 'You interested in Hebrew Literature too?'

Rostov said, 'No, I'm here to study bourgeois economics.'

Dickstein laughed loudly. Cortone did not see the joke. Dickstein explained, 'Rostov is from Smolensk. He's a member of the CPSU – the Communist Party of the Soviet Union.' Cortone still did not see the joke.

'I thought nobody was allowed to leave Russia,' Cortone said.

Rostov went into a long and involved explanation which had to do with his father's having been a diplomat in Japan when the war broke out. He had an earnest expression which occasionally gave way to a sly smile. Although his English was imperfect, he managed to give Cortone the impression that he was condescending. Cortone turned off, and began to think about how you could love a man as if he was your own brother, fighting side by side with him, and then he could go off and study Hebrew Literature and you would realize you never really knew him at all.

Eventually Rostov said to Dickstein, 'Have you decided yet, about going to Palestine?'

Cortone said, 'Palestine? What for?'

Dickstein looked troubled. 'I haven't decided.'

'You should go,' said Rostov. 'The Jewish National Home will help to break up the last remnants of the British Empire in the Middle East.'

'Is that the Party line?' Dickstein asked with a faint smile.

'Yes,' Rostov said seriously. 'You're a socialist—'

'Of sorts.'

'—and it is important that the new State should be socialist.'

Cortone was incredulous. 'The Arabs are murdering you people out there. Jeez, Nat, you only just escaped from the Germans!'

'I haven't decided,' Dickstein repeated. He shook his head irritably. 'I don't know what to do.' It seemed he did not want to talk about it.

They were walking briskly. Cortone's face was freezing, but he was perspiring beneath his winter uniform. The other two began to discuss a scandal: a man called Mosley – the name meant nothing to Cortone – had been persuaded to enter Oxford in a van and make a speech at the Martyr's Memorial. Mosley was a Fascist, he gathered a moment later. Rostov was arguing that the incident proved how social democracy was closer to Fascism than Communism. Dickstein claimed the undergraduates who organized the event were just trying to be 'shocking'.

Cortone listened and watched the two men. They

11

were an odd couple: tall Rostov, his scarf like a striped bandage, taking long strides, his too-short trousers flapping like flags; and diminutive Dickstein with big eyes and round spectacles, wearing a demob suit, looking like a skeleton in a hurry. Cortone was no academic, but he figured he could smell out bullshit in any language, and he knew that neither of them was saying what he believed: Rostov was parroting some kind of official dogma, and Dickstein's brittle unconcern masked a different, deeper attitude. When Dickstein laughed about Mosley, he sounded like a child laughing after a nightmare. They both argued cleverly but without emotion: it was like a fencing match with blunted swords.

Eventually Dickstein seemed to realize that Cortone was being left out of the discussion and began to talk about their host. 'Stephen Ashford is a bit eccentric, but a remarkable man,' he said. 'He spent most of his life in the Middle East. Made a small fortune and lost it, by all accounts. He used to do crazy things, like crossing the Arabian Desert on a camel.'

'That might be the least crazy way to cross it,' Cortone said.

Rostov said, 'Ashford has a Lebanese wife.'

Cortone looked at Dickstein. 'She's—'

'She's younger than he is,' Dickstein said hastily. 'He brought her back to England just before the war and became Professor of Semitic Literature here. If he gives you Marsala instead of sherry it means you've overstayed your welcome.'

'People know the difference?' Cortone said.

'This is his house.'

Cortone was half expecting a Moorish villa, but the Ashford home was imitation Tudor, painted white with green woodwork. The garden in front was a jungle of shrubs. The three young men walked up a brick pathway to the house. The front door was open. They entered a small, square hall. Somewhere in the house several people laughed: the party had started. A pair of double doors opened and the most beautiful woman in the world came out.

Cortone was transfixed. He stood and stared as she came across the carpet to welcome them. He heard Dickstein say, 'This is my friend Alan Cortone,' and suddenly he was touching her long brown hand, warm and dry and fine-boned, and he never wanted to let go.

She turned away and led them into the drawing room. Dickstein touched Cortone's arm and grinned: he had known what was going on in his friend's mind.

Cortone recovered his composure sufficiently to say, 'Wow.'

Small glasses of sherry were lined up with military precision on a little table. She handed one to Cortone, smiled, and said, 'I'm Eila Ashford, by the way.'

Cortone took in the details as she handed out the drinks. She was completely unadorned: there was no make-up on her astonishing face, her black hair was straight, and she wore a white dress and sandals – yet the effect was almost like nakedness, and Cortone was embarrassed at the animal thoughts that rushed through his mind as he looked at her.

He forced himself to turn away and study his

surroundings. The room had the unfinished elegance of a place where people are living slightly beyond their means. The rich Persian carpet was bordered by a strip of peeling grey linoleum; someone had been mending the radio, and its innards were all over a kidney table; there were a couple of bright rectangles on the wallpaper where pictures had been taken down; and some of the sherry glasses did not quite match the set. There were about a dozen people in the room.

An Arab wearing a beautiful pearl-grey Western suit was standing at the fireplace, looking at a wooden carving on the mantelpiece. Eila Ashford called him over. 'I want you to meet Yasif Hassan, a friend of my family from home,' she said. 'He's at Worcester College.'

Hassan said, 'I know Dickstein.' He shook hands all around.

Cortone thought he was fairly handsome, for a nigger, and haughty, the way they were when they made some money and got invited to white homes.

Rostov asked him, 'You're from Lebanon?'

'Palestine.'

'Ah!' Rostov became animated. 'And what do you think of the United Nations partition plan?'

'Irrelevant,' the Arab said languidly. 'The British must leave, and my country will have a democratic government.'

'But then the Jews will be in a minority,' Rostov argued.

'They are in a minority in England. Should they be given Surrey as a national home?'

'Surrey has never been theirs. Palestine was, once.'

Hassan shrugged elegantly. 'It was – when the Welsh had England, the English had Germany, and the Norman French lived in Scandinavia.' He turned to Dickstein. 'You have a sense of justice – what do you think?'

Dickstein took off his glasses. 'Never mind justice. I want a place to call my own.'

'Even if you have to steal mine?' Hassan said.

'You can have the rest of the Middle East.'

'I don't want it.'

Rostov said, 'This discussion proves the necessity for partition.'

Eila Ashford offered a box of cigarettes. Cortone took one, and lit hers. While the others argued about Palestine, Eila asked Cortone, 'Have you known Dickstein long?'

'We met in 1943,' Cortone said. He watched her brown lips close around the cigarette. She even smoked beautifully. Delicately, she picked a fragment of tobacco from the tip of her tongue.

'I'm terribly curious about him,' she said.

'Why?'

'Everyone is. He's only a boy, and yet he seems so old. Then again, he's obviously a Cockney, but he's not in the least intimidated by all these upper-class Englishmen. But he'll talk about anything except himself.'

Cortone nodded. 'I'm finding out that I don't really know him, either.'

'My husband says he's a brilliant student.'

'He saved my life.'

'Good Lord.' She looked at him more closely, as if she were wondering whether he was just being melodramatic. She seemed to decide in his favour. 'I'd like to hear about it.'

A middle-aged man in baggy corduroy trousers touched her shoulder and said, 'How is everything, my dear?'

'Fine,' she said. 'Mr Cortone, this is my husband, Professor Ashford.'

Cortone said, 'How are you.' Ashford was a balding man in ill-fitting clothes. Cortone had been expecting Lawrence of Arabia. He thought: Maybe Nat has a chance after all.

Eila said, 'Mr Cortone was telling me how Nat Dickstein saved his life.'

'Really!' Ashford said.

'It's not a long story,' Cortone said. He glanced over at Dickstein, now deep in conversation with Hassan and Rostov; and noted how the three men displayed their attitudes by the way they stood: Rostov with his feet apart, wagging a finger like a teacher, sure in his dogma; Hassan leaning against a bookcase, one hand in his pocket, smoking, pretending that the international debate about the future of his country was of merely academic interest; Dickstein with arms folded tightly, shoulders hunched, head bowed in concentration, his stance giving the lie to the dispassionate character of his remarks. Cortone heard *The British promised Palestine to the Jews*, and the reply, *Beware the gifts of a thief.* He turned back to the Ashfords and began to tell them the story.

'It was in Sicily, near a place called Ragusa, a hill town,' he said. 'I'd taken a T-force around the outskirts. To the north of the town we came on a German tank in a little hollow, on the edge of a clump of trees. The tank looked abandoned but I put a grenade into it to make sure. As we drove past there was a shot – only one – and a German with a machine gun fell out of a tree. He'd been hiding up there, ready to pick us off as we passed. It was Nat Dickstein who shot him.'

Eila's eyes sparkled with something like excitement, but her husband had gone white. Obviously the professor had no stomach for tales of life and death. Cortone thought: If that upsets you, pop, I hope Dickstein never tells you any of *his* stories.

'The British had come around the town from the other side,' Cortone went on. 'Nat had seen the tank, like I did, and smelled a trap. He had spotted the sniper and was waiting to see if there were any more when we turned up. If he hadn't been so damn smart I'd be dead.'

The other two were silent for a moment. Ashford said, 'It's not long ago, but we forget so fast.'

Eila remembered her other guests. 'I want to talk to you some more before you go,' she said to Cortone. She went across the room to where Hassan was trying to open a pair of doors that gave on to the garden.

Ashford brushed nervously at the wispy hair behind his ears. 'The public hears about the big battles, but I suppose the soldier remembers those little personal incidents.'

Cortone nodded, thinking that Ashford clearly had

no conception of what war was like, and wondering if the professor's youth had really been as adventurous as Dickstein claimed. 'Later, I took him to meet my cousins – the family comes from Sicily. We had pasta and wine, and they made a hero of Nat. We were together only for a few days, but we were like brothers, you know?'

'Indeed.'

'When I heard he was taken prisoner, I figured I'd never see him again.'

'Do you know what happened to him?' Ashford said. 'He doesn't say much . . .'

Cortone shrugged. 'He survived the camps.'

'He was fortunate.'

'Was he?'

Ashford looked at Cortone for a moment, confused, then turned away and looked around the room. After a moment he said, 'This is not a very typical Oxford gathering, you know. Dickstein, Rostov and Hassan are somewhat unusual students. You should meet Toby – he's the archetypal undergraduate.' He caught the eye of a red-faced youth in a tweed suit and a very wide paisley tie. 'Toby, come and meet Dickstein's comrade-in-arms – Mr Cortone.'

Toby shook hands and said abruptly, 'Any chance of a tip from the stable? Will Dickstein win?'

'Win what?' Cortone said.

Ashford explained, 'Dickstein and Rostov are to play a chess match – they're both supposed to be terribly good. Toby thinks you might have inside information – he probably wants to bet on the outcome.'

Cortone said, 'I thought chess was an old man's game.'

Toby said, 'Ah!' rather loudly, and emptied his glass. He and Ashford seemed nonplussed by Cortone's remark. A little girl, four or five years old, came in from the garden carrying an elderly grey cat. Ashford introduced her with the coy pride of a man who has become a father in middle age.

'This is Suza,' he said.

The girl said, 'And this is Hezekiah.'

She had her mother's skin and hair; she too would be beautiful. Cortone wondered whether she was really Ashford's daughter. There was nothing of him in her looks. She held out the cat's paw, and Cortone obligingly shook it and said, 'How are you, Hezekiah?'

Suza went over to Dickstein. 'Good morning, Nat. Would you like to stroke Hezekiah?'

'She's very cute,' Cortone said to Ashford. 'I have to talk to Nat. Would you excuse me?' He went over to Dickstein, who was kneeling down and stroking the cat.

Nat and Suza seemed to be pals. He told her, 'This is my friend Alan.'

'We've met,' she said, and fluttered her eyelashes. Cortone thought: She learned that from her mother.

'We were in the war together,' Dickstein continued.

Suza looked directly at Cortone. 'Did you kill people?'

He hesitated. 'Sure.'

'Do you feel bad about it?'

'Not too bad. They were wicked people.'

'Nat feels bad about it. That's why he doesn't like to talk about it too much.'

The kid had got more out of Dickstein than all the grown-ups put together.

The cat jumped out of Suza's arms with surprising agility. She chased after it. Dickstein stood up.

'I wouldn't say Mrs Ashford is out of reach,' Cortone said quietly.

'Wouldn't you?' Dickstein said.

'She can't be more than twenty-five. He's at least twenty years older, and I'll bet he's no pistol. If they got married before the war, she must have been around seventeen at the time. And they don't seem affectionate.'

'I wish I could believe you,' Dickstein said. He was not as interested as he should have been. 'Come and see the garden.'

They went through the French doors. The sun was stronger, and the bitter cold had gone from the air. The garden stretched in a green-and-brown wilderness down to the edge of the river. They walked away from the house.

Dickstein said, 'You don't much like this crowd.'

'The war's over,' Cortone said. 'You and me, we live in different worlds now. All this – professors, chess matches, sherry parties . . . I might as well be on Mars. My life is doing deals, fighting off the competition, making a few bucks. I was fixing to offer you a job in my business, but I guess I'd be wasting my time.'

'Alan . . .'

'Listen, what the hell. We'll probably lose touch now

– I'm not much of a letter writer. But I won't forget that I owe you my life. One of these days you might want to call in the debt. You know where to find me.'

Dickstein opened his mouth to speak, then they heard the voices.

'Oh . . . no, not here, not now . . .' It was a woman.

'Yes!' A man.

Dickstein and Cortone were standing beside a thick box hedge which cut off a corner of the garden: someone had begun to plant a maze and never finished the job. A few steps from where they were a gap opened, then the hedge turned a right angle and ran along the river bank. The voices came clearly from the other side of the foliage.

The woman spoke again, low and throaty. 'Don't, damn you, or I'll scream.'

Dickstein and Cortone stepped through the gap.

Cortone would never forget what he saw there. He stared at the two people and then, appalled, he glanced at Dickstein. Dickstein's face was grey with shock, and he looked ill; his mouth dropped open as he gazed in horror and despair. Cortone looked back at the couple.

The woman was Eila Ashford. The skirt of her dress was around her waist, her face was flushed with pleasure, and she was kissing Yasif Hassan.

CHAPTER ONE

T HE PUBLIC-ADDRESS system at Cairo airport
made a noise like a doorbell, and then the
arrival of the Alitalia flight from Milan was announced
in Arabic, Italian, French and English. Towfik el-Masiri
left his table in the buffet and made his way out to the
observation deck. He put on his sunglasses to look over
the shimmering concrete apron. The Caravelle was
already down and taxiing.

Towfik was there because of a cable. It had come
that morning from his 'uncle' in Rome, and it had been
in code. Any business could use a code for international
telegrams, provided it first lodged the key to the code
with the post office. Such codes were used more and
more to save money – by reducing common phrases to
single words – than to keep secrets. Towfik's uncle's
cable, transcribed according to the registered code
book, gave details of his late aunt's will. However,
Towfik had another key, and the message he read was:

OBSERVE AND FOLLOW PROFESSOR FRIEDRICH
SCHULZ ARRIVING CAIRO FROM MILAN
WEDNESDAY 28 FEBRUARY 1968 FOR SEVERAL.
DAYS. AGE 51 HEIGHT 180 CM WEIGHT 150

23

POUNDS HAIR WHITE EYES BLUE NATIONALITY
AUSTRIAN COMPANIONS WIFE ONLY.

The passengers began to file out of the aircraft, and
Towfik spotted his man almost immediately. There was
only one tall, lean white-haired man on the flight. He
was wearing a light blue suit, a white shirt and a tie,
and carrying a plastic shopping bag from a duty-free
store and a camera. His wife was much shorter, and
wore a fashionable mini-dress and a blonde wig. As they
crossed the airfield they looked about them and sniffed
the warm, dry desert air the way most people did the
first time they landed in North Africa.

The passengers disappeared into the arrivals hall.
Towfik waited on the observation deck until the baggage came off the plane, then he went inside and
mingled with the small crowd of people waiting just
beyond the customs barrier.

He did a lot of waiting. That was something they did
not teach you – how to wait. You learned to handle
guns, memorize maps, break open safes and kill people
with your bare hands, all in the first six months of the
training course; but there were no lectures in patience,
no exercises for sore feet, no seminars on tedium. And
it was beginning to seem like *There is something wrong
here* beginning to seem *Lookout lookout* beginning to—

There was another agent in the crowd.

Towfik's subconscious hit the fire alarm while he was
thinking about patience. The people in the little crowd,
waiting for relatives and friends and business acquaint-

ances off the Milan plane, were impatient. They smoked, shifted their weight from one foot to the other, craned their necks and fidgeted. There was a middle-class family with four children, two men in the traditional striped cotton *galabiya* robes, a businessman in a dark suit, a young white woman, a chauffeur with a sign saying FORD MOTOR COMPANY, and—

And a patient man.

Like Towfik, he had dark skin and short hair and wore a European-style suit. At first glance he seemed to be with the middle-class family – just as Towfik would seem, to a casual observer, to be with the businessman in the dark suit. The other agent stood nonchalantly, with his hands behind his back, facing the exit from the baggage hall, looking unobtrusive. There was a streak of paler skin alongside his nose, like an old scar. He touched it, once, in what might have been a nervous gesture, then put his hand behind his back again.

The question was, had he spotted Towfik?

Towfik turned to the businessman beside him and said, 'I never understand why this has to take so long.' He smiled, and spoke quietly, so that the businessman leaned closer to hear him and smiled back; and the pair of them looked like acquaintances having a casual conversation.

The businessman said, 'The formalities take longer than the flight.'

Towfik stole another glance at the other agent. The man stood in the same position, watching the exit. He had not attempted any camouflage. Did that mean that he had not spotted Towfik? Or was it just that he had second-guessed Towfik, by deciding that a piece of camouflage would give him away?

The passengers began to emerge, and Towfik realized there was nothing he could do, either way. He hoped the people the agent was meeting would come out before Professor Schulz.

It was not to be. Schulz and his wife were among the first little knot of passengers to come through.

The other agent approached them and shook hands.

Of course, of course.

The agent was there to meet Schulz.

Towfik watched while the agent summoned porters and ushered the Schulzes away; then he went out by a different exit to his car. Before getting in he took off his jacket and tie and put on sunglasses and a white cotton cap. Now he would not be easily recognizable as the man who had been waiting at the meeting point.

He figured the agent would have parked in a no-waiting zone right outside the main entrance, so he drove that way. He was right. He saw the porters loading the Schulz baggage into the boot of a five-year-old grey Mercedes. He drove on.

He steered his dirty Renault on to the main highway which ran from Heliopolis, where the airport was, to Cairo. He drove at 60 kph and kept to the slow lane. The grey Mercedes passed him two or three minutes later, and he accelerated to keep it within sight. He memorized its number, as it was always useful to be able to recognize the opposition's cars.

The sky began to cloud over. As he sped down the straight, palm-lined highway, Towfik considered what he had found out so far. The cable had told him nothing about Schulz except what the man looked like and the fact that he was an Austrian professor. The meeting at the airport meant a great deal, though. It had been a kind of clandestine VIP treatment. Towfik had the agent figured for a local: everything pointed to that – his clothes, his car, his style of waiting. That meant Schulz was probably here by invitation of the government, but either he or the people he had come to see wanted the visit kept secret.

It was not much. What was Schulz professor *of?* He could be a banker, arms manufacturer, rocketry expert or cotton buyer. He might even be with Al Fatah, but Towfik could not quite see the man as a resurrected Nazi. Still, anything was possible.

Certainly Tel Aviv did not think Schulz was important: if they had, they would not have used Towfik, who was young and inexperienced, for this surveillance. It was even possible that the whole thing was yet another training exercise.

They entered Cairo on the Shari Ramses, and Towfik closed the gap between his car and the Mercedes until there was only one vehicle between them. The grey car turned right on to the Corniche al-Nil, then crossed the river by the 26 July Bridge and entered the Zamalek district of Gezira island.

There was less traffic in the wealthy, dull suburb, and Towfik became edgy about being spotted by the agent at the wheel of the Mercedes. However, two minutes later the other car turned into a residential street near the Officers' Club and stopped outside an apartment block with a jacaranda tree in the garden. Towfik immediately took a right turn and was out of sight before the doors of the other car could open. He parked, jumped out, and walked back to the corner. He was in time to see the agent and the Schulzes disappear into the building followed by a caretaker in *galabiya* struggling with their luggage.

Towfik looked up and down the street. There was nowhere a man could convincingly idle. He returned to his car, backed it around the corner and parked between two other cars on the same side of the road as the Mercedes.

Half an hour later the agent came out alone, got into his car, and drove off.

Towfik settled down to wait.

It went on for two days, then it broke.

Until then the Schulzes behaved like tourists, and seemed to enjoy it. On the first evening they had dinner in a nightclub and watched a troupe of belly-dancers. Next day they did the Pyramids and the Sphinx, with lunch at Groppi's and dinner at the Nile Hilton. In the morning on the third day they got up early and took a taxi to the mosque of Ibn Tulun.

Towfik left his car near the Gayer-Anderson Museum and followed them. They took a perfunctory look around the mosque and headed east on the Shari al-Salibah. They were dawdling, looking at fountains and buildings, peering into dark tiny shops, watching *baladi* women buy onions and peppers and camel's feet at street stalls.

They stopped at a crossroads and went into a tea-shop. Towfik crossed the street to the *sebeel*, a domed fountain behind windows of iron lace, and studied the baroque relief around its walls. He moved on up the street, still within sight of the tea-shop, and spent some time buying four misshapen giant tomatoes from a white-capped stallholder whose feet were bare.

The Schulzes came out of the tea-shop and turned north, following Towfik, into the street market. Here it was easier for Towfik to idle, sometimes ahead of them and sometimes behind. Frau Schulz bought slippers and a gold bangle, and paid too much for a sprig of mint from a half-naked child. Towfik got far enough in front of them to drink a small cup of strong, unsweetened Turkish coffee under the awning of a café called Nasif's.

They left the street market and entered a covered *souq* specializing in saddlery. Schulz glanced at his wristwatch and spoke to his wife – giving Towfik the first faint tremor of anxiety – and then they walked a little faster until they emerged at Bab Zuweyla, the gateway to the original walled city.

For a few moments the Schulzes were obscured from Towfik's view by a donkey pulling a cart loaded with Ali-Baba jars, their mouths stoppered with crumpled paper. When the cart passed, Towfik saw that Schulz was saying goodbye to his wife and getting into an oldish grey Mercedes.

Towfik cursed under his breath.

The car door slammed and it pulled away. Frau Schulz waved. Towfik read the licence plate – it was the car he had followed from Heliopolis – and saw it go west, then turn left into the Shari Port Said.

Forgetting Frau Schulz, he turned around and broke into a run.

They had been walking for about an hour, but they had covered only a mile. Towfik sprinted through the saddlery *souq* and the street market, dodging around the stalls and bumping into robed men and women in black, dropping his bag of tomatoes in a collision with a Nubian sweeper, until he reached the museum and his car.

He dropped into the driver's seat, breathing hard and grimacing at the pain in his side. He started the engine and pulled away on an interception course for the Shari Port Said.

The traffic was light, so when he hit the main road he guessed he must be behind the Mercedes. He continued southwest, over the island of Roda and the Giza Bridge onto the Giza Road.

Schulz had not been deliberately trying to shake a tail, Towfik decided. Had the professor been a pro he would have lost Towfik decisively and finally. No, he had simply been taking a morning walk through the market before meeting someone at a landmark. But Towfik was sure that the meeting place, and the walk beforehand, had been suggested by the agent.

They might have gone anywhere, but it seemed likely they were leaving the city – otherwise Schulz could simply have taken a taxi at Bab Zuweyla – and this was the major road westward. Towfik drove very fast. Soon there was nothing in front of him but the arrow-straight grey road, and nothing either side but yellow sand and blue sky.

He reached the Pyramids without catching the Mercedes. Here the road forked, leading north to Alexandria or south to Faiyum. From where the Mercedes had picked up Schulz, this would have been an unlikely, roundabout route to Alexandria; so Towfik plumped for Faiyum.

When at last he saw the other car it was behind him, coming up very fast. Before it reached him it turned right off the main road. Towfik braked to a halt and reversed the Renault to the turnoff. The other car was already a mile ahead on the side road. He followed.

This was dangerous, now. The road probably went deep into the Western Desert, perhaps all the way to the oil field at Qattara. It seemed little used, and a strong wind might obscure it under a layer of sand. The agent in the Mercedes was sure to realize he was being followed. If he were a good agent, the sight of the Renault might even trigger memories of the journey from Heliopolis.

This was where the training broke down, and all the careful camouflage and tricks of the trade became useless; and you had to simply get on someone's tail and stick with him whether he saw you or not, because the whole point was to find out where he was going, and if you could not manage that you were no use at all.

So he threw caution to the desert wind and followed; and still he lost them.

The Mercedes was a faster car, and better designed for the narrow, bumpy road, and within a few minutes it was out of sight. Towfik followed the road, hoping he might catch them when they stopped or at least come across something that might be their destination.

Sixty kilometres on, deep in the desert and beginning to worry about getting petrol, he reached a tiny oasis village at a crossroads. A few scrawny animals grazed in sparse vegetation around a muddy pool. A jar of fava beans and three Fanta cans on a makeshift table outside a hut signified the local café. Towfik got out of the car and spoke to an old man watering a bony buffalo.

'Have you seen a grey Mercedes?'

The peasant stared at him blankly, as if he were speaking a foreign language.

'Have you seen a grey car?'

The old man brushed a large black fly off his forehead and nodded, once.

'When?'

'Today.'

That was probably as precise an answer as he could hope for. 'Which way did it go?'

The old man pointed west, into the desert.

Towfik said, 'Where can I get petrol?'

The man pointed east, toward Cairo.

Towfik gave him a coin and returned to the car. He started the engine and looked again at the petrol gauge. He had enough fuel to get back to Cairo, just; if he went farther west he would run out on the return journey.

He had done all he could, he decided. Wearily, he turned the Renault around and headed back toward the city.

Towfik did not like his work. When it was dull he was bored, and when it was exciting he was frightened. But they had told him that there was important, dangerous work to be done in Cairo, and that he had the qualities necessary to be a good spy, and that there were not enough Egyptian Jews in Israel for them to be able just to go out and find another one with all the qualities if he said no; so, of course, he had agreed. It was not out of idealism that he risked his life for his country. It was more like self-interest: the destruction of Israel would mean his own destruction; in fighting for Israel he was fighting for himself; he risked his life to save his life. It was the logical thing to do. Still, he looked forward to the time – in five years? Ten? Twenty? – when he would be too old for field work, and they would bring him home and sit him behind a desk, and he could find a nice Jewish girl and marry her and settle down to enjoy the land he had fought for.

Meanwhile, having lost Professor Schulz, he was following the wife.

She continued to see the sights, escorted now by a young Arab who had presumably been laid on by the Egyptians to take care of her while her husband was away. In the evening the Arab took her to an Egyptian restaurant for dinner, brought her home, and kissed her cheek under the jacaranda tree in the garden.

The next morning Towfik went to the main post office and sent a coded cable to his uncle in Rome:

SCHULZ MET AT AIRPORT BY SUSPECTED LOCAL AGENT. SPENT TWO DAYS SIGHTSEEING. PICKED UP BY AFORESAID AGENT AND DRIVEN DIRECTION QATTARA. SURVEILLANCE ABORTED. NOW WATCHING WIFE.

He was back in Zamalek at nine A.M. At eleven-thirty he saw Frau Schulz on a balcony, drinking coffee, and was able to figure out which of the apartments was the Schulzes'.

By lunchtime the interior of the Renault had become very hot. Towfik ate an apple and drank tepid beer from a bottle.

Professor Schulz arrived late in the afternoon, in the same grey Mercedes. He looked tired and a little rumpled, like a middle-aged man who had travelled too far. He left the car and went into the building without looking back. After dropping him, the agent drove past the Renault and looked straight at Towfik for an instant. There was nothing Towfik could do about it.

Where had Schulz been? It had taken him most of a day to get there, Towfik speculated; he had spent a night, a full day and a second night there; and it had taken most of today to get back. Qattara was only one of several possibilities: the desert road went all the way to Matruh on the Mediterranean coast; there was a turnoff to Karkur Tohl in the far south; with a change of car and a desert guide they could even have gone to a rendezvous on the border with Libya.

At nine P.M. the Schulzes came out again. The professor looked refreshed. They were dressed for dinner. They walked a short distance and hailed a taxi.

Towfik made a decision. He did not follow them.

He got out of the car and entered the garden of the building. He stepped on to the dusty lawn and found a vantage point behind a bush from where he could see into the hall through the open front door. The Nubian caretaker was sitting on a low wooden bench, picking his nose.

Towfik waited.

Twenty minutes later the man left his bench and disappeared into the back of the building.

Towfik hurried through the hall and ran, soft-footed, up the staircase.

He had three Yale-type skeleton keys, but none of them fitted the lock of apartment three. In the end he got the door open with a piece of bendy plastic broken off a college set-square.

He entered the apartment and closed the door behind him.

It was now quite dark outside. A little light from a streetlamp came through the unshaded windows. Towfik drew a small flashlight from his trousers pocket, but he did not switch it on yet.

The apartment was large and airy, with white-painted walls and English-colonial furniture. It had the sparse, chilly look of a place where nobody actually lived.

There was a big drawing room, a dining room, three bedrooms and a kitchen. After a quick general survey Towfik started snooping in earnest.

The two smaller bedrooms were bare. In the larger one, Towfik went rapidly through all the drawers and cupboards. A wardrobe held the rather gaudy dresses of a woman past her prime: bright prints, sequinned gowns, turquoise and orange and pink. The labels were American. Schulz was an Austrian national, the cable had said, but perhaps he lived in the USA. Towfik had never heard him speak.

On the bedside table were a guide to Cairo in English, a copy of *Vogue* and a reprinted lecture on isotopes.

So Schulz was a scientist.

Towfik glanced through the lecture. Most of it was over his head. Schulz must be a top chemist or physicist, he thought. If he was here to work on weaponry, Tel Aviv would want to know.

There were no personal papers – Schulz evidently had his passport and wallet in his pocket. The airline labels had been removed from the matching set of tan suitcases.

On a low table in the drawing room, two empty glasses smelled of gin: they had had a cocktail before going out.

In the bathroom Towfik found the clothes Schulz had worn into the desert. There was a lot of sand in the shoes, and on the trouser cuffs he found small dusty grey smears which might have been cement. In the breast pocket of the rumpled jacket was a blue plastic container, about one-and-a-half inches square, very slender. It contained a light-tight envelope of the kind used to protect photographic film.

Towfik pocketed the plastic box.

The airline labels from the luggage were in a waste basket in the little hall. The Schulzes' address was in Boston, Massachusetts, which probably meant that the professor taught at Harvard, MIT or one of the many lesser universities in the area. Towfik did some rapid arithmetic. Schulz would have been in his twenties during World War Two: he could easily be one of the German rocketry experts who went to the USA after the war.

Or not. You did not have to be a Nazi to work for the Arabs.

Nazi or not, Schulz was a cheapskate: his soap, toothpaste and after-shave were all taken from airlines and hotels.

On the floor beside a rattan chair, near the table with the empty cocktail glasses, lay a lined foolscap notepad, its top sheet blank. There was a pencil lying on the pad. Perhaps Schulz had been making notes on his trip while he sipped his gin sling. Towfik searched the apartment for sheets torn from the pad.

He found them on the balcony, burned to cinders in a large glass ashtray.

The night was cool. Later in the year the air would be warm and fragrant with the blossom of the jacaranda tree in the garden below. The city traffic snored in the distance. It reminded Towfik of his father's apartment in Jerusalem. He wondered how long it would be before he saw Jerusalem again.

He had done all he could here. He would look again at that foolscap pad, to see whether Schulz's pencil had pressed hard enough to leave an impression on the next page. He turned away from the parapet and crossed the balcony to the French windows leading back into the drawing room.

He had his hand on the door when he heard the voices.

Towfik froze.

'I'm sorry, honey, I just couldn't face another overdone steak.'

'We could have eaten something, for God's sake.'

The Schulzes were back.

Towfik rapidly reviewed his progress through the rooms: bedrooms, bathroom, drawing room, kitchen . . . he had replaced everything he had touched, except the little plastic box. He had to keep that anyway. Schulz would have to assume he had lost it.

If Towfik could get away unseen now, they might never know he had been there.

He bellied over the parapet and hung at full length by his fingertips. It was too dark for him to see the ground. He dropped, landed lightly and strolled away.

It had been his first burglary, and he felt pleased. It had gone as smoothly as a training exercise, even to the early return of the occupant and sudden exit of spy by prearranged emergency route. He grinned in the dark. He might yet live to see that desk job.

He got into his car, started the engine and switched on the lights.

Two men emerged from the shadows and stood on either side of the Renault.

Who . . . ?

He did not pause to figure out what was going on. He rammed the gearshift into first and pulled away. The two men hastily stepped aside.

They had made no attempt to stop him. So why had they been there? To make sure he stayed in the car . . . ?

He jammed on the brakes and looked into the back seat, and then he knew, with unbearable sadness, that he would never see Jerusalem again.

A tall Arab in a dark suit was smiling at him over the snout of a small handgun.

'Drive on,' the man said in Arabic, 'but not quite so fast, please.'

Q: What is your name?
A: Towfik el-Masiri.
Q: Describe yourself.
A: Age twenty-six, five-foot-nine, one hundred and eighty pounds, brown eyes, black hair, Semitic features, light brown skin.
Q: Who do you work for?
A: I am a student.
Q: What day is today?
A: Saturday.
Q: What is your nationality?
A: Egyptian.

Q: What is twenty minus seven?

A: Thirteen.

The above questions are designed to facilitate fine calibration of the lie detector.

Q: You work for the CIA.

A: No. (TRUE)

Q: The Germans?

A: No. (TRUE)

Q: Israel, then.

A: No. (FALSE)

Q: You really are a student?

A: Yes. (FALSE)

Q: Tell me about your studies.

A: I'm doing chemistry at Cairo University. (TRUE) I'm interested in polymers. (TRUE) I want to be a petrochemical engineer. (FALSE)

Q: What are polymers?

A: Complex organic compounds with long-chain molecules – the commonest is polythene. (TRUE)

Q: What is your name?

A: I told you, Towfik el-Masiri. (FALSE)

Q: The pads attached to your head and chest measure your pulse, heartbeat, breathing and perspiration. When you tell untruths, your metabolism betrays you – you breathe faster, sweat more, and so on. This machine, which was given to us by our Russian friends, tells me when you are lying. Besides, I happen to know that Towfik el-Masiri is dead. Who are you?

A: (no reply)

Q: The wire taped to the tip of your penis is part of a

different machine. It is connected to this button here. When I press the button—

A: (scream)

Q: —an electric current passes through the wire and gives you a shock. We have put your feet in a bucket of water to improve the efficiency of the apparatus. What is your name?

A: Avram Ambache.

The electrical apparatus interferes with the functioning of the lie detector.

Q: Have a cigarette.

A: Thank you.

Q: Believe it or not, I hate this work. The trouble is, people who like it are never any good at it – you need sensitivity, you know. I'm a sensitive person . . . I hate to see people suffer. Don't you?

A: (no reply)

Q: You're now trying to think of ways to resist me. Please don't bother. There is no defence against modern techniques of . . . interviewing. What is your name?

A: Avram Ambache. (TRUE)

Q: Who is your control?

A: I don't know what you mean. (FALSE)

Q: Is it Bosch?

A: No, Friedman. (READING INDETERMINATE)

Q: It is Bosch.

A: Yes. (FALSE)

Q: No, it's not Bosch. It's Krantz.

A: Okay, it's Krantz – whatever you say. (TRUE)

Q: How do you make contact?

A: I have a radio. (FALSE)

Q: You're not telling me the truth.

A: (scream)

Q: How do you make contact?

A: A dead-letter box in the *faubourg*.

Q: You are thinking that when you are in pain, the lie detector will not function properly, and that there is therefore safety in torture. You are only partly right. This is a very sophisticated machine, and I spent many months learning to use it properly. After I have given you a shock, it takes only a few moments to readjust the machine to your faster metabolism; and then I can once more tell when you are lying. How do you make contact?

A: A dead-letter – (scream)

Q: Ali! He's kicked his feet free – these convulsions are very strong. Tie him again, before he comes round. Pick up that bucket and put more water in it.

(pause)

Right, he's waking, get out. Can you hear me, Towfik?

A: (indistinct)

Q: What is your name?

A: (no reply)

Q: A little jab to help you—

A: (scream)

Q: —to think.

A: Avram Ambache.

Q: What day is today?

A: Saturday.

Q: What did we give you for breakfast?

A: Fava beans.

Q: What is twenty minus seven?

A: Thirteen.

Q: What is your profession?

A: I'm a student. No don't please and a spy yes I'm a spy don't touch the button please oh god oh god—

Q: How do you make contact?

A: Coded cables.

Q: Have a cigarette. Here . . . oh, you don't seem to be able to hold it between your lips – let me help . . . there.

A: Thank you.

Q: Just try to be calm. Remember, as long as you're telling the truth, there will be no pain.
(pause)
Are you feeling better?

A: Yes.

Q: So am I. Now then, tell me about Professor Schulz. Why were you following him?

A: I was ordered to. (TRUE)

Q: By Tel Aviv?

A: Yes. (TRUE)

Q: Who in Tel Aviv?

A: I don't know. (READING INDETERMINATE)

Q: But you can guess.

A: Bosch. (READING INDETERMINATE)

Q: Or Krantz?

A: Perhaps. (TRUE)

Q: Krantz is a good man. Dependable. How's his wife?

A: Very well, I—(scream)

Q: His wife died in 1958. Why do you make me hurt you? What did Schulz do?

A: Went sightseeing for two days, then disappeared into the desert in a grey Mercedes.

Q: And you burglarized his apartment.

A: Yes. (TRUE)

Q: What did you learn?

A: He is a scientist. (TRUE)

Q: Anything else?

A: American. (TRUE) That's all. (TRUE)

Q: Who was your instructor in training?

A: Ertl. (READING INDETERMINATE)

Q: That wasn't his real name, though.

A: I don't know. (FALSE) No! Not the button let me think it was just a minute I think somebody said his real name was Manner. (TRUE)

Q: Oh, Manner. Shame. He's the old-fashioned type. He still believes you can train agents to resist interrogation. It's his fault you're suffering so much, you know. What about your colleagues? Who trained with you?

A: I never knew their real names. (FALSE)

Q: Didn't you?

A: (scream)

Q: Real names.

A: Not all of them—

Q: Tell me the ones you did know.

A: (no reply)
(scream)

The prisoner fainted.
(pause)

Q: What is your name?
A: Uh . . . Towfik. (scream)
Q: What did you have for breakfast?
A: Don't know.
Q: What is twenty minus seven?
A: Twenty-seven.
Q: What did you tell Krantz about Professor Schulz?
A: Sightseeing . . . Western Desert . . . surveillance aborted . . .
Q: Who did you train with?
A: (no reply)
Q: Who did you train with?
A: (scream)
Q: Who did you train with?
A: Yea, though I walk through the valley of the shadow of death—
Q: Who did you train with?
A: (scream)
The prisoner died.

When Kawash asked for a meeting, Pierre Borg went. There was no discussion about times and places: Kawash sent a message giving the rendezvous, and Borg made sure to be there. Kawash was the best double agent Borg had ever had, and that was that.

The head of the Mossad stood at one end of the northbound Bakerloo Line platform in Oxford Circus underground station, reading an advertisement for a course of lectures in Theosophy, waiting for Kawash. He had no idea why the Arab had chosen London for this meeting; no idea what he told his masters he was doing in the city; no idea, even, why Kawash was a traitor. But this man had helped the Israelis win two wars and avoid a third, and Borg needed him.

Borg glanced along the platform, looking for a high brown head with a large, thin nose. He had an idea he knew what Kawash wanted to talk about. He hoped his idea was right.

Borg was very worried about the Schulz affair. It had started out as a piece of routine surveillance, just the right kind of assignment for his newest, rawest agent in Cairo: a high-powered American physicist on vacation in Europe decides to take a trip to Egypt. The first warning sign came when Towfik lost Schulz. At that point Borg had stepped up activity on the project. A freelance journalist in Milan who occasionally made inquiries for German Intelligence had established that Schulz's air ticket to Cairo had been paid for by the wife of an Egyptian diplomat in Rome. Then the CIA had routinely passed to the Mossad a set of satellite photographs of the area around Qattara which seemed to show signs of construction work – and Borg had remembered that Schulz had been heading in the direction of Qattara when Towfik lost him.

Something was going on, and he did not know what, and that worried him.

He was always worried. If it was not the Egyptians, it was the Syrians; if it was not the Syrians it was the Fedayeen; if it was not his enemies it was his friends and the question of how long they would continue to be his friends. He had a worrying job. His mother had

once said, 'Job, *nothing* – you were *born* worrying, like
your poor father – if you were a *gardener* you would
worry about your job.' She might have been right, but
all the same, paranoia was the only rational frame of
mind for a spymaster.

Now Towfik had broken contact, and that was the
most worrying sign of all.

Maybe Kawash would have some answers.

A train thundered in. Borg was not waiting for a
train. He began to read the credits on a movie poster.
Half the names were Jewish. Maybe I should have been
a movie producer, he thought.

The train pulled out, and a shadow fell over Borg.
He looked up into the calm face of Kawash.

The Arab said, 'Thank you for coming.' He always
said that.

Borg ignored it: he never knew how to respond to
thanks. He said, 'What's new?'

'I had to pick up one of your youngsters in Cairo on
Friday.'

'You *had* to?'

'Military Intelligence were bodyguarding a VIP, and
they spotted the kid tailing them. Military don't have
operational personnel in the city, so they asked my
department to pick him up. It was an official request.'

'God *damn*,' Borg said feelingly. 'What happened to
him?'

'I had to do it by the book,' Kawash said. He looked
very sad. 'The boy was interrogated and killed. His
name was Avram Ambache, but he worked as Towfik
el-Masiri.'

47

Borg frowned. 'He told you his real name?'

'He's dead, Pierre.'

Borg shook his head irritably: Kawash always wanted to linger over personal aspects. 'Why did he tell you his name?'

'We're using the Russian equipment – the electric shock and the lie detector together. You're not training them to cope with it.'

Borg gave a short laugh. 'If we told them about it, we'd never get any fucking recruits. What else did he give away?'

'Nothing we didn't know. He would have, but I killed him first.'

'*You* killed him?'

'I conducted the interrogation, in order to make sure he did not say anything important. All these interviews are taped now, and the transcripts filed. We're learning from the Russians.' The sadness deepened in the brown eyes. 'Why – would you prefer that I should have someone else kill your boys?'

Borg stared at him, then looked away. Once again he had to steer the conversation away from the sentimental. 'What did the boy discover about Schulz?'

'An agent took the professor into the Western Desert.'

'Sure, but what for?'

'I don't know.'

'You must know, you're in Egyptian Intelligence!' Borg controlled his irritation. Let the man do things at his own pace, he told himself; whatever information he's got, he'll tell.

'I don't know what they're doing out there, because they've set up a special group to handle it,' Kawash said. 'My department isn't informed.'

'Any idea why?'

The Arab shrugged. 'I'd say they don't want the Russians to know about it. These days Moscow gets everything that goes through us.'

Borg let his disappointment show. 'Is that all Towfik could manage?'

Suddenly there was anger in the soft voice of the Arab. 'The kid died for you,' he said.

'I'll thank him in heaven. Did he die in vain?'

'He took this from Schulz's apartment.' Kawash drew a hand from inside his coat and showed Borg a small, square box of blue plastic.

Borg took the box. 'How do you know where he got it?'

'It has Schulz's fingerprints on it. And we arrested Towfik right after he broke into the apartment.'

Borg opened the box and fingered the light-proof envelope. It was unsealed. He took out the photographic negative.

The Arab said, 'We opened the envelope and developed the film. It's blank.'

With a deep sense of satisfaction, Borg reassembled the box and put it into his pocket. Now it all made sense; now he understood; now he knew what he had to do. A train came in. 'You want to catch this one?' he said.

Kawash frowned slightly, nodded assent, and moved to the edge of the platform as the train stopped and the doors opened. He boarded, and stood just inside. He said, 'I don't know what on earth the box is.'

Borg thought, You don't like me, but I think you're just great. He smiled thinly at the Arab as the doors of the underground train began to slide shut. 'I do,' he said.

CHAPTER TWO

THE AMERICAN girl was quite taken with Nat Dickstein.

They worked side by side in a dusty vineyard, weeding and hoeing, with a light breeze blowing over them from the Sea of Galilee. Dickstein had taken off his shirt and worked in shorts and sandals, with the contempt for the sun which only the city-born possess.

He was a thin man, small-boned, with narrow shoulders, a shallow chest, and knobby elbows and knees. Karen would watch him when she stopped for a break – which she did often, although he never seemed to need a rest. Stringy muscles moved like knotted rope under his brown, scarred skin. She was a sensual woman, and she wanted to touch those scars with her fingers and ask him how he got them.

Sometimes he would look up and catch her staring, and he would grin, unembarrassed, and carry on working. His face was regular and anonymous in repose. He had dark eyes behind cheap round spectacles of the kind which Karen's generation liked because John Lennon wore them. His hair was dark, too, and short: Karen would have liked him to grow it. When he grinned that lopsided grin, he looked younger; though at any time it was hard to say just how old he might be. He had the strength and energy of a young man, but she had seen the concentration camp tattoo under his wristwatch, so he could not be much less than forty, she thought.

He had arrived at the kibbutz shortly after Karen, in the summer of 1967. She had come, with her deodorants and her contraceptive pills, looking for a place where she could live out hippy ideals without getting stoned twenty-four hours a day. He had been brought here in an ambulance. She assumed he had been wounded in the Six-Day War, and the other kibbutzniks agreed, vaguely, that it was something like that.

His welcome had been very different from hers. Karen's reception had been friendly but wary: in her philosophy they saw their own, with dangerous additions. Nat Dickstein returned like a long-lost son. They clustered around him, fed him soup and came away from his wounds with tears in their eyes.

If Dickstein was their son, Esther was their mother. She was the oldest member of the kibbutz. Karen had said, 'She looks like Golda Meir's mother,' and one of the others had said, 'I think she's Golda's *father*,' and they all laughed affectionately. She used a walking stick, and stomped about the village giving unsolicited advice, most of it very wise. She had stood guard outside Dickstein's sickroom chasing away noisy children, waving her stick and threatening beatings which even the children knew would never be administered.

Dickstein had recovered very quickly. Within a few days he was sitting out in the sun, peeling vegetables for the kitchen and telling vulgar jokes to the older children. Two weeks later he was working in the fields, and soon he was labouring harder than all but the youngest men.

His past was vague, but Esther had told Karen the story of his arrival in Israel in 1948, during the War of Independence.

Nineteen forty-eight was part of the recent past for Esther. She had been a young woman in London in the first two decades of the century, and had been an activist in half a dozen radical left-wing causes from suffragism to pacifism before emigrating to Palestine; but her memory went back further, to pogroms in Russia which she recalled vaguely in monstrous nightmare images. She had sat under a fig tree in the heat of the day, varnishing a chair she had made with her own gnarled hands, and talked about Dickstein like a clever but mischievous schoolboy.

'There were eight or nine of them, some from the university, some working men from the East End. If they ever had any money, they'd spent it before they got to France. They hitched a ride on a truck to Paris, then jumped a freight train to Marseilles. From there, it seems, they walked most of the way to Italy. Then they stole a huge car, a German Army staff car, a Mercedes, and drove all the way to the toe of Italy.' Esther's face was creased in smiles, and Karen thought: She would love to have been there with them.

'Dickstein had been to Sicily in the war, and it seems he knew the Mafia there. They had all the guns left over from the war. Dickstein wanted guns for Israel, but he had no money. He persuaded the Sicilians to sell a boatload of submachine guns to an Arab purchaser, and then to tell the Jews where the pickup would take place. They knew what he was up to, and they loved it. The deal was done, the Sicilians got their money, and then Dickstein and his friend stole the boat with its cargo and sailed to Israel!'

Karen had laughed aloud, there under the fig tree, and a grazing goat looked up at her balefully.

'Wait,' said Esther, 'you haven't heard the end of it. Some of the university boys had done a bit of rowing, and one of the other lot was a docker, but that was all the experience they had of the sea, and here they were sailing a five-thousand-ton cargo vessel on their own. They figured out a little navigation from first principles: the ship had charts and a compass. Dickstein had looked up in a book how to start the ship, but he says the book did not tell how to stop it. So they steamed into Haifa, yelling and waving and throwing their hats into the air, just like it was a varsity rag – and ploughed straight into the dock.

'They were forgiven instantly, of course – the guns were more precious than gold, literally. And that's when they started to call Dickstein "The Pirate".'

He did not look much like a pirate, working in the vineyard in his baggy shorts and his spectacles, Karen thought. All the same, he was attractive. She wanted to seduce him, but she could not figure out how. He obviously liked her, and she had taken care to let him know she was available. But he never made a move.

Perhaps he felt she was too young and innocent. Or maybe he was not interested in women.

His voice broke into her thoughts. 'I think we've finished.'

She looked at the sun: it was time to go. 'You've done twice as much as me.'

'I'm used to the work. I've been here, on and off, for twenty years. The body gets into the habit.'

They walked back toward the village as the sky turned purple and yellow. Karen said, 'What else do you do – when you're not here?'

'Oh . . . poison wells, kidnap Christian children.'

Karen laughed.

Dickstein said, 'How does this life compare with California?'

'This is a wonderful place,' she told him. 'I think there's a lot of work still to be done before the women are genuinely equal.'

'That seems to be the big topic at the moment.'

'You never have much to say about it.'

'Listen, I think you're right; but it's better for people to take their freedom rather than be given it.'

Karen said, 'That sounds like a good excuse for doing nothing.'

Dickstein laughed.

As they entered the village they passed a young man on a pony, carrying a rifle, on his way to patrol the borders of the settlement. Dickstein called out, 'Be careful, Yisrael.' The shelling from the Golan Heights had stopped, of course, and the children no longer had to sleep underground; but the kibbutz kept up the patrols. Dickstein had been one of those in favour of maintaining vigilance.

'I'm going to read to Mottie,' Dickstein said.

'Can I come?'

'Why not?' Dickstein looked at his watch. 'We've just got time to wash. Come to my room in five minutes.'

They parted, and Karen went into the showers. A kibbutz was the best place to be an orphan, she thought as she took off her clothes. Mottie's parents were both dead – the father blown up in the attack on the Golan Heights during the last war, the mother killed a year earlier in a shootout with Fedayeen. Both had been close friends of Dickstein. It was a tragedy for the child, of course; but he still slept in the same bed, ate in the same room, and had almost one hundred other adults to love and care for him – he was not foisted on to unwilling aunts or ageing grandparents or, worst of all, an orphanage. And he had Dickstein.

When she had washed off the dust Karen put on clean clothes and went to Dickstein's room. Mottie was already there, sitting on Dickstein's lap, sucking his thumb and listening to *Treasure Island* in Hebrew. Dickstein was the only person Karen had ever met who spoke Hebrew with a Cockney accent. His speech was even more strange now, because he was doing different voices for the characters in the story: a high-pitched boy's voice for Jim, a deep snarl for Long John Silver, and a half whisper for the mad Ben Gunn. Karen sat and watched the two of them in the yellow electric light, thinking how boyish Dickstein appeared, and how grown-up the child was.

When the chapter was finished they took Mottie to his dormitory, kissed him goodnight, and went into the dining room. Karen thought: If we continue to go about together like this, everyone will think we're lovers already.

They sat with Esther. After dinner she told them a story, and there was a young woman's twinkle in her eye. 'When I first went to Jerusalem, they used to say that if you owned a feather pillow, you could buy a house.'

Dickstein willingly took the bait. 'How was that?'

'You could sell a good feather pillow for a pound. With that pound you could join a loan society, which entitled you to borrow ten pounds. Then you found a plot of land. The owner of the land would take ten pounds deposit and the rest in promissory notes. Now you were a landowner. You went to a builder and said, "Build a house for yourself on this plot of land. All I want is a small flat for myself and my family."'

They all laughed. Dickstein looked toward the door. Karen followed his glance and saw a stranger, a stocky man in his forties with a coarse, fleshy face. Dickstein got up and went to him.

Esther said to Karen, 'Don't break your heart, child. That one is not made to be a husband.'

Karen looked at Esther, then back at the doorway. Dickstein had gone. A few moments later she heard the sound of a car starting up and driving away.

Esther put her old hand on Karen's young one, and squeezed.

Karen never saw Dickstein again.

Nat Dickstein and Pierre Borg sat in the back seat of a big black Citroën. Borg's bodyguard was driving, with his machine pistol lying on the front seat beside him. They travelled through the darkness with nothing ahead but the cone of light from the headlamps. Nat Dickstein was afraid.

He had never come to see himself the way others did, as a competent, indeed brilliant, agent who had proved his ability to survive just about anything. Later, when the game was on and he was living by his wits, grappling at close quarters with strategy and problems and personalities, there would be no room in his mind for fear; but now, when Borg was about to brief him, he had no plans to make, no forecasts to refine, no characters to assess. He knew only that he had to turn his back on peace and simple hard work, the land and the sunshine and caring for growing things; and that ahead of him there were terrible risks and great danger, lies and pain and bloodshed and, perhaps, his death. So he sat in the corner of the seat, his arms and legs crossed tightly, watching Borg's dimly lit face, while fear of the unknown knotted and writhed in his stomach and made him nauseous.

In the faint, shifting light, Borg looked like the giant in a fairy story. He had heavy features: thick lips, broad cheeks, and protruding eyes shadowed by thick brows.

As a child he had been told he was ugly, and so he had grown into an ugly man. When he was uneasy – like now – his hands went continually to his face, covering his mouth, rubbing his nose, scratching his forehead, in a subconscious attempt to hide his unsightliness. Once, in a relaxed moment, Dickstein had asked him, 'Why do you yell at everybody?' and he had replied, 'Because they're all so fucking handsome.'

They never knew what language to use when they spoke. Borg was French-Canadian originally, and found Hebrew a struggle. Dickstein's Hebrew was good and his French only passable. Usually they settled for English.

Dickstein had worked under Borg for ten years, and still he did not like the man. He felt he understood Borg's troubled, unhappy nature; and he respected his professionalism and his obsessional devotion to Israeli Intelligence; but in Dickstein's book this was not enough cause to like a person. When Borg lied to him, there were always good sound reasons, but Dickstein resented the lie no less.

He retaliated by playing Borg's tactics back against him. He would refuse to say where he was going, or he would lie about it. He never checked in on schedule while he was in the field: he simply called or sent messages with peremptory demands. And he would sometimes conceal from Borg part or all of his game plan. This prevented Borg from interfering with schemes of his own, and it was also more secure – for what Borg knew, he might be obliged to tell to politicians, and what they knew might find its way to the opposition. Dickstein knew the strength of his position – he was responsible for many of the triumphs which had distinguished Borg's career – and he played it for all it was worth.

The Citroën roared through the Arab town of Nazareth – deserted now, presumably under curfew – and went on into the night, heading for Tel Aviv. Borg lit a thin cigar and began to speak.

'After the Six-Day War, one of the bright boys in the Ministry of Defence wrote a paper entitled "The Inevitable Destruction of Israel." The argument went like this. During the War of Independence, we bought arms from Czechoslovakia. When the Soviet bloc began to take the Arab side, we turned to France, and later West Germany. Germany called off all deals as soon as the Arabs found out. France imposed an embargo after the Six-Day War. Both Britain and the United States have consistently refused to supply us with arms. We are losing our sources one by one.

'Suppose we are able to make up those losses, by continually finding new suppliers and by building our own munitions industry: even then, the fact remains that Israel must be the loser in a Middle East arms race. The oil countries will be richer than us throughout the foreseeable future. Our defence budget is already a terrible burden on the national economy whereas our enemies have nothing better to spend their billions on. When they have ten thousand tanks, we'll need six thousand; when they have twenty thousand tanks, we'll need twelve thousand; and so on. Simply by doubling their arms expenditure every year, they will be able to cripple our national economy without firing a shot.

'Finally, the recent history of the Middle East shows a pattern of limited wars about once a decade. The logic of this pattern is against us. The Arabs can afford to lose a war from time to time. We can't: our first defeat will be our last war.

'Conclusion: the survival of Israel depends on our breaking out of the vicious spiral our enemies have prescribed for us.'

Dickstein nodded. 'It's not a novel line of thought. It's the usual argument for "peace at any price." I should think the bright boy got fired from the Ministry of Defence for that paper.'

'Wrong both times. He went on to say, "We must inflict, or have the power to inflict, permanent and crippling damage to the next Arab army that crosses our borders. We must have nuclear weapons."'

Dickstein was very still for a moment; then he let out his breath in a long whistle. It was one of those devastating ideas that seems completely obvious as soon as it has been said. It would change everything. He was silent for a while, digesting the implications. His mind teemed with questions. Was it technically feasible? Would the Americans help? Would the Israeli Cabinet approve it? Would the Arabs retaliate with their own bomb? What he said was, 'Bright boy in the Ministry, hell. That was Moshe Dayan's paper.'

'No comment,' said Borg.

'Did the Cabinet adopt it?'

'There has been a long debate. Certain elder statesmen argued that they had not come this far to see the Middle East wiped out in a nuclear holocaust. But the opposition faction relied mainly on the argument that if we have a bomb, the Arabs will get one too, and we will be back at square one. As it turned out, that was their big mistake.' Borg reached into his pocket and took out a small plastic box. He handed it to Dickstein.

Dickstein switched on the interior light and examined the box. It was about an inch and a half square, thin, and blue in colour. It opened to reveal a small envelope made of heavy light-proof paper. 'What's this?' he said.

Borg said, 'A physicist named Friedrich Schulz visited Cairo in February. He is Austrian but he works in the United States. He was apparently on holiday in Europe, but his plane ticket to Egypt was paid for by the Egyptian government.

'I had him followed, but he gave our boy the slip and disappeared into the Western Desert for forty-eight hours. We know from CIA satellite pictures that there is a major construction project going on in that part of the desert. When Schulz came back, he had that in his pocket. It's a personnel dosimeter. The envelope, which is light-tight, contains a piece of ordinary photographic film. You carry the box in your pocket, or pinned to your lapel or trouser belt. If you're exposed to radiation, the film will show fogging when it's developed. Dosimeters are carried, as a matter of routine, by everyone who visits or works in a nuclear power station.'

Dickstein switched off the light and gave the box back to Borg. 'You're telling me the Arabs are already making atom bombs,' he said softly.

'That's right.' Borg spoke unnecessarily loudly.

'So the Cabinet gave Dayan the go-ahead to make a bomb of his own.'

'In principle, yes.'

'How so?'

'There are some practical difficulties. The mechanics of the business are simple – the actual clockwork of the bomb, so to speak. Anyone who can make a conventional bomb can make a nuclear bomb. The problem is getting hold of the explosive material, plutonium. You get plutonium out of an atomic reactor. It's a by-product. Now, we have a reactor, at Dimona in the Negev Desert. Did you know that?'

'Yes.'

'It's our worst-kept secret. However, we don't have the equipment for extracting the plutonium from the spent fuel. We could build a reprocessing plant, but the problem is that we have no uranium *of our own* to put through the reactor.'

'Wait a minute.' Dickstein frowned. 'We must have uranium, to fuel the reactor for normal use.'

'Correct. We get it from France, and it's supplied to us on condition we return the spent fuel to them for reprocessing, so they get the plutonium.'

'Other suppliers?'

'Would impose the same condition – it's part of all the nuclear non-proliferation treaties.'

Dickstein said, 'But the people at Dimona could siphon off some of the spent fuel without anyone noticing.'

'No. Given the quantity of uranium originally supplied, it's possible to calculate precisely how much plutonium comes out the other end. And they weigh it very carefully – it's expensive stuff.'

'So the problem is to get hold of some uranium.'

'Right.'

'And the solution?'

'The solution is, you're going to steal it.'

Dickstein looked out of the window. The moon came out, revealing a flock of sheep huddled in a corner of a field, watched by an Arab shepherd with a staff: a Biblical scene. So this was the game: stolen uranium for the land of milk and honey. Last time it had been the murder of a terrorist leader in Damascus; the time before, blackmailing a wealthy Arab in Monte Carlo to stop him funding the Fedayeen.

Dickstein's feelings had been pushed into the background while Borg talked about politics and Schulz and nuclear reactors. Now he was reminded that this involved *him*; and the fear came back, and with it a memory. After his father died the family had been desperately poor, and when creditors called, Nat had been sent to the door to say mummy was out. At the age of thirteen, he had found it unbearably humiliating, because the creditors knew he was lying, and he knew they knew, and they would look at him with a mixture of contempt and pity which pierced him to the quick.

He would never forget that feeling – and it came back, like a reminder from his unconscious, when somebody like Borg said something like, 'Little Nathaniel, go steal some uranium for your motherland.'

To his mother he had always said, 'Do I have to?' And now he said to Pierre Borg, 'If we're going to steal it anyway, why not buy it and simply refuse to send it back for reprocessing?'

'Because that way, everyone would know what we're up to.'

'So?'

'Reprocessing takes time – many months. During that time two things could happen: one, the Egyptians would hurry their programme; and two, the Americans would pressure us not to build the bomb.'

'Oh!' It was worse. 'So you want me to steal this stuff without anyone knowing that it's us.'

'More than that.' Borg's voice was harsh and throaty. 'Nobody must even know it's been stolen. It must look as if the stuff has just been lost. I want the owners, and the international agencies, to be so embarrassed about the stuff disappearing that they will hush it up. Then, when they discover they've been robbed, they will be compromised by their own cover-up.'

'It's bound to come out eventually.'

'Not before we've got our bomb.'

They had reached the coast road from Haifa to Tel Aviv, and as the car butted through the night Dickstein could see, over to the right, occasional glimpses of the Mediterranean, glinting like jewellery in the moonlight.

When he spoke he was surprised at the note of weary resignation in his voice. 'How much uranium do we need?'

'They want twelve bombs. In the yellowcake form – that's the uranium ore – it would mean about a hundred tons.'

'I won't be able to slip it into my pocket, then.' Dickstein frowned. 'What would all that cost if we bought it?'

'Something over one million US dollars.'

'And you think the losers will just hush it up?'

'If it's done right.'

'How?'

'That's your job, Pirate.'

'I'm not so sure it's possible,' Dickstein said.

'It's got to be. I told the Prime Minister we could pull it off. I laid my career on the line, Nat.'

'Don't talk to me about your bleeding career.'

Borg lit another cigar – a nervous reaction to Dickstein's scorn. Dickstein opened his window an inch to let the smoke out. His sudden hostility had nothing to do with Borg's clumsy personal appeal: that was typical of the man's inability to understand how people felt toward him. What had unnerved Dickstein was a sudden vision of mushroom clouds over Jerusalem and Cairo, of cotton fields by the Nile and vineyards beside the Sea of Galilee blighted by fallout, the Middle East wasted by fire, its children deformed for generations.

He said, 'I still think peace is an alternative.'

Borg shrugged. 'I wouldn't know. I don't get involved in politics.'

'Bullshit. '

Borg sighed. 'Look, if they have a bomb, we have to have one too, don't we?'

'If that was all there was to it, we could just hold a press conference, announce that the Egyptians are making a bomb, and let the rest of the world stop them. I think our people want the bomb anyway. I think they're glad of the excuse.'

'And maybe they're right!' Borg said. 'We can't go on fighting a war every few years – one of these days we might lose one.'

'We could make peace.'

Borg snorted. 'You're so fucking naive.'

'If we gave way on a few things – the Occupied Territories, the Law of Return, equal rights for Arabs in Israel—'

'The Arabs have equal rights.'

Dickstein smiled mirthlessly. 'You're so fucking naive.'

'Listen!' Borg made an effort at self-control. Dickstein understood his anger: it was a reaction he had in common with many Israelis. They thought that if these liberal ideas should ever take hold, they would be the thin edge of the wedge, and concession would follow concession until the land was handed back to the Arabs on a plate – and that prospect struck at the very roots of their identity. 'Listen,' Borg said again. 'Maybe we should sell our birthright for a mess of potage. But this is the real world, and the people of this country won't vote for peace-at-any-price; and in your heart you know that the Arabs aren't in any great hurry for peace either. So, in the real world, we still have to fight them; and if we're going to fight them we'd better win; and if we're to be sure of winning, you'd better steal us some uranium.'

Dickstein said, 'The thing I dislike most about you is, you're usually right.'

Borg wound down his window and threw away the stub of his cigar. It made a trail of sparks on the road, like a firecracker. The lights of Tel Aviv became visible ahead: they were almost there.

Borg said, 'You know, with most of my people I don't feel obliged to argue politics every time I give them an assignment. They just take orders, like operatives are supposed to.'

'I don't believe you,' Dickstein said. 'This is a nation of idealists, or it's nothing.'

'Maybe.'

'I once knew a man called Wolfgang. He used to say, "I just take orders." Then he used to break my leg.'

'Yeah,' Borg said. 'You told me.'

When a company hires an accountant to keep the books, the first thing he does is announce that he has so much work to do on the overall direction of the company's financial policy that he needs to hire a junior accountant to keep the books. Something similar happens with spies. A country sets up an intelligence service to find out how many tanks its neighbour has and where they are kept, and before you can say MI5 the intelligence service announces that it is so busy spying on subversive elements at home that a separate service is needed to deal with military intelligence.

So it was in Egypt in 1955. The country's fledgling intelligence service was divided into two directorates. Military Intelligence had the job of counting Israel's tanks; General Investigations had all the glamour.

The man in charge of both these directorates was called the Director of General Intelligence, just to be confusing; and he was supposed – in theory – to report to the Minister of the Interior. But another thing that always happens to spy departments is that the Head of State tries to take them over. There are two reasons for this. One is that the spies are continually hatching lunatic schemes of murder, blackmail and invasion which can be terribly embarrassing if they ever get off the ground, so Presidents and Prime Ministers like to keep a personal eye on such departments. The other reason is that intelligence services are a source of power, especially in unstable countries, and the Head of State wants that power for himself.

So the Director of General Intelligence in Cairo always, in practice, reported either to the President or to the Minister of State at the Presidency.

Kawash, the tall Arab who interrogated and killed Towfik and subsequently gave the personnel dosimeter to Pierre Borg, worked in the Directorate of General Investigations, the glamorous civilian half of the service. He was an intelligent and dignified man of great integrity, but he was also deeply religious – to the point of mysticism. His was the solid, powerful kind of mysticism which could support the most unlikely – not to say bizarre – beliefs about the real world. He adhered to a brand of Christianity which held that the return of the Jews to the Promised Land was ordained in the Bible, and was a portent of the end of the world. To work against the return was therefore a sin; to work for it, a holy task. This was why Kawash was a double agent.

The work was all he had. His faith had led him into the secret life, and there he had gradually cut himself off from friends, neighbors, and – with exceptions – family. He had no personal ambitions except to go to heaven. He lived ascetically, his only earthly pleasure being to score points in the espionage game. He was a lot like Pierre Borg, with this difference: Kawash was happy.

At present, though, he was troubled. So far he was losing points in the affair which had begun with Professor Schulz, and this depressed him. The problem was that the Qattara project was being run not by General Investigations but by the other half of the intelligence effort – Military Intelligence. However, Kawash had fasted and meditated, and in the long watches of the night he had developed a scheme for penetrating the secret project.

He had a second cousin, Assam, who worked in the office of the Director of General Intelligence – the body which coordinated Military Intelligence and General Investigations. Assam was more senior than Kawash, but Kawash was smarter.

The two cousins sat in the back room of a small, dirty coffee house near the Sherif Pasha in the heat of the day, drinking lukewarm lime cordial and blowing tobacco smoke at the flies. They looked alike in their lightweight suits and Nasser moustaches. Kawash wanted to use Assam to find out about Qattara. He had devised a plausible line of approach which he thought Assam would go for, but he knew he had to put the matter very delicately in order to win Assam's support. He appeared his usual imperturbable self, despite the anxiety he felt inside.

He began by seeming to be very direct. 'My cousin, do you know what is happening at Qattara?'

A rather furtive look came over Assam's handsome face. 'If you don't know, I can't tell you.'

Kawash shook his head, as if Assam had misunderstood him. 'I don't want you to reveal secrets. Besides, I can guess what the project is.' This was a lie. 'What bothers me is that Maraji has control of it.'

'Why?'

'For your sake. I'm thinking of your career.'

'I'm not worried—'

'Then you should be. Maraji wants your job, you must know that.'

The café proprietor brought a dish of olives and two flat loaves of pita bread. Kawash was silent until he went out. He watched Assam as the man's natural insecurity fed on the lie about Maraji.

Kawash continued, 'Maraji is reporting directly to the Minister, I gather.'

'I see all the documents, though,' Assam said defensively.

'You don't know what he is saying privately to the Minister. He is in a very strong position.'

Assam frowned. 'How did you find out about the project, anyway?'

Kawash leaned back against the cool concrete wall. 'One of Maraji's men was doing a bodyguarding job in Cairo and realized he was being followed. The tail was an Israeli agent called Towfik. Maraji doesn't have any field men in the city, so the bodyguard's request for action was passed to me. I picked Towfik up.'

Assam snorted with disgust. 'Bad enough to let himself be followed. Worse to call the wrong department for help. This is terrible.'

'Perhaps we can do something about it, my cousin.'

Assam scratched his nose with a hand heavy with rings. 'Go on.'

'Tell the Director about Towfik. Say that Maraji, for all his considerable talents, makes mistakes in picking his men, because he is young and inexperienced by comparison with someone such as yourself. Insist that you should have charge of personnel for the Qattara project. Then put a man loyal to us into a job there.'

Assam nodded slowly. 'I see.'

The taste of success was in Kawash's mouth. He leaned forward. 'The Director will be grateful to you for having discovered this area of slackness in a top-security matter. And you will be able to keep track of everything Maraji does.'

'This is a very good plan,' Assam said. 'I will speak to the Director today. I'm grateful to you, cousin.'

Kawash had one more thing to say – the most important thing – and he wanted to say it at the best possible moment. It would wait a few minutes, he decided. He stood up and said, 'Haven't you always been my patron?'

They went arm-in-arm out into the heat of the city. Assam said, 'And I will find a suitable man immediatcly.'

'Ah, yes,' Kawash said, as if that reminded him of another small detail. 'I have a man who would be ideal. He is intelligent, resourceful, and very discreet – and the son of my late wife's brother.'

Assam's eyes narrowed. 'So he would report to you, too.'

Kawash looked hurt. 'If this is too much for me to ask . . .' He spread his hands in a gesture of resignation.

'No,' Assam said. 'We have always helped one another.'

They reached the corner where they parted company. Kawash struggled to keep his feeling of triumph from showing in his face. 'I will send the man to see you. You will find him completely reliable.'

'So be it,' said Assam.

Pierre Borg had known Nat Dickstein for twenty years. Back in 1948 Borg had been sure the boy was not agent material, despite that stroke with the boatload of rifles. He had been thin, pale, awkward, unprepossessing. But it had not been Borg's decision, and they had given Dickstein a trial. Borg had rapidly come to acknowledge that the kid might not look much but he was smart as shit. He also had an odd charm that Borg never understood. Some of the women in the Mossad were crazy about him – while others, like Borg, failed to see the attraction. Dickstein showed no interest either way – his dossier said, 'Sex life: none.'

Over the years Dickstein had grown in skill and confidence, and now Borg would rely on him more than any other agent. Indeed, if Dickstein had been more personally ambitious he could have had the job Borg now held.

Nevertheless, Borg did not see how Dickstein could fulfil his brief. The result of the policy debate over nuclear weapons had been one of those asinine political compromises which bedevilled the work of all civil servants: they had agreed to steal the uranium only if it could be done in such a way that nobody would know, at least for many years, that Israel had been the thief. Borg had fought the decision – he had been all for a sudden, swift piece of buccaneering and to hell with the consequences. A more judicious view had prevailed in the Cabinet; but it was Borg and his team who had to put the decision into effect.

There were other men in the Mossad who could carry out a prescribed scheme as well as Dickstein – Mike, the head of Special Operations, was one, and Borg himself was another. But there was nobody else to whom Borg could say, as he had said to Dickstein: This is the problem – go solve it.

The two men spent a day in a Mossad safe house in the town of Ramat Gan, just outside Tel Aviv. Security-vetted Mossad employees made coffee, served meals, and patrolled the garden with revolvers under their jackets. In the morning Dickstein saw a young physics teacher from the Weizmann Institute at Rehovot. The scientist had long hair and a flowered tie, and he explained the chemistry of uranium, the nature of radioactivity and the working of an atomic pile with limpid clarity and endless patience. After lunch Dickstein talked to an administrator from Dimona about uranium mines, enrichment plants, fuel fabrication works, storage and transport; about safety rules and international regulations; and about the International Atomic Energy Agency, the US Atomic Energy Commission, the United Kingdom Atomic Energy Authority and Euratom.

In the evening Borg and Dickstein had dinner together. Borg was on a halfhearted diet, as usual: he ate no bread with his skewered lamb and salad, but he drank most of the bottle of red Israeli wine. His excuse was that he was calming his nerves so that he would not reveal his anxiety to Dickstein.

After dinner he gave Dickstein three keys. 'There are spare identities for you in safety-deposit boxes in London, Brussels and Zurich,' he said. 'Passports, driving licences, cash and a weapon in each. If you have to switch, leave the old documents in the box.'

Dickstein nodded. 'Do I report to you or Mike?'

Borg thought: You never report anyway, you bastard. He said, 'To me, please. Whenever possible, call me direct and use the jargon. If you can't reach me, contact any embassy and use the code for a meeting – I'll try to get to you, wherever you are. As a last resort, send coded letters via the diplomatic bags.'

Dickstein nodded expressionlessly: all this was routine. Borg stared at him, trying to read his mind. How did *he* feel? Did he think he could do it? Did he have any ideas? Did he plan to go through the motions of trying it and then report that it was impossible? Was he really convinced the bomb was the right thing for Israel?

Borg could have asked, but he would have got no answers.

Dickstein said, 'Presumably there's a deadline.'

'Yes, but we don't know what it is.' Borg began to pick onions out of the remains of the salad. 'We must have our bomb before the Egyptians get theirs. That means your uranium has to go on stream in the reactor before the Egyptian reactor goes operational. After that point, everything is chemistry – there's nothing either side can do to hurry subatomic particles. The first to start will be the first to finish.'

'We need an agent in Qattara,' Dickstein said.

'I'm working on it.'

Dickstein nodded. 'We must have a very good man in Cairo.'

This was not what Borg wanted to talk about. 'What are you trying to do, pump me for information?' he said crossly.

'Thinking aloud.'

There was silence for a few moments. Borg crunched some more onions. At last he said, 'I've told you what I want, but I've left to you all the decisions about how to get it.'

'Yes, you have, haven't you.' Dickstein stood up. 'I think I'll go to bed.'

'Have you got any idea where you're going to start?'

Dickstein said, 'Yes, I have. Goodnight.'

CHAPTER THREE

NAT DICKSTEIN never got used to being a secret agent. It was the continual deceit that bothered him. He was always lying to people, hiding, pretending to be someone he was not, surreptitiously following people and showing false documents to officials at airports. He never ceased to worry about being found out. He had a daytime nightmare in which he was surrounded suddenly by policemen who shouted, 'You're a spy! You're a spy!' and took him off to prison where they broke his leg.

He was uneasy now. He was at the Jean-Monnet building in Luxembourg, on the Kirchberg Plateau across a narrow river valley from the hilltop city. He sat in the entrance to the offices of the Euratom Safeguards Directorate, memorizing the faces of the employees as they arrived at work. He was waiting to see a press officer called Pfaffer but he had intentionally come much too early. He was looking for weakness. The disadvantage of this ploy was that all the staff got to see his face, too; but he had no time for subtle precautions.

Pfaffer turned out to be an untidy young man with an expression of disapproval and a battered brown briefcase. Dickstein followed him into an equally untidy office and accepted his offer of coffee. They spoke French. Dickstein was accredited to the Paris office of an obscure journal called *Science International.* He told Pfaffer that it was his ambition to get a job on *Scientific American.*

Pfaffer asked him, 'Exactly what are you writing about at the moment?'

'The article is called "MUF".' Dickstein explained in English, 'Material Unaccounted For.' He went on, 'In the United States radioactive fuel is continually getting lost. Here in Europe, I'm told, there's an international system for keeping track of all such material.'

'Correct,' Pfaffer said. 'The member countries hand over control of fissile substances to Euratom. We have, first of all, a complete list of civilian establishments where stocks are held – from mines through prep-aration and fabrication plants, stores, and reactors, to reprocessing plants.'

'You said civilian establishments.'

'Yes. The military are outside our scope.'

'Go on.' Dickstein was relieved to get Pfaffer talking before the press officer had a chance to realize how limited was Dickstein's knowledge of these subjects.

'As an example,' Pfaffer continued, 'take a factory making fuel elements from ordinary yellowcake. The raw material coming into the factory is weighed and analyzed by Euratom inspectors. Their findings are programmed into the Euratom computer and checked against the information from the inspectors at the dispatching installation – in this case, probably a ura-nium mine. If there is a discrepancy between the quantity that left the dispatching installation and the quantity that arrived at the factory, the computer will say so. Similar measurements are made of the material leaving the factory – quantity and quality. These figures will in turn be checked against information supplied by inspectors at the premises where the fuel is to be used – a nuclear power station, probably. In addition, all waste at the factory is weighed and analyzed.

'This process of inspection and double-checking is carried on up to and including the final disposal of radioactive wastes. Finally, stocktaking is done at least twice a year at the factory.'

'I see.' Dickstein looked impressed and felt desperately discouraged. No doubt Pfaffer was exaggerating the efficiency of the system – but even if they made half the checks they were supposed to, how could anyone spirit away one hundred tons of yellowcake without their computer noticing? To keep Pfaffer talking, he said, 'So, at any given moment, your computer knows the location of every scrap of uranium in Europe.'

'Within the member countries – France, Germany, Italy, Belgium, the Netherlands and Luxembourg. And it's not just uranium, it's all radioactive material.'

'What about details of transportation?'

'All have to be approved by us.'

Dickstein closed his notebook. 'It sounds like a good system. Can I see it in operation?'

'That wouldn't be up to us. You'd have to contact the atomic energy authority in the member country and ask permission to visit an installation. Some of them do guided tours.'

'Can you let me have a list of phone numbers?'

'Certainly.' Pfaffer stood up and opened a filing cabinet.

Dickstein had solved one problem only to be confronted with another. He had wanted to know where he could go to find out the location of stockpiles of radioactive material, and he now had the answer: Euratom's computer. But all the uranium the computer knew about was subject to the rigorous monitoring system, and therefore extremely difficult to steal. Sitting in the untidy little office, watching the smug Herr Pfaffer rummage through his old press releases, Dickstein thought: If only you knew what's in my mind, little bureaucrat, you'd have a blue fit; and he suppressed a grin and felt a little more cheerful.

Pfaffer handed him a cyclostyled leaflet. Dickstein folded it and put it in his pocket. He said, 'Thank you for your help.'

Pfaffer said, 'Where are you staying?'

'The Alfa, opposite the railway station.'

Pfaffer saw him to the door. 'Enjoy Luxembourg.'

'I'll do my best,' Dickstein said, and shook his hand.

The memory thing was a trick. Dickstein had picked it up as a small child, sitting with his grandfather in a smelly room over a pie shop in the Mile End Road, struggling to recognize the strange characters of the Hebrew alphabet. The idea was to isolate one unique feature of the shape to be remembered and ignore everything else. Dickstein had done that with the faces of the Euratom staff.

He waited outside the Jean-Monnet building in the late afternoon, watching people leave for home. Some of them interested him more than others. Secretaries, messengers and coffee-makers were no use to him, nor were senior administrators. He wanted the people in between: computer programmers, office managers, heads of small departments, personal assistants and assistant chiefs. He had given names to the likeliest ones, names which reminded him of their memorable feature: Diamante, Stiffcollar, Tony Curtis, No-nose, Snowhead, Zapata, Fatbum.

Diamante was a plump woman in her late thirties without a wedding ring. Her name came from the crystal glitter on the rims of her spectacles. Dickstein followed her to the car park, where she squeezed herself into the driving seat of a white Fiat 500. Dickstein's rented Peugeot was parked nearby.

She cross the Pont-Adolphe, driving badly but slowly, and went about fifteen kilometers southeast, finishing up at a small village called Mondorf-les-Bains. She parked in the cobbled yard of a square Luxembour-geois house with a nail-studded door. She let herself in with a key.

The village was a tourist attraction, with thermal springs. Dickstein slung a camera around his neck and wandered about, passing Diamante's house several times. On one pass he saw, through a window, Dia-mante serving a meal to an old woman.

The baby Fiat stayed outside the house until after midnight, when Dickstein left.

She had been a poor choice. She was a spinster living with her elderly mother, neither rich nor poor – the house was probably the mother's – and apparently without vices. If Dickstein had been a different kind of man he might have seduced her, but otherwise there was no way to get at her.

He went back to his hotel disappointed and frustrated – unreasonably so, for he had made the best guess he could on the information he had. Nevertheless he felt he had spent a day skirting the problem and he was impatient to get to grips with it so he could stop worrying vaguely and start worrying specifically.

He spent three more days getting nowhere. He drew blanks with Zapata, Fatbum and Tony Curtis.

But Stiffcollar was perfect.

He was about Dickstein's age, a slim, elegant man in a dark blue suit, plain blue tie, and white shirt with starched collar. His dark hair, a little longer than was usual for a man of his age, was greying over the ears. He wore handmade shoes.

He walked from the office across the Alzette River and uphill into the old town. He went down a narrow cobbled street and entered an old terraced house. Two minutes later a light went on in an attic window.

Dickstein hung around for two hours.

When Stiffcollar came out he was wearing close-fitting light trousers and an orange scarf around his neck. His hair was combed forward, making him look younger, and his walk was jaunty.

Dickstein followed him to the Rue Dicks, where he ducked into an unlit doorway and disappeared. Dickstein stopped outside. The door was open but there was nothing to indicate what might be inside. A bare flight of stairs went down. After a moment, Dickstein heard faint music.

Two young men in matching yellow jeans passed him and went in. One of them grinned back at him and said, 'Yes, this is the place.' Dickstein followed them down the stairs.

It was an ordinary-looking nightclub with tables and chairs, a few booths, a small dance floor and a jazz trio in a corner. Dickstein paid an entrance fee and sat at a booth, within sight of Stiffcollar. He ordered beer.

He had already guessed why the place had such a discreet air, and now, as he looked around, his theory was confirmed: it was a homosexual club. It was the first club of this kind he had been to, and he was mildly surprised to find it so unexceptionable. A few of the men wore light make-up, there were a couple of outrageous queens camping it up by the bar, and a very pretty girl was holding hands with an older woman in trousers; but most of the customers were dressed normally by the standards of peacock Europe, and there was no one in drag.

Stiffcollar was sitting close to a fair-haired man in a maroon double-breasted jacket. Dickstein had no feelings about homosexuals as such. He was not offended when people supposed, wrongly, that he might be homosexual because he was a bachelor in his early forties. To him, Stiffcollar was just a man who worked at Euratom and had a guilty secret.

He listened to the music and drank his beer. A waiter came across and said, 'Are you on your own, dear?'

Dickstein shook his head. 'I'm waiting for my friend.'

A guitarist replaced the trio and began to sing vulgar folk songs in German. Dickstein missed most of the jokes, but the rest of the audience roared with laughter. After that several couples danced.

Dickstein saw Stiffcollar put his hand on his companion's knee. He got up and walked across to their booth.

'Hello,' he said cheerfully, 'didn't I see you at the Euratom office the other day?'

Stiffcollar went white. 'I don't know . . .'

Dickstein stuck out his hand. 'Ed Rodgers,' he said, giving the name he had used with Pfaffer. 'I'm a journalist.'

Stiffcollar muttered, 'How do you do.' He was shaken, but he had the presence of mind not to give his name.

'I've got to rush away,' Dickstein said. 'It was nice to see you.'

'Goodbye, then.'

Dickstein turned away and went out of the club. He had done all that was necessary, for now: Stiffcollar knew that his secret was out, and he was frightened.

Dickstein walked towards his hotel, feeling grubby and ashamed.

He was followed from the Rue Dicks.

The tail was not a professional, and made no attempt at camouflage. He stayed fifteen or twenty steps behind, his leather shoes making a regular slap-slap on the pavement. Dickstein pretended not to notice. Crossing the road, he got a look at the tail: a large youth, long hair, worn brown leather jacket.

Moments later another youth stepped out of the shadows and stood squarely in front of Dickstein, blocking the pavement. Dickstein stood still and waited, thinking: What the hell is this? He could not imagine who could be tailing him already, nor why anyone who wanted him tailed would use clumsy amateurs from off the streets.

The blade of a knife glinted in the street light. The tail came up behind.

The youth in front said, 'All right, nancy-boy, give us your wallet.'

Dickstein was deeply relieved. They were just thieves who assumed that anyone coming out of that nightclub would be easy game.

'Don't hit me,' Dickstein said, 'I'll give you my money.' He took out his wallet.

'The wallet,' the youth said.

Dickstein did not want to fight them; but, while he could get more cash easily, he would be greatly inconvenienced if he lost all his papers and credit cards. He removed the notes from the wallet and offered them. 'I need my papers. Just take the money, and I won't report this.'

The boy in front snatched the notes.

The one behind said, 'Get the credit cards.'

The one in front was the weaker. Dickstein looked squarely at him and said, 'Why don't you quit while you're ahead, sonny?' Then he walked forward, passing the youth on the outside of the pavement.

Leather shoes beat a brief tattoo as the other rushed Dickstein, and then there was only one way for the encounter to end.

Dickstein spun about, grabbed the boy's foot as he aimed a kick, pulled and twisted, and broke the boy's ankle. The kid shouted with pain and fell down.

The one with the knife came at Dickstein then. He danced back, kicked the boy's shin, danced back, and kicked again. The boy lunged with the knife. Dickstein dodged and kicked him a third time in exactly the same place. There was a noise like a bone snapping, and the boy fell down.

Dickstein stood for a moment looking at the two injured muggers. He felt like a parent whose children had pushed him until he was obliged to strike them. He thought: Why did you make me do it? They *were* children: about seventeen, he guessed. They were vicious – they preyed on homosexuals; but that was exactly what Dickstein had been doing this night.

He walked away. It was an evening to forget. He decided to leave town in the morning.

When Dickstein was working he stayed in his hotel room as much as possible to avoid being seen. He might have been a heavy drinker, except it was unwise to drink during an operation – alcohol blunted the sharp edge of his vigilance – and at other times he felt no need of it. He spent a lot of time looking out of windows or sitting in front of a flickering television screen. He did not walk around the streets, did not sit in hotel bars, did not even eat in hotel restaurants – he always used room service. But there were limits to the precautions a man could take: he could not be invisible. In the lobby of the Alfa Hotel in Luxembourg he bumped into someone who knew him.

He was standing at the desk, checking out. He had looked over the bill and presented a credit card in the name of Ed Rodgers, and he was waiting to sign the American Express slip when a voice behind him said in English, 'My God! It's Nat Dickstein, isn't it?'

It was the moment he dreaded. Like every agent who used cover identities, he lived in constant fear of accidentally coming up against someone from his distant past who could unmask him. It was the nightmare of the policemen who shouted. 'You're a spy!' and it was the debt-collector saying, 'But your mother *is* in, I just saw her, through the window, hiding under the kitchen table.'

Like every agent he had been trained for this moment. The rule was simple: *Whoever it is, you don't know him.* They made you practise in the school. They would say, 'Today you are Chaim Meyerson, engineering student,' and so on; and you would have to walk around and do your work and be Chaim Meyerson; and then, late in the afternoon, they would arrange for you to bump into your cousin, or your old college professor, or a rabbi who knew your whole family. The first time, you always smiled and said 'Hello,' and talked about old times for a while, and then that evening your tutor told you that you were dead. Eventually you learned to look old friends straight in the eye and say, 'Who the hell are you?'

Dickstein's training came into play now. He looked first at the desk clerk, who was at that moment checking him out in the name of Ed Rodgers. The clerk did not react: presumably either he did not understand, or he had not heard, or he did not care.

A hand tapped Dickstein's shoulder. He started an apologetic smile and turned around, saying in French, 'I'm afraid you've got the wrong—'

The skirt of her dress was around her waist, her face was flushed with pleasure, and she was kissing Yasif Hassan.

'It *is* you!' said Yasif Hassan.

And then, because of the dreadful impact of the memory of that morning in Oxford twenty years ago, Dickstein lost control for an instant, and his training deserted him, and he made the biggest mistake of his career. He stared in shock, and he said, 'Christ. Hassan.'

Hassan smiled, and stuck out his hand, and said, 'How long . . . it must be . . . more than twenty years!'

Dickstein shook the proffered hand mechanically, conscious that he had blundered, and tried to pull himself together. 'It must be,' he muttered. 'What are you doing here?'

'I live here. You?'

'I'm just leaving.' Dickstein decided the only thing to do was get out, fast, before he did himself any more harm. The clerk handed him the credit-card form and he scribbled 'Ed Rodgers' on it. He looked at his wristwatch. 'Damn, I've got to catch this plane.'

'My car's outside,' Hassan said. 'I'll take you to the airport. We *must* talk.'

'I've ordered a taxi . . .'

Hassan spoke to the desk clerk. 'Cancel that cab – give this to the driver for his trouble.' He handed over some coins.

Dickstein said, 'I really am in a rush.'

'Come on, then!' Hassan picked up Dickstein's case and went outside.

Feeling helpless, foolish and incompetent, Dickstein followed.

They got into a battered two-seater English sports car. Dickstein studied Hassan as he steered the car out of a no-waiting zone and into the traffic. The Arab had changed, and it was not just age. The grey streaks in his moustache, the thickening of his waist, his deeper voice – these were to be expected. But something else was different. Hassan had always seemed to Dickstein to be the archetypal aristocrat. He had been slow-moving, dispassionate and faintly bored when everyone else was young and excitable. Now his hauteur seemed to have gone. He was like his car: somewhat the worse for wear, with a rather hurried air. Still, Dickstein had sometimes wondered how much of his upper-class appearance was cultivated.

Resigning himself to the consequences of his error, Dickstein tried to find out the extent of the damage. He asked Hassan, 'You live here now?'

'My bank has its European headquarters here.'

So, maybe he's still rich, Dickstein thought. 'Which bank is that?'

'The Cedar Bank of Lebanon.'

'Why Luxembourg?'

'It's a considerable financial centre,' Hassan replied. 'The European Investment Bank is here, and they have an international stock exchange. But what about you?'

'I live in Israel. My kibbutz makes wine – I'm sniffing at the possibilities of European distribution.'

'Taking coals to Newcastle.'

'I'm beginning to think so.'

'Perhaps I can help you, if you're coming back. I have a lot of contacts here. I could set up some appointments for you.'

'Thank you. I'm going to take you up on that offer.' If the worst came to the worst, Dickstein thought, he could always keep the appointments and sell some wine.

Hassan said, 'So, now your home is in Palestine and

my home is in Europe.' His smile was forced, Dickstein thought.

'How is the bank doing?' Dickstein asked, wondering whether 'my bank' had meant 'the bank I own' or 'the bank I manage' or 'the bank I work for'.

'Oh, remarkably well.'

They seemed not to have much more to say to each other. Dickstein would have liked to ask what had happened to Hassan's family in Palestine, how his affair with Eila Ashford had ended, and why he was driving a sports car; but he was afraid the answers might be painful, either for Hassan or for himself.

Hassan asked, 'Are you married?'

'No. You?'

'No.'

'How odd,' Dickstein said.

Hassan smiled. 'We're not the type to take on responsibilities, you and I.'

'Oh, I've got responsibilities,' Dickstein said, thinking of the orphan Mottie who had not yet finished *Treasure Island.*

'But you have a roving eye, eh?' Hassan said with a wink.

'As I recall, you were the ladies' man,' Dickstein said uncomfortably.

'Ah, those were the days.'

Dickstein tried not to think about Eila. They reached the airport, and Hassan stopped the car.

Dickstein said, 'Thank you for the lift.'

Hassan swivelled around in the bucket seat. He

stared at Dickstein. 'I can't get over this,' he said. 'You actually look younger than you did in 1947.'

Dickstein shook his hand. 'I'm sorry to be in such a rush.' He got out of the car.

'Don't forget – call me next time you're here,' Hassan said.

'Goodbye.' Dickstein closed the car door and walked into the airport.

Then, at last, he allowed himself to remember.

The four people in the chilly garden were still for one long heartbeat. Then Hassan's hands moved on Eila's body. Instantly Dickstein and Cortone moved away, through the gap in the hedge and out of sight. The lovers never saw them.

They walked toward the house. When they were well out of earshot Cortone said, 'Jesus, that was hot stuff.'

'Let's not talk about it,' Dickstein said. He felt like a man who, looking backward over his shoulder, has walked into a lamp-post: there was pain and rage, and nobody to blame but himself.

Fortunately the party was breaking up. They left without speaking to the cuckold, Professor Ashford, who was in a corner deep in conversation with a graduate student. They went to the George for lunch. Dickstein ate very little but drank some beer.

Cortone said, 'Listen, Nat, I don't know why you're getting so down in the mouth about it. I mean, it just goes to show she's available, right?'

'Yes,' Dickstein said, but he did not mean it.

The bill came to more than ten shillings. Cortone paid it. Dickstein walked him to the railway station. They shook hands solemnly, and Cortone got on the train.

Dickstein walked in the park for several hours, hardly noticing the cold, trying to sort out his feelings. He failed. He knew he was not envious of Hassan, or disillusioned with Eila, nor disappointed in his hopes, for he had never been hopeful. He was shattered, and he had no words to say why. He wished he had somebody to whom he could talk about it.

Soon after this he went to Palestine, although not just because of Eila.

In the next twenty-one years he never had a woman; but that, too, was not entirely because of Eila.

Yasif Hassan drove away from Luxembourg airport in a black rage. He could picture, as clearly as if it were yesterday, the young Dickstein: a pale Jew in a cheap suit, thin as a girl, always standing slightly hunched as if he expected to be flogged, staring with adolescent longing at the ripe body of Eila Ashford, arguing doggedly that his people would have Palestine whether the Arabs consented or not. Hassan had thought him ridiculous, a child. Now Dickstein lived in Israel, and grew grapes to make wine: he had found a home, and Hassan had lost one.

Hassan was no longer rich. He had never been fabulously wealthy, even by Levantine standards, but he had always had fine food, expensive clothes and the best education, and he had consciously adopted the manners of Arab aristocracy. His grandfather had been a successful doctor who set up his elder son in medicine and his younger son in business. The younger, Hassan's father, bought and sold textiles in Palestine, Lebanon and Transjordan. The business prospered under British rule, and Zionist immigration swelled the market. By 1947 the family had shops all over the Levant and owned their native village near Nazareth.

The 1948 war ruined them.

When the State of Israel was declared and the Arab armies attacked, the Hassan family made the fatal mistake of packing their bags and fleeing to Syria. They never came back. The warehouse in Jerusalem burned down; the shops were destroyed or taken over by Jews; and the family lands became 'administered' by the Israeli government. Hassan had heard that the village was now a kibbutz.

Hassan's father had lived ever since in a United Nations refugee camp. The last positive thing he had done was to write a letter of introduction for Yasif to his Lebanese bankers. Yasif had a university degree and spoke excellent English: the bank gave him a job.

He applied to the Israeli government for compensation under the 1953 Land Acquisition Act, and was refused.

He visited his family in the camp only once, but what he saw there stayed with him for the rest of his life. They lived in a hut made of boards and shared the communal toilets. They got no special treatment: they were just one among thousands of families without a home, a purpose or a hope. To see his father who had been a clever, decisive man ruling a large business with a firm hand, reduced now to queuing for food and wasting his life playing backgammon, made Yasif want to throw bombs at school buses.

The women fetched water and cleaned house much as always, but the men shuffled around in secondhand clothes, waiting for nothing, their bodies getting flabby while their minds grew dull. Teenagers strutted and squabbled and fought with knives, for there was nothing ahead of them but the prospect of their lives shrivelling to nothing in the baking heat of the sun.

The camp smelled of sewage and despair. Hassan never returned to visit, although he continued to write to his mother. He had escaped the trap, and if he was deserting his father, well, his father had helped him do it, so it must have been what he wanted.

He was a modest success as a bank clerk. He had intelligence and integrity, but his upbringing did not fit him for careful, calculating work involving much shuffling of memoranda and keeping of records in triplicate. Besides, his heart was elsewhere.

He never ceased bitterly to resent what had been taken from him. He carried his hatred through life like a secret burden. Whatever his logical mind might tell him, his soul said he had abandoned his father in time of need, and the guilt fed his hatred of Israel. Each year he expected the Arab armies to destroy the Zionist invaders, and each time they failed he grew more wretched and more angry.

In 1957 he began to work for Egyptian Intelligence.

He was not a very important agent, but as the bank expanded its European business he began to pick up the occasional titbit, both in the office and from general banking gossip. Sometimes Cairo would ask him for specific information about the finances of an arms manufacturer, a Jewish philanthropist, or an Arab millionaire; and if Hassan did not have the details in his bank's files he could often get them from friends and business contacts. He also had a general brief to keep an eye on Israeli businessmen in Europe, in case they were agents; and that was why he had approached Nat Dickstein and pretended to be friendly.

Hassan thought Dickstein's story was probably true. In his shabby suit, with the same round spectacles and the same inconspicuous air, he looked exactly like an underpaid salesman with a product he could not promote. However, there was that odd business in the Rue Dicks the previous night: two youths, known to the police as petty thieves, had been found in the gutter savagely disabled. Hassan had got all the details from a contact on the city police force. Clearly they had picked on the wrong sort of victim. Their injuries were professional: the man who had inflicted them had to be a soldier, a policeman, a bodyguard . . . or an agent. After an incident like that, any Israeli who flew out in a hurry the next morning was worth checking up on.

Hassan drove back to the Alfa Hotel and spoke to the desk clerk. 'I was here an hour ago when one of your guests was checking out,' he said. 'Do you remember?'

'I think so, sir.'

Hassan gave him two hundred Luxembourg francs. 'Would you tell me what name he was registered under?'

'Certainly, sir.' The clerk consulted a file. 'Edward Rodgers, from *Science International* magazine.'

'Not Nathaniel Dickstein?'

The clerk shook his head patiently.

'Would you just see whether you had a Nathaniel Dickstein, from Israel, registered at all?'

'Certainly.' The clerk took several minutes to look through a wad of papers. Hassan's excitement rose. If Dickstein had registered under a false name, then he was not a wine salesman – so what else could he be but an Israeli agent? Finally the clerk closed his file and looked up. 'Definitely not, sir.'

'Thank you.' Hassan left. He was jubilant as he drove back to his office: he had used his wits and discovered something important. As soon as he got to his desk he composed a message.

SUSPECTED ISRAELI AGENT SEEN HERE. NAT DICKSTEIN ALIAS ED RODGERS. FIVE FOOT SIX, SMALL BUILD, DARK HAIR, BROWN EYES, AGE ABOUT 40.

He encoded the message, added an extra code word at its top and sent it by telex to the bank's Egyptian headquarters. It would never get there: the extra code word instructed the Cairo post office to reroute the telex to the Directorate of General Investigations.

Sending the message was an anticlimax, of course. There would be no reaction, no thanks from the other end. Hassan had nothing to do but get on with his bank work, and try not to daydream.

Then Cairo called him on the phone.

It had never happened before. Sometimes they sent him cables, telexes, and even letters, all in code, of course. Once or twice he had met with people from Arab embassies and been given verbal instructions. But they had never phoned. His report must have caused more of a stir than he had anticipated.

The caller wanted to know more about Dickstein. 'I want to confirm the identity of the customer referred to in your message,' he said. 'Did he wear round spectacles?'

'Yes.'

'Did he speak English with a Cockney accent? Would you recognize such an accent?'

'Yes, and yes.'

'Did he have a number tattooed on his forearm?'

'I didn't see it today, but I know he has it . . . I was at Oxford University with him, years ago. I'm quite sure it is him.'

'You *know* him?' There was astonishment in the voice from Cairo. 'Is this information on your file?'

'No, I've never—'

'Then it should be,' the man said angrily. 'How long have you been with us?'

'Since 1957.'

'That explains it . . . those were the old days. Okay, now listen. This man is a very important . . . client. We want you to stay with him twenty-four hours a day, do you understand?'

'I can't,' Hassan said miserably. 'He left town.'

'Where did he go?'

'I dropped him at the airport, I don't know where he went.'

'Then find out. Phone the airlines, ask which flight he was on, and call me back in fifteen minutes.'

'I'll do my best—'

'I'm not interested in your best,' said the voice from Cairo. 'I want his destination, and I want it before he gets there. Just be sure you call me in fifteen minutes. Now that we've contacted him, *we must not lose him again.*'

'I'll get on to it right away,' said Hassan, but the line was dead before he could finish the sentence.

He cradled the phone. True, he had got no thanks from Cairo; but this was better. Suddenly he was important, his work was urgent, they were depending on him. He had a chance to do something for the Arab cause, a chance to strike back at last.

He picked up the phone again and started calling the airlines.

CHAPTER FOUR

NAT DICKSTEIN chose to visit a nuclear power station in France simply because French was the only European language he spoke passably well, except for English, but England was not part of Euratom. He travelled to the power station in a bus with an assorted party of students and tourists. The countryside slipping past the windows was a dusty southern green, more like Galilee than Essex, which had been 'the country' to Dickstein as a boy. He had travelled the world since, getting on planes as casually as any jet-setter, but he could remember the time when his horizons had been Park Lane in the west and Southend-on-Sea in the east. He could also remember how suddenly those horizons had receded, when he began to try to think of himself as a man, after his bar mitzvah and the death of his father. Other boys of his age saw themselves getting jobs on the docks or in printing plants, marrying local girls, finding houses within a quarter of a mile of their parents' homes and settling down; their ambitions were to breed a champion grey-hound, to see West Ham win the Cup Final, to buy a motor car. Young Nat thought he might go to California or Rhodesia or Hong Kong and become a brain surgeon or an archaeologist or a millionaire. It was partly that he was cleverer than most of his contemporaries; partly that to them foreign languages were alien, mysterious, a school subject like algebra rather than a way of talking; but mainly the difference had to do with being Jewish. Dickstein's boyhood chess partner, Harry Chieseman, was brainy and forceful and quick-witted, but he saw himself as a working-class Londoner and believed he would always be one. Dickstein knew – although he could not remember anyone actually telling him this – that wherever they were born, Jews were able to find their way into the greatest universities, to start new industries like motion pictures, to become the most successful bankers and lawyers and manufacturers; and if they could not do it in the country where they were born, they would move somewhere else and try again. It was curious, Dickstein thought as he recollected his boyhood, that a people who had been persecuted for centuries should be so convinced of their ability to achieve anything they set their minds to. Like, when they needed nuclear bombs, they went out and got them.

The tradition was a comfort, but it gave him no help with the ways and means.

The power station loomed in the distance. As the bus got closer, Dickstein realized that the reactor was going to be bigger than he had imagined. It occupied a ten-storey building. Somehow he had imagined the thing fitting into a small room.

The external security was on an industrial, rather than military, level. The premises were surrounded by one high fence, not electrified. Dickstein looked into the gatehouse while the tour guide went through the formalities: the guards had only two closed-circuit television screens. Dickstein thought: I could get fifty men inside the compound in broad daylight without the guards noticing anything amiss. It was a bad sign, he decided glumly: it meant they had other reasons to be confident.

He left the bus with the rest of the party and walked across the tar-macadamed parking lot to the reception building. The place had been laid out with a view to the public image of nuclear energy: there were well-kept lawns and flower beds and lots of newly planted trees; everything was clean and natural, white-painted and smokeless. Looking back toward the gatehouse, Dickstein saw a grey Opel pull up on the road. One of the two men in it got out and spoke to the security guards, who appeared to give directions. Inside the car, something glinted briefly in the sun.

Dickstein followed the tour party into the lounge. There in a glass case was a rugby football trophy won by the power station's team. An aerial photograph of the establishment hung on the wall. Dickstein stood in front of it, imprinting its details on his mind, idly figuring out how he would raid the place while the back of his mind worried about the grey Opel.

They were led around the power station by four hostesses in smart uniforms. Dickstein was not interested in the massive turbines, the space-age control room with its banks of dials and switches, or the water-intake system designed to save the fish and return them to the river. He wondered if the men in the Opel had been following him, and if so, why.

He was enormously interested in the delivery bay. He asked the hostess, 'How does the fuel arrive?'

'On trucks,' she said archly. Some of the party giggled nervously at the thought of uranium running around the countryside on trucks. 'It's not dangerous,' she went on as soon as she had got the expected laugh. 'It isn't even radioactive until it is fed into the atomic pile. It is taken off the truck straight into the elevator and up to the fuel store on the seventh floor. From there, everything is automatic.'

'What about checking the quantity and quality of the consignment?' Dickstein said.

'This is done at the fuel fabrication plant. The consignment is sealed there, and only the seals are checked here.'

'Thank you.' Dickstein nodded, pleased. The system was not quite as rigorous as Mr Pfaffer of Euratom had claimed. One or two schemes began to take vague shape in Dickstein's mind.

They saw the reactor loading machine in operation. Worked entirely by remote control, it took the fuel element from the store to the reactor, lifted the concrete lid of a fuel channel, removed the spent element, inserted the new one, closed the lid and dumped the used element into a water-filled shaft which led to the cooling ponds.

The hostess, speaking perfect Parisian French in an oddly seductive voice, said, 'The reactor has three thousand fuel channels, each channel containing eight fuel rods. The rods last four to seven years. The loading machine renews five channels in each operation.'

They went on to see the cooling ponds. Under twenty feet of water the spent fuel elements were loaded into pannets, then – cool, but still highly radioactive – they were locked into fifty-ton lead flasks, two hundred elements to a flask, for transport by road and rail to a reprocessing plant.

As the hostesses served coffee and pastries in the lounge Dickstein considered what he had learned. It had occurred to him that, since plutonium was ulti-mately what was wanted, he might steal used fuel. Now he knew why nobody had suggested it. It would be easy enough to hijack the truck – he could do it single-handed – but how would he sneak a fifty-ton lead flask out of the country and take it to Israel without anyone noticing?

Stealing uranium from inside the power station was no more promising an idea. Sure, the security was flimsy – the very fact that he had been permitted to make this reconnaissance, and had even been given a guided tour, showed that. But fuel inside the station was locked into an automatic, remote-controlled system. The only way it could come out was by going right through the nuclear process and emerging in the cooling ponds; and then he was back with the problem of sneaking a huge flask of radioactive material through some European port.

There had to be a way of breaking into the fuel store, Dickstein supposed; then you could manhandle the stuff into the elevator, take it down, put it on a truck and drive away; but that would involve holding some or all of the station personnel at gunpoint for some time, and his brief was to do this thing surreptitiously.

A hostess offered to refill his cup, and he accepted. Trust the French to give you good coffee. A young engineer began a talk on nuclear safety. He wore unpressed trousers and a baggy sweater. Scientists and technicians all had a look about them, Dickstein had observed: their clothes were old, mismatched and comfortable, and if many of them wore beards, it was usually a sign of indifference rather than vanity. He thought it was because in their work, force of personality generally counted for nothing, brains for everything, so there was no point in trying to make a good visual impression. But perhaps that was a romantic view of science.

He did not pay attention to the lecture. The physicist from the Weizmann Institute had been much more concise. 'There is no such thing as a safe level of radiation,' he had said. 'Such talk makes you think of radiation like water in a pool: if it's four feet high you're safe, if it's eight feet high you drown. But in fact radiation levels are much more like speed limits on the highway – thirty miles per hour is safer than eighty, but not as safe as twenty, and the only way to be completely safe is not to get in the car.'

Dickstein turned his mind back to the problem of stealing uranium. It was the requirement of *secrecy* that defeated every plan he dreamed. Maybe the whole thing was doomed to failure. After all, impossible is impossible, he thought. No, it was too soon to say that. He went back to first principles.

He would have to take a consignment in transit: that much was clear from what he had seen today. Now, the fuel elements were not checked at this end, they were fed straight into the system. He could hijack a truck, take the uranium out of the fuel elements, close them up again, reseal the consignment and bribe or frighten the truck driver to deliver the empty shells. The dud elements would gradually find their way into the reactor, five at a time, over a period of months. Eventually the reactor's output would fall marginally. There would be an investigation. Tests would be done. Perhaps no conclusions would be reached before the empty elements ran out and new, genuine fuel elements went in, causing output to rise again. Maybe no one would understand what had happened until the duds were reprocessed and the plutonium recovered was too little, by which time – four to seven years later – the trail to Tel Aviv would have gone cold.

But they might find out sooner. And there was still the problem of getting the stuff out of the country.

Still, he had the outline of one possible scheme, and he felt a bit more cheerful.

The lecture ended. There were a few desultory questions, then the party trooped back to the bus. Dickstein sat at the back. A middle-aged woman said to him, 'That was my seat,' and he stared at her stonily until she went away.

Driving back from the power station, Dickstein kept looking out of the rear window. After about a mile the grey Opel pulled out of a turnoff and followed the bus. Dickstein's cheerfulness vanished.

He had been spotted. It had happened either here or in Luxembourg, probably Luxembourg. The spotter might have been Yasif Hassan – no reason why he should not be an agent – or someone else. They must be following him out of general curiosity because there was no way – was there? – that they could know what he was up to. All he had to do was lose them.

He spent a day in and around the town near the nuclear power station, travelling by bus and taxi, driving a rented car, and walking. By the end of the day he had identified the three vehicles – the grey Opel, a dirty little flatbed truck, and a German Ford – and five of the men in the surveillance team. The men looked vaguely Arabic, but in this part of France many of the criminals were North African: somebody might have hired local help. The size of the team explained why he had not sniffed the surveillance earlier. They had been able continually to switch cars and personnel. The trip to the power station, a long there-and-back journey on a country road with very little traffic, explained why the team had finally blown themselves.

The next day he drove out of town and on to the autoroute. The Ford followed him for a few miles, then the grey Opel took over. There were two men in each car. There would be two more in the flatbed truck, plus one at his hotel.

The Opel was still with him when he found a

pedestrian bridge over the road in a place where there were no turnoffs from the highway for four or five miles in either direction. Dickstein pulled over to the shoulder, stopped the car, got out and lifted the hood. He looked inside for a few minutes. The grey Opel disappeared up ahead, and the Ford went by a minute later. The Ford would wait at the next turnoff, and the Opel would come back on the opposite side of the road to see what he was doing. That was what the textbook prescribed for this situation.

Dickstein hoped these people would follow the book, otherwise his scheme would not work.

He took a collapsible warning triangle from the trunk of the car and stood it behind the offside rear wheel.

The Opel went by on the opposite side of the highway.

They were following the book.

Dickstein began to walk.

When he got off the highway he caught the first bus he saw and rode it until it came to a town. On the journey he spotted each of the three surveillance vehicles at different times. He allowed himself to feel a little premature triumph: they were going for it.

He took a taxi from the town and got out close to his car but on the wrong side of the highway. The Opel went by, then the Ford pulled off the road a couple of hundred yards behind him.

Dickstein began to run.

He was in good condition after his months of out-door work in the kibbutz. He sprinted to the pedestrian bridge, ran across it and raced along the shoulder on the other side of the road. Breathing hard and sweating, he reached his abandoned car in under three minutes.

One of the men from the Ford had got out and started to follow him. The man now realized he had been taken in. The Ford moved off. The man ran back and jumped into it as it gathered speed and swung into the slow lane.

Dickstein got into his car. The surveillance vehicles were now on the wrong side of the highway and would have to go all the way to the next junction before they could cross over and come after him. At sixty miles per hour the round trip would take them ten minutes, which meant he had at least five minutes start on them. They would not catch him.

He pulled away, heading for Paris, humming a musical chant that came from the football terraces of West Ham: 'Easy, easy, eeeezeee.'

There was a godalmighty panic in Moscow when they heard about the Arab atom bomb.

The Foreign Ministry panicked because they had not heard of it earlier, the KGB panicked because they had not heard about it first, and the Party Secretary's office panicked because the last thing they wanted was another who's-to-blame row between the Foreign Ministry and the KGB; the previous one had made life hell in the Kremlin for eleven months.

Fortunately, the way the Egyptians chose to make

their revelation allowed for a certain amount of covering of rears. The Egyptians wanted to make the point that they were not diplomatically obliged to tell their allies about this secret project, and the technical help they were asking for was not crucial to its success. Their attitude was 'Oh, by the way, we're building this nuclear reactor in order to get some plutonium to make atom bombs to blow Israel off the face of the earth, so would you like to give us a hand, or not?' The message, trimmed and decorated with ambassadorial niceties, was delivered, in the manner of an afterthought, at the end of a routine meeting between the Egyptian Ambassador in Moscow and the deputy chief of the Middle East desk at the Foreign Ministry.

The deputy chief who received the message considered very carefully what he should do with the information. His first duty, naturally, was to pass the news to his chief, who would then tell the Secretary. However, the credit for the news would go to his chief, who would also not miss the opportunity for scoring points off the KGB. Was there a way for the deputy chief to gain some advantage to himself out of the affair?

He knew that the best way to get on in the Kremlin was to put the KGB under some obligation to yourself. He was now in a position to do the boys a big favour. If he warned them of the Egyptian Ambassador's message, they would have a little time to get ready to pretend they knew all about the Arab atom bomb and were about to reveal the news themselves.

He put on his coat, thinking to go out and phone

his acquaintance in the KGB from a phone booth in case his own phone were tapped – then he realized how silly that would be, for he was going to call the KGB, and it was they who tapped people's phones anyway; so he took off his coat and used his office phone.

The KGB desk man he talked to was equally expert at working the system. In the new KGB building on the Moscow ring road, he kicked up a huge fuss. First he called his boss's secretary and asked for an urgent meeting in fifteen minutes. He carefully avoided speaking to the boss himself. He fired off half a dozen more noisy phone calls, and sent secretaries and messengers scurrying about the building to take memos and collect files. But his master stroke was the agenda. It so happened that the agenda for the next meeting of the Middle East political committee had been typed the previous day and was at this moment being run off on a duplicating machine. He got the agenda back and at the top of the list added a new item: 'Recent Developments in Egyptian Armaments – Special Report,' followed by his own name in brackets. Next he ordered the new agenda to be duplicated, still bearing the previous day's date, and sent around to the interested departments that afternoon by hand.

Then when he had made certain that half Moscow would associate his name and no one else's with the news, he went to see his boss.

The same day a much less striking piece of news came in. As part of the routine exchange of information between Egyptian Intelligence and the KGB, Cairo sent notice that an Israeli agent named Nat Dickstein had been spotted in Luxembourg and was now under surveillance. Because of the circumstances, the report got less attention than it deserved. There was only one man in the KGB who entertained the mildest suspicion that the two items might be connected.

His name was David Rostov.

David Rostov's father had been a minor diplomat whose career was stunted by a lack of connections, particularly secret service connections. Knowing this, the son, with the remorseless logic which was to characterize his decisions all his life, joined what was then called the NKVD, later to become the KGB.

He had already been an agent when he went to Oxford. In those idealistic times, when Russia had just won the war and the extent of the Stalin purge was not comprehended, the great English universities had been ripe recruiting-grounds for Soviet Intelligence. Rostov had picked a couple of winners, one of whom was still sending secrets from London in 1968. Nat Dickstein had been one of his failures.

Young Dickstein had been some kind of socialist, Rostov remembered, and his personality was suited to espionage: he was withdrawn, intense and mistrustful. He had brains, too. Rostov recalled debating the Middle East with him, and with Professor Ashford and Yasif Hassan, in the green-and-white house by the river. And the Rostov–Dickstein chess match had been a hard-fought affair.

But Dickstein did not have the light of idealism in

his eyes. He had no evangelical spirit. He was secure in his convictions, but he had no wish to convert the rest of the world. Most of the war veterans had been like that. Rostov would lay the bait – 'Of course, if you *really* want to join the struggle for world socialism, you have to work for the Soviet Union' – and the veterans would say 'Bullshit.'

After Oxford Rostov had worked in Russian embassies in a series of European capitals – Rome, Amsterdam, Paris. He never got out of the KGB and into the diplomatic service. Over the years he came to realize that he did not have the breadth of political vision to become the great statesman his father wanted him to be. The earnestness of his youth disappeared. He still thought, on balance, that socialism was probably the political system of the future; but this credo no longer burned inside him like a passion. He believed in Communism the way most people believed in God: he would not be greatly surprised or disappointed if he turned out to be wrong, and meanwhile it made little difference to the way he lived.

In his maturity he pursued narrower ambitions with, if anything, greater energy. He became a superb technician, a master of the devious and cruel skills of the intelligence game; and – equally important in the USSR as well as the West – he learned how to manipulate the bureaucracy so as to gain maximum kudos for his triumphs.

The First Chief Directorate of the KGB was a kind of Head Office, responsible for collection and analysis of information. Most of the field agents were attached to the Second Chief Directorate, the largest department of the KGB, which was involved in subversion, sabotage, treason, economic espionage and any internal police work considered politically sensitive. The Third Chief Directorate, which had been called Smersh until that name got a lot of embarrassing publicity in the West, did counter-espionage and special operations, and it employed some of the bravest, cleverest, nastiest agents in the world.

Rostov worked in the Third, and he was one of its stars.

He held the rank of colonel. He had gained a medal for liberating a convicted agent from a British jail called Wormwood Scrubs. Over the years he had also acquired a wife, two children and a mistress. The mistress was Olga, twenty years his junior, a blonde Viking goddess from Murmansk and the most exciting woman he had ever met. He knew she would not have been his lover without the KGB privileges that came with him; all the same he thought she loved him. They were alike, and each knew the other to be coldly ambitious, and somehow that had made their passion all the more frantic. There was no passion in his marriage any more, but there were other things: affection, companionship, stability and the fact that Mariya was still the only person in the world who could make him laugh helplessly, convulsively, until he fell down. And the boys: Yuri Davidovitch, studying at Moscow State University and listening to smuggled Beatles records; and Vladimir Davidovitch, the young genius, already considered a potential world champion chess player. Vladimir had applied for a place at the prestigious Phys-Mat School No. 2, and Rostov was sure he would succeed: he deserved the place on merit, and a colonel in the KGB had a little influence too.

Rostov had risen high in the Soviet meritocracy, but he reckoned he could go a little higher. His wife no longer had to queue up in markets with the hoi polloi – she shopped at the Beryozka stores with the elite – and they had a big apartment in Moscow and a little dacha on the Baltic; but Rostov wanted a chauffeur-driven Volga limousine, a second dacha at a Black Sea resort where he could keep Olga, invitations to private showings of decadent Western movies, and treatment in the Kremlin Clinic when old age began to creep up on him.

His career was at a crossroads. He was fifty this year. He spent about half his time behind a desk in Moscow, the other half in the field with his own small team of operatives. He was already older than any other agent still working abroad. From here he would go in one of two directions. If he slowed up, and allowed his past victories to be forgotten, he would end his career lecturing to would-be agents at KGB school No. 311 in Novosibirsk, Siberia. If he continued to score spectacular points in the intelligence game, he would be promoted to a totally administrative job, get appointed to one or two committees, and begin a challenging – but safe – career in the organization of the Soviet Union's intelligence effort – and *then* he would get the Volga limousine and the Black Sea dacha.

Sometime in the next two or three years he would

need to pull off another great coup. When the news about Nat Dickstein came in, he wondered for a while whether this might be his chance.

He had watched Dickstein's career with the nostalgic fascination of a mathematics teacher whose brightest pupil has decided to go to art school. While still at Oxford he had heard stories about the stolen boatload of guns, and as a result had himself initiated Dickstein's KGB file. Over the years additions had been made to the file by himself and others, based on occasional sightings, rumours, guesswork and good old-fashioned espionage. The file made it clear that Dickstein was now one of the most formidable agents in the Mossad. If Rostov could bring home his head on a platter, the future would be assured.

But Rostov was a careful operator. When he was able to pick his targets, he picked easy ones. He was no death-or-glory man: quite the reverse. One of his more important talents was the ability to become invisible when chancy assignments were being handed out. A contest between himself and Dickstein would be uncomfortably even.

He would read with interest any further reports from Cairo on what Nat Dickstein was doing in Luxembourg; but he would take care not to get involved.

He had not come this far by sticking his neck out.

The forum for discussion of the Arab bomb was the Middle East political committee. It could have been any one of eleven or twelve Kremlin committees, for the same factions were represented on all the interested committees, and they would have said the same things; and the result would have been the same, because this issue was big enough to override factional considerations.

The committee had nineteen members, but two were abroad, one was ill and one had been run over by a truck on the day of the meeting. It made no difference. Only three people counted: one from the Foreign Ministry, one KGB man and one man who represented the Party Secretary. Among the supernumeraries were David Rostov's boss, who collected all the committee memberships he could just on general principles, and Rostov himself, acting as aide. (It was by signs such as this that Rostov knew he was being considered for the next promotion.)

The KGB was against the Arab bomb, because the KGB's power was clandestine and the bomb would shift decisions into the overt sphere and out of the range of KGB activity. For that very reason the Foreign Ministry was in favour – the bomb would give them more work and more influence. The Party Secretary was against, because if the Arabs were to win decisively in the Middle East, how then would the USSR retain a foothold there?

The discussion opened with the reading of the KGB report 'Recent Developments in Egyptian Armaments'. Rostov could imagine exactly how the one fact in the report had been spun out with a little background gleaned from a phone call to Cairo, a good deal of guesswork and much bullshit, into a screed which took twenty minutes to read. He had done that kind of thing himself more than once.

A Foreign Ministry underling then stated, at some length, his interpretation of Soviet policy in the Middle East. Whatever the motives of the Zionist settlers, he said, it was clear that Israel had survived only because of the support it had received from Western capitalism; and capitalism's purpose had been to build a Middle East outpost from which to keep an eye on its oil interests. Any doubts about this analysis had been swept away by the Anglo-Franco-Israeli attack on Egypt in 1956. Soviet policy was to support the Arabs in their natural hostility to this rump of colonialism. Now, he said, although it might have been imprudent – in terms of global politics – for the USSR to *initiate* Arab nuclear armament, nevertheless once such armament had commenced it was a straightforward extension of Soviet policy to *support* it. The man talked for ever.

Everyone was so bored by this interminable statement of the obvious that the discussion thereafter became quite informal: so much so, in fact, that Rostov's boss said, 'Yes, but, shit, we can't give atom bombs to those fucking lunatics.'

'I agree,' said the Party Secretary's man, who was also chairman of the committee. 'If they have the bomb, they'll use it. That will force the Americans to attack the Arabs, with or without nukes – I'd say with. Then the Soviet Union has only two options: let down its allies, or start World War Three.'

'Another Cuba,' someone muttered.

The man from the Foreign Ministry said, 'The answer to that might be a treaty with the Americans under which both sides agree that in no circumstances will they use nuclear weapons in the Middle East.' If he could get started on a project like that, his job would be safe for twenty-five years.

The KGB man said, 'Then if the Arabs dropped the bomb, would that count as our breaking the treaty?'

A woman in a white apron entered, pulling a trolley of tea, and the committee took a break. In the interval the Party Secretary's man stood by the trolley with a cup in his hand and a mouth full of fruitcake and told a joke. 'It seems there was a captain in the KGB whose stupid son had great difficulty understanding the concepts of the Party, the Motherland, the Unions and the People. The captain told the boy to think of his father as the Party, his mother as the Motherland, his grandmother as the Unions and himself as the People. Still the boy did not understand. In a rage the father locked the boy in a wardrobe in the parental bedroom. That night the boy was still in the wardrobe when the father began to make love to the mother. The boy, watching through the wardrobe keyhole, said, "Now I understand! The Party rapes the Motherland while the Unions sleep and the People have to stand and suffer!"'

Everybody roared with laughter. The tea-lady shook her head in mock disgust. Rostov had heard the joke before.

When the committee went reluctantly back to work, it was the Party Secretary's man who asked the crucial question. 'If we refuse to give the Egyptians the technical help they're asking for, will they still be able to build the bomb?'

The KGB man who had presented the report said, 'There is not enough information to give a definite answer, sir. However, I have taken background briefing from one of our scientists on this point, and it seems that to build a crude nuclear bomb is actually no more difficult, technically, than to build a conventional bomb.'

The Foreign Ministry man said, 'I think we must assume that they will be able to build it without our help, if perhaps more slowly.'

'I can do my own guessing,' the chairman said sharply.

'Of course,' said the Foreign Ministry man, chastened.

The KGB man continued, 'Their only serious problem would be to obtain a supply of plutonium. Whether they have one or not, we simply do not know.'

David Rostov took in all this with great interest. In his opinion there was only one decision the committee could possibly take. The chairman now confirmed his view.

'My reading of the situation is as follows,' he began. 'If we help the Egyptians build their bomb, we continue and strengthen our existing Middle East policy, we improve our influence in Cairo, and we are in a position to exert some control over the bomb. If we refuse to help, we estrange ourselves from the Arabs, and we possibly leave a situation in which they still have a bomb but we have no control over it.'

The Foreign Ministry man said, 'In other words, if they're going to have a bomb anyway, there had better be a Russian finger on the trigger.'

The chairman threw him a look of irritation, and continued, 'We might, then, recommend to the Secretariat as follows: the Egyptians should be given technical help with their nuclear reactor project, such help always to be structured with a view to Soviet personnel gaining ultimate control of the weaponry.'

Rostov permitted himself the ghost of a satisfied smile: it was the conclusion he had expected.

The Foreign Ministry man said, 'So move.'

The KGB man said, 'Seconded.'

'All in favour?'

They were all in favour.

The committee proceeded to the next item on the agenda.

It was not until after the meeting that Rostov was struck by this thought: if the Egyptians were in fact *not* able to build their bomb unaided – for lack of uranium, for instance – then they had done a very expert job of bluffing the Russians into giving them the help they needed.

Rostov liked his family, in small doses. The advantage of his kind of job was that by the time he got bored with them – and it *was* boring, living with children – he was off on another trip abroad, and by the time he came back he was missing them enough to put up with them for a few more months. He was fond of Yuri, the elder boy, despite his cheap music and contentious views about dissident poets; but Vladimir, the younger, was the apple of his eye. As a baby Vladimir had been so pretty that people thought he was a girl. From the start Rostov had taught the boy games of logic, spoken to him in complex sentences, discussed with him the geography of distant countries, the mechanics of engines, and the workings of radios, flowers, water taps and political parties. He had come to the top of every class he was put into – although now, Rostov thought, he might find his equals at Phys-Mat No. 2.

Rostov knew he was trying to instil in his son some of the ambitions he himself had failed to fulfil. Fortunately this meshed with the boy's own inclinations: he knew he was clever, he liked being clever, and he wanted to be a Great Man. The only thing he balked at was the work he had to do for the Young Communist League: he thought this was a waste of time. Rostov had often said, 'Perhaps it is a waste of time, but you will never get anywhere in any field of endeavour unless you also make progress in the Party. If you want to change the system, you'll have to get to the top and change it from within.' Vladimir accepted this and went to the Young Communist League meetings: he had inherited his father's unbending logic.

Driving home through the rush-hour traffic, Rostov looked forward to a dull, pleasant evening at home. The four of them would have dinner together, then watch a television serial about heroic Russian spies outwitting the CIA. He would have a glass of vodka before bed.

Rostov parked in the road outside his home. His building was occupied by senior bureaucrats, about half of whom had small Russian-built cars like his, but there were no garages. The apartments were spacious by Moscow standards: Yuri and Vladimir had a bedroom each, and nobody had to sleep in the living room.

There was a row going on when he entered his home. He heard Mariya's voice raised in anger, the sound of something breaking, and a shout; then he heard Yuri call his mother a foul name. Rostov flung open the kitchen door and stood there, briefcase still in hand, face as black as thunder.

Mariya and Yuri confronted one another across the kitchen table: she was in a rare rage and close to hysterical tears, he was full of ugly adolescent resentment. Between them was Yuri's guitar, broken at the neck. Mariya has smashed it, Rostov thought instantly; then, a moment later: but this is not what the row is about.

They both appealed to him immediately.

'She broke my guitar!' Yuri said.

Mariya said, 'He has brought disgrace upon the family with this decadent music.'

Then Yuri again called his mother the same foul name.

Rostov dropped his briefcase, stepped forward and slapped the boy's face.

Yuri rocked backward with the force of the blow, and his cheeks reddened with pain and humiliation. The son was as tall as his father, and broader: Rostov had not struck him like this since the boy became a man. Yuri struck back immediately, his fist shooting out: if the blow had connected it would have knocked Rostov cold. Rostov moved quickly aside with the instincts of many years' training and, as gently as possible, threw Yuri to the floor.

'Leave the house,' he said quietly. 'Come back when you're ready to apologize to your mother.'

Yuri scrambled to his feet. 'Never!' he shouted. He went out, slamming the door.

Rostov took off his hat and coat and sat down at the kitchen table. He removed the broken guitar and set it carefully on the floor. Mariya poured tea and gave it to him: his hand was shaking as he took the cup. Finally he said, 'What was that all about?'

'Vladimir failed the exam.'

'Vladimir? What has that to do with Yuri's guitar? What exam did he fail?'

'For the Phys-Mat. He was rejected.'

Rostov stared at her dumbly.

Mariya said, 'I was so upset, and Yuri laughed – he is a little jealous, you know, of his younger brother – and then Yuri started playing this Western music, and I thought it could not be that Vladimir is not clever enough, it must be that his family has not enough influence, perhaps we are considered unreliable because of Yuri and his opinions and his music; I know this is foolish, but I broke his guitar in the heat of the moment.'

Rostov was no longer listening. Vladimir rejected? Impossible. The boy was smarter than his teachers, much too smart for ordinary schools, they could not handle him. The school for exceptionally gifted children was the Phys-Mat. Besides, the boy had said the examination was not difficult, he thought he had scored one hundred per cent, and he *always* knew how he had done in examinations.

'Where's Vladimir?' Rostov asked his wife.

'In his room.'

Rostov went along the corridor and knocked at the bedroom door. There was no answer. He went in. Vladimir was sitting on the bed, staring at the wall, his face red and streaked with tears.

Rostov said, 'What did you score in that exam?'

Vladimir looked up at his father, his face a mask of childish incomprehension. 'One hundred per cent,' he said. He handed over a sheaf of papers. 'I remember the questions. I remember my answers. I've checked them all twice: no mistakes. And I left the examination room five minutes before the time was up.'

Rostov turned to leave.

'Don't you *believe* me?'

'Yes, of course I do,' Rostov told him. He went into the living room, where the phone was. He called the school. The head teacher was still at work.

'Vladimir got full marks in that test,' Rostov said.

The head teacher spoke soothingly. 'I'm sorry, Comrade Colonel. Many very talented youngsters apply for places here—'

'Did they all get one hundred per cent in the exam?'

'I'm afraid I can't divulge—'

'You know who I am,' Rostov said bluntly. 'You know I can find out.'

'Comrade Colonel, I like you and I want to have your son in my school. Please don't make trouble for yourself by creating a storm about this. If your son would apply again in one year's time, he would have an excellent chance of gaining a place.'

People did not warn KGB officers against making trouble for themselves. Rostov began to understand. 'But he *did* score full marks.'

'Several applicants scored full marks in the written paper—'

'Thank you,' Rostov said. He hung up.

The living room was dark, but he did not put the lights on. He sat in his armchair, thinking. The head teacher could easily have told him that all the applicants had scored full marks; but lies did not come easily to people on the spur of the moment, evasions were easier. However, to question the results would create trouble for Rostov.

So. Strings had been pulled. Less talented youngsters had gained places because their fathers had used more influence. Rostov refused to be angry. Don't get mad at the system, he told himself: use it.

He had some strings of his own to pull.

He picked up the phone and called his boss, Feliks Vorontsov, at home. Feliks sounded a little odd, but Rostov ignored it. 'Listen, Feliks, my son has been turned down for the Phys-Mat.'

'I'm sorry to hear that,' Vorontsov said. 'Still, not everybody can get in.'

It was not the expected response. Now Rostov paid

attention to Vorontsov's tone of voice. 'What makes you say that?'

'My son was accepted.'

Rostov was silent for a moment. He had not known that Feliks's son had even applied. The boy was smart, but not half as clever as Vladimir. Rostov pulled himself together. 'Then let me be the first to congratulate you.'

'Thank you,' Feliks said awkwardly. 'What did you call about, though?'

'Oh . . . look, I won't interrupt your celebration. It will keep until morning.'

'All right. Goodbye.'

Rostov hung up and put the phone gently down on the floor. If the son of some bureaucrat or politico had got into the school because of string-pulling, Rostov could have fought it: everyone's file had something nasty in it. The only kind of person he could not fight was a more senior KGB man. There was no way he could overturn this year's awards of places.

So, Vladimir would apply again next year. But the same thing could happen again. Somehow, by this time next year, he had to get into a position where the Vorontsovs of this world could not nudge him aside. Next year he would handle the whole thing differently. He would call on the head teacher's KGB file, for a start. He would get the complete list of applicants and work on any who might be a threat. He would have phones tapped and mail opened to find out who was putting on the pressure.

But first he had to get into a position of strength.

And now he realized that his complacency about his career so far had been erroneous. If they could do this to him, his star must be fading fast.

That coup which he was so casually scheduling for some time in the next two or three years had to be brought forward.

He sat in the dark living room, planning his first moves.

Mariya came in after a while and sat beside him, not speaking. She brought him food on a tray and asked him if he wanted to watch TV. He shook his head and put the food aside. A little later, she went quietly to bed.

Yuri came in at midnight, a little drunk. He entered the living room and switched on the light. He was surprised to see his father sitting there. He took a frightened step back.

Rostov stood up and looked at his elder son, remembering the growing pains of his own teenage years, the misdirected anger, the clear, narrow vision of right and wrong, the quick humiliations and the slow acquisition of knowledge. 'Yuri,' he said, 'I want to apologize for hitting you.'

Yuri burst into tears.

Rostov put an arm around his broad shoulders and led him toward his room. 'We were both wrong, you and I,' he continued. 'Your mother, too. I'm going away again soon, I'll try to bring back a new guitar.'

He wanted to kiss his son, but they had got like Westerners, afraid to kiss. Gently, he pushed him into the bedroom and closed the door on him.

Going back to the living room, he realized that in the last few minutes his plans had hardened into shape in his mind. He sat in the armchair again, this time with a soft pencil and a sheet of paper, and began to draft a memorandum.

To: Chairman, Committee for State Security
From: Acting Chief, European Desk
Copy: Chief, European Desk
Date: 24 May 1968

Comrade Andropov:

My department chief, Feliks Vorontsov, is absent today and I feel that the following matters are too urgent to await his return.

An agent in Luxembourg has reported the sighting there of the Israeli operative Nathaniel ('Nat') David Jonathan Dickstein, alias Edward ('Ed') Rodgers, known as The Pirate.

Dickstein was born in Stepney, East London, in 1925, the son of a shopkeeper. The father died in 1938, the mother in 1951. Dickstein joined the British Army in 1943, fought in Italy, was promoted sergeant and taken prisoner at La Molina. After the war he went to Oxford University to read Semitic Languages. In 1948 he left Oxford without graduating and emigrated to Palestine, where he began almost immediately to work for the Mossad.

At first he was involved in stealing and secretly buying arms for the Zionist state. In the Fifties he mounted an operation against an Egyptian-

supported group of Palestinian freedom fighters
based in the Gaza Strip, and was personally
responsible for the booby-trap bomb which killed
Commander Aly. In the late Fifties and early Sixties
he was a leading member of the assassination team
which hunted escaped Nazis. He directed the
terrorist effort against German rocket scientists
working for Egypt in 1963–4.

On his file the entry under 'Weaknesses' reads:
'None known.' He appears to have no family, either
in Palestine or elsewhere. He is not interested in
alcohol, narcotics or gambling. He has no known
romantic liaisons, and there is on his file a
speculation that he may be sexually frozen as a
result of being the subject of medical experiments
conducted by Nazi scientists.

I, personally, knew Dickstein intimately in the
formative years 1947–8, when we were both at
Oxford University. I played chess with him. I
initiated his file. I have followed his subsequent
career with special interest. He now appears to be
operating in the territory which has been my
speciality for twenty years. I doubt if there is anyone
among the 110,000 employees of your committee
who is as well qualified as I am to oppose this
formidable Zionist operative.

I therefore recommend that you assign me to
discover what Dickstein's mission is and, if
appropriate, to stop him.

(Signed)
David Rostov.

To: Acting Chief, European Desk
From: Chairman, Committee for State Security
Copy: Chief, European Desk
Date: 24 May 1968

Comrade Rostov:
    Your recommendation is approved.
               (Signed)
             Yuri Andropov.

To: Chairman, Committee for State Security
From: Chief, European Desk
Copy: Deputy Chief, European Desk
Date: 26 May 1968

Comrade Andropov:
    I refer to the exchange of memoranda which
took place between yourself and my deputy, David
Rostov, during my recent short absence on State
business in Novosibirsk.
    Naturally I agree wholeheartedly with Comrade
Rostov's concern and your approval thereof,
although I feel there was no good reason for his
haste.
    As a field agent Rostov does not, of course, see
things in quite the same broad perspective as his
superiors, and there is one aspect of the situation
which he failed to bring to your attention.
    The current investigation of Dickstein was
initiated by our Egyptian allies, and indeed at this
moment remains exclusively their undertaking. For

political reasons I would not recommend that we
brush them aside without a second thought, as
Rostov seems to think we can. At most, we should
offer them our cooperation.

Needless to say, this latter undertaking, involving
as it would international liaison between
intelligence services, ought to be handled at chief-
of-desk level rather than deputy-chief level.

(Signed)
Feliks Vorontsov.

To: Chief, European Desk
From: Office of the Chairman, Committee for
        State Security
Copy: Deputy Chief, European Desk
Date: 28 May 1968

Comrade Vorontsov:

Comrade Andropov has asked me to deal with
your memorandum of 26 May.

He agrees that the political implications of
Rostov's scheme must be taken into account, but he
is unwilling to leave the initiative in Egyptian hands
while we merely 'cooperate'. I have now spoken
with our allies in Cairo and they have agreed that
Rostov should command the team investigating
Dickstein on condition that one of their agents
serves as a full member of the team.

(Signed)
Maksim Bykov, personal assistant to the Chairman.

(pencilled addendum)

Feliks: Don't bother me with this again until you've got a result. And keep an eye on Rostov – he wants your job, and unless you shape up I'm going to give it to him. Yuri.

To: Deputy Chief, European Desk
From: Office of the Chairman, Committee for
         State Security
Copy: Chief, European Desk
Date: 29 May 1968

Comrade Rostov:

Cairo has now nominated the agent to serve with your team in the Dickstein investigation. He is in fact the agent who first spotted Dickstein in Luxembourg. His name is Yasif Hassan.

(Signed)

Maksim Bykov, personal assistant to the Chairman.

When he gave lectures at the training school, Pierre Borg would say, 'Call in. Always call in. Not just when you need something, but every day if possible. We need to know what you're doing – and we may have vital information for you.' Then the trainees went into the bar and heard that Nat Dickstein's motto was: 'Never call in for less than $100,000.'

Borg was angry with Dickstein. Anger came easily to him, especially when he did not know what was happening. Fortunately anger rarely interfered with his judgment. He was angry with Kawash, too. He could understand why Kawash had wanted to meet in Rome – the Egyptians had a big team here, so it was easy for Kawash to find an excuse to visit – but there was no reason why they should meet in a goddamn bathhouse.

Borg got angry by sitting in his office in Tel Aviv, wondering and worrying about Dickstein and Kawash and the others, waiting for messages, until he began to think they would not call because they did not like him; and so he got mad and broke pencils and fired his secretary.

A bathhouse in Rome, for God's sake – the place was bound to be full of queers. Also, Borg did not like his body. He slept in pyjamas, never went swimming, never tried on clothes in shops, never went naked except to take a quick shower in the morning. Now he stood in the steam-room, wearing around his waist the largest towel he could find, conscious that he was white except for his face and hands, his flesh softly plump, with a pelt of greying hair across his shoulders.

He saw Kawash. The Arab's body was lean and dark brown, with very little hair. Their eyes met across the steamroom and, like secret lovers, they went side by side, not looking at one another, into a private room with a bed.

Borg was relieved to get out of public view and impatient to hear Kawash's news. The Arab switched on the machine that made the bed vibrate: its hum would swamp a listening device, if there were one. The two men stood close together and spoke in low voices.

Embarrassed, Borg turned his body so that he was facing away from Kawash and had to speak over his shoulder.

'I've got a man into Qattara,' Kawash said.

'*Formidable*,' Borg said, pronouncing it the French way in his great relief. 'Your department isn't even involved in the project.'

'I have a cousin in Military Intelligence.'

'Well done. Who is the man in Qattara?'

'Saman Hussein, one of yours.'

'Good, good, *good*. What did he find?'

'The construction work is finished. They've built the reactor housing, plus an administration block, staff quarters, and an airstrip. They're much farther ahead than anyone imagined.'

'What about the reactor itself? That's what counts.'

'They're working on it now. It's hard to say how long it will take – there's a certain amount of precision work.'

'Are they going to be able to manage that?' Borg wondered. 'I mean, all those complex control systems . . .'

'The controls don't need to be sophisticated, I understand. You slow the speed of the nuclear reaction simply by pushing metal rods into the atomic pile. Anyway, there's been another development. Saman found the place crawling with Russians.'

Borg said, 'Oh, fuck.'

'So now I guess they'll have all the fancy electronics they need.'

Borg sat on the chair, forgetting the bathhouse and the vibrating bed and his soft white body. 'This is bad news,' he said.

'There's worse. Dickstein is blown.'

Borg stared at Kawash, thunderstruck. 'Blown?' he said as if he did not know what the word meant. 'Blown?'

'Yes.'

Borg felt furious and despairing by turns. After a moment he said, 'How did he manage that ... the prick?'

'He was recognized by an agent of ours in Luxembourg.'

'What was he doing there?'

'*You* should know.'

'Skip it.'

'Apparently it was just a chance meeting. The agent is called Yasif Hassan. He's small fry – works for a Lebanese bank and keeps an eye on visiting Israelis. Of course, our people recognized the name Dickstein—'

'He's using his real name?' Borg said incredulously. It got worse and worse.

'I don't think so,' Kawash said. 'This Hassan knew him from way back.'

Borg shook his head slowly. 'You wouldn't think we were the Chosen People, with our luck.'

'We put Dickstein under surveillance and informed Moscow,' Kawash continued. 'He lost the surveillance team quite quickly, of course, but Moscow is putting together a big effort to find him again.'

Borg put his chin in his hand and stared without

seeing at the erotic frieze on the tiled wall. It was as if there were a world-wide conspiracy to frustrate Israeli policy in general and his plans in particular. He wanted to give it all up and go back to Quebec; he wanted to hit Dickstein over the head with a blunt instrument; he wanted to wipe that imperturbable look off Kawash's handsome face.

He made a gesture of throwing something away. 'Great,' he said. 'The Egyptians are well ahead with their reactor; the Russians are helping them; Dickstein is blown; and the KGB has put a team on him. We could lose this race, do you realize that? Then they'll have a nuclear bomb and we won't. And do you think they will use it?' He had Kawash by the shoulders now, shaking him. 'They're your people, you tell me, will they drop the bomb on Israel? You bet your ass they will!'

'Stop shouting,' Kawash said calmly. He detached Borg's hands from his shoulders. 'There's a long road ahead before one side or the other has won.'

'Yeah.' Borg turned away.

'You'll have to contact Dickstein and warn him,' Kawash said. 'Where is he now?'

'Fucked if I know,' said Pierre Borg.

CHAPTER FIVE

THE ONLY completely innocent person whose
life was ruined by the spies during the affair of
the yellowcake was the Euratom official whom Dickstein
named Stiffcollar.

After losing the surveillance team in France Dickstein returned to Luxembourg by road, guessing they
would have set a twenty-four-hours-a-day watch for him
at Luxembourg airport. And, since they had the
number of his rented car, he stopped off in Paris to
turn it in and hire another from a different company.

On his first evening in Luxembourg he went to the
discreet nightclub in the Rue Dicks and sat alone,
sipping beer, waiting for Stiffcollar to come in. But it
was the fair-haired friend who arrived first. He was a
younger man, perhaps twenty-five or thirty, broad-
shouldered and in good shape underneath his maroon
double-breasted jacket. He walked across to the booth
they had occupied last time. He was graceful, like a
dancer: Dickstein thought he might be the goalkeeper
on a soccer team. The booth was vacant. If the couple
met here every night it was probably kept for them.

The fair-haired man ordered a drink and looked at
his watch. He did not see Dickstein observing him.

Stiffcollar entered a few minutes later. He wore a red V-necked sweater and a white shirt with a button-down collar. As before, he went straight to the table where his friend sat waiting. They greeted each other with a double handshake. They seemed happy. Dickstein prepared to shatter their world.

He called a waiter. 'Please take a bottle of champagne to that table, for the man in the red sweater. And bring me another beer.'

The waiter brought his beer first, then took the champagne in a bucket of ice to Stiffcollar's table. Dickstein saw the waiter point him out to the couple as the donor of the champagne. When they looked at him, he raised his beer glass in a toast, and smiled. Stiffcollar recognized him and looked worried.

Dickstein left his table and went to the cloakroom. He washed his face, killing time. After a couple of minutes Stiffcollar's friend came in. The young man combed his hair, waiting for a third man to leave the room. Then he spoke to Dickstein.

'My friend wants you to leave him alone.'

Dickstein gave a nasty smile. 'Let him tell me so himself.'

'You're a journalist, aren't you? What if your editor were to hear that you come to places like this?'

'I'm freelance.'

The young man came closer. He was five inches taller than Dickstein and at least thirty pounds heavier. 'You're to leave us alone,' he said.

'No.'

'Why are you doing this? What do you want?'

'I'm not interested in you, pretty boy. You'd better go home while I talk to your friend.'

'Damn you,' the young man said, and he grabbed the lapels of Dickstein's jacket in one large hand. He drew back his other arm and made a fist. He never landed the punch.

With his fingers Dickstein poked the young man in the eyes. The blond head jerked back and to the side reflexively. Dickstein stepped inside the swinging arm and hit him in the belly, very hard. The breath rattled out of him and he doubled over, turning away. Dickstein punched him once again, very precisely, on the bridge of the nose. Something snapped, and blood spurted. The young man collapsed on the tiled floor.

It was enough.

Dickstein went out quickly, straightening his tie and smoothing his hair on the way. In the club the cabaret had begun and the German guitarist was singing a song about a gay policeman. Dickstein paid his bill and left. As he went he saw Stiffcollar, looking worried, making his way to the cloakroom.

On the street it was a mild summer night, but Dickstein was shivering. He walked a little way, then went into a bar and ordered brandy. It was a noisy, smoky place with a television set on the counter. Dickstein carried his drink to a corner table and sat facing the wall.

The fight in the cloakroom would not be reported to the police. It would look like a quarrel over a lover, and neither Stiffcollar nor the club management would want to bring that sort of thing to official notice.

Stiffcollar would take his friend to a doctor, saying he had walked into a door.

Dickstein drank the brandy and stopped shivering. There was, he thought, no way to be a spy without doing things like this. And there was no way to be a nation, in this world, without having spies. And without a nation Nat Dickstein could not feel safe.

It did not seem possible to live honourably. Even if he gave up this profession, others would become spies and do evil on his behalf, and that was almost as bad. You had to be bad to live. Dickstein recalled that a Nazi camp doctor called Wolfgang had said much the same.

He had long ago decided that life was not about right and wrong, but about winning and losing. Still there were times when that philosophy gave him no consolation.

He left the bar and went into the street, heading for Stiffcollar's home. He had to press his advantage while the man was demoralized. He reached the narrow cobbled street within a few minutes and stood guard opposite the old terraced house. There was no light in the attic window.

The night became cooler as he waited. He began to pace up and down. European weather was dismal. At this time of year Israel would be glorious: long sunny days and warm nights, hard physical work by day and companionship and laughter in the evenings. Dickstein wished he could go home.

At last Stiffcollar and his friend returned. The friend's head was wrapped in bandages, and he was obviously having trouble seeing: he walked with one hand on Stiffcollar's arm, like a blind man. They stopped outside the house while Stiffcollar fumbled for a key. Dickstein crossed the road and approached them. They had their backs to him, and his shoes made no noise.

Stiffcollar opened the door, turned to help his friend, and saw Dickstein. He jumped with shock. 'Oh, God!'

The friend said, 'What is it? What is it?'

'It's him.'

Dickstein said, 'I have to talk to you.'

'Call the police,' said the friend.

Stiffcollar took his friend's arm and began to lead him through the door. Dickstein put out a hand and stopped them. 'You'll have to let me in,' he said. 'Otherwise I'll create a scene in the street.'

Stiffcollar said, 'He'll make our lives miserable until he gets what he wants.'

'But what does he want?'

'I'll tell you in a minute,' Dickstein said. He walked into the house ahead of them and started up the stairs.

After a moment's hesitation, they followed.

The three men climbed the stairs to the top. Stiffcollar unlocked the door of the attic flat, and they went in. Dickstein looked around. It was bigger than he imagined, and very elegantly decorated with period furniture, striped wallpaper, and many plants and pictures. Stiffcollar put his friend in a chair, then took a cigarette from a box, lit it with a table lighter and put it in his friend's mouth. They sat close together, waiting for Dickstein to speak.

'I'm a journalist,' Dickstein began.

Stiffcollar interrupted, 'Journalists interview people, they don't beat them up.'

'I didn't beat him up. I hit him twice.'

'Why?'

'He attacked me, didn't he tell you?'

'I don't believe you,' said Stiffcollar.

'How much time would you like to spend arguing about it?'

'None.'

'Good. I want a story about Euratom. A good story – my career needs it. Now then, one possibility is the prevalence of homosexuals in positions of responsibility within the organization.'

'You're a lousy bastard,' said Stiffcollar's friend.

'Quite so,' Dickstein said. 'However, I'll drop the story if I get a better one.'

Stiffcollar ran a hand across his grey-tipped hair, and Dickstein noticed that he wore clear nail polish. 'I think I understand this,' he said.

'What? What do you understand?' said his friend.

'He wants information.'

'That's right,' said Dickstein. Stiffcollar was looking relieved. Now was the time to be a little friendly, to come across as a human being, to let them think that things might not be so bad after all. Dickstein got up. There was whisky in a decanter on a highly polished side table. He poured small shots into three glasses as he said, 'Look, you're vulnerable and I've picked on you, and I expect you to hate me for that; but I'm not going to pretend that I hate you. I'm a bastard and I'm using you, and that's all there is to it. Except that I'm drinking your booze as well.' He handed them drinks and sat down again.

There was a pause, then Stiffcollar said, 'What is it that you want to know?'

'Well, now.' Dickstein took the tiniest sip of whisky: he hated the taste. 'Euratom keeps records of all movements of fissionable materials into, out of and within the member countries, right?'

'Yes.'

'To be more precise: before anyone can move an ounce of uranium from A to B he has to ask your permission.'

'Yes.'

'Complete records are kept of all permits given.'

'The records are on a computer.'

'I know. If asked, the computer would print out a list of all future uranium shipments for which permission has been given.'

'It does, regularly. A list is circulated once a month within the office.'

'Splendid,' said Dickstein. 'All I want is that list.'

There was a long silence. Stiffcollar drank some whisky. Dickstein left his alone: the two beers and one large brandy he had already drunk this evening were more than he normally took in a fortnight.

The friend said, 'What do you want the list *for*?'

'I'm going to check all the shipments in a given month. I expect to be able to prove that what people do in reality bears little or no relation to what they tell Euratom.'

Stiffcollar said, 'I don't believe you.'

The man was not stupid, Dickstein thought. He shrugged. 'What do you think I want it for?'

'I don't know. You're not a journalist. Nothing you've said has been true.'

'It makes no difference, does it?' Dickstein said. 'Believe what you like. You've no choice but to give me the list.'

'I have,' Stiffcollar said. 'I'm going to resign the job.'

'If you do,' Dickstein said slowly, 'I will beat your friend to a pulp.'

'We'll go to the police!' the friend said.

'I would go away,' Dickstein said. 'Perhaps for a year. But I would come back. And I'd find you. And I will very nearly kill you. Your face will be unrecognizable.'

Stiffcollar stared at Dickstein. 'What *are* you?'

'It really doesn't matter what I am, does it? You know I can do what I threaten.'

'Yes,' Stiffcollar said. He buried his face in his hands.

Dickstein let the silence build. Stiffcollar was cornered, helpless. There was only one thing he could do, and he was now realizing this. Dickstein let him take his time. It was several moments before Dickstein spoke.

'The printout will be bulky,' he said gently.

Stiffcollar nodded without looking up.

'Is your briefcase checked as you leave the office?'

He shook his head.

'Are the printouts supposed to be kept under lock and key?'

'No. 'Stiffcollar gathered his wits with a visible effort. 'No,' he said wearily, 'this information is not classified. It's merely confidential, not to be made public.'

'Good. Now, you'll need tomorrow to think about the details – which copy of the printout to take, exactly what you'll tell your secretary, and so on. The day after tomorrow you will bring the printout home. You'll find a note from me waiting for you. The note will tell you how to deliver the document to me.' Dickstein smiled. 'After that, you'll probably never see me again. '

Stiffcollar said, 'By God, I hope so.'

Dickstein stood up. 'You'd rather not be bothered by phone calls for a while,' he said. He found the telephone and pulled the cord out of the wall. He went to the door and opened it.

The friend looked at the disconnected wire. His eyes seemed to be recovering. He said, 'Are you afraid he'll change his mind?'

Dickstein said, 'You're the one who should be afraid of that.' He went out, closing the door softly behind him.

Life is not a popularity contest, especially in the KGB. David Rostov was now very unpopular with his boss and with all those in the section who were loyal to his boss. Feliks Vorontsov was boiling with anger at the way he had been bypassed: from now on he would do anything he could to destroy Rostov.

Rostov had anticipated this. He did not regret his decision to go for broke on the Dickstein affair. On the contrary, he was rather glad. He was already planning the finely stitched, stylishly cut dark blue English suit he would buy when he got his pass for Section 100 on the third floor of the GUM department store in Moscow.

What he did regret was leaving a loophole for Vorontsov. He should have thought of the Egyptians and their reaction. That was the trouble with the Arabs, they were so clumsy and useless that you tended to ignore them as a force in the intelligence world. Fortunately Yuri Andropov, head of the KGB and confidant of Leonid Brezhnev, had seen what Feliks Vorontsov was trying to do, namely win back control of the Dickstein project; and he had not permitted it.

So the only consequence of Rostov's error was that he would be forced to work with the wretched Arabs.

That was bad enough. Rostov had his own little team, Nik Bunin and Pyotr Tyrin, and they worked well together. And Cairo was as leaky as a sieve: half the stuff that went through them got back to Tel Aviv.

The fact that the Arab in question was Yasif Hassan might or might not help.

Rostov remembered Hassan very clearly: a rich kid, indolent and haughty, smart enough but with no drive, shallow politics, and too many clothes. His wealthy father had got him into Oxford, not his brains; and

Rostov resented that more now than he had then. Still, knowing the man should make it easier to control him. Rostov planned to start by making it clear Hassan was essentially superfluous, and was on the team for purely political reasons. He would need to be very clever about what he told Hassan and what he kept secret: say too little, and Cairo would bitch to Moscow; too much, and Tel Aviv would be able to frustrate his every move.

It was damned awkward, and he had only himself to blame for it.

He was uneasy about the whole affair by the time he reached Luxembourg. He had flown in from Athens, having changed identities twice and planes three times since Moscow. He took this little precaution because, if you came direct from Russia, the local intelligence people sometimes made a note of your arrival and kept an eye on you, and that could be a nuisance.

There was nobody to meet him at the airport, of course. He took a taxi to his hotel.

He had told Cairo he would be using the name David Roberts. When he checked into the hotel under that name, the desk clerk gave him a message. He opened the envelope as he went up in the lift with the porter. It said simply 'Room 179.'

He tipped the porter, picked up the room phone and dialled 179. A voice said, 'Hello?'

'I'm in 142. Give me ten minutes, then come here for a conference.'

'Fine. Listen, is that—'

'Shut up!' Rostov snapped. 'No names. Ten minutes.'

'Of course, I'm sorry, I—'

Rostov hung up. What kind of idiots was Cairo hiring now? The kind that used your real name over the hotel phone system, obviously. It was going to be even worse than he had feared.

There was a time when he would have been over-professional, and turned out the lights and sat watching the doorway with a gun in his hand until the other man arrived, in case of a trap. Nowadays he considered that sort of behaviour to be obsessive and left it to the actors in the television shows. Elaborate personal precautions were not his style, not any more. He did not even carry a gun, in case customs officials searched his luggage at airports. But there were precautions and precautions, weapons and weapons: he did have one or two KGB gadgets subtly concealed – including an electric tooth-brush that gave out a hum calculated to jam listening devices, a miniature Polaroid camera, and a bootlace garrotte.

He unpacked his small case quickly. There was very little in it: a safety razor, the toothbrush, two American-made wash-and-wear shirts and a change of underwear. He made himself a drink from the room bar – Scotch whisky was one of the perks of working abroad. After exactly ten minutes there was a knock on the door. Rostov opened it, and Yasif Hassan came in.

Hassan smiled broadly. 'How are you?'

'How do you do,' said Rostov, and shook his hand.

'It's twenty years . . . how have you been?'

'Busy.'

'That we should meet again, after so long, and because of Dickstein!'

'Yes. Sit down. Let's talk about Dickstein.' Rostov sat, and Hassan followed suit. 'Bring me up to date,' Rostov continued. 'You spotted Dickstein, then your people picked him up again at Nice airport. What happened next?'

'He went on a guided tour of a nuclear power station, then shook off the tail,' Hassan said. 'So we've lost him again.'

Rostov gave a grunt of disgust. 'We'll have to do better than that.'

Hassan smiled – a salesman's smile, Rostov thought – and said, 'If he wasn't the sort of agent who is bound to spot a tail and lose it, we wouldn't be so concerned about him, would we?'

Rostov ignored that. 'Was he using a car?'

'Yes. He hired a Peugeot.'

'Okay. What do you know about his movements before that, when he was here in Luxembourg?'

Hassan spoke briskly, adopting Rostov's businesslike air. 'He stayed at the Alfa Hotel for a week under the name Ed Rodgers. He gave as his address the Paris bureau of a magazine called *Science International*. There is such a magazine; they do have a Paris address, but it's only a forwarding address for mail; they do use a freelance called Ed Rodgers, but they haven't heard from him for over a year.'

Rostov nodded. 'As you may know, that is a typical Mossad cover story. Nice and tight. Anything else?'

'Yes. The night before he left there was an incident in the Rue Dicks. Two men were found quite savagely beaten. It had the look of a professional job – neatly broken bones, you know the kind of thing. The police aren't doing anything about it: the men were known thieves, thought to have been lying in wait close to a homosexual nightclub.'

'Robbing the queers as they come out?'

'That's the general idea. Anyway, there's nothing to connect Dickstein with the incident, except that he is capable of it and he was here at the time.'

'That's enough for a strong presumption,' Rostov said. 'Do you think Dickstein is a homosexual?'

'It's possible, but Cairo says there's nothing like that in his file, so he must have been very discreet about it all these years.'

'And therefore too discreet to go to queer clubs while he's on assignment. Your argument is self-defeating, isn't it?'

A trace of anger showed in Hassan's face. 'So what do you think?' he said defensively.

'My guess is that he had an informant who is queer.' He stood up and began to pace the room. He felt he had made the right start with Hassan, but enough was enough: no point in making the man surly. It was time to ease up a little. 'Let's speculate for a moment. Why would he want to look around a nuclear power station?'

Hassan said, 'The Israelis have been on bad terms

with the French since the Six-Day War. De Gaulle cut off the supply of arms. Maybe the Mossad plans some retaliation: like blowing up the reactor?'

Rostov shook his head. 'Even the Israelis aren't that irresponsible. Besides, why then would Dickstein be in Luxembourg?'

'Who knows?'

Rostov sat down again. 'What is there, here in Luxembourg? What makes it an important place? Why is your bank here, for example?'

'It's an important European capital. My bank is here because the European Investment Bank is here. But there are also several Common Market institutions – in fact, there's a European Centre over on the Ritchberg.'

'Which institutions?'

'The Secretariat of the European Parliament, the Council of Ministers, and the Court of Justice. Oh, and Euratom.'

Rostov stared at Hassan. 'Euratom?'

'It's short for the European Atomic Energy Community, but everybody—'

'I know what it is,' Rostov said. 'Don't you see the connection? He comes to Luxembourg, where Euratom has its headquarters, then he goes to visit a nuclear reactor.'

Hassan shrugged. 'An interesting hypothesis. What's that you're drinking?'

'Whisky. Help yourself. As I recall, the French helped the Israelis build their nuclear reactor. Now they've probably cut off their aid. Dickstein may be after scientific secrets.'

Hassan poured himself a drink and sat down again. 'How shall we operate, you and I? My orders are to cooperate with you.'

'My team is arriving this evening,' Rostov said. He was thinking: Cooperate, hell – you'll follow my orders. He said, 'I always use the same two men – Nik Bunin and Pyotr Tyrin. We operate very well together. They know how I like things done. I want you to work with them, do what they say – you'll learn a lot, they're very good agents.'

'And my people . . .'

'We won't need them much longer,' Rostov said briskly. 'A small team is best. Now, our first job is to make sure we see Dickstein if and when he comes back to Luxembourg.'

'I've got a man at the airport twenty-four hours a day.'

'He'll have thought of that, he won't fly in. We must cover some other spots. He might go to Euratom . . .'

'The Jean-Monnet building, yes.'

'We can cover the Alfa Hotel by bribing the desk clerk, but he won't go back there. And the nightclub in the Rue Dicks. Now, then, you said he hired a car.'

'Yes, in France.'

'He'll have dumped it by now – he knows that you know the number. I want you to call the rental company and find out where it was left – that may tell us what direction he's travelling in.'

'Very well.'

'Moscow has put his photograph on the wire, so our people will be looking out for him in every capital city in the world.' Rostov finished his drink. 'We'll catch him. One way or another.'

'Do you really think so?' Hassan asked.

'I've played chess with him, I know how his mind works. His opening moves are routine, predictable; then suddenly he does something completely unexpected, usually something highly risky. You just have to wait for him to stick out his neck – then you chop his head off.'

Hassan said, 'As I recall, you lost that chess match.'

Rostov gave a wolfish grin. 'Yes, but this is real life,' he said.

There are two kinds of shadow: pavement artists and bulldogs. Pavement artists regard the business of shadowing people as a skill of the highest order, comparable with acting or cellular biophysics or poetry. They are perfectionists, capable of being almost invisible. They have wardrobes of unobtrusive clothes, they practise blank expressions in front of their mirrors, they know dozens of tricks with shop doorways and bus queues, policemen and children, spectacles and shopping bags and hedges. They despise the bulldogs, who think that shadowing someone is the same as following him, and trail the mark the way a dog follows its master.

Nik Bunin was a bulldog. He was a young thug, the type of man who always becomes either a policeman or a criminal, depending on his luck. Luck had brought Nik into the KGB: his brother, back in Georgia, was a dope dealer, running hashish from Tbilisi to Moscow

University (where it was consumed by – among others – Rostov's son Yuri). Nik was officially a chauffeur, unofficially a bodyguard, and even more unofficially a full-time professional ruffian.

It was Nik who spotted The Pirate.

Nik was a little under six feet tall, and very broad. He wore a leather jacket across his wide shoulders. He had short blond hair and watery green eyes, and he was embarrassed about the fact that at the age of twenty-five he still did not need to shave every day.

At the nightclub in the Rue Dicks they thought he was cute as hell.

He came in at seven-thirty, soon after the club opened, and sat in the same corner all night, drinking iced vodka with lugubrious relish, just watching. Somebody asked him to dance, and he told the man to piss off in bad French. When he turned up the second night they wondered if he was a jilted lover lying in wait for a showdown with his ex. He had about him the air of what the gays called rough trade, what with those shoulders and the leather jacket and his dour expression.

Nik knew nothing of these undercurrents. He had been shown a photograph of a man and told to go to a club and look out for the man; so he memorized the face, then went to the club and looked. It made little difference to him whether the place was a whorehouse or a cathedral. He liked occasionally to get the chance to beat people up, but otherwise all he asked was regular pay and two days off every week to devote to his enthusiasms, which were vodka and colouring books.

When Nat Dickstein came into the nightclub, Nik felt no sense of excitement. When he did well, Rostov always assumed it was because he had scrupulously obeyed precise orders, and he was generally right. Nik watched the mark sit down alone, order a drink, get served and sip his beer. It looked like he, too, was waiting.

Nik went to the phone in the lobby and called the hotel. Rostov answered.

'This is Nik. The mark just came in.'

'Good!' said Rostov. 'What's he doing?'

'Waiting.'

'Good. Alone?'

'Yes.'

'Stay with him and call me if he does anything.'

'Sure.'

'I'm sending Pyotr down. He'll wait outside. If the mark leaves the club you follow him, doubling with Pyotr. The Arab will be with you in a car, well back. It's a ... wait a minute ... it's a green Volkswagen hatchback.'

'Okay.'

'Get back to him now.'

Nik hung up and returned to his table, not looking at Dickstein as he crossed the club.

A few minutes later a well-dressed, good-looking man of about forty came into the club. He looked around, then walked past Dickstein's table and went to the bar. Nik saw Dickstein pick up a piece of paper from the table and put it in his pocket. It was all very discreet:

only someone who was carefully observing Dickstein
would know anything had happened.

Nik went to the phone again.

'A queer came in and gave him something – it
looked like a ticket,' he told Rostov.

'Like a theatre ticket, maybe?'

'Don't know.'

'Did they speak?'

'No, the queer just dropped the ticket on the table
as he went by. They didn't even look at each other.'

'All right. Stay with it. Pyotr should be outside by
now.'

'Wait,' Nik said. 'The mark just came into the lobby.
Hold on ... he's going to the desk ... he's handed
over the ticket, that's what it was, it was a cloakroom
ticket.'

'Stay on the line, tell me what happens.' Rostov's
voice was deadly calm.

'The guy behind the counter is giving him a briefcase. He leaves a tip ...'

'It's a delivery. Good.'

'The mark is leaving the club.'

'Follow him.'

'Shall I snatch the briefcase?'

'No, I don't want us to show ourselves until we know
what he's doing, just find out where he goes, and stay
low. Go!'

Nik hung up. He gave the cloakroom attendant
some notes, saying: 'I have to rush, this will cover my
bill.' Then he went up the staircase after Nat Dickstein.

Out on the street it was a bright summer evening, and there were plenty of people making their way to restaurants and cinemas or just strolling. Nik looked left and right, then saw the mark on the opposite side of the road, fifty yards away. He crossed over and followed.

Dickstein was walking quickly, looking straight ahead, carrying the briefcase under his arm. Nik plodded after him for a couple of blocks. During this time, if Dickstein looked back he would see some distance behind him a man who had also been in the nightclub, and he would begin to wonder if he were being shadowed. Then Pyotr came alongside Nik, touched his arm, and went on ahead. Nik dropped back to a position from which he could see Pyotr but not Dickstein. If Dickstein looked again now, he would not see Nik and he would not recognize Pyotr. It was very difficult for the mark to sniff this kind of surveillance; but of course, the longer the distance for which the mark was shadowed, the more men were needed to keep up the regular switches.

After another half mile the green Volkswagen pulled to the kerb beside Nik. Yasif Hassan leaned across from the driving seat and opened the door. 'New orders,' he said. 'Jump in.'

Nik got into the car and Hassan steered back toward the nightclub in the Rue Dicks.

'You did very well,' Hassan said.

Nik ignored this.

'We want you to go back to the club, pick out the delivery man and follow him home,' Hassan said.

'Colonel Rostov said this?'

'Yes.'

'Okay.'

Hassan stopped the car close to the club. Nik went in. He stood in the doorway, looking carefully all about the club.

The delivery man had gone.

The computer printout ran to more than one hundred pages. Dickstein's heart sank as he flicked through the prized sheets of paper he had worked so hard to get. None of it made sense.

He returned to the first page and looked again. There were a lot of jumbled numbers and letters. Could it be in code? No – this printout was used every day by the ordinary office workers of Euratom, so it had to be fairly easily comprehensible.

Dickstein concentrated. He saw 'U234'. He knew that to be an isotope of uranium. Another group of letters and numbers was 'I80KG' – one hundred and eighty kilograms. 'I7F68' would be a date, the seventeenth of February this year. Gradually the lines of computer-alphabet letters and numbers began to yield up their meanings: he found place-names from various European countries, words such as TRAIN and TRUCK with distances affixed next to them, and names with suffixes 'SA' or 'INC', indicating companies. Eventually the layout of the entries became clear: the first line gave the quantity and type of material, the second line the name and address of the sender, and so on.

His spirits lifted. He read on with growing comprehension and a sense of achievement. About sixty consignments were listed in the printout. There seemed to be three main types: large quantities of crude uranium ore coming from mines in South Africa, Canada and France to European refineries; fuel elements – oxides, uranium metal or enriched mixtures – moving from fabrication plants to reactors; and spent fuel from reactors going for reprocessing and disposal. There were a few non-standard shipments, mostly of plutonium and transuranium elements extracted from spent fuel and sent to laboratories in universities and research institutes.

Dickstein's head ached and his eyes were bleary by the time he found what he was looking for. On the very last page there was one shipment headed 'NON-NUCLEAR.'

He had been briefly told, by the Rehovot physicist with the flowered tie, about the non-nuclear uses of uranium and its compounds in photography, in dyeing, as colouring agents for glass and ceramics and as industrial catalysts. Of course the stuff always had the potential for fission no matter how mundane and innocent its use, so the Euratom regulations still applied. However, Dickstein thought it likely that in ordinary industrial chemistry the security would be less strict.

The entry on the last page referred to two hundred tons of yellowcake, or crude uranium oxide. It was in Belgium, at a metal refinery in the countryside near the Dutch border, a site licenced for storage of fissionable material. The refinery was owned by the Société Générale de la Chimie, a mining conglomerate with head-quarters in Brussels. SGC had sold the yellowcake to a German concern called F.A. Pedler of Wiesbaden. Pedler planned to use it for 'manufacture of uranium compounds, especially uranium carbide, in commercial quantities.' Dickstein recalled that the carbide was a catalyst for the production of synthetic ammonia.

However, it seemed that Pedler were not going to work the uranium themselves, at least not initially. Dickstein's interest sharpened as he read that they had not applied for their own works in Wiesbaden to be licenced, but instead for permission to ship the yellow-cake to Genoa by sea. There it was to undergo 'non-nuclear processing' by a company called Angeluzzi e Bianco.

By sea! The implications struck Dickstein instantly: the load would be passed through a European port by someone else.

He read on. Transport would be by railway from SGC's refinery to the docks at Antwerp. There the yellowcake would be loaded on to the motor vessel *Coparelli* for shipment to Genoa. The short journey from the Italian port to the Angeluzzi e Bianco works would be made by road.

For the trip the yellowcake – looking like sand but yellower – would be packed into five hundred and sixty 200-litre oil drums with heavily sealed lids. The train would require eleven cars, the ship would carry no other cargo for this voyage, and the Italians would use six trucks for the last leg of the journey.

It was the sea journey that excited Dickstein: through

the English Channel, across the Bay of Biscay, down the Atlantic coast of Spain, through the Strait of Gibraltar and across one thousand miles of the Mediterranean.

A lot could go wrong in that distance.

Journeys on land were straightforward, controlled: a train left at noon one day and-arrived at eight-thirty the following morning; a truck travelled on roads that always carried other traffic including police cars; a plane was continually in contact with someone or other on the ground. But the sea was unpredictable, with its own laws – a trip could take ten days or twenty, there might be storms and collisions and engine trouble, unscheduled ports of call and sudden changes of direction. Hijack a plane and the whole world would see it on television an hour later; hijack a ship and no one would know about it for days, weeks, perhaps for ever.

The sea was the inevitable choice for The Pirate.

Dickstein thought on, with growing enthusiasm and a sense that the solution to his problem was within his reach. Hijack the *Coparelli* . . . then what? Transfer the cargo to the hold of the pirate ship. The *Coparelli* would probably have its own derricks. But transferring a cargo at sea could be chancy. Dickstein looked on the print-out for the proposed date of the voyage. November. That was bad. There might be storms – even the Mediterranean could blow up a gale in November. What, then? Take over the *Coparelli* and sail her to Haifa? It would be hard to dock a stolen ship secretly, even in top-security Israel.

Dickstein glanced at his wristwatch. It was past midnight. He began to undress for bed. He needed to know more about the *Coparelli*: her tonnage, how many crew, present whereabouts, who owned her, and if possible her layout. Tomorrow he would go to London. You could find out anything about ships at Lloyd's of London.

There was something else he needed to know: who was following him around Europe? There had been a big team in France. Tonight as he left the nightclub in the Rue Dicks a thuggish face had been behind him. He had suspected a tail, but the face had disappeared – coincidence, or another big team? It rather depended on whether Hassan was in the game. He could make inquiries about that, too, in England.

He wondered how to travel. If somebody had picked up his scent tonight he ought to take some precautions tomorrow. Even if the thuggish face were nobody, Dickstein had to make sure he was not spotted at Luxembourg airport.

He picked up the phone and dialled the desk. When the clerk answered, he said, 'Wake me at six-thirty, please.'

'Very good, sir.'

He hung up and got into bed. At last he had a definite target: the *Coparelli*. He did not yet have a plan, but he knew in outline what had to be done. Whatever other difficulties came up, the combination of a non-nuclear consignment and a sea journey was irresistible.

He turned out the light and closed his eyes, thinking: What a good day.

*

David Rostov had always been a condescending bastard, and he had not improved with age, thought Yasif Hassan. 'What you probably don't realize . . .' he would say with a patronizing smile; and, 'We won't need your people much longer – a small team is better;' and, 'You can tag along in the car and keep out of sight;' and now, 'Man the phone while I go to the Embassy.'

Hassan had been prepared to work under Rostov's orders as one of the team, but it seemed his status was lower than that. It was, to say the least, insulting to be considered inferior to a man like Nik Bunin.

The trouble was, Rostov had some justification. It was not that the Russians were smarter than the Arabs; but the KGB was undoubtedly a larger, richer, more powerful and more professional organization than Egyptian Intelligence.

Hassan had no choice but to suffer Rostov's attitude, justified or not. Cairo was delighted to have the KGB hunting one of the Arab world's greatest enemies. If Hassan were to complain, he rather than Rostov would be taken off the case.

Rostov might remember, thought Hassan, that it was the Arabs who had first spotted Dickstein; there would be no investigation at all had it not been for my original discovery.

All the same, he wanted to win Rostov's respect; to have the Russian confide in him, discuss developments, ask his opinion. He would have to prove to Rostov that he was a competent and professional agent, easily the equal of Nik Bunin and Pyotr Tyrin.

The phone rang. Hassan picked it up hastily. 'Hello?'

'Is the other one there?' It was Tyrin's voice.

'He's out. What's happening?'

Tyrin hesitated. 'When will he be back?'

'I don't know,' Hassan lied. 'Give me your report.'

'Okay. The client got off the train at Zurich.'

'Zurich? Go on.'

'He took a taxi to a bank, entered and went down into the vault. This particular bank has safe-deposit boxes. He came out carrying a briefcase.'

'And then?'

'He went to a car dealer on the outskirts of the city and bought a used E-type Jaguar, paying with cash he had in the case.'

'I see.' Hassan thought he knew what was coming next.

'He drove out of Zurich in the car, got onto the El7 autobahn and increased his speed to one hundred and forty miles per hour.'

'And you lost him,' said Hassan, feeling gratification and anxiety in equal parts.

'We had a taxi and an embassy Mercedes.'

Hassan was visualizing the road map of Europe. 'He could be headed for anywhere in France, Spain, Germany, Scandinavia . . . unless he doubles back, in which case Italy, Austria . . . He's vanished, then. All right – come back to base.' He hung up before Tyrin could question his authority.

So, he thought, the great KGB is not invincible after

all. Much as he liked to see them fall on their collective face, his malicious pleasure was overshadowed by the fear that they had lost Dickstein permanently.

He was still thinking about what they ought to do next when Rostov came back.

'Anything?' the Russian asked.

'Your people lost Dickstein,' Hassan said, suppressing a smile.

Rostov's face darkened. 'How?'

Hassan told him.

Rostov asked, 'So what are they doing now?'

'I suggested they might come back here. I guess they're on their way.'

Rostov grunted.

Hassan said, 'I've been thinking about what we should do next.'

'We've got to find Dickstein again.' Rostov was fiddling with something in his suitcase, and his replies were distracted.

'Yes, but apart from that.'

Rostov turned around. 'Get to the point.'

'I think we should pick up the delivery man and ask him what he passed to Dickstein.'

Rostov stood still, considering. 'Yes,' he said thoughtfully. Hassan was delighted.

'We'll have to find him . . .'

'That shouldn't be impossible,' Rostov said. 'If we keep watch on the nightclub, the airport, the Alfa Hotel and the Jean-Monnet building for a few days . . .'

Hassan watched Rostov, studying his tall thin figure, and his impassive, unreadable face with its high forehead and close-cropped greying hair. I'm right, Hassan thought, and he's got to admit it.

'You're right,' Rostov said. 'I should have thought of that.'

Hassan felt a glow of pride, and thought: maybe he's not such a bastard after all.

CHAPTER SIX

THE CITY of Oxford had not changed as much as the people. The city was predictably different: it was bigger, the cars and shops were more numerous and more garish, and the streets were more crowded. But the predominant characteristic of the place was still the cream-coloured stone of the college buildings, with the occasional glimpse, through an arch, of the startling green turf of a deserted quadrangle. Dickstein noticed also the curious pale English light, such a contrast with the brassy glare of Israeli sunshine: of course it had always been there, but as a native he had never seen it. However, the students seemed a totally new breed. In the Middle East and all over Europe Dickstein had seen men with hair growing over their ears, with orange and pink neckerchiefs, with bell-bottom trousers and high-heeled shoes; and he had not been expecting people to be dressed as they were in 1948, in tweed jackets and corduroy trousers, with Oxford shirts and Paisley ties from Hall's. All the same he was not prepared for this. Many of them were barefoot in the streets, or wore peculiar open sandals without socks. Men and women had trousers which seemed to Dickstein to be vulgarly tight-fitting. After observing several women whose breasts wobbled freely inside loose, colourful shirts, he concluded that brassieres were out of fashion. There was a great deal of blue denim – not just jeans but shirts, jackets, skirts and even coats. And the hair! It was this that really shocked him. The men grew it not just over their ears but sometimes halfway down their backs. He saw two chaps with pigtails. Others, male and female, grew it upward and outward in great masses of curls so that they always looked as if they were peering through a hole in a hedge. This apparently being insufficiently outrageous for some, they had added Jesus beards, Mexican moustaches, or swooping side-whiskers. They might have been men from Mars.

He walked through the city centre, marvelling, and headed out. It was twenty years since he had followed this route, but he remembered the way. Little things about his college days came back to him: the discovery of Louis Armstrong's astonishing cornet-playing; the way he had been secretly self-conscious about his Cockney accent; wondering why everyone but he liked so much to get drunk; borrowing books faster than he could read them so that the pile on the table in his room always grew higher.

He wondered whether the years had changed him. Not much, he thought. Then he had been a frightened man looking for a fortress: now he had Israel for a fortress, but instead of hiding there he had to come out and fight to defend it. Then as now he had been a lukewarm socialist, knowing that society was unjust, not sure how it might be changed for the better. Growing older, he had gained skills but not wisdom. In fact, it seemed to him that he knew more and understood less.

He was somewhat happier now, he decided. He knew who he was and what he had to do; he had figured out what life was about and discovered that he could cope with it; although his attitudes were much the same as they had been in 1948, he was now more sure of them. However, the young Dickstein had hoped for certain other kinds of happiness which, in the event, had not come his way; indeed, the possibility had receded as the years passed. This place reminded him uncomfortably of all that. This house, especially.

He stood outside, looking at it. It had not changed at all: the paintwork was still green and white, the garden still a jungle in the front. He opened the gate, walked up the path to the door, and knocked.

This was not the efficient way to do it. Ashford might have moved away, or died, or simply gone on holiday. Dickstein should perhaps have called the university to check. However, if the inquiry was to be casual and discreet it was necessary to risk wasting a little time. Besides, he had rather liked the idea of seeing the old place again after so many years.

The door opened and the woman said, 'Yes?'

Dickstein went cold with shock. His mouth dropped open. He staggered slightly, and put a hand against the wall to steady himself. His face creased into a frown of astonishment.

It was she, and she was still twenty-five years old.

In a voice full of incredulity, Dickstein said, 'Elia . . . ?'

She stared at the odd little man on the doorstep. He looked like a don, with his round spectacles and his old grey suit and his bristly short hair. There had been nothing wrong with him when she opened the door, but as soon as he set eyes on her he had turned quite grey.

This kind of thing had happened to her once before, walking down the High Street. A delightful old gentleman had stared at her, doffed his hat, stopped her and said, 'I say, I know we haven't been introduced but . . .'

This was obviously the same phenomenon, so she said, 'I'm not Eila. I'm Suza.'

'Suza!' said the stranger.

'They say I look exactly like my mother did when she was my age. You obviously knew her. Will you come in?'

The man stayed where he was. He seemed to be recovering from the surprise, although he was still pale. 'I'm Nat Dickstein,' he said with a little smile.

'How do you do,' Suza said. 'Won't you—' Then she realized what he had said. It was her turn to be surprised. 'Mister Dickstein!' she said, her voice rising almost to a squeal. She threw her arms around his neck and kissed him.

'You remembered,' he said when she let go. He looked pleased and embarrassed.

'Of course!' she said. 'You used to pet Hezekiah. You

were the only one who could understand what he was saying.'

He gave that little smile again. 'Hezekiah the cat . . . I'd forgotten.'

'Well, come in!'

He stepped past her into the house, and she closed the door. Taking his arm, she led him across the square hall. 'This is wonderful,' she said. 'Come into the kitchen, I've been messing about trying to make a cake.'

She gave him a stool. He sat down and looked about slowly, giving little nods of recognition at the old kitchen table, the fireplace, the view through the window.

'Let's have some coffee,' Suza said. 'Or would you prefer tea?'

'Coffee, please. Thank you.'

'I expect you want to see daddy. He's teaching this morning, but he'll be back soon for lunch.' She poured coffee beans into a hand-operated grinder.

'And your mother?'

'She died fourteen years ago. Cancer.' Suza looked at him, expecting the automatic 'I'm sorry.' The words did not come, but the thought showed on his face. Somehow she liked him more for that. She ground the beans. The noise filled the silence.

When she had finished, Dickstein said, 'Professor Ashford is still teaching . . . I was just trying to work out his age.'

'Sixty-five,' she said. 'He doesn't do a lot.' Sixty-five sounded ancient but daddy didn't seem old, she thought fondly: his mind was still sharp as a knife. She wondered what Dickstein did for a living. 'Didn't you emigrate to Palestine?' she asked him.

'Israel. I live on a kibbutz. I grow grapes and make wine.'

Israel. In this house it was always called Palestine. How would daddy react to this old friend who now stood for everything daddy stood against? She knew the answer: it would make no difference, for daddy's politics were theoretical, not practical. She wondered why Dickstein had come. 'Are you on holiday?'

'Business. We now think the wine is good enough to export to Europe.'

'That's very good. And you're selling it?'

'Looking out the possibilities. Tell me about yourself. I'll bet you're not a university professor.'

The remark annoyed her a little, and she knew she was blushing faintly just below her ears: she did not want this man to think she was not clever enough to be a don. 'What makes you say that?' she said coolly.

'You're so . . . warm.' Dickstein looked away, as if he immediately regretted the choice of word. 'Anyway, too young.'

She had misjudged him. He had not been condescending. 'I have my father's ear for languages, but not his academic turn of mind, so I'm an air hostess,' she said, and wondered if it were true that she did not have an academic mind, whether she really was not clever enough to be a don. She poured boiling water into a filter, and the smell of coffee filled the room. She did not know what to say next. She glanced up at Dickstein and discovered that he was openly gazing at her, deep in thought. His eyes were large and dark brown. Suddenly she felt shy – which was most unusual. She told him so.

'Shy?' he said. 'That's because I've been staring at you as if you were a painting, or something. I'm trying to get used to the fact that you're not Eila, you're the little girl with the old grey cat.'

'Hezekiah died, it must have been soon after you left.'

'There's a lot that's changed.'

'Were you great friends with my parents?'

'I was one of your father's students. I admired your mother from a distance. Eila . . .' Again he looked away, as if to pretend that it was someone else speaking. 'She wasn't just beautiful – she was *striking.*'

Suza looked into his face. She thought: You loved her. The thought came unbidden; it was intuitive; she immediately suspected it might be wrong. However, it would explain the severity of his reaction on the doorstep when he saw her. She said, 'My mother was the original hippy – did you know that?'

'I don't know what you mean.'

'She wanted to be free. She rebelled against the restrictions put on Arab women, even though she came from an affluent, liberal home. She married my father to get out of the Middle East. Of course she found that Western society had its own ways of repressing women – so she proceeded to break most of the rules.' As she spoke Suza remembered how she had realized, while she was becoming a woman and beginning to understand passion, that her mother was promiscuous. She had been shocked, she was sure, but somehow she could not recall the feeling.

'That makes her a hippy?' Dickstcin said.

'Hippies believe in free love.'

'I see.'

And from his reaction to *that* she knew that her mother had not loved Nat Dickstein. For no reason at all this made her sad. 'Tell me about your parents,' she said. She was talking to him as if they were the same age.

'Only if you pour the coffee.'

She laughed. 'I was forgetting.'

'My father was a cobbler,' Dickstein began. 'He was good at mending boots but he wasn't much of a businessman. Still, the Thirties were good years for cobblers in the East End of London. People couldn't afford new boots, so they had their old ones mended year after year. We were never rich, but we had a little more money than most of the people around us. And, of course, there was some pressure on my father from his family to expand the business, open a second shop, employ other men.'

Suza passed him his coffee. 'Milk, sugar?'

'Sugar, no milk. Thank you.'

'Do go on.' It was a different world, one she knew nothing about: it had never occurred to her that a shoe repairer would do well in a depression.

'The leather dealers thought my father was a tartar – they could never sell him anything but the best. If there was a second-rate hide they would say, "Don't bother giving that to Dickstein, he'll send it straight back." So I was told, anyway.' He gave that little smile again.

'Is he still alive?' Suza asked.

'He died before the war.'

'What happened?'

'Well. The Thirties were the Fascist years in London. They used to hold open-air meetings every night. The speakers would tell them how Jews the world over were sucking the blood of working people. The speakers, the organizers, were respectable middle-class men, but the crowds were unemployed ruffians. After the meetings they would march through the streets, breaking windows and roughing-up passersby. Our house was a perfect target for them. We were Jews; my father was a shopkeeper and therefore a bloodsucker; and, true to their propaganda, we were slightly better off than the people around us.'

He stopped, staring into space. Suza waited for him to go on. As he told this story, he seemed to huddle – crossing his legs tightly, wrapping his arms around his body, hunching his back. Sitting there on the kitchen stool, in his ill-fitting suit of clerical grey, with his elbows and knees and shoulders pointing at all angles, he looked like a bundle of sticks in a bag.

'We lived over the shop. Every damn night I used to lie awake, waiting for them to go past. I was blind terrified, mainly because I knew my father was so frightened. Sometimes they did nothing, just went by. Usually they shouted out slogans. Often, often they broke the windows. A couple of times they got into the shop and smashed it up. I thought they were going to come up the stairs. I put my head under the pillow, crying, and cursed God for making me Jewish.'

'Didn't the police do anything?'

'What they could. If they were around they stopped it. But they had a lot to do in those days. The Communists were the only people who would help us fight back, and my father didn't want their help. All the political parties were against the Fascists, of course – but it was the Reds who gave out pickaxe handles and crowbars and built barricades. I tried to join the Party but they wouldn't have me – too young.'

'And your father?'

'He just sort of lost heart. After the shop was wrecked the second time there was no money to fix it. It seemed he didn't have the energy to start again somewhere else. He went on the dole, and just kind of wasted. He died in 1938.'

'And you?'

'Grew up fast. Joined the army as soon as I looked old enough. Got taken prisoner early. Came to Oxford after the war, then dropped out and went to Israel.'

'Have you got a family out there?'

'The whole kibbutz is my family . . . but I never married.'

'Because of my mother?'

'Perhaps. Partly. You're very direct.'

She felt the glow of a faint blush below her ears again: it had been a very intimate question to ask someone who was practically a stranger. Yet it had come quite naturally. She said, 'I'm sorry.'

'Don't apologize,' Dickstein said. 'I rarely talk like this. Actually, this whole trip is, I don't know, full of the past. There's a word for it. Redolent.'

'That means smelling of death.'

Dickstein shrugged.

There was a silence. I like this man at lot, Suza thought. I like his conversation and his silences, his big eyes and his old suit and his memories. I hope he'll stay a while.

She picked up the coffee cups and opened the dishwasher. A spoon slid off a saucer and bounced under the large old freezer. She said, 'Damn.'

Dickstein got down on his knees and peered underneath.

'It's there for ever, now,' Suza said. 'That thing is too heavy to move.'

Dickstein lifted one end of the freezer with his right hand and reached underneath it with his left. He lowered the end of the freezer, stood up and handed the spoon to Suza.

She stared at him. 'What are you – Captain America? That thing is *heavy*.'

'I work in the fields. How do you know about Captain America? He was the rage in my boyhood.'

'He's the rage now. The art in those comics is fantastic.'

'Well, stone the crows,' he said. 'We had to read them in secret because they were trash. Now they're art. Quite right, too.'

She smiled. 'Do you really work in the fields?' He looked like a clerk, not a field hand.

'Of course.'

'A wine salesman who actually gets dirt under his fingernails in the vineyard. That's unusual.'

'Not in Israel. We're a little . . . obsessive, I suppose . . . about the soil.'

Suza looked at her watch and was surprised to see how late it was. 'Daddy should be home any minute. You'll eat with us, won't you? I'm afraid it's only a sandwich.'

'That would be lovely.'

She sliced a French loaf and began to make salad. Dickstein offered to wash lettuce, and she gave him an apron. After a while she caught him watching her again, smiling. 'What are you thinking?'

'I was remembering something that would embarrass you,' he said.

'Tell me anyway.'

'I was here one evening, around six,' he began. 'Your mother was out. I had come to borrow a book from your father. You were in your bath. Your father got a phone call from France, I can't remember why. While he was talking you began to cry. I went upstairs, took you out of the bath, dried you and put you into your nightdress. You must have been four or five years old.'

Suza laughed. She had a sudden vision of Dickstein in a steamy bathroom, reaching down and effortlessly lifting her out of a hot bath full of soap bubbles. In the vision she was not a child but a grown woman with wet breasts and foam between her thighs, and his hands were strong and sure as he drew her against his chest. Then the kitchen door opened and her father came in, and the dream vanished, leaving only a sense of intrigue and a trace of guilt.

Nat Dickstein thought Professor Ashford had aged well. He was now bald except for a monkish fringe of white hair. He had put on a little weight and his movements were slower, but he still had the spark of intellectual curiosity in his eyes.

Suza said, 'A surprise guest, daddy.'

Ashford looked at him and, without hesitation, said, 'Young Dickstein! Well, I'm blessed! My dear fellow.'

Dickstein shook his hand. The grip was firm. 'How are you, professor?'

'In the pink, dear boy, especially when my daughter's here to look after me. You remember Suza?'

'We've spent the morning reminiscing,' Dickstein said.

'I see she's put you in an apron already. That's fast, even for her. I've told her she'll never get a husband this way. Take it off, dear boy, and come and have a drink.'

With a rueful grin at Suza, Dickstein did as he was told and followed Ashford into the drawing room.

'Sherry?' Ashford asked.

'Thank you, a small one.' Dickstein suddenly remembered he was here for a purpose. He had to get information out of Ashford without the old man realizing it. He had been, as it were, off-duty, for a couple of hours, and now he had to turn his mind back to work. But softly, softly, he thought.

Ashford handed him a small glass of pale sherry. 'Now tell me, what have you been up to all these years?'

Dickstein sipped the sherry. It was very dry, the way they liked it at Oxford. He told the professor the story he had given to Hassan and to Suza, about finding export markets for Israeli wine. Ashford asked informed questions. Were young people leaving the kibbutzim for the cities? Had time and prosperity eroded the communalist ideas of the kibbutzniks? Did European Jews mix and intermarry with African and Levantine Jews? Dickstein's answers were yes, no, and not much. Ashford courteously avoided the question of their opposing views on the political morality of Israel, but nevertheless there was, underlying his detached inquiries about Israeli problems, a detectable trace of eagerness for bad news.

Suza called them to the kitchen for lunch before Dickstein had an opportunity to ask his own questions. Her French sandwiches were vast and delicious. She had opened a bottle of red wine to go with them. Dickstein could see why Ashford had put on weight.

Over coffee Dickstein said, 'I ran into a contemporary of mine a couple of weeks ago – in Luxembourg, of all places.'

Ashford said, 'Yasif Hassan?'

'How did you know?'

'We've kept in touch. I know he lives in Luxembourg.'

'Have you seen him much?' Dickstein asked, thinking: Softly, softly.

'Several times, over the years.' Ashford paused. 'It

needs to be said, Dickstein, that the wars which have given you everything took everything away from him. His family lost all their money and went into a refugee camp. He's understandably bitter about Israel.'

Dickstein nodded. He was now almost certain that Hassan was in the game. 'I had very little time with him – I was on my way to catch a plane. How is he otherwise?'

Ashford frowned. 'I find him a bit . . . *distrait*,' he finished, unable to find the right English word. 'Sudden errands he has to run, cancelled appointments, odd phone calls at all times, mysterious absences. Perhaps it's the behaviour of a dispossessed aristocrat.'

'Perhaps,' Dickstein said. In fact it was the typical behaviour of an agent, and he was now one hundred per cent sure that the meeting with Hassan had blown him. He said, 'Do you see anyone else from my year?'

'Only old Toby. He's on the Conservative Front Bench now.'

'Perfect!' Dickstein said delightedly. 'He always did talk like an Opposition spokesman – pompous and defensive at the same time. I'm glad he's found his niche.'

Suza said, 'More coffee, Nat?'

'No, thank you.' He stood up. 'I'll help you clear away, then I must get back to London. I'm so glad I dropped in on you.'

'Daddy will clear up,' Suza said. She grinned. 'We have an agreement.'

'I'm afraid it is so,' Ashford confessed. 'She won't be anybody's drudge, least of all mine.' The remark surprised Dickstein because it was so obviously untrue. Perhaps Suza didn't wait on him hand and foot, but she seemed to look after him the way a working wife would.

'I'll walk into town with you,' Suza said. 'Let me get my coat.'

Ashford shook Dickstein's hand. 'A real pleasure to see you, dear boy, a real pleasure.'

Suza came back wearing a velvet jacket. Ashford saw them to the door and waved, smiling.

As they walked along the street Dickstein talked just to have an excuse to keep looking at her. The jacket matched her black velvet trousers, and she wore a loose cream-coloured shirt that looked like silk. Like her mother, she knew how to dress to make the most of her shining dark hair and perfect tan skin. Dickstein gave her his arm, feeling rather old-fashioned, just to have her touching him. There was no doubt that she had the same physical magnetism as her mother: there was that something about her which filled men with the desire to possess her, a desire not so much like lust as greed; the need to *own* such a beautiful object, so that it would never be taken away. Dickstein was old enough now to know how false such desires were, and to know that Eila Ashford would not have made him happy. But the daughter seemed to have something the mother had lacked, and that was warmth. Dickstein was sorry he would never see Suza again. Given time, he might . . .

Well. It was not to be.

When they reached the station he asked her, 'Do you ever go to London?'

'Of course,' she said. 'I'm going tomorrow.'
'What for?'
'To have dinner with you,' she said.

When Suza's mother died, her father was wonderful.

She was eleven years of age: old enough to understand death, but too young to cope with it. Daddy had been calm and comforting. He had known when to leave her to weep alone and when to make her dress up and go out to lunch. Quite unembarrassed, he had talked to her about menstruation and gone with her cheerfully to buy new brassieres. He gave her a new role in life: she became the woman of the house, giving instructions to the cleaner, writing the laundry list, handing out sherry on Sunday mornings. At the age of fourteen she was in charge of the household finances. She took care of her father better than Eila ever had. She would throw away worn shirts and replace them with identical new ones without daddy ever knowing. She learned that it was possible to be alive and secure and loved even without a mother.

Daddy gave her a role, just as he had her mother; and, like her mother, she had rebelled against the role while continuing to play it.

He wanted her to stay at Oxford, to be first an undergraduate, then a graduate student, then a teacher. It would have meant that she was always around to take care of him. She said she was not smart enough, with an uneasy feeling that this was an excuse for something else, and took a job that obliged her to be away from home and unable to look after daddy for weeks at a time. High in the air and thousands of miles from Oxford, she served drinks and meals to middle-aged men, and wondered if she really had changed anything.

Walking home from the railway station. she thought about the groove she was in and whether she would ever get out of it.

She was at the end of a love affair which, like the rest of her life, had wearily followed a familiar pattern. Julian was in his late thirties, a philosophy lecturer specializing in the pre-Socratic Greeks: brilliant, dedicated and helpless. He took drugs for everything – cannabis to make love, amphetamine to work, Mogadon to sleep. He was divorced, without children. At first she had found him interesting, charming and sexy. When they were in bed he liked her to get on top. He took her to fringe theatres in London and bizarre student parties. But it all wore off: she realized that he wasn't really very interested in sex, that he took her out because she looked good on his arm, that he liked her company just because she was so impressed by his intellect. One day she found herself ironing his clothes while he took a tutorial; and then it was as good as over.

Sometimes she went to bed with men her own age or younger, mostly because she was consumed with lust for their bodies. She was usually disappointed and they all bored her eventually.

She was already regretting the impulse which had led her to make a date with Nat Dickstein. He was depressingly true to type: a generation older than she and patently in need of care and attention. Worst of all, he had been in love with her mother. At first sight he was a father-figure like all the rest.

But he was different in some ways, she told herself. He was a farmer, not an academic – he would probably be the least well-read person she had ever dated. He had gone to Palestine instead of sitting in Oxford coffee shops talking about it. He could pick up one end of the freezer with his right hand. In the time they had spent together he had more than once surprised her by not conforming to her expectations.

Maybe Nat Dickstein will break the pattern, she thought.

And maybe I'm kidding myself, again.

Nat Dickstein called the Israeli Embassy from a phone booth at Paddington Station. When he got through he asked for the Commercial Credit Office. There was no such department: this was a code for the Mossad message centre. He was answered by a young man with a Hebrew accent. This pleased Dickstein, for it was good to know there were people for whom Hebrew was a native tongue and not a dead language. He knew the conversation would automatically be tape-recorded, so he went straight into his message: 'Rush to Bill. Sale jeopardized by presence of opposition team. Henry.' He hung up without waiting for an acknowledgment.

He walked to his hotel from the station, thinking about Suza Ashford. He was to meet her at Paddington tomorrow evening. She would spend the night at the flat of a friend. Dickstein did not really know where to begin – he could not remember ever taking a woman out to dinner just for pleasure. As a teenager he had been too poor; after the war he had been too nervous and awkward; as he grew older he somehow never got into the habit. There had been dinners with colleagues, of course, and with kibbutzniks after shopping expeditions in Nazareth; but to take a woman, just the two of you, for nothing more than the pleasure of each other's company . . .

What did you do? You were supposed to pick her up in your car, wearing your dinner jacket, and give her a box of chocolates tied with a big ribbon. Dickstein was meeting Suza at the railway station, and he had neither car nor dinner jacket. Where would he take her? He did not know any posh restaurants in Israel, let alone England.

Walking alone through Hyde Park, he smiled broadly. This was a laughable situation for a man of forty-three to be in. She knew he was no sophisticate, and obviously she did not care, for she had invited herself to dinner. She would also know the restaurants and what to order. It was hardly a matter of life and death. Whatever happened, he was going to enjoy it.

There was now a hiatus in his work. Having discovered that he was blown, he could do nothing until he had talked to Pierre Borg and Borg had decided whether or not to abort. That evening he went to see a French film called *Un Homme et Une Femme*. It was a simple love story, beautifully told, with an insistent

Latin-American tune on the soundtrack. He left before the movie was halfway through, because the story made him want to cry; but the tune ran through his mind all night.

In the morning he went to a phone booth in the street near his hotel and phoned the Embassy again. When he got through to the message centre he said, 'This is Henry. Any reply?'

The voice said, 'Go to ninety-three thousand and confer tomorrow.'

Dickstein said, 'Reply: conference agenda at airport information.'

Pierre Borg would be flying in at nine-thirty tomorrow.

The four men sat in the car with the patience of spies, silent and watchful, as the day darkened.

Pyotr Tyrin was at the wheel, a stocky middle-aged man in a raincoat, drumming his fingernails on the dashboard, making a noise like pigeons' feet on a roof. Yasif Hassan sat beside him. David Rostov and Nik Bunin were in the back.

Nik had found the delivery man on the third day, the day he spent watching the Jean-Monnet building on the Kirchberg. He had reported a positive identification. 'He doesn't look quite so much of a nancy-boy in his office suit, but I'm quite sure it's him. I should say he must work here.'

'I should have guessed,' Rostov had said. 'If Dickstein is after secrets his informants won't be from the airport or the Alfa Hotel. I should have sent Nik to Euratom first.'

He was addressing Pyotr Tyrin, but Hassan heard and said, 'You can't think of everything.'

'Yes, I can,' Rostov told him.

He had instructed Hassan to get hold of a large dark car. The American Buick they now sat in was a little conspicuous, but it was black and roomy. Nik had followed the Euratom man home, and now the four spies waited in the cobbled street close to the old terraced house.

Rostov hated this cloak-and-dagger stuff. It was so old-fashioned. It belonged to the Twenties and Thirties, to places like Vienna and Istanbul and Beirut, not to western Europe in 1968. It was just *dangerous* to snatch a civilian off the street, bundle him into a car, and beat him until he gave you information. You might be seen by passersby who were not afraid to go to the police and tell what they had observed. Rostov liked things to be straightforward and clear-cut and predictable, and he preferred to use his brains rather than his fists. But this delivery man had gained in importance with each day that Dickstein failed to surface. Rostov had to know what he had delivered to Dickstein, and he had to know today.

Pyotr Tyrin said, 'I wish he would come out.'

'We're in no hurry,' Rostov said. It was not true, but he did not want the team to get edgy and impatient and make mistakes. To relieve the tension he continued speaking. 'Dickstein did this, of course. He did what we've done and what we're doing. He watched the

Jean-Monnet building, he followed this man home, and he waited here in the street. The man came out and went to the homosexual club, and then Dickstein knew the man's weakness and used it to turn him into an informant.'

Nik said, 'He hasn't been at the club the past two nights.'

Rostov said, 'He's discovered that everything has its price, especially love.'

'Love?' Nik said with scorn in his voice.

Rostov did not reply.

The darkness thickened and the street lights came on. The air coming through the open car window tasted faintly damp: Rostov saw a swirl or two of mist around the lights. The vapour came from the river. A fog would be too much to hope for in June.

Tyrin said, 'What's this?'

A fair-haired man in a double-breasted jacket was walking briskly along the street toward them.

'Quiet, now,' Rostov said.

The man stopped at the house they were watching. He rang a doorbell.

Hassan put a hand on the door handle.

Rostov hissed: 'Not yet.'

A net curtain was briefly drawn aside in the attic window.

The fair-haired man waited, tapping his foot.

Hassan said, 'The lover, perhaps?'

'For God's sake shut up,' Rostov told him.

After a minute the front door opened and the fair-haired man stepped inside. Rostov got a glimpse of the person who had opened up: it was the delivery man. The door closed and their chance was gone.

'Too quick,' Rostov said. 'Damn it.'

Tyrin began to drum his fingers again, and Nik scratched himself. Hassan gave an exasperated sigh, as if he had known all along that it was foolish to wait. Rostov decided that it was time to bring him down a peg or two.

Nothing happened for an hour.

Tyrin said, 'They're spending an evening indoors.'

'If they've had a brush with Dickstein they're probably afraid to go out at night,' Rostov said.

Nik asked, 'Do we go in?'

'There's a problem,' Rostov answered. 'From the window they can see who's at the door. I guess they won't open up for strangers.'

'The lover might stay the night,' Tyrin said.

'Quite.'

Nik said, 'We'll just have to bust in.'

Rostov ignored him. Nik always wanted to bust in, but he would not start any rough stuff until he was told to. Rostov was thinking that they might now have to snatch two people, which was more tricky and more dangerous. 'Have we got any firearms?' he said.

Tyrin opened the glove box in front of him and drew out a pistol.

'Good,' Rostov said. 'So long as you don't fire it.'

'It's not loaded,' Tyrin said. He stuffed the gun into his raincoat pocket.

Hassan said, 'If the lover stays the night do we take them in the morning?'

'Certainly not,' Rostov said. 'We can't do this sort of thing in broad daylight.'

'What, then?'

'I haven't decided.'

He thought about it until midnight, and then the problem solved itself.

Rostov was watching the doorway through half-closed eyes. He saw the first movement of the door as it began to open. He said: 'Now.'

Nik was first out of the car. Tyrin was next. Hassan took a moment to realize what was happening, then he followed suit.

The two men were saying goodnight, the younger one on the pavement, the older just inside the door wearing a robe. The older one, the delivery man, reached out and gave his lover's arm a farewell squeeze. They both looked up, alarmed, as Nik and Tyrin burst out of the car and came at them.

'Don't move, be silent,' Tyrin said softly in French, showing them the gun.

Rostov noticed that Nik's sound tactical instinct had led him to stand beside and slightly behind the younger man.

The older one said, 'Oh, my God, no, no more please.'

'Get in the car,' Tyrin said.

The younger man said, 'Why can't you fuckers leave us alone?'

Watching and listening from the back seat of the car, Rostov thought: This is the moment they decide whether to come quietly or make trouble. He glanced quickly up and down the darkened street. It was empty.

Nik, sensing that the younger man was thinking of disobedience, seized both his arms just below the shoulders and held him tightly.

'Don't hurt him, I'll go,' said the older man. He stepped out of the house.

His friend said, 'The hell you will!'

Rostov thought: *Damn.*

The younger man struggled in Nik's grip, then tried to stamp on Nik's foot. Nik stepped back a pace and hit the boy in the kidney with his right fist.

'No, Pierre!' the older one said, too loud.

Tyrin jumped him and put a big hand over the man's mouth. He struggled, got his head free, and shouted 'Help!' before Tyrin gagged him again.

Pierre had fallen to one knee and was groaning.

Rostov leaned across the back seat of the car and called through the open window, 'Let's *go*!'

Tyrin lifted the older man off his feet and carried him bodily across the pavement toward the car. Pierre suddenly recovered from Nik's punch and sprinted away. Hassan stuck out a leg and tripped him. The boy went sprawling on to the cobbled road.

Rostov saw a light go on in an upstairs window at a neighbouring house. If the fracas continued much longer they would all get arrested.

Tyrin bundled the delivery man into the back of the car. Rostov grabbed hold of him and said to Tyrin: 'I've got him. Start the car. Quick.'

Nik had picked up the younger one and was carrying him to the car. Tyrin got into the driver's seat and Hassan opened the other door. Rostov said, 'Hassan, shut the door of the house, idiot!'

Nik pushed the young man into the car next to his friend, then got into the back seat so that the two captives were between Rostov and himself. Hassan closed the door of the house and jumped into the front passenger seat of the car. Tyrin gunned the car away from the kerb.

Rostov said in English, 'Jesus Christ almighty, what a fuck-up.'

Pierre was still groaning. The older prisoner said, 'We haven't done anything to hurt you.'

'Haven't you?' Rostov replied. 'Three nights ago, at the club in the Rue Dicks, you delivered a briefcase to an Englishman.'

'Ed Rodgers?'

'That's not his name,' Rostov said.

'Are you the police?'

'Not exactly.' Rostov would let the man believe what he wanted to. 'I'm not interested in collecting evidence, building a case, and bringing you to a trial. I'm interested in what was in that briefcase.'

There was a silence. Tyrin spoke over his shoulder. 'Want me to head out of town, look for a quiet spot?'

'Wait,' Rostov said.

The older man said, 'I'll tell you.'

'Just drive around town,' Rostov told Tyrin. He looked at the Euratom man. 'So tell me.'

'It was a Euratom computer printout.'

'And the information on it?'

'Details of licenced shipments of fissionable materials.'

'Fissionable? You mean nuclear stuff?'

'Yellowcake, uranium metal, nuclear waste, plutonium . . .'

Rostov sat back in the seat and looked out of the window at the lights of the city going by. His blood raced with excitement: Dickstein's operation was becoming visible. Licenced shipments of fissionable matcrials . . . the Israelis wanted nuclear fuel. Dickstein would be looking for one of two things on that list – either a holder of uranium who might be prepared to sell some on the black market, or a consignment of uranium he might be able to steal.

As for what they would *do* with the stuff once they got it . . .

The Euratom man interrupted his thoughts. 'Will you let us go home now?'

Rostov said, 'I'll have to have a copy of that printout.'

'I can't take another one, the disappearance of the first was suspicious enough!'

'I'm afraid you'll have to,' Rostov said. 'But if you like, you can take it back to the office after we've photographed it.'

'Oh, God,' the man groaned.

'You've got no choice.'

'All right.'

'Head back to the house,' Rostov told Tyrin. To the

Euratom man he said, 'Bring the printout home tomorrow night. Someone will come to your house during the evening to photograph it.'

The big car moved through the streets of the city. Rostov felt the snatch had not been such a disaster after all. Nik Bunin said to Pierre, 'Stop looking at me.'

They reached the cobbled street. Tyrin stopped the car. 'Okay,' Rostov said. 'Let the older man out. His friend stays with us.'

The Euratom man yelped as if hurt. 'Why?'

'In case you're tempted to break down and confess everything to your bosses tomorrow. Young Pierre will be our hostage. Get out.' Nik opened the door and let the man out. He stood on the pavement for a moment. Nik got back in and Tyrin drove off.

Hassan said, 'Will he be all right? Will he do it?'

'He'll work for us until he gets his friend back,' Rostov said.

'And then?'

Rostov said nothing. He was thinking that it would probably be prudent to kill them both.

This is Suza's nightmare.

It is evening at the green-and-white house by the river. She is alone. She takes a bath, lying for a long time in the hot scented water. Afterwards she goes into the master bedroom, sits in front of the three-sided mirror, and dusts herself with powder from an onyx box that belonged to her mother.

She opens the wardrobe, expecting to find her

mother's clothes moth-eaten, falling away from the hangers in dun-coloured tatters, transparent with age; but it is not so: they are all clean and new and perfect, except for a faint odour of mothballs. She chooses a nightgown, white as a shroud, and puts it on. She gets into the bed.

She lies still for a long time, waiting for Nat Dickstein to come to his Eila. The evening becomes night. The river whispers. The door opens. The man stands at the foot of the bed and takes off his clothes. He lies on top of her, and her panic begins like the first small spark of a conflagration as she realizes that it is not Nat Dickstein but her father; and that she is, of course, long dead: and as the nightgown crumbles to dust and her hair falls out and her flesh withers and the skin of her face dries and shrinks baring the teeth and the skull and she becomes, even as the man thrusts at her, a skeleton, so she screams and screams and screams and wakes up, and she lies perspiring and shivering and frightened, wondering why nobody comes rushing in to ask what is wrong, until she realizes with relief that even the screams were dreamed; and consoled, she wonders vaguely about the meaning of the dream while she drifts back into sleep.

In the morning she is her usual cheerful self, except perhaps for a small imprecise darkness, like a smudge of cloud in the sky of her mood, not remembering the dream at all, only aware that there was once something that troubled her, not worrying any more, though, because, after all, dreaming is instead of worrying.

CHAPTER SEVEN

'NAT DICKSTEIN is going to steal some uranium,' said Yasif Hassan.

David Rostov nodded agreement. His mind was elsewhere. He was trying to figure out how to get rid of Yasif Hassan.

They were walking through the valley at the foot of the crag which was the old city of Luxembourg. Here, on the banks of the Petrusse River, were lawns and ornamental trees and footpaths. Hassan was saying, 'They've got a nuclear reactor at a place called Dimona in the Negev Desert. The French helped them build it, and presumably supplied them with fuel for it. Since the Six-Day War, de Gaulle has cut off their supplies of guns, so perhaps he's cut off the uranium as well.'

This much was obvious, Rostov thought, so it was best to allay Hassan's suspicions by agreeing vehemently. 'It would be a completely characteristic Mossad move to just go out and steal the uranium they need,' he said. 'That's exactly how those people think. They have this backs-to-the-wall mentality which enables them to ignore the niceties of international diplomacy.'

Rostov was able to guess a little farther than Hassan – which was why he was at once so elated and so anxious to get the Arab out of the way for a while. Rostov knew about the Egyptian nuclear project at Qattara: Hassan almost certainly did not – why should they tell such secrets to an agent in Luxembourg?

However, because Cairo was so leaky it was likely the Israelis also knew about the Egyptian bomb. And what would they do about it? Build their own – for which they needed, in the Euratom man's phrase, 'fissionable material'. Rostov thought Dickstein was going to try to get some uranium for an Israeli atom bomb. But Hassan would not be able to reach that conclusion, not yet; and Rostov was not going to help him, for he did not want Tel Aviv to discover how close he was.

When the printout arrived that night it would take him farther still. For it was the list from which Dickstein would probably choose his target. Rostov did not want Hassan to have that information, either.

David Rostov's blood was up. He felt the way he did in a chess game at the moment when three or four of the opponent's moves began to form a pattern and he could see from where the attack would come and how he would have to turn it into a rout. He had not forgotten the reasons why he had entered into battle with Dickstein – that other conflict inside the KGB between himself and Feliks Vorontsov, with Yuri Andropov as umpire and a place at the Phys-Mat School as the prize – but that receded to the back of his mind. What moved him now, what kept him tense and alert and sharpened the edge of his ruthlessness, was the thrill of the chase and the scent of the quarry in his nostrils.

Hassan stood in his way. Eager, amateur, touchy, bungling Hassan, reporting back to Cairo, was at this moment a more dangerous enemy than Dickstein himself. For all his faults, he was not stupid – indeed, Rostov thought, he had a sly intelligence that was typically Levantine, inherited no doubt from his capitalist father. He would know that Rostov wanted him out of the way. Therefore Rostov would have to give him a real job to do.

They passed beneath the Pont Adolphe, and Rostov stopped to look back, admiring the view through the arch of the bridge. It reminded him of Oxford, and then, suddenly, he knew what to do about Hassan.

Rostov said, 'Dickstein knows someone has been following him, and presumably he's connected that fact with his meeting with you.'

'You think so?' Hassan said.

'Well, look. He goes on an assignment, he bumps into an Arab who knows his real name and suddenly he's tailed.'

'He's sure to speculate, but he doesn't *know*.'

'You're right.' Looking at Hassan's face, Rostov realized that the Arab just loved him to say *You're right*. Rostov thought: He doesn't like me, but he wants my approval – wants it badly. He's a proud man – I can use that. 'Dickstein has to check,' Rostov went on. 'Now, are you on file in Tel Aviv?'

Hassan shrugged, with a hint of his old aristocratic nonchalance. 'Who knows?'

'How often have you had face-to-face contacts with other agents – Americans, British, Israelis?'

'Never,' Hassan said. 'I'm too careful.'

Rostov almost laughed out loud. The truth was that Hassan was too insignificant an agent to have come to the notice of the major intelligence services, and had never done anything important enough to have met other spies. 'If you're not on file,' Rostov said, 'Dickstein has to talk to your friends. Have you any acquaintances in common?'

'No. I haven't seen him since college. Anyway, he could learn nothing from my friends. They know nothing of my secret life. I don't go around telling people—'

'No, no,' Rostov said, suppressing his impatience. 'But all Dickstein would have to do is ask casual questions about your general behaviour to see whether it conforms to the pattern of clandestine work – for example, do you have mysterious phone calls, sudden absences, friends whom you don't introduce around . . . Now, is there anybody from Oxford whom you still see?'

'None of the students.' Hassan's tone had become defensive, and Rostov knew he was about to get what he wanted 'I've kept in touch with some of the faculty, on and off: Professor Ashford, in particular – once or twice he has put me in touch with people who are prepared to give money to our cause.'

'Dickstein knew Ashford, if I remember rightly.'

'Of course. Ashford had the chair of Semitic Languages, which was what both Dickstein and I read.'

'There. All Dickstein has to do is call on Ashford and mention your name in passing. Ashford will tell him what you're doing and how you behave. Then Dickstein will know you're an agent.'

'It's a bit hit-and-miss,' Hassan said dubiously.

'Not at all,' Rostov said brightly, although Hassan was right. 'It's a standard technique. I've done it myself. It works.'

'And if he has contacted Ashford . . .'

'We have a chance of picking up his trail again. So I want you to go to Oxford.'

'Oh!' Hassan had not seen where the conversation was leading, and now was boxed in. 'Dickstein might have just called on the phone . . .'

'He might, but that kind of inquiry is easier to make in person. Then you can say you were in town and just dropped by to talk about old times . . . It's hard to be that casual on the international telephone. For the same reasons, you must go there rather than call.'

'I suppose you're right,' Hassan said reluctantly. 'I was planning to make a report to Cairo as soon as we've read the printout . . .'

That was exactly what Rostov was trying to avoid. 'Good idea,' he said. 'But the report will look so much better if you can also say that you have picked up Dickstein's trail again.'

Hassan stood staring at the view, peering into the distance as if he was trying to see Oxford. 'Let's go back,' he said abruptly. 'I've walked far enough.'

It was time to be chummy. Rostov put an arm around Hassan's shoulders. 'You Europeans are soft.'

'Don't try to tell me the KGB have a tough life in Moscow.'

'Want to hear a Russian joke?' Rostov said as they climbed the side of the valley toward the road. 'Brezhnev was telling his old mother how well he had done. He showed her his apartment – huge, with Western furniture, dishwasher, freezer, servants, everything. She didn't say a word. He took her to his dacha on the Black Sea – a big villa with a swimming pool, private beach, more servants. Still she wasn't impressed. He took her to his hunting lodge in his Zil limousine, showed off the beautiful grounds, the guns, the dogs. Finally he said, "Mother, mother, why don't you say something? Aren't you proud?" So she said, "It's wonderful, Leonid. But what will you do if the Communists come back?"'

Rostov roared with laughter at his own story, but Hassan only smiled.

'You don't think it's funny?' Rostov said.

'Not very,' Hassan told him. 'It's guilt that makes you laugh at that joke. I don't feel guilty, so I don't find it funny.'

Rostov shrugged, thinking: Thank you Yasif Hassan, Islam's answer to Sigmund Freud. They reached the road and stood there for a while, watching the cars speed by as Hassan caught his breath. Rostov said, 'Oh, listen, there's something I've always wanted to ask you. Did you really screw Ashford's wife?'

'Only four or five times a week,' Hassan said, and he laughed, loudly.

Rostov said, 'Who feels guilty now?'

*

He arrived at the station early, and the train was late, so he had to wait for a whole hour. It was the only time in his life he read *Newsweek* from cover to cover. She came through the ticket barrier at a half-run, smiling broadly. Just like yesterday, she threw her arms around him and kissed him; but this time the kiss was longer. He had vaguely expected to see her in a long dress and a mink wrap, like a banker's wife on a night out at the 61 Club in Tel Aviv; but of course Suza belonged to another country and another generation, and she wore high boots which disappeared under the hem of her below-the-knee skirt, with a silk shirt under an embroidered waistcoat such as a matador might wear. Her face was not made up. Her hands were empty: no coat, no handbag, no overnight case. They stood still, smiling at each other, for a moment. Dickstein, not quite sure what to do, gave her his arm as he had the day before, and that seemed to please her. They walked to the taxi stand.

As they got into the cab Dickstein said, 'Where do you want to go?'

'You haven't booked?'

I should have reserved a table, he thought. He said, 'I don't know London restaurants.'

'Kings Road,' Suza said to the driver.

As the cab pulled away she looked at Dickstein and said, 'Hello, Nathaniel.'

Nobody ever called him Nathaniel. He liked it.

The Chelsea restaurant she chose was small, dim and trendy. As they walked to a table Dickstein thought he saw one or two familiar faces, and his stomach tightened as he strove to place them; then he realized they were pop singers he had seen in magazines, and he relaxed again. He was glad his reflexes still worked like this in spite of the atypical way he was spending his time this evening. He was also pleased that the other diners in the place were of all ages, for he had been a little afraid he might be the oldest man in sight.

They sat down, and Dickstein said, 'Do you bring all your young men here?'

Suza gave him a cold smile. 'That's the first witless thing you've said.'

'I stand corrected.' He wanted to kick himself.

She said, 'What do you like to eat?' and the moment passed.

'At home I eat a lot of plain, wholesome, communal food. When I'm away I live in hotels, where I get junk tricked out as haute cuisine. What I like is the kind of food you don't get in either sort of place: roast leg of lamb, steak and kidney pudding, Lancashire hot-pot.'

'What I like about you,' she grinned, 'is that you have no idea whatsoever about what is trendy and what isn't; and furthermore you don't give a damn.'

He touched his lapels. 'You don't like the suit?'

'I love it,' she said. 'It must have been out-of-date when you bought it.'

He decided on roast beef from the trolley, and she had some kind of sautéed liver which she ate with enormous relish. He ordered a bottle of Burgundy: a more delicate wine would not have gone well with the liver. His knowledge of wine was the only polite accomplishment he possessed. Still, he let her drink most of it: his appetites were small.

She told him about the time she took LSD. 'It was quite unforgettable. I could feel my whole body, inside and out. I could hear my heart. My skin felt wonderful when I touched it. And the colours, of everything . . . Still, the question is, did the drug show me amazing things, or did it just make me amazed? Is it a new way of seeing the world, or does it merely synthesize the sensations you would have if you really saw the world in a new way?'

'You didn't need more of it, afterwards?' he asked.

She shook her head. 'I don't relish losing control of myself to that extent. But I'm glad I know what it's like.'

'That's what I hate about getting drunk – the loss of self-possession. Although I'm sure it's not in the same league. At any rate, the couple of times I've been drunk I haven't felt I've found the key to the universe.'

She made a dismissing gesture with her hand. It was a long, slender hand, just like Eila's; and suddenly Dickstein remembered Eila making exactly the same graceful gesture. Suza said, 'I don't believe in drugs as the solution to the world's problems.'

'What do you believe in, Suza?'

She hesitated, looking at him, smiling faintly. 'I believe that all you need is love.' Her tone was a little defensive, as if she anticipated scorn.

'That philosophy is more likely to appeal to a swinging Londoner than an embattled Israeli.'

'I guess there's no point in trying to convert you.'

'I should be so lucky.'

She looked into his eyes. 'You never know your luck.'

He looked down at the menu and said, 'It's got to be strawberries.'

Suddenly, she said, 'Tell me who you love, Nathaniel.'

'An old woman, a child and a ghost,' he said immediately, for he had been asking himself the same question. 'The old woman is called Esther, and she remembers the pogroms in Czarist Russia. The child is a boy called Mottie. He likes *Treasure Island*. His father died in the Six-Day War.'

'And the ghost?'

'You will have some strawberries?'

'Yes, please.'

'Cream?'

'No, thanks. You're not going to tell me about the ghost, are you?'

'As soon as I know, you'll know.'

It was June, and the strawberries were perfect. Dickstein said, 'Now tell me who you love.'

'Well,' she said, and then she thought for a minute. 'Well . . .' She put down her spoon. 'Oh, shit, Nathaniel, I think I love you.'

Her first thought was: What the *hell* has got into me? Why did I say that?

Then she thought: I don't care, it's true.

And finally: But *why* do I love him?

She did not know why, but she knew when. There

had been two occasions when she had been able to look inside him and see the real Dickstein: once when he spoke about the London Fascists in the Thirties, and once when he mentioned the boy whose father had been killed in the Six-Day War. Both times he had dropped his mask. She had expected to see a small, frightened man, cowering in a corner. In fact, he had appeared to be strong, confident and determined. At those moments she could sense his strength as if it were a powerful scent. It made her feel a little dizzy.

The man was weird, intriguing and powerful. She wanted to get close to him, to understand his mind, to know his secret thoughts. She wanted to touch his bony body, and feel his strong hands grasping her, and look into his sad brown eyes when he cried out in passion. She wanted his love.

It had never been like this for her before.

Nat Dickstein knew it was all wrong.

Suza had formed an attachment to him when she was five years old and he was a kind grown-up who knew how to talk to children and cats. Now he was exploiting that childhood affection.

He had loved Eila, who had died. There was something unhealthy about his relationship with her look-alike daughter.

He was not just a Jew, but an Israeli; not just an Israeli, but a Mossad agent. He of all people could not love a girl who was half Arab.

Whenever a beautiful girl falls in love with a spy, the

spy is obliged to ask himself which enemy intelligence
service she might be working for.

Over the years, each time a woman had become
fond of Dickstein, he had found reasons like these for
being cool to her, and sooner or later she had understood and gone away disappointed; and the fact that
Suza had outmanoeuvred his subconscious by being too
quick for his defences was just another reason to be
suspicious.

It was all wrong.

But Dickstein did not care.

They took a taxi to the flat where she planned to stay
the night. She invited him in – her friends, the owners
of the flat, were away on holiday – and they went to bed
together; and that was when their problems began.

At first Suza thought he was going to be too eagerly
passionate when, standing in the little hallway, he
gripped her arms and kissed her roughly, and when he
groaned, 'Oh, God,' as she took his hands and placed
them on her breasts. There flashed through her mind
the cynical thought: I've seen this act before, he is so
overcome by my beauty that he practically rapes me,
and five minutes after getting into bed he is fast asleep
and snoring. Then she pulled away from his kiss and
looked into his soft, big, brown eyes, and she thought:
Whatever happens, it won't be an act.

She led him into the little single bedroom at the
back of the flat, overlooking the courtyard. She stayed
here so often that it was regarded as her room; indeed

some of her clothes were in the wardrobe and the drawers. She sat on the edge of the single bed and took off her shoes. Dickstein stood in the doorway, watching. She looked up at him and smiled. 'Undress,' she said.

He turned out the light.

She was intrigued: it ran through her like the first tingle of a cannabis high. What was he really like? He was a Cockney, but an Israeli; he was a middle-aged schoolboy; a thin man as strong as a horse; a little gauche and nervous superficially, but confident and oddly powerful underneath. What did a man like *that* do in bed?

She got in beneath the sheet, curiously touched that he wanted to make love in the dark. He got in beside her and kissed her, gently this time. She ran her hands over his hard, bony body, and opened her mouth to his kisses. After a momentary hesitation, he responded; and she guessed he had not kissed like that before, or at least not for a long time.

He touched her tenderly now, with his fingertips, exploring, and he said 'Oh!' with a sense of wonder in his voice when he found her nipple taut. His caresses had none of the facile expertise so familiar to her from previous affairs: he was like . . . well, he was like a virgin. The thought made her smile in the darkness.

'Your breasts are beautiful,' he said.

'So are yours,' she said, touching them.

The magic began to work, and she became immersed in sensation: the roughness of his skin, the hair on his legs, the faint masculine smell of him. Then, suddenly, she sensed a change in him. There was no apparent reason for it, and for a moment she wondered if she might be imagining it, for he continued to caress her; but she knew that now it was mechanical, he was thinking of something else, she had lost him.

She was about to speak of it when he withdrew his hands and said, 'It's not working. I can't do it.'

She felt panic, and fought it down. She was frightened, not for herself – *You've known enough stiff pricks in your time, girl, not to mention a few limp ones* – but for him, for his reaction, in case he should be defeated or ashamed and—

She put both arms around him and held him tightly, saying, 'Whatever you do, please don't go away.'

'I won't.'

She wanted to put the light on, to see his face, but it seemed like the wrong thing to do right now. She pressed her cheek against his chest. 'Have you got a wife somewhere?'

'No.'

She put out her tongue and tasted his skin. 'I just think you might feel guilty about something. Like, me being half an Arab?'

'I don't think so.'

'Or, me being Eila Ashford's daughter? You loved her, didn't you?'

'How did you know?'

'From the way you talked about her.'

'Oh. Well, I don't think I feel guilty about that, but I could be wrong, doctor.'

'Mmm.' He was coming out of his shell. She kissed his chest. 'Will you tell me something?'

'I expect so.'

'When did you last have sex?'

'Nineteen forty-four.'

'You're kidding!' she said, genuinely astonished.

'That's the first witless thing you've said.'

'I . . . you're right, I'm sorry.' She hesitated. 'But why?'

He sighed. 'I can't . . . I'm not able to talk about it.'

'But you *must*.' She reached out to the bedside lamp and turned on the light. Dickstein closed his eyes against the glare. Suza propped herself up on one elbow. 'Listen,' she said, 'there are no rules. We're grown-ups, we're naked in bed, and this is nineteen sixty-eight: nothing is wrong, it's whatever turns you on.'

'There isn't anything.' His eyes were still closed.

'And there are no secrets. If you're frightened or disgusted or inflamed, you can say so, and you must. I've never said "I love you" before tonight, Nat. Speak to me, please.'

There was a long silence. He lay still, impassive, eyes closed. At last he began to talk.

'I didn't know where I was – still don't. I was taken there in a cattle truck, and in those days I couldn't tell one country from another by the landscape. It was a special camp, a medical research centre. The prisoners were selected from other camps. We were all young, healthy and Jewish.

'Conditions were better than in the first camp I was at. We had food, blankets, cigarettes; there was no thieving, no fighting. At first I thought I had struck lucky. There were lots of tests – blood, urine, blow into this tube, catch this ball, read the letters on the card. It was like being in a hospital. Then the experiments began.

'To this day I don't know whether there was any real scientific curiosity behind it. I mean, if somebody did those things with animals, I could see that it might be, you know, quite interesting, quite revealing. On the other hand, the doctors must have been insane. I don't know.'

He stopped, and swallowed. It was becoming more difficult for him to speak calmly. Suza whispered, 'You must tell me what happened – everything.'

He was pale, and his voice was very low. Still he kept his eyes shut. 'They took me to this laboratory. The guards who escorted me kept winking and nudging and telling me I was *glücklich* – lucky. It was a big room with a low ceiling and very bright lights. There were six or seven of them there, with a movie camera. In the middle of the room was a low bed with a mattress on it, no sheets. There was a woman on the mattress. They told me to fuck her. She was naked, and shivering – she was a prisoner too. She whispered to me, "You save my life and I'll save yours." And then we did it. But that was only the beginning.'

Suza ran her hand over his loins and found his penis taut. *Now* she understood. She stroked him, gently at first, and waited for him to go on – for she knew that now he would tell all of the story.

'After that they did variations on the experiment. Every day for months, there was something. Drugs, sometimes. An old woman. A man, once. Intercourse in different positions – standing up, sitting, everything. Oral sex, anal sex, masturbation, group sex. If you didn't perform, you were flogged or shot. That's why the story never came out after the war, do you see? Because all the survivors were guilty.'

Suza stroked him harder. She was certain, without knowing why, that this was the right thing to do. 'Tell me. All of it.'

He was breathing faster. His eyes opened and he stared up at the blank white ceiling, seeing another place and another time. 'At the end ... the most shameful of all ... she was a nun. At first I thought they were lying to me, they had just dressed her up, but then she started praying, in French. She had no legs ... they had amputated her, just to observe the effect on me ... it was horrible, and I ... and I ...'

Then he jerked, and Suza bent and closed her mouth over his penis, and he said, 'Oh, no, no, no!' in rhythm with his spasms, and then it was all over and he wept.

She kissed his tears, and told him it was all right, over and over again. Slowly he calmed down, and eventually he seemed to sleep for a few minutes. She lay there watching his face as the tension seeped away and he became peaceful. Then he opened his eyes and said, 'Why did you do that?'

'Well.' At the time she had not understood exactly why, but now she thought she did. 'I could have given you a lecture,' she said. 'I could have told you that there is nothing to be ashamed of; that everybody has grisly fantasies, that women dream of being flogged and men have visions of flogging them; that you can buy, here in London, pornographic books about sex with amputees, including full-colour pictures. I could have told you that many men would have been able to summon up enough bestiality to perform in that Nazi laboratory. I could have argued with you, but it wouldn't have made any difference. I had to show you. Besides—' She smiled ruefully. 'Besides, I have a dark side, too.'

He touched her cheek, then leaned forward and kissed her lips. 'Where did you get this wisdom, child?'

'It isn't wisdom, it's love.'

Then he held her very tightly and kissed her and called her darling and after a while they made love, very simply, hardly speaking, without confessions or dark fantasies or bizarre lusts, giving and taking pleasure with the familiarity of an old couple who know each other very well; and afterwards they went to sleep full of peace and joy.

David Rostov was bitterly disappointed with the Euratom printout. After he and Pyotr Tyrin had spent hours getting it doped out, it became clear that the list of consignments was very long. They could not possibly cover every target. The only way they could discover which one would be hit was to pick up Dickstein's trail again.

Yasif Hassan's mission to Oxford thereupon assumed much greater importance.

They waited for the Arab to call. At ten o'clock Nik Bunin, who enjoyed sleep the way other people enjoy sunbathing, went to bed. Tyrin stuck it out until midnight, then he too retired. Rostov's phone finally rang at one A.M. He jumped as if frightened, grabbed the phone, then waited a few moments before speaking in order to compose himself.

'Yes?'

Hassan's voice came three hundred miles along the international telephone cables. 'I did it. The man was here. Two days ago.'

Rostov clenched a fist in suppressed excitement. 'Jesus. What a piece of luck.'

'What now?'

Rostov considered. 'Now, he knows that we know.'

'Yes. Shall I come back to base?'

'I don't think so. Did the professor say how long the man plans to be in England?'

'No. I asked the question directly. The professor didn't know: the man didn't tell him.'

'He wouldn't.' Rostov frowned, calculating. 'First thing the man has to do now is report that he's blown. That means he has to contact his London office.'

'Perhaps he already has.'

'Yes, but he may want a meeting. This man takes precautions, and precautions take time. All right, leave it with me. I'll be in London later today. Where are you now?'

'I'm still in Oxford. I came straight here off the plane. I can't get back to London until the morning.'

'All right. Check into the Hilton and I'll contact you there around lunchtime.'

'Check. *A bientôt.*'

'Wait.'

'Still here.'

'Don't do anything on your own initiative, now. Wait until I get there. You've done well, don't screw it up.'

Hassan hung up.

Rostov sat still for a moment, wondering whether Hassan was planning some piece of foolishness or simply resented being told to be a good boy. The latter, he decided. Anyway, there was no damage he could do over the next few hours.

Rostov turned his mind back to Dickstein. The man would not give them a second chance to pick up his trail. Rostov had to move fast and he had to move now. He put on his jacket, left the hotel and took a taxi to the Russian Embassy.

He had to wait some time, and identify himself to four different people, before they would let him in in the middle of the night. The duty operator stood at attention when Rostov entered the communications room. Rostov said, 'Sit down. There's work to do. Get the London office first.'

The operator picked up the scrambler phone and began to call the Russian Embassy in London. Rostov took off his jacket and rolled up his sleeves.

The operator said, 'Comrade Colonel David Rostov

will speak to the most senior security officer there.' He motioned Rostov to pick up the extension.

'Colonel Petrov.' It was the voice of a middle-aged soldier.

'Petrov, I need some help,' Rostov said without preamble. 'An Israeli agent named Nat Dickstein is believed to be in England.'

'Yes, we've had his picture sent to us in the diplomatic pouch – but we weren't notified he was thought to be here.'

'Listen. I think he may contact his embassy. I want you to put all known Israeli legals in London under surveillance from dawn today.'

'Hang on, Rostov,' said Petrov with a half laugh. 'That's a lot of manpower.'

'Don't be stupid. You've got hundreds of men, the Israelis only have a dozen or two.'

'Sorry, Rostov, I can't mount an operation like that on your say-so.'

Rostov wanted to get the man by the throat. 'This is urgent!'

'Let me have the proper documentation, and I'm at your disposal.'

'By then he'll be somewhere else!'

'Not my fault, comrade.'

Rostov slammed the phone down, furious, and said, 'Bloody Russians! Never do anything without six sets of authorization. Get Moscow, tell them to find Feliks Vorontsov and patch him through to me wherever he is.'

The operator got busy. Rostov drummed his fingers

on the desk impatiently. Petrov was probably an old soldier close to retirement, with no ambition for anything but his pension. There were too many men like that in the KGB.

A few minutes later the sleepy voice of Rostov's boss, Feliks, came on the line. 'Yes, who is it?'

'David Rostov. I'm in Luxembourg. I need some backing. I think The Pirate is about to contact the Israeli Embassy in London and I want their legals watched.'

'So call London.'

'I did. They want authorization.'

'Then apply for it.'

'For God's sake, Feliks, I'm applying for it now!'

'There's nothing I can do at this time of night. Call me in the morning.'

'What is this? Surely you can—' Suddenly Rostov realized what was happening. He controlled himself with an effort. 'All right, Feliks. In the morning.'

'Goodbye.'

'Feliks—'

'Yes?'

'I'll remember this.'

The line went dead.

'Where next?' the operator asked.

Rostov frowned. 'Keep the Moscow line open. Give me a minute to think.' He might have guessed he would get no help from Feliks. The old fool wanted him to fail on this mission, to prove that he, Feliks, should have been given control of it in the first place. It was even possible that Feliks was pally with Petrov in

London and had unofficially told Petrov not to cooperate.

There was only one thing for Rostov to do. It was a dangerous course of action and might well get him pulled off the case – in fact it could even be what Feliks was hoping for. But he could not complain if the stakes were high, for it was he who had raised them.

He thought for a minute or two about exactly how he should do it. Then he said, 'Tell Moscow to put me through to Yuri Andropov's apartment at number twenty-six Kutuzov Prospekt.' The operator raised his eyebrows – it was probably the first and last time he would be instructed to get the head of the KGB on the phone – but he said nothing. Rostov waited, fidgeting. 'I bet it isn't like this working for the CIA,' he muttered.

The operator gave him the sign, and he picked up the phone. A voice said, 'Yes?'

Rostov raised his voice and barked: 'Your name and rank!'

'Major Pyotr Eduardovitch Scherbitsky.'

'This is Colonel Rostov. I want to speak to Andropov. It's an emergency, and if he isn't on this phone within one hundred and twenty seconds you'll spend the rest of your life building dams in Bratsk, do I make myself clear?'

'Yes, colonel. Please hold the line.'

A moment later Rostov heard the deep, confident voice of Yuri Andropov, one of the most powerful men in the world. 'You certainly managed to panic young Eduardovitch, David.'

'I had no alternative, sir.'

'All right, let's have it. It had better be good.'

'The Mossad are after uranium.'

'Good God.'

'I think The Pirate is in England. He may contact his embassy. I want surveillance on the Israelis there, but an old fool called Petrov in London is giving me the runaround.'

'I'll talk to him now, before I go back to bed.'

'Thank you, sir.'

'And, David?'

'Yes?'

'It was worth waking me up – but only just.'

There was a click as Andropov hung up. Rostov laughed as the tension drained out of him, and he thought: Let them do their worst – Dickstein, Hassan, Feliks – I can handle them.

'Success?' the operator asked with a smile.

'Yes,' Rostov said. 'Our system is inefficient and cumbersome and corrupt, but in the end, you know, we get what we want.'

CHAPTER EIGHT

IT WAS quite a wrench for Dickstein to leave Suza in the morning and go back to work.

He was still ... well, stunned ... at eleven A.M., sitting in the window of a restaurant in the Fulham Road waiting for Pierre Borg to show. He had left a message with airport information at Heathrow telling Borg to go to a café opposite the one where Dickstein now sat. He thought he was likely to stay stunned for a long time, maybe permanently.

He had awakened at six o'clock, and suffered a moment of panic wondering where he was. Then he saw Suza's long brown hand lying on the pillow beside his head, curled up like a small animal sleeping, and the night had come flooding back, and he could hardly believe his good fortune. He thought he should not wake her, but suddenly he could not keep his hands off her body. She opened her eyes at his touch, and they made love playfully, smiling at one another, laughing sometimes, and looking into each other's eyes at the moment of climax. Then they fooled around in the kitchen, half-dressed, making the coffee too weak and burning the toast.

Dickstein wanted to stay there for ever.

Suza had picked up his undershirt with a cry of horror. 'What's this?'

'My undershirt.'

'Undershirt? I forbid you to wear undershirts. They're old-fashioned and unhygienic and they'll get in the way when I want to feel your nipples.'

Her expression was so lecherous that he burst out laughing. 'All right,' he said. 'I won't wear them.'

'Good.' She opened the window and threw the undershirt out into the street, and he laughed all over again.

He said, 'But you mustn't wear trousers.'

'Why not?'

It was his turn to leer.

'But all my trousers have flies.'

'No good,' he said. 'No room to manoeuvre.'

And like that.

They acted as if they had just invented sex. The only faintly unhappy moment came when she looked at his scars and asked how he got them. 'We've had three wars since I went to Israel,' he said. It was the truth, but not the whole truth.

'What made you go to Israel?'

'Safety.'

'But it's just the opposite of *safe* there.'

'It's a different kind of safety.' He said this dismissively, not wanting to explain it, then he changed his mind, for he wanted her to know all about him. 'There had to be a place where nobody could say, "You're different, you're not a human being, you're a Jew," where nobody could break my windows or experiment on my body just because I'm Jewish. You see . . .' She had been looking at him with that clear-eyed, frank gaze of hers, and he had struggled to tell her the whole truth, without evasions, without trying to make it look better than it was. 'It didn't matter to me whether we chose Palestine or Uganda or Manhattan Island – wherever it was, I would have said, "That place is *mine*," and I would have fought tooth and nail to keep it. That's why I never try to argue the moral rights and wrongs of the establishment of Israel. Justice and fair play never entered into it. After the war . . . well, the suggestion that the concept of fair play had any role in international politics seemed like a sick joke to me. I'm not pretending this is an admirable attitude, I'm just telling you how it is for me. Any other place Jews live – New York, Paris, Toronto – no matter how good it is, how assimilated they are, they never know how long it's going to last, how soon will come the next crisis that can conveniently be blamed on them. In Israel I know that whatever happens, I won't be a victim of *that*. So, with that problem out of the way, we can get on and deal with the realities that are part of everyone's life: planting and reaping, buying and selling, fighting and dying. That's why I went, I think . . . Maybe I didn't see it all so clearly back then – in fact, I've never put it into words like this – but that's how I felt, anyway.'

After a moment Suza said, 'My father holds the opinion that Israel itself is now a racist society.'

'That's what the youngsters say. They've got a point. If . . .'

She looked at him, waiting.

'If you and I had a child, they would refuse to classify him as Jewish. He would be a second-class citizen. But I don't think that sort of thing will last for ever. At the moment the religious zcalots are powerful in the government: it's inevitable, Zionism was a religious movement. As the nation matures that will fade away. The race laws are already controversial. We're fighting them, and we'll win in the end.'

She came to him and put her head on his shoulder, and they held each other in silence. He knew that she did not care about Israeli politics: it was the mention of a son that had moved her.

Sitting in the restaurant window, remembering, he knew that he wanted Suza in his life always, and he wondered what he would do if she refused to go to his country. Which would he give up, Israel or Suza? He did not know.

He watched the street. It was typical June weather: raining steadily and quite cold. The familiar red buses and black cabs swished up and down, butting through the rain, splashing in the puddles on the road. A country of his own, a woman of his own: maybe he could have both.

I should be so lucky.

A cab drew up outside the café opposite, and Dickstein tensed, leaning closer to his window and peering through the rain. He recognized the bulky figure of Pierre Borg, in a dark short raincoat and a trilby hat, climbing out of the cab. He did not recognize the

second man, who got out and paid the driver. The two
men went into the café. Dickstein looked up and down
the road.

A grey Mark II Jaguar had stopped on a double
yellow line fifty yards from the café. Now it reversed
and backed into a side street, parking on the corner
within sight of the café. The passenger got out and
walked toward the café.

Dickstein left his table and went to the phone booth
in the restaurant entrance. He could still see the café
opposite. He dialled its number.

'Yes?'

'Let me speak to Bill, please.'

'Bill? Don't know him.'

'Would you just ask, please?'

'Sure. Hey, anybody here called Bill?' A pause. 'Yes,
he's coming.'

After a moment Dickstein heard Borg's voice. 'Yes?'

'Who's the face with you?'

'Head of London Station. Do you think we can trust
him?'

Dickstein ignored the sarcasm. 'One of you picked
up a shadow. Two men in a grey Jaguar.'

'We saw them.'

'Lose them.'

'Of course. Listen, you know this town – what's the
best way?'

'Send the Head of Station back to the Embassy in a
cab. That should lose the Jaguar. Wait ten minutes,
then take a taxi to . . .'

Dickstein hesitated, trying to think of a quiet street not too far away. 'To Redcliffe Street. I'll meet you there.'

'Okay.'

Dickstein looked across the road. 'Your tail is just going into your café.' He hung up.

He went back to his window seat and watched. The other man came out of the café, opened an umbrella, and stood at the kerb looking for a cab. The tail had either recognized Borg at the airport or had been following the Head of Station for some other reason. It did not make any difference. A taxi pulled up. When it left, the grey Jaguar came out of the side street and followed. Dickstein left the restaurant and hailed a cab for himself. Taxi drivers do well out of spies, he thought.

He told the cabbie to go to Redcliffe Street and wait. After eleven minutes another taxi entered the street and Borg got out. 'Flash your lights,' Dickstein said. 'That's the man I'm meeting.' Borg saw the lights and waved acknowledgment. As he was paying, a third taxi entered the street and stopped. Borg spotted it.

The shadow in the third taxi was waiting to see what happened. Borg realized this, and began to walk away from his cab. Dickstein told his driver not to flash his lights again.

Borg walked past them. The tail got out of his taxi, paid the driver and walked after Borg. When the tail's cab had gone Borg turned, came back to Dickstein's cab, and got in. Dickstein said, 'Okay, let's go.' They pulled away, leaving the tail on the pavement looking for another taxi. It was a quiet street: he would not find one for five or ten minutes.

Borg said, 'Slick.'

'Easy,' Dickstein replied.

The driver said, 'What was all that about, then?'

'Don't worry,' Dickstein told him. 'We're secret agents.'

The cabbie laughed. 'Where to now – MI5?'

'The Science Museum.'

Dickstein sat back in his seat. He smiled at Borg. 'Well, Bill, you old fart, how the hell are you?'

Borg frowned at him. 'What have you got to be so fucking cheerful about?'

They did not speak again in the cab, and Dickstein realized he had not prepared himself sufficiently for this meeting. He should have decided in advance what he wanted from Borg and how he was going to get it.

He thought: What *do* I want? The answer came up out of the back of his mind and hit him like a slap. I want to give Israel the bomb – and then I want to go home.

He turned away from Borg. Rain streaked the cab window like tears. He was suddenly glad they could not speak because of the driver. On the pavement were three coatless hippies, soaking wet, their faces and hands upturned to enjoy the rain. *If I could do this, if I could finish this assignment, I could rest.*

The thought made him unaccountably happy. He looked at Borg and smiled. Borg turned his face to the window.

They reached the museum and went inside. They
stood in front of a reconstructed dinosaur. Borg said,
'I'm thinking of taking you off this assignment.'

Dickstein nodded, suppressing his alarm, thinking
fast. Hassan must be reporting to Cairo, and Borg's
man in Cairo must be getting the reports and passing
them to Tel Aviv. 'I've discovered I'm blown,' he told
Borg.

'I knew that weeks ago,' Borg said. 'If you'd keep in
touch you'd be up-to-date on these things.'

'If I kept in touch I'd be blown more often.'

Borg grunted and walked on. He took out a cigar,
and Dickstein said, 'No smoking in here.' Borg put the
cigar away.

'Blown is nothing,' Dickstein said. 'It's happened to
me half a dozen times. What counts is how much they
know.'

'You were fingered by this Hassan, who knows you
from years back. He's working with the Russians now.'

'But what do they *know?*'

'You've been in Luxembourg and France.'

'That's not much.'

'I realize it's not much. I know you've been in
Luxembourg and France too, and *I* have no idea what
you did there.'

'So you'll leave me in,' Dickstein said, and looked
hard at Borg.

'That depends. What *have* you been doing?'

'Well.' Dickstein continued looking at Borg. The
man had become fidgety, not knowing what to do with
his hands now that he could not smoke. The bright

lights on the displays illuminated his bad complexion: his troubled face was like a gravel parking lot. Dickstein needed to judge very carefully how much he told Borg: enough to give the impression that a great deal had been achieved; not so much that Borg would think he could get another man to operate Dickstein's plan . . . 'I've picked a consignment of uranium for us to steal,' he began. 'It's going by ship from Antwerp to Genoa in November. I'm going to hijack the ship.'

'Shit!' Borg seemed both pleased and afraid at the audacity of the idea. He said, 'How the hell will you keep that secret?'

'I'm working on that.' Dickstein decided to tell Borg just a tantalizing little bit more. 'I have to visit Lloyd's, here in London. I'm hoping the ship will turn out to be one of a series of identical vessels – I'm told most ships are built that way. If I can buy an identical vessel, I can switch the two somewhere in the Mediterranean.'

Borg rubbed his hand across his close-cropped hair twice, then pulled at his ear. 'I don't see . . .'

'I haven't figured out the details yet, but I'm sure this is the only way to do the thing clandestinely.'

'So get on and figure out the details.'

'But you're thinking of pulling me out.'

'Yeah . . .' Borg tilted his head from one side to the other, a gesture of indecision. 'If I put an experienced man in to replace you, he may be spotted too.'

'And if you put in an unknown he won't be experienced.'

'Plus, I'm really not sure there is anyone, experienced or otherwise, who can pull this off apart from you. And there is something else you don't know.'

They stopped in front of a model of a nuclear reactor.

'Well?' Dickstein said.

'We've had a report from Qattara. The Russians are helping them now. We're in a hurry, Dickstein. I can't afford delay, and changes of plan cause delay.'

'Will November be soon enough?'

Borg considered. 'Just,' he said. He seemed to come to a decision. 'All right, I'm leaving you in. You'll have to take evasive action.'

Dickstein grinned broadly and slapped Borg on the back. 'You're a pal, Pierre. Don't you worry now. I'll run rings around them.'

Borg frowned. 'Just what is it with you? You can't stop grinning.'

'It's seeing you that does it. Your face is like a tonic. Your sunny disposition is infectious. When you smile, Pierre, the whole world smiles with you.'

'You're crazy, you prick,' said Borg.

Pierre Borg was vulgar, insensitive, malicious, and boring, but he was not stupid. 'He may be a bastard,' people would say, 'but he's a clever bastard.' By the time they parted company he knew that something important had changed in Nat Dickstein's life.

He thought about it, walking back to the Israeli Embassy at No. 2 Palace Green in Kensington. In the twenty years since they had first met, Dickstein had hardly changed. It was still only rarely that the force of the man showed through. He had always been quiet and withdrawn; he continued to look like an out-of-work bank clerk; and, except for occasional flashes of rather cynical wit, he was still dour.

Until today.

At first he had been his usual self – brief to the point of rudeness. But toward the end he had come on like the stereotyped chirpy Cockney sparrow in a Hollywood movie.

Borg had to know why.

He would tolerate a lot from his agents. Provided they were efficient, they could be neurotic, or aggressive, or sadistic, or insubordinate – so long as he knew about it. He could make allowances for faults: but he could not allow for unknown factors. He would be unsure of his hold over Dickstein until he had figured out the cause of the change. That was all. He had no objection in principle to one of his agents acquiring a sunny disposition.

He came within sight of the embassy. He would put Dickstein under surveillance, he decided. It would take two cars and three teams of men working in eight-hour shifts. The Head of London Station would complain. The hell with *him*.

The need to know why Dickstein's disposition had changed was only one reason Borg had decided not to pull him out. The other reason was more important. Dickstein had half a plan; another man might not be able to complete it. Dickstein had a mind for this sort of thing. Once Dickstein had figured it all out, *then* somebody else could take over. Borg had decided to take him off the assignment at the first opportunity. Dickstein would be furious: he would consider he had been shafted.

The hell with him, too.

Major Pyotr Alekseivitch Tyrin did not actually like Rostov. He did not like any of his superiors: in his view, you had to be a rat to get promoted above the rank of major in the KGB. Still, he had a sort of awestruck affection for his clever, helpful boss. Tyrin had considerable skills, particularly with electronics, but he could not manipulate people. He was a major only because he was on Rostov's incredibly successful team.

Abba Allon. High Street exit. Fifty-two, or nine? Where are you, fifty-two?

Fifty-two. We're close. We'll take him. What does he look like?

Plastic raincoat, green hat, moustache.

As a friend Rostov was not much; but he was a lot worse as an enemy. This Colonel Petrov in London had discovered that. He had tried to mess around with Rostov and had been surprised by a middle-of-the-night phone call from the head of the KGB, Yuri Andropov himself. The people in the London Embassy said Petrov had looked like a ghost when he hung up. Since then Rostov could have anything he wanted: if he sneezed five agents rushed out to buy handkerchiefs.

Okay, this is Ruth Davisson, and she's going . . . north . . .

Nineteen, we can take her—

Relax, nineteen. False alarm. It's a secretary who looks like her.

Rostov had commandeered all Petrov's best pavement artists and most of his cars. The area around the Israeli Embassy in London was crawling with agents – someone had said, 'There are more Reds here than in the Kremlin Clinic' – but it was hard to spot them. They were in cars, vans, minicabs, trucks and one vehicle that looked remarkably like an unmarked Metropolitan Police bus. There were more on foot, some in public buildings and others walking the streets and the footpaths of the park. There was even one inside the Embassy, asking in dreadfully broken English what he had to do to emigrate to Israel.

The Embassy was ideally suited for this kind of exercise. It was in a little diplomatic ghetto on the edge of Kensington Gardens. So many of the lovely old houses belonged to foreign legations that it was known as Embassy Row. Indeed, the Soviet Embassy was close by in Kensington Palace Gardens. The little group of streets formed a private estate, and you had to tell a policeman your business before you could get in.

Nineteen, this time it is Ruth Davisson . . . nineteen, do you hear me?

Nineteen here, yes.

Are you still on the north side?

Yes. And we know what she looks like.

None of the agents was actually in sight of the Israeli Embassy. Only one member of the team could see the door – Rostov, who was a half mile away, on the twentieth floor of a hotel, watching through a powerful Zeiss telescope mounted on a tripod. Several high buildings in the West End of London had clear views across the park to Embassy Row. Indeed, certain suites in certain hotels fetched inordinately high prices because of rumours that from them you could see into Princess Margaret's backyard at the neighbouring palace, which gave its name to Palace Green and Kensington Palace Gardens.

Rostov was in one of those suites, and he had a radio transmitter as well as the telescope. Each of his sidewalk squads had a walkie-talkie. Petrov spoke to his men in fast Russian, using confusing codewords, and the wavelength on which he transmitted and on which the men replied was changed every five minutes according to a computer program built into all the sets. The system was working very well, Tyrin thought – he had invented it – except that somewhere in the cycle everyone was subjected to five minutes of BBC Radio One.

Eight, move up to the north side.

Understood.

If the Israelis had been in Belgravia, the home of the more senior embassies, Rostov's job would have been more difficult. There were almost no shops, cafés or public offices in Belgravia – nowhere for agents to make themselves unobtrusive; and because the whole district was quiet, wealthy and stuffed with ambassadors it was easy for the police to keep an eye open for suspicious activities. Any of the standard surveillance ploys – telephone repair van, road crew with striped tent – would have drawn a crowd of bobbies in minutes.

By contrast the area around the little oasis of Embassy Row was Kensington, a major shopping area with several colleges and four museums.

Tyrin himself was in a pub in Kensington Church Street. The resident KGB men had told him that the pub was frequented by detectives from 'Special Branch' – the rather coy name for Scotland Yard's political police. The four youngish men in rather sharp suits drinking whisky at the bar were probably detectives. They did not know Tyrin, and would not have been much interested in him if they had. Indeed, if Tyrin were to approach them and say, 'By the way, the KGB is tailing every Israeli legal in London at the moment,' they would probably say, 'What, again?' and order another round of drinks.

In any event Tyrin knew he was not a man to attract second glances. He was small and rather rotund, with a big nose and a drinker's veined face. He wore a grey raincoat over a green sweater. The rain had removed the last memory of a crease from his charcoal flannel trousers. He sat in a corner with a glass of English beer and a small bag of potato chips. The radio in his shirt pocket was connected by a fine, flesh-coloured wire to the plug – it looked like a hearing aid – in his left ear. His left side was to the wall. He could talk to Rostov by pretending to fumble in the inside pocket of his raincoat, turning his face away from the room and muttering into the perforated metal disc on the top edge of the radio.

He was watching the detectives drink whisky and thinking that the Special Branch must have better expense accounts than its Russian equivalent: he was allowed one pint of beer per hour, the potato crisps he had to buy himself. At one time agents in England had even been obliged to buy beer in half pints, until the accounts department had been told that in many pubs a man who drank halves was as peculiar as a Russian who took his vodka in sips instead of gulps.

Thirteen, pick up a green Volvo, two men, High Street.

Understood.

And one on foot . . . I think that's Yigael Meier . . . Twenty?

Tyrin was 'Twenty.' He turned his face into his shoulder and said, 'Yes. Describe him.'

Tall, grey hair, umbrella, belted coat. High Street gate.

Tyrin said, 'I'm on my way.' He drained his glass and left the pub.

It was raining. Tyrin took a collapsible umbrella from his raincoat pocket and opened it. The wet pavements were crowded with shoppers. At the traffic lights he spotted the green Volvo and, three cars behind it, 'Thirteen' in an Austin.

Another car. Five, this one's yours. Blue Volkswagen Beetle.

Understood.

Tyrin reached Palace Gate, looked up Palace Avenue, saw a man fitting the description heading toward him, and walked on without pausing. When he had calculated that the man had had time to reach the street he stood at the kerb, as if about to cross, and looked up and down. The mark emerged from Palace Avenue and turned west, away from Tyrin.

Tyrin followed.

Along High Street tailing was made easier by the crowds. Then they turned south into a maze of side streets, and Tyrin became a bit nervous; but the Israeli did not seem to be watching for a shadow. He simply butted ahead through the rain, a tall, bent figure under an umbrella, walking fast, intent on his destination.

He did not go far. He turned into a small modern hotel just off the Cromwell Road. Tyrin walked past the entrance and, glancing through the glass door, saw the mark step into a phone booth in the lobby. A little farther along the road Tyrin passed the green Volvo, and concluded that the Israeli and his colleagues in the Volvo were staking out the hotel.

He crossed the road and came back on the opposite side, just in case the mark were to come out again immediately. He looked for the blue Volkswagen Beetle and did not see it, but he was quite sure it would be close by.

He spoke into his shirt pocket. 'This is Twenty. Meier and the green Volvo have staked out the Jacobean Hotel.'

Confirmed, Twenty. Five and Thirteen have the Israeli cars covered. Where is Meier?

'In the lobby.' Tyrin looked up and down and saw the Austin which was following the green Volvo.

Stay with him.

'Understood.' Tyrin now had a difficult decision to make. If he went straight into the hotel Meier might spot him, but if he took the time to find the back entrance Meier might go away in the meanwhile.

He decided to chance the back entrance, on the

grounds that he was supported by two cars which could cover for a few minutes if the worst happened. Beside the hotel there was a narrow alley for delivery vans. Tyrin walked along it and came to an unlocked fire exit in the blank side wall of the building. He went in and found himself in a concrete stairwell, obviously built to be used only as a fire escape. As he climbed the stairs he collapsed his umbrella, put it in his raincoat pocket and took off the raincoat. He folded it and left it in a little bundle on the first half landing, where he could quickly pick it up if he needed to make a fast exit. He went to the second floor and took the elevator down to the lobby. When he emerged in his sweater and trousers he looked like a guest at the hotel.

The Israeli was still in the phone booth.

Tyrin went up to the glass door at the front of the lobby, looked out, checked his wristwatch and returned to the waiting area to sit down as if he were meeting someone. It did not seem to be his lucky day. The object of the whole exercise was to find Nat Dickstein. He was known to be in England, and it was hoped that he would have a meeting with one of the legals. The Russians were following the legals in order to witness that meeting and pick up Dickstein's trail. The Israeli team at this hotel was clearly not involved in a meeting. They were staking out someone, presumably with a view to tailing him as soon as he showed, and that someone was not likely to be one of their own agents. Tyrin could only hope that what they *were* doing would at least turn out to be of some interest.

He watched the mark come out of the phone booth

and walk off in the direction of the bar. He wondered if the lobby could be observed from the bar. Apparently not, because the mark came back a few minutes later with a drink in his hand, then sat down across from Tyrin and picked up a newspaper.

The mark did not have time to drink his beer.

The elevator doors hissed open, and out walked Nat Dickstein.

Tyrin was so surprised that he made the mistake of staring straight at Dickstein for several seconds. Dickstein caught his eye, and nodded politely. Tyrin smiled weakly and looked at his watch. It occurred to him – more in hope than conviction – that staring was such a bad mistake that Dickstein might take it as proof that Tyrin was *not* an agent.

There was no time for reflection. Moving quickly with – Tyrin thought – something of a spring in his step, Dickstein crossed to the counter and dropped a room key, then proceeded quickly out into the street. The Israeli tail, Meier, put his newspaper on the table and followed. When the plate-glass door closed behind Meier, Tyrin got up, thinking: I'm an agent following an agent following an agent. Well, at least we keep each other in employment.

He went into the elevator and pressed the button for the first floor. He spoke into his radio. 'This is Twenty. I have Pirate.' There was no reply – the walls of the building were blocking his transmission. He got out of the elevator at the first floor and ran down the fire stairs, picking up his raincoat at the half landing. As soon as he was outside he tried the radio again. 'This is Twenty, I have the Pirate.'

All right, Twenty. Thirteen has him too.

Tyrin saw the mark crossing Cromwell Road. 'I'm following Meier,' he said into his radio.

Five and Twenty, both of you listen to me. Do not follow. Have you got that – Five?

Yes.

Twenty?

Tyrin said, 'Understood.' He stopped walking and stood on the corner watching Meier and Dickstein disappear in the direction of Chelsea.

Twenty, go back into the hotel. Get his room number. Book a room close to his. Call me on the telephone as soon as it's done.

'Understood.' Tyrin turned back, rehearsing his dialogue: Excuse me, the fellow that just walked out of here, short man with glasses, I think I know him but he got into a cab before I could catch up with him . . . his name is John but we all used to call him Jack, what room . . . ? As it turned out, none of that was necessary. Dickstein's key was still on the desk. Tyrin memorized the number.

The desk clerk came over. 'Can I help you?'

'I'd like a room,' Tyrin said.

He kissed her, and he was like a man who has been thirsty all day. He savoured the smell of her skin and the soft motions of her lips. He touched her face and said, 'This, this, this is what I need.' They stared into each other's eyes, and the truth between them was like nakedness. He thought: I can do anything I want. The idea ran through his mind again and again like an incantation, a magic spell. He touched her body greedily. He stood face to face with her in the little blue-and-yellow kitchen, looking into her eyes while he fingered the secret places of her body. Her red mouth opened a fraction and he felt her breath coming faster and hot on his face; he inhaled deeply so as to breathe the air from her. He thought: If I can do anything I want, so can she; and, as if she had read his mind, she opened his shirt, and bent to his chest, and took his nipple between her teeth, and sucked. The sudden, astonishing pleasure of it made him gasp aloud. He held her head gently in his hands and rocked to and fro a little to intensify the sensation. He thought: Anything I want! He reached behind her, lifted her skirt, and feasted his eyes on the white panties clinging to her curves and contrasting with the brown skin of her long legs. His right hand stroked her face and gripped her shoulder and weighed her breasts; his left hand moved over her hips and inside her panties and between her legs; and everything felt so good, so good, that he wished he had four hands to feel her with, six. Then, suddenly, he wanted to see her face, so he gripped her shoulders and made her stand upright, saying, 'I want to look at you.' Her eyes filled with tears, and he knew that these were signs not of sadness but of intense pleasure. Again they stared into each other's eyes, and this time it was not just truth between them but raw emotion gushing from one to another in rivers, in torrents. Then he knelt at her feet like a supplicant. First he laid his head on her thighs, feeling the heat of her body through her clothing. Then he reached beneath her skirt with both hands, found the waist of her panties, and drew them down slowly, holding the shoes on her feet as she stepped out. He got up from the floor. They were still standing on the spot where they had kissed when he had first come into the room. Just there, standing up, they began to make love. He watched her face. She looked peaceful, and her eyes were half closed. He wanted to do this, moving slowly, for a long time: but his body would not wait. He was compelled to thrust harder and faster. He felt himself losing his balance, so he put both arms around her, lifted her an inch off the floor, and without withdrawing from her body moved two paces so that her back was against the wall. She pulled his shirt out of his waistband and dug her fingers into the hard muscles of his back. He linked his hands beneath her buttocks and took her weight. She lifted her legs high, her thighs gripping his hips, her ankles crossed behind his back, and, incredibly, he seemed to penetrate even deeper inside her. He felt he was being wound up like a clockwork motor, and everything she did, every look on her face, tightened the spring. He watched her through a haze of lust. There came into her eyes an expression of something like panic; a wild, wide-eyed animal emotion; and it pushed him over the edge, so that he knew that it was coming, the beautiful thing was going to happen now, and he wanted to tell her, so he said, 'Suza, here it comes,' and she said, 'Oh, and me,' and she dug her nails into the skin of his back and drew them down his spine in a long sharp tear which went through him like an electric shock and he felt the earthquake in her body just as his own erupted and he was still looking at her and he saw her mouth open wide, wide as she drew breath and the peak of delight overtook them both and she *screamed.*

'We follow the Israelis and the Israelis follow Dickstein. All it needs is for Dickstein to start following us and we can all go around in a circle for the rest of the day,' Rostov said. He strode down the hotel corridor. Tyrin hurried beside him, his short plump legs almost running to keep up.

Tyrin said, 'I was wondering what, exactly, was your thinking in abandoning the surveillance as soon as we saw him?'

'It's obvious,' Rostov said irritably; then he reminded himself that Tyrin's loyalty was valuable, and he decided to explain. 'Dickstein has been under surveillance a great deal during the last few weeks. Each time he has eventually spotted us and thrown us off. Now a certain amount of surveillance is inevitable for someone who has been in the game as long as Dickstein. But on a particular operation, the more he is followed the more likely he is to abandon what he's doing and hand it over to someone else – and we might not know who. All too often the information we gain by following someone is cancelled out because they discover that we're following them and therefore they know that we've got the information in question. This way – by abandoning the surveillance as we have done today – we know where he is but he doesn't know we know.'

'I see,' said Tyrin.

'He'll spot those Israelis in no time at all,' Rostov added. 'He must be hypersensitive by now.'

'Why do you suppose they're following their own man?'

'I really can't understand that.' Rostov frowned, thinking aloud. 'I'm sure Dickstein met Borg this morning – which would explain why Borg threw off his tail with that taxi manoeuvre. It's possible Borg pulled Dickstein out and now he's simply checking that Dickstein really does come out, and doesn't try to carry on unofficially.' He shook his head, a gesture of frustration. 'That doesn't convince me. But the alternative is that Borg doesn't trust Dickstein any more, and I find that unlikely, too. Careful, now.'

They were at the door to Dickstein's hotel room. Tyrin took out a small, powerful flashlight and shone it around the edges of the door. 'No telltales,' he said.

Rostov nodded, waiting. This was Tyrin's province. The little round man was the best general technician in the KGB, in Rostov's opinion. He watched as Tyrin took from his pocket a skeleton key, one of a large collection of such keys that he had. By trying several on the door of his own room here, he had already established which one fitted the locks of the Jacobean Hotel. He opened Dickstein's door slowly and stayed outside, looking in.

'No booby traps,' he said after a minute.

He stepped inside and Rostov followed, closing the door. This part of the game gave Rostov no pleasure at all. He liked to watch, to speculate, to plot: burglary was not his style. He felt exposed and vulnerable. If a maid should come in now, or the hotel manager, or even Dickstein who might evade the sentry in the lobby . . . it would be so undignified, so humiliating. 'Let's make it fast,' he said.

The room was laid out according to the standard plan: the door opened into a little passage with the bathroom on one side and the wardrobe opposite. Beyond the bathroom the room was square, with the single bed against one wall and the television set against the other. There was a large window in the exterior wall opposite the door.

Tyrin picked up the phone and began to unscrew the mouthpiece. Rostov stood at the foot of the bed, looking around, trying to get an impression of the man who was staying in this room. There was not much to go on. The room had been cleaned and the bed made. On the bedside table were a book of chess problems and an evening newspaper. There were no signs of tobacco or alcohol. The wastepaper basket was empty. A small black vinyl suitcase on a stool contained clean underwear and one clean shirt. Rostov muttered, 'The man travels with one spare shirt!' The drawers of the dresser were empty. Rostov looked into the bathroom. He saw a toothbrush, a rechargeable electric shaver with spare plugs for different kinds of electrical outlets, and – the only personal touch – a pack of indigestion tablets.

Rostov went back into the bedroom, where Tyrin was reassembling the telephone. 'It's done.'

'Put one behind the headboard,' Rostov said.

Tyrin was taping a bug to the wall behind the bed when the phone rang.

If Dickstein returned the sentry in the lobby was to call Dickstein's room on the house phone, let it ring twice, then hang up.

It rang a second time. Rostov and Tyrin stood still, silent, waiting.

It rang again.

They relaxed.

It stopped after the seventh ring.

Rostov said, 'I wish he had a car for us to bug.'

'I've got a shirt button.'

'What?'

'A bug like a shirt button.'

'I didn't know such things existed.'

'It's new.'

'Got a needle? And thread?'

'Of course.'

'Then go ahead.'

Tyrin went to Dickstein's case and without taking the shirt out snipped off the second button, carefully removing all the loose thread. With a few swift strokes he sewed on the new button. His pudgy hands were surprisingly dexterous.

Rostov watched but his thoughts were elsewhere. He wanted desperately to do more to ensure that he would hear what Dickstein said and did. The Israeli might find the bugs in the phone and the headboard; he would not wear the bugged shirt all the time. Rostov liked to be sure of things, and Dickstein was maddeningly slippery: there was nowhere you could hook on to him. Rostov had harboured a faint hope that somewhere in this room there would be a photograph of someone Dickstein loved.

'There.' Tyrin showed him his handiwork. The shirt was plain white nylon with the commonest sort of white button. The new one was indistinguishable from the others.

'Good,' Rostov said. 'Close the case.'

Tyrin did so. 'Anything else?'

'Take another quick look around for telltales. I can't believe Dickstein would go out without taking any precautions at all.'

They searched again, quickly, silently, their movements practised and economical, showing no signs of the haste they both felt. There were dozens of ways of planting telltales. A hair lightly stuck across the crack of the door was the most simple; a scrap of paper jammed against the back of a drawer would fall out when the drawer was opened; a lump of sugar under a thick carpet would be silently crushed by a footstep; a penny behind the lining of a suitcase lid would slide from front to back if the case were opened . . .

They found nothing.

Rostov said, 'All Israelis are paranoid. Why should he be different?'

'Maybe he's been pulled out.'

Rostov grunted. 'Why else would he suddenly get careless?'

'He could have fallen in love,' Tyrin suggested.

Rostov laughed. 'Sure,' he said. 'And Joe Stalin could have been canonized by the Vatican. Let's get out of here.'

He went out, and Tyrin followed, closing the door softly behind him.

So it was a woman.

Pierre Borg was shocked, amazed, mystified, intrigued and deeply worried.

Dickstein *never* had women.

Borg sat on a park bench under an umbrella. He had been unable to think in the Embassy, with phones ringing and people asking him questions all the time, so he had come out here, despite the weather. The rain blew across the empty park in sheets, and every now and then a drop would land on the tip of his cigar and he would have to relight it.

It was the tension in Dickstein that made the man so fierce. The last thing Borg wanted was for him to learn how to relax.

The pavement artists had followed Dickstein to a small apartment house in Chelsea where he had met a woman. 'It's a sexual relationship,' one of them had said. 'I heard her orgasm.' The caretaker of the building had been interviewed, but he knew nothing about the woman except that she was a close friend of the people who owned the apartment.

The obvious conclusion was that Dickstein owned the flat (and had bribed the caretaker to lie); that he used it as a rendezvous; that he met someone from the opposition, a woman; that they made love and he told her secrets.

Borg might have bought that idea if he had found out about the woman some other way. But if Dickstein had suddenly become a traitor he would not have allowed Borg to become suspicious. He was too clever. He would have covered his tracks. He would not have led the pavement artists straight to the flat without once looking over his shoulder. His behaviour had innocence written all over it. He had met with Borg, looking like the cat that got at the cream, either not knowing or not caring that his mood was all over his face. When Borg asked what was going on, Dickstein made jokes. Borg was bound to have him tailed. Hours later Dickstein was screwing some girl who liked it so much you could hear her out in the fucking *street*. The whole thing was so damn naïve it had to be true.

All right, then. Some woman had found a way to get past Dickstein's defences and seduce him. Dickstein was reacting like a teenager because he never had a teenage. The important question was, who was she?

The Russians had files, too, and they ought to have assumed, like Borg, that Dickstein was invulnerable to a sexual approach. But maybe they thought it was worth a try. And maybe they were right.

Once again, Borg's instinct was to pull Dickstein out immediately. And once again, he hesitated. If it had been any project other than this one, any agent other than Dickstein, he would have known what to do. But Dickstein was the only man who could solve this problem. Borg had no option but to stick to his original scheme: wait until Dickstein had fully conceived his plan, then pull him out.

He could at least have the London Station investigate the woman and find out all they could about her.

Meanwhile he would just have to hope that if she were an agent Dickstein would have the sense not to tell her anything.

It would be a dangerous time, but there was no more Borg could do.

His cigar went out, but he hardly noticed. The park was completely deserted now. Borg sat on his bench, his body uncharacteristically still, holding the umbrella over his head, looking like a statue, worrying himself to death.

The fun was over, Dickstein told himself: it was time to get back to work.

Entering his hotel room at ten o'clock in the morning, he realized that – incredibly – he had left no telltales. For the first time in twenty years as an agent, he had simply forgotten to take elementary precautions. He stood in the doorway, looking around, thinking about the shattering effect that she had had on him. Leaving her and going back to work was like climbing into a familiar car which has been garaged for a year: he had to let the old habits, the old instincts, the old paranoia seep back into his mind.

He went into the bathroom and ran a tub. He now had a kind of emotional breathing-space. Suza was going back to work today. She was with BOAC, and this tour of duty would take her all the way around the world. She expected to be back in twenty-one days, but it might be longer. He had no idea where he might be in three weeks' time; which meant he did not know when he would see her again. But see her again he would, if he lived.

Everything looked different now, past and future. The last twenty years of his life seemed dull, despite the fact that he had shot people and been shot at, travelled all over the world, disguised himself and deceived people and pulled off outrageous, clandestine coups. It all seemed trivial.

Sitting in the tub he wondered what he would do with the rest of his life. He had decided he would not be a spy any more – but what would he be? It seemed all possibilities were open to him. He could stand for election to the Knesset, or start his own business, or simply stay on the kibbutz and make the best wine in Israel. Would he marry Suza? If he did, would they live in Israel? He found the uncertainty delicious, like wondering what you would be given for your birthday.

If I live, he thought. Suddenly there was even more at stake. He was afraid to die. Until now death had been something to avoid with all skill only because it constituted, so to speak, a losing move in the game. Now he wanted desperately to live: to sleep with Suza again, to make a home with her, to learn all about her, her idiosyncrasies and her habits and her secrets, the books she liked and what she thought about Beethoven and whether she snored.

It would be terrible to lose his life so soon after she had saved it.

He got out of the bath, rubbed himself dry and dressed. The way to keep his life was to win this fight.

His next move was a phone call. He considered the hotel phone, decided to start being extra careful here and now, and went out to find a call box.

The weather had changed. Yesterday had emptied the sky of rain, and now it was pleasantly sunny and warm. He passed the phone booth nearest to the hotel and went on to the next one: extra careful. He looked up Lloyd's of London in the directory and dialled their number.

'Lloyd's, good morning.'

'I need some information about a ship.'

'That's Lloyd's of London Press – I'll put you through.'

While he waited Dickstein looked out of the windows of the phone booth at the London traffic, and wondered whether Lloyd's would give him what he wanted. He hoped so – he could not think where else to go for the information. He tapped his foot nervously.

'Lloyd's of London Press.'

'Good morning, I'd like some information about a ship.'

'What sort of information?' the voice said, with – Dickstein thought – a trace of suspicion.

'I want to know whether she was built as part of a series; and if so, the names of her sister ships, who owns them, and their present locations. Plus plans, if possible.'

'I'm afraid I can't help you there.'

Dickstein's heart sank. 'Why not?'

'We don't keep plans, that's Lloyd's Register, and they only give them out to owners.'

'But the other information? The sister ships?'

'Can't help you there either.'

Dickstein wanted to get the man by the throat. 'Then who can?'

'We're the only people who have such information.'

'And you keep it secret?'

'We don't give it out over the phone.'

'Wait a minute, you mean you can't help me *over the phone*.'

'That's right.'

'But you can if I write or call personally.'

'Um . . . yes, this inquiry shouldn't take too long, so you could call personally.'

'Give me the address.' He wrote it down. 'And you could get these details while I wait?'

'I think so.'

'All right. I'll give you the name of the ship now, and you should have all the information ready by the time I get there. Her name is *Coparelli*.' He spelled it.

'And your name?'

'Ed Rodgers.'

'The company?'

'*Science International*.'

'Will you want us to bill the company?'

'No, I'll pay by personal cheque.'

'So long as you have some identification.'

'Of course. I'll be there in an hour. Goodbye.'

Dickstein hung up and left the phone booth, thinking: Thank God for that. He crossed the road to a café and ordered coffee and a sandwich.

He had lied to Borg, of course: he knew exactly how he would hijack the *Coparelli*. He would buy one of the sister ships – if there were such – and take his team on to meet the *Coparelli* at sea. After the hijack, instead of the dicey business of transferring the cargo from one ship to another offshore, he would sink his own ship and transfer its papers to the *Coparelli*. He would also paint out the *Coparelli*'s name and over it put the name of the sunken sister ship. And then he would sail what would appear to be his own ship into Haifa.

This was good, but it was still only the rudiments of a plan. What would he do about the crew of the *Coparelli*? How would the apparent loss of the *Coparelli* be explained? How would he avoid an international inquiry into the loss at sea of tons of uranium ore?

The more he thought about it, the bigger this last problem seemed. There would be a major search for any large ship which was thought to have sunk. With uranium aboard, the search would attract publicity and consequently be even more thorough. And what if the searchers found not the *Coparelli* but the sister ship which was supposed to belong to Dickstein?

He chewed over the problem for a while without coming up with any answers. There were still too many unknowns in the equation. Either the sandwich or the problem had stuck in his stomach: he took an indigestion tablet.

He turned his mind to evading the opposition. Had

he covered his tracks well enough? Only Borg could know of his plans. Even if his hotel room were bugged – even if the phone booth nearest the hotel were bugged – still nobody else could know of his interest in the *Coparelli*. He had been extra careful.

He sipped his coffee; then another customer, on his way out of the café, jogged Dickstein's elbow and made him spill coffee all down the front of his clean shirt.

'*Coparelli*,' said David Rostov excitedly. 'Where have I heard of a ship called the *Coparelli*?'

Yasif Hassan said, 'It's familiar to me, too.'

'Let me see that computer printout.'

They were in the back of a listening van parked near the Jacobean Hotel. The van, which belonged to the KGB, was dark blue, without markings, and very dirty. Powerful radio equipment occupied most of the space inside, but there was a small compartment behind the front seats where Rostov and Hassan could squeeze in. Pyotr Tyrin was at the wheel. Large speakers above their heads were giving out an undertone of distant conversation and the occasional clink of crockery. A moment ago there had been an incomprehensible exchange, with someone apologizing for something and Dickstein saying it was all right, it had been an accident. Nothing distinct had been said since then.

Rostov's pleasure at being able to listen to Dickstein's conversation was marred only by the fact that Hassan was listening too. Hassan had become self-confident since his triumph in discovering that Dickstein was in

England: now he thought he was a professional spy like everyone else. He had insisted on being in on every detail of the London operation, threatening to complain to Cairo if he were excluded. Rostov had considered calling his bluff, but that would have meant another head-on collision with Feliks Vorontsov, and Rostov did not want to go over Feliks's head to Andropov again so soon after the last time. So he had settled on an alternative: he would allow Hassan to come along, and caution him against reporting anything to Cairo.

Hassan, who had been reading the printout, passed it across to Rostov. While the Russian was looking through the sheets, the sound from the speakers changed to street noises for a minute or two, followed by more dialogue.

Where to, guv?

Dickstein's voice: *Lime Street.*

Rostov looked up and spoke to Tyrin. 'That'll be Lloyd's, the address he was given over the phone. Let's go there.'

Tyrin started the van and moved off, heading east toward the City district. Rostov returned to the printout.

Hassan said pessimistically, 'Lloyd's will probably give him a written report.'

Tyrin said, 'The bug is working very well . . . so far.' He was driving with one hand and biting the fingernails of the other.

Rostov found what he was looking for. 'Here it is!' he said. 'The *Coparelli.* Good, good, good!' He thumped his knee in enthusiasm.

Hassan said, 'Show me.'

Rostov hesitated momentarily, realized there was no way he could get out of it, and smiled at Hassan as he pointed to the last page. 'Under NON-NUCLEAR. Two hundred tons of yellowcake to go from Antwerp to Genoa aboard the motor vessel *Coparelli*.'

'That's *it*, then,' said Hassan. 'That's Dickstein's target.'

'But if you report this to Cairo, Dickstein will probably switch to a different target. Hassan—'

Hassan's colour deepened with anger. 'You've said all that once,' he said coldly.

'Okay,' Rostov said. He thought: Damn it, you have to be a diplomat too. He said, 'Now we know what he's going to steal, and who he's going to steal it from. I call that some progress.'

'We don't know when, where, or how,' Hassan said.

Rostov nodded. 'All this business about sister ships must have something to do with it.' He pulled his nose. 'But I don't see how.'

Two and sixpence, please, guv.

Keep the change.

'Find somewhere to park, Tyrin,' said Rostov.

'That's not so easy around here,' Tyrin complained.

'If you can't find a space, just stop. Nobody cares if you get a parking ticket,' Rostov said impatiently.

Good morning. My name's Ed Rodgers.

Ah, yes. Just a moment, please . . .

Your report has just been typed, Mr Rodgers. And here's the bill.

You're very efficient.

Hassan said, 'It *is* a written report.'

Thank you very much.

Goodbye, Mr Rodgers.

'He's not very chatty, is he?' said Tyrin.

Rostov said, 'Good agents never are. You might bear that in mind.'

'Yes, sir.'

Hassan said, 'Damn. Now we won't know the answers to his questions.'

'Makes no difference,' Rostov told him. 'It's just occurred to me.' He smiled. 'We know the questions. All we have to do is ask the same questions ourselves and we get the answers he got. Listen, he's on the street again. Go around the block, Tyrin, let's try to spot him.'

The van moved off, but before it had completed a circuit of the block the street noises faded again.

Can I help you, sir?

'He's gone into a shop,' Hassan said.

Rostov looked at Hassan. When he forgot about his pride, the Arab was as thrilled as a schoolboy about all this – the van, the bugs, the tailing. Maybe he would keep his mouth shut, if only so that he could continue to play spies with the Russians.

I need a new shirt.

'Oh, no!' said Tyrin.

I can see that, sir. What is it?

Coffee.

It should have been sponged right away, sir. It will be very difficult to get the stain out now. Did you want a similar shirt?

Yes. Plain white nylon, button cuffs, collar size fourteen and a half.

Here we are. This one is thirty-two and sixpence.

That's fine.

Tyrin said, 'I'll bet he charges it to expenses.'

Thank you. Would you like to put it on now, perhaps?

Yes, please.

The fitting room is just through here.

Footsteps, then a brief silence.

Would you like a bag for the old one, sir?

Perhaps you'd throw it away for me.

'That button cost two thousand roubles!' Tyrin said.

Certainly, sir.

'That's it,' Hassan said. 'We won't get any more now.'

'Two thousand rubles!' Tyrin said again.

Rostov said, 'I think we got our money's worth.'

'Where are we heading?' Tyrin asked.

'Back to the Embassy,' Rostov told him. 'I want to stretch my legs. I can't feel the left one at all. Damn, but we've done a good morning's work.'

As Tyrin drove west, Hassan said thoughtfully, 'We need to find out where the *Coparelli* is right now.'

'The squirrels can do that,' Rostov said.

'Squirrels?'

'Desk workers in Moscow Centre. They sit on their behinds all day, never doing anything more risky than crossing Granovsky Street in the rush hour, and get paid more than agents in the field.' Rostov decided to use the opportunity to further Hassan's education. 'Remember, an agent should never spend time acquiring information that is public knowledge. Anything in books, reports and files can be found by the squirrels. Since a squirrel is cheaper to run than an agent – not because of salaries but because of support work – the Committee always prefers a squirrel to do a given job of work if he can. Always use the squirrels. Nobody will think you're being lazy.'

Hassan smiled nonchalantly, an echo of his old, languid self. 'Dickstein doesn't work that way.'

'The Israelis have a completely different approach. Besides, I suspect Dickstein isn't a team man.'

'How long will the squirrels take to get us the *Coparelli*'s location?'

'Maybe a day. I'll put in the inquiry as soon as we get to the Embassy.'

Tyrin spoke over his shoulder. 'Can you put through a fast requisition at the same time?'

'What do you need?'

'Six more shirt buttons.'

'Six?'

'If they're like the last lot, five won't work.'

Hassan laughed. 'Is this Communist efficiency?'

'There's nothing wrong with Communist efficiency,' Rostov told him. 'It's Russian efficiency we suffer from.'

The van entered Embassy Row and was waved on by the duty policeman. Hassan asked, 'What do we do when we've located the *Coparelli*?'

'Obviously,' said Rostov, 'we put a man aboard.'

CHAPTER NINE

THE DON had had a bad day.

It had started at breakfast with the news that some of his people had been busted in the night. The police had stopped and searched a truck containing two thousand five hundred pairs of fur-lined bedroom slippers and five kilos of adulterated heroin. The load, on its way from Canada to New York City, had been hit at Albany. The smack was confiscated and the driver and co-driver jailed.

The stuff did not belong to the don. However, the team that did the run paid dues to him, and in return expected protection. They would want him to get the men out of jail and get the heroin back. It was close to impossible. He might have been able to do it if the bust had involved only the state police; but if only the state police had been involved, the bust would not have happened.

And that was just the start. His eldest son had wired from Harvard for more money, having gambled away the whole of his next semester's allowance weeks before classes started. He had spent the morning finding out why his chain of restaurants was losing money, and the afternoon explaining to his mistress why he could not take her to Europe this year. Finally his doctor told him he had gonorrhoea, again.

He looked in his dressing-room mirror, adjusting his bow tie, and said to himself, 'What a shitty day.'

It had turned out that the New York City police had been behind the bust: they had passed the tip to the state police in order to avoid trouble with the city Mafia. The city police could have ignored the tip, of course: the fact that they did not was a sign that the tip had originated with someone important, perhaps the Drug Enforcement Agency of the Treasury Department. The don had assigned lawyers to the jailed drivers, sent people to visit their families, and opened negotiations to buy back the heroin from the police.

He put on his jacket. He liked to change for dinner; he always had. He did not know what to do about his son Johnny. Why wasn't he home for the summer? College boys were supposed to come home for the summer. The don had thought of sending somebody to see Johnny; but then the boy would think his father was only worried about the money. It looked like he would have to go himself.

The phone rang, and the don picked it up. 'Yes.'

'Gate here, sir. I got an Englishman asking for you, won't give his name.'

'So send him anyway,' said the don, still thinking about Johnny.

'He said to tell you he's a friend from Oxford University.'

'I don't know anybody . . . wait a minute. What's he look like?'

'Little guy with glasses, looks like a bum.'

'No kidding!' The don's face broke into a smile. 'Bring him in – and put out the red carpet!'

It had been a year for seeing old friends and observing how they had changed; but Al Cortone's appearance was the most startling yet. The increase in weight which had just begun when he returned from Frankfurt seemed to have continued steadily through the years, and now he weighed at least two hundred and fifty pounds. There was a look of sensuality about his puffy face that had been only hinted at in 1947 and totally absent during the war. And he was completely bald. Dickstein thought this was unusual among Italians.

Dickstein could remember, as clearly as if it were yesterday, the occasion when he had put Cortone under an obligation. In those days he had been learning about the psychology of a cornered animal. When there is no longer any possibility of running away, you realize how fiercely you can fight. Landed in a strange country, separated from his unit, advancing across unknown terrain with his rifle in his hand, Dickstein had drawn on reserves of patience, cunning and ruthlessness he did not know he had. He had lain for half an hour in that thicket, watching the abandoned tank which he *knew* – without understanding how – was the bait in a trap. He had spotted the one sniper and was looking for another when the Americans came roaring up. That made it safe for Dickstein to shoot – if there were another sniper, he would fire at the obvious target, the

Americans, rather than search the bushes for the source of the shot.

So, with no thought for anything but his own survival, Dickstein had saved Al Cortone's life.

Cortone had been even more new to the war than Dickstein, and learning just as fast. They were both streetwise kids applying old principles to new terrain. For a while they fought together, and cursed and laughed and talked about women together. When the island was taken, they had sneaked off during the buildup for the next push and visited Cortone's Sicilian cousins.

Those cousins were the focus of Dickstein's interest now.

They had helped him once before, in 1948. There had been profit for them in that deal, so Dickstein had gone straight to them with the plan. This project was different: he wanted a favour and he could offer no percentage. Consequently he had to go to Al and call in the twenty-four-year-old debt.

He was not at all sure it would work. Cortone was rich now. The house was large – in England it would have been called a mansion – with beautiful grounds inside a high wall and guards at the gate. There were three cars in the gravel drive, and Dickstein had lost count of the servants. A rich and comfortable middle-aged American might not be in a hurry to get involved in Mediterranean political shenanigans, even for the sake of a man who had saved his life.

Cortone seemed very pleased to see him, which was a good start. They slapped each other on the back, just as they had on that November Sunday in 1947, and kept saying, 'How the hell are you?' to each other.

Cortone looked Dickstein up and down. 'You're the same! I lost all my hair and gained a hundred pounds, and you haven't even turned grey. What have you been up to?'

'I went to Israel. I'm sort of a farmer. You?'

'Doing business, you know? Come on, let's eat and talk.'

The meal was a strange affair. Mrs Cortone sat at the foot of the table without speaking or being spoken to throughout. Two ill-mannered boys wolfed their food and left early with a roar of sports-car exhaust. Cortone ate large quantities of the heavy Italian food and drank several glasses of California red wine. But the most intriguing character was a well-dressed, shark-faced man who behaved sometimes like a friend, sometimes like an adviser and sometimes like a servant: once Cortone called him a counsellor. No business was talked about during dinner. Instead they told war stories – Cortone told most of them. He also told the story of Dickstein's 1948 coup against the Arabs: he had heard it from his cousins and had been as delighted as they. The tale had become embroidered in the retelling.

Dickstein decided that Cortone was genuinely glad to see him. Maybe the man was bored. He should be, if he ate dinner every night with a silent wife, two surly boys and a shark-faced counsellor. Dickstein did all he could to keep the bonhomie going: he wanted Cortone in a good mood when he asked his favour.

Afterwards Cortone and Dickstein sat in leather

armchairs in a den and a butler brought brandy and cigars. Dickstein refused both.

'You used to be a hell of a drinker,' Cortone said.

'It was a hell of a war,' Dickstein replied. The butler left the room. Dickstein watched Cortone sip brandy and pull on the cigar, and thought that the man ate, drank and smoked joylessly, as though he thought that if he did these things long enough he would eventually acquire the taste. Recalling the sheer fun the two of them had had with the Sicilian cousins, Dickstein wondered whether there were any real people left in Cortone's life.

Suddenly Cortone laughed out loud. 'I remember every minute of that day in Oxford. Hey, did you ever make it with that professor's wife, the Ay-rab?'

'No.' Dickstein barely smiled. 'She's dead, now.'

'I'm sorry.'

'A strange thing happened. I went back there, to that house by the river, and met her daughter . . . She looks just like Eila used to.'

'No kidding. And . . .' Cortone leered. 'And you made it with the daughter – I don't believe it!'

Dickstein nodded. 'We made it in more ways than one. I want to marry her. I plan to ask her next time I see her.'

'Will she say yes?'

'I'm not sure. I think so. I'm older than she is.'

'Age doesn't matter. You could put on a little weight, though. A woman likes to have something to get hold of.'

The conversation was annoying Dickstein, and now

he realized why: Cortone was set on keeping it trivial. It might have been the habit of years of being close-mouthed; it might have been that so much of his 'family business' was criminal business and he did not want Dickstein to know it (but Dickstein had already guessed); or there might have been something else he was afraid of revealing, some secret disappointment he could not share: anyhow, the open, garrulous, excitable young man had long since disappeared inside this fat man. Dickstein longed to say, Tell me what gives you joy, and who you love, and how your life runs on.

Instead he said, 'Do you remember what you said to me in Oxford?'

'Sure. I told you I owe you a debt, you saved my life.' Cortone inhaled on his cigar.

At least that had not changed. 'I'm here to ask for your help.'

'Go ahead and ask.'

'Mind if I put the radio on?'

Cortone smiled. 'This place is swept for bugs about once a week.'

'Good,' said Dickstein, but he put the radio on all the same. 'Cards on the table, Al. I work for Israeli Intelligence.'

Cortone's eyes widened. 'I should have guessed.'

'I'm running an operation in the Mediterranean in November. It's . . .' Dickstein wondered how much he needed to tell, and decided very little. 'It's something that could mean the end of the wars in the Middle

East.' He paused, remembering a phrase Cortone had used habitually. 'And I ain't shittin' you.'

Cortone laughed. 'If you were going to shit me, I figure you would have been here sooner than twenty years.'

'It's important that the operation should not be traceable back to Israel. I need a base from which to work. I need a big house on the coast with a landing for small boats and an anchorage not too far offshore for a big ship. While I'm there – a couple of weeks, maybe more – I need to be protected from inquiring police and other nosy officials. I can think of only one place where I could get all that, and only one person who could get it for me.'

Cortone nodded. 'I know a place – a derelict house in Sicily. It's not exactly plush, kid ... no heat, no phone – but it could fill the bill.'

Dickstein smiled broadly. 'That's terrific,' he said. 'That's what I came to ask for.'

'You're kidding,' said Cortone. 'That's *all*?'

To: Head of Mossad
From: Head of London Station
Date: 29 July 1968

Suza Ashford is almost certainly an agent of an Arab intelligence service.

She was born in Oxford, England, 17 June 1944, the only child of Mr (now Professor) Stephen Ashford (born Guildford, England, 1908) and Eila

Zuabi (born Tripoli, Lebanon, 1925). The mother, who died in 1954, was a full-blooded Arab. The father is what is known in England as an 'Arabist'; he spent most of the first forty years of his life in the Middle East and was an explorer, entrepreneur and linguist. He now teaches Semitic Languages at Oxford University, where he is well known for his moderately pro-Arab views.

Therefore, although Suza Ashford is strictly speaking a U.K. national, her loyalties may be assumed to lie with the Arab cause.

She works as an air hostess for BOAC on intercontinental routes, travelling frequently to Tehran, Singapore and Zurich, among other places. Consequently, she has numerous opportunities to make clandestine contacts with Arab diplomatic staff.

She is a strikingly beautiful young woman (see attached photograph – which, however, does not do her justice, according to the field agent on this case). She is promiscuous, but not unusually so by the standards of her profession nor by those of her generation in London. To be specific: for her to have sexual relations with a man for the purpose of obtaining information might be an unpleasant experience but not a traumatic one.

Finally – and this is the clincher – Yasif Hassan, the agent who spotted Dickstein in Luxembourg, studied under her father, Professor Ashford, at the same time as Dickstein, and has remained in occasional contact with Ashford in the intervening

years. He may have visited Ashford – a man
answering his description certainly *did* visit – about
the time Dickstein's affair with Suza Ashford began.

I recommend that surveillance be continued.

(Signed)

Robert Jakes

To: Head of London Station
From: Head of Mossad
Date: 30 July 1968

With all that against her, I cannot understand
why you do not recommend we kill her.

(Signed)

Pierre Borg

To: Head of Mossad
From: Head of London Station
Date: 31 July 1968

I do not recommend eliminating Suza Ashford
for the following reasons:

1. The evidence against her is strong but
circumstantial.

2. From what I know of Dickstein, I doubt very
much that he has given her any information, even if
he is romantically involved.

3. If we eliminate her the other side will begin
looking for another way to get at Dickstein. Better
the devil we know.

4. We may be able to use her to feed false information to the other side.

5. I do not like to kill on the basis of circumstantial evidence. We are not barbarians. We are Jews.

6. If we kill a woman Dickstein loves, I think he will kill you, me and everyone else involved.

(Signed)
Robert Jakes

To: Head of London Station
From: Head of Mossad
Date: 1 August 1968
    Do it your way.

(Signed)
Pierre Borg
POSTSCRIPT (marked Personal):
    Your point 5 is very noble and touching, but remarks like that won't get you promoted in this man's army. – P.B.

She was a small, old, ugly, dirty, cantankerous bitch.

Rust bloomed like a skin rash in great orange blotches all over her hull. If there had ever been any paint on her upperworks it had long ago been peeled away and blasted off and dissolved by the wind and the rain and the sea. Her starboard gunwale had been badly buckled just aft of the prow in an old collision, and nobody had ever bothered to straighten it out. Her funnel bore a layer of grime ten years thick. Her deck was scored and dented and stained; and although it was swabbed often, it was never swabbed thoroughly, so that there were traces of past cargoes – grains of corn, splinters of timber, bits of rotting vegetation and fragments of sacking – hidden behind lifeboats and under coils of rope and inside cracks and joints and holes. On a warm day she smelled foul.

She was some 2,500 tons, 200 feet long and a little over 30 feet broad. There was a tall radio mast in her blunt prow. Most of her deck was taken up by two large hatches opening into the main cargo holds. There were three cranes on deck: one forward of the hatches, one aft and one in between. The wheelhouse, officers' cabins, galley and crew's quarters were in the stern, clustered around the funnel. She had a single screw driven by a six-cylinder diesel engine theoretically capable of developing 2,450 b.h.p. and maintaining a service speed of thirteen knots.

Fully loaded, she would pitch badly. In ballast she would yaw like the very devil. Either way she would troll through seventy degrees of arc at the slightest provocation. The quarters were cramped and poorly ventilated, the galley was often flooded and the engine room had been designed by Hieronymus Bosch.

She was crewed by thirty-one officers and men, not one of whom had a good word to say for her.

The only passengers were a colony of cockroaches in the galley, a few mice and several hundred rats.

Nobody loved her, and her name was *Coparelli.*

CHAPTER TEN

NAT DICKENSTEIN went to New York to become a shipping tycoon. It took him all morning.

He looked in the Manhattan phone book and selected a lawyer with an address on the lower East Side. Instead of calling on the phone he went there personally, and was satisfied when he saw that the lawyer's office was one room over a Chinese restaurant. The lawyer's name was Mr Chung.

Dickstein and Chung took a cab to the Park Avenue offices of Liberian Corporation Services Inc., a company set up to assist people who wanted to register a Liberian corporation but had no intention of ever going within three thousand miles of Liberia. Dickstein was not asked for references, and he did not have to establish that he was honest or solvent or sane. For a fee of five hundred dollars – which Dickstein paid in cash – they registered the Savile Shipping Corporation of Liberia. The fact that at this stage Dickstein did not own so much as a rowboat was of no interest to anyone.

The company's headquarters was listed as No. 80 Broad Street, Monrovia, Liberia; and its directors were P. Satia, E.K. Nugba and J.D. Boyd, all residents of

Liberia. This was also the headquarters address of most Liberian corporations, and the address of the Liberian Trust Company. Satia, Nugba and Boyd were founding directors of many such corporations; indeed this was the way they made their living. They were also employees of the Liberian Trust Company.

Mr Chung asked for fifty dollars and cab fare. Dickstein paid him in cash and told him to take the bus.

So, without so much as giving an address, Dickstein had created a fully legitimate shipping company which could not be traced back either to him or to the Mossad.

Satia, Nugba and Boyd resigned twenty-four hours later, as was the custom; and that same day the notary public of Montserrado County, Liberia, stamped an affidavit which said that total control of the Savile Shipping Corporation now lay in the hands of one Andre Papagopolous.

By that time Dickstein was riding the bus from Zurich airport into town, on his way to meet Papagopolous for lunch.

When he had time to reflect on it, even he was shaken by the complexity of his plan, the number of pieces that had to be made to fit into the jigsaw puzzle, the number of people who had to be persuaded, bribed or coerced into performing their parts. He had been successful so far, first with Stiffcollar and then with Al Cortone, not to mention Lloyd's of London and Liberian Corporation Services, Inc., but how long could it go on?

Papagopolous was in some ways the greatest challenge: a man as elusive, as powerful, and as free of weakness as Dickstein himself.

He had been born in 1912 in a village that during his boyhood was variously Turkish, Bulgarian and Greek. His father was a fisherman. In his teenage he graduated from fishing to other kinds of maritime work, mostly smuggling. After World War Two he turned up in Ethiopia, buying for knock-down prices the piles of surplus military supplies which had suddenly become worthless when the war ended. He bought rifles, handguns, machine guns, anti-tank guns, and ammunition for all of these. He then contacted the Jewish Agency in Cairo and sold the arms at an enormous profit to the underground Israeli Army. He arranged shipping – and here his smuggling background was invaluable – and delivered the goods to Palestine. Then he asked if they wanted more.

This was how he had met Nat Dickstein.

He soon moved on, to Farouk's Cairo and then to Switzerland. His Israeli deals had marked a transition from totally illegal business to dealings which were at worst shady and at best pristine. Now he called himself a ship broker and that was most, though by no means all, of his business.

He had no address. He could be reached via half a dozen telephone numbers all over the world, but he was never *there* – always, somebody took a message and Papagopolous called you back. Many people knew him and trusted him, especially in the shipping business, for he never let anyone down; but this trust was based on reputation, not personal contact. He lived well but quietly, and Nat Dickstein was one of the few people in the world who knew of his single vice, which was that he liked to go to bed with lots of girls – but *lots*: like, ten or twelve. He had no sense of humour.

Dickstein got off the bus at the railway station, where Papagopolous was waiting for him on the pavement. He was a big man, olive-skinned with thin dark hair combed over a growing bald patch. On a bright summer day in Zurich he wore a navy-blue suit, pale blue shirt and dark blue striped tie. He had small dark eyes.

They shook hands. Dickstein said, 'How's business?'

'Up and down.' Papagopolous smiled. 'Mostly up.'

They walked through the clean, tidy streets, looking like a managing director and his accountant. Dickstein inhaled the cold air. 'I like this town,' he said.

'I've booked a table at the Veltliner Keller in the old city,' Papagopolous said. 'I know you don't care about food, but I do.'

Dickstein said, 'You've been to the Pelikanstrasse?'

'Yes.'

'Good.' The Zurich office of Liberian Corporation Services, Inc., was in the Pelikanstrasse. Dickstein had asked Papagopolous to go there to register himself as president and chief executive of Savile Shipping. For this he would receive ten thousand U.S. dollars, paid out of Mossad's account in a Swiss bank to Papagopolous's account in the same branch of the same bank – a transaction very difficult for anyone to uncover.

Papagopolous said, 'But I didn't promise to do anything else. You may have wasted your money.'

'I'm sure I didn't.'

They reached the restaurant. Dickstein had expected that Papagopolous would be known there, but there was no sign of recognition from the head waiter, and Dickstein thought: Of course, he's not known anywhere.

They ordered food and wine. Dickstein noted with regret that the domestic Swiss white wine was still better than the Israeli.

While they ate, Dickstein explained Papagopolous's duties as president of Savile Shipping.

'One: buy a small, fast ship, a thousand or fifteen hundred tons, small crew. Register her in Liberia.' This would involve another visit to the Pelikanstrasse and a fee of about a dollar per ton. 'For the purchase, take your percentage as a broker. Do some business with the ship, and take your broker's percentage on that. I don't care what the ship does so long as she completes a voyage by docking in Haifa on or before October 7. Dismiss the crew at Haifa. Do you want to take notes?'

Papagopolous smiled. 'I think not.'

The implication was not lost on Dickstein. Papagopolous was listening, but he had not yet agreed to do the job. Dickstein continued. 'Two: buy any one of the ships on this list.' He handed over a single sheet of paper bearing the names of the four sister ships of the *Coparelli*, with their owners and last known locations – the information he had got from Lloyd's. 'Offer whatever price is necessary: I must have one of them. Take your broker's percentage. Deliver her to Haifa by October 7. Dismiss the crew.'

Papagopolous was eating chocolate mousse, his smooth face imperturbable. He put down his spoon and put on gold-rimmed glasses to read the list. He folded the sheet of paper in half and set it on the table without comment.

Dickstein handed him another sheet of paper. 'Three: buy this ship – the *Coparelli*. But you must buy her at exactly the right time. She sails from Antwerp on Sunday, November 17. We must buy her *after* she sails but *before* she passes through the Strait of Gibraltar.'

Papapopolous looked dubious. 'Well . . .'

'Wait, let me give you the rest of it. Four: early in 1969 you sell ship No. 1, the little one, and ship No. 3, the *Coparelli*. You get from me a certificate showing that ship No. 2 has been sold for scrap. You send that certificate to Lloyd's. You wind up Savile Shipping.' Dickstein smiled and sipped his coffee.

'What you want to do is make a ship disappear without a trace.'

Dickstein nodded. Papagopolous was as sharp as a knife.

'As you must realize,' Papagopolous went on, 'all this is straightforward except for the purchase of the *Coparelli* while she is at sea. The normal procedure for the sale of a ship is as follows: negotiations take place, a price is agreed, and the documents are drawn up. The ship goes into dry dock for inspection. When she has been pronounced satisfactory the documents are signed, the money is paid and the new owner takes her out of dry dock. Buying a ship while she is sailing is most irregular.'

'But not impossible.'

'No, not impossible.'

Dickstein watched him. He became thoughtful, his gaze distant: he was grappling with the problem. It was a good sign.

Papagopolous said, 'We would have to open negotiations, agree on the price and have the inspection arranged for a date after her November voyage. Then, when she has sailed, we say that the purchaser needs to spend the money immediately, perhaps for tax reasons. The buyer would then take out insurance against any major repairs which might prove necessary after the inspection, but this is not the seller's concern. He is concerned about his reputation as a shipper. He will want cast-iron guarantees that his cargo will be delivered by the new owner of the *Coparelli*.'

'Would he accept a guarantee based on your personal reputation?'

'Of course. But why would I give such a guarantee?'

Dickstein looked him in the eye. 'I can promise you that the owner of the cargo will not complain.'

Papagopolous made an open-handed gesture. 'It is obvious that you are perpetrating some kind of a swindle here. You need me as a respectable front. That I can do. But you also want me to lay my reputation on the line and take your word that it will not suffer?'

'Yes. Listen. Let me ask you one thing. You trusted the Israelis once before, remember?'

'Of course.'

'Did you ever regret it?'

Papagopolous smiled, remembering the old days. 'It was the best decision I ever made.'

'So, will you trust us again?' Dickstein held his breath.

'I had less to lose in those days. I was . . . thirty-five. We used to have a lot of fun. This is the most intriguing offer I've had in twenty years. What the hell, I'll do it.'

Dickstein extended his hand across the restaurant table. Papagopolous shook it.

A waitress brought a little bowl of Swiss chocolates for them to eat with their coffee. Papagopolous took one, Dickstein refused.

'Details,' Dickstein said. 'Open an account for Savile Shipping at your bank here. The Embassy will put funds in as they are required. You report to me simply by leaving a written message at the bank. The note will be picked up by someone from the Embassy. If we need to meet and talk, we use the usual phone numbers.'

'Agreed.'

'I'm glad we're doing business together again.'

Papagopolous was thoughtful. 'Ship No. 2 is a sister ship of the *Coparelli*,' he mused. 'I think I can guess what you're up to. There's one thing I'd like to know, although I'm sure you won't tell me. What the hell kind of cargo will the *Coparelli* be carrying – uranium?'

Pyotr Tyrin looked gloomily at the *Coparelli* and said, 'She's a grubby old ship.'

Rostov did not reply. They were sitting in a rented

Ford on a quay at Cardiff docks. The squirrels at Moscow Centre had informed them that the *Coparelli* would make port there today, and they were now watching her tie up. She was to unload a cargo of Swedish timber and take on a mixture of small machinery and cotton goods: it would take her some days.

'At least the mess decks aren't in the foc'sle,' Tyrin muttered, more or less to himself.

'She's not *that* old,' Rostov said.

Tyrin was surprised Rostov knew what he was talking about. Rostov continually surprised him with odd bits of knowledge.

From the rear seat of the car Nik Bunin said, 'Is that the front or the back of the boat?'

Rostov and Tyrin looked at one another and grinned at Nik's ignorance. 'The back,' Tyrin said. 'We call it the stern.'

It was raining. The Welsh rain was even more persistent and monotonous than the English, and colder. Pyotr Tyrin was unhappy. It so happened that he had done two years in the Soviet Navy. That, plus the fact that he was the radio and electronics expert, made him the obvious choice as the man to be planted aboard the *Coparelli*. He did not want to go back to sea. In truth, the main reason he had applied to join the KGB was to get out of the navy. He hated the damp and the cold and the food and the discipline. Besides, he had a warm, comfortable wife in an apartment in Moscow, and he missed her.

Of course, there was no question of his saying no to Rostov.

'We'll get you on as radio operator, but you must take your own equipment as a fallback,' Rostov said.

Tyrin wondered how this was to be managed. His approach would have been to find the ship's radio man, knock him on the head, throw him in the water, and board the ship to say, 'I hear you need a new radio operator.' No doubt Rostov would be able to come up with something a little more subtle: that was why he was a colonel.

The activity on deck had died down, and the *Coparelli*'s engines were quiet. Five or six sailors came across the gangplank in a bunch, laughing and shouting, and headed for the town. Rostov said, 'See which pub they go to, Nik.' Bunin got out of the car and followed the sailors.

Tyrin watched him go. He was depressed by the scene: the figures crossing the wet concrete quay with their raincoat collars turned up; the sounds of tugs hooting and men shouting nautical instructions and chains winding and unwinding; the stacks of pallets; the bare cranes like sentries; the smell of engine oil and the ship's ropes and salt spray. It all made him think of the Moscow flat, the chair in front of the paraffin heater, salt fish and black bread, beer and vodka in the refrigerator, and an evening of television.

He was unable to share Rostov's irrepressible cheerfulness about the way the operation was going. Once again they had no idea where Dickstein was – even though they had not exactly lost him, they had deliberately let him go. It had been Rostov's decision: he was afraid of getting too close to Dickstein, of scaring the man off. 'We'll follow the *Coparelli*, and Dickstein will come to us,' Rostov had said. Yasif Hassan had argued with him, but Rostov had won. Tyrin, who had no contribution to make to such strategic discussions, thought Rostov was correct, but also thought he had no reason to be so confident.

'Your first job is to befriend the crew,' Rostov said. interrupting Tyrin's thoughts. 'You're a radio operator. You suffered a minor accident aboard your last ship, the *Christmas Rose* – you broke your arm – and you were discharged here in Cardiff to convalesce. You got an excellent compensation payment from the owners. You are spending the money and having a good time while it lasts. You say vaguely that you'll look for another job when your money runs out. You must discover two things: the identity of the radio man, and the anticipated date and time of departure of the ship.'

'Fine,' said Tyrin, though it was far from fine. Just *how* was he to 'befriend' these people? He was not much of an actor, in his view. Would he have to play the part of a hearty hail-fellow-well-met? Suppose the crew of this ship thought him a bore, a lonely man trying to attach himself to a jolly group? What if they just plain did not like him?

Unconsciously he squared his broad shoulders. Either he would do it, or there would be some reason why it could not be done. All he could promise was to try his best.

Bunin came back across the quay. Rostov said, 'Get in the back, let Nik drive.' Tyrin got out and held the door for Nik. The young man's face was streaming with rain. He started the car. Tyrin got in.

As the car pulled away Rostov turned around to speak to Tyrin in the back seat. 'Here's a hundred pounds,' he said, and handed over a roll of banknotes. 'Don't spend it too carefully.'

Bunin stopped the car opposite a small dockland pub on a corner. A sign outside, flapping gently in the wind, read, 'Brains Beers'. A smoky yellow light glowed behind the frosted-glass windows. There were worse places to be on a day like this, Tyrin thought.

'What nationality are the crew?' he said suddenly.

'Swedish,' Bunin said.

Tyrin's false papers made him out to be Austrian. 'What language should I use with them?'

'All Swedes speak English,' Rostov told him. There was a moment of silence. Rostov said, 'Any more questions? I want to go back to Hassan before he gets up to any mischief.'

'No more questions.' Tyrin opened the car door.

Rostov said, 'Speak to me when you get back to the hotel tonight – no matter how late.'

'Sure.'

'Good luck.'

Tyrin slammed the car door and crossed the road to the pub. As he reached the entrance someone came out, and the warm smell of beer and tobacco engulfed Tyrin for a moment. He went inside.

It was a poky little place, with hard wooden benches around the walls and plastic tables nailed to the floor.

Four of the sailors were playing darts in the corner and a fifth was at the bar calling out encouragement to them.

The barman nodded to Tyrin. 'Good morning,' Tyrin said. 'A pint of lager, a large whisky and a ham sandwich.'

The sailor at the bar turned around and nodded pleasantly. Tyrin smiled. 'Have you just made port?'

'Yes. The *Coparelli*,' the sailor replied.

'*Christmas Rose*,' Tyrin said. 'She left me behind.'

'You're lucky.'

'I broke my arm.'

'So?' said the Swedish sailor with a grin. 'You can drink with the other one.'

'I like that,' Tyrin said. 'Let me buy you a drink. What will it be?'

Two days later they were still drinking. There were changes in the composition of the group as some sailors went on duty and others came ashore; and there was a short period between four A.M. and opening time when there was nowhere in the city, legal or illegal, where one could buy a drink; but otherwise life was one long pub crawl. Tyrin had forgotten how sailors could drink. He was dreading the hangover. He was glad, however, that he had not got into a situation where he felt obliged to go with prostitutes: the Swedes were interested in women, but not in whores. Tyrin would never have been able to convince his wife that he had caught venereal disease in the service of Mother Russia. The Swedes' other vice was gambling. Tyrin had lost about fifty pounds of KGB money at poker. He was so well in with the crew of the *Coparelli* that the previous night he had been invited aboard at two A.M. He had fallen asleep on the mess deck and they had left him there until eight bells.

Tonight would not be like that. The *Coparelli* was to sail on the morning tide, and all officers and men had to be aboard by midnight. It was now ten past eleven. The landlord of the pub was moving about the room collecting glasses and emptying ashtrays. Tyrin was playing dominoes with Lars, the radio operator. They had abandoned the proper game and were now competing to see who could stand the most blocks in a line without knocking the lot down. Lars was very drunk, but Tyrin was pretending. He was also very frightened about what he had to do in a few minutes' time.

The landlord called out, 'Time, gentlemen, please! Thank you very much.'

Tyrin knocked his dominoes down, and laughed. Lars said, 'You see – I am smaller alcoholic than you.'

The other crew were leaving. Tyrin and Lars stood up. Tyrin put his arm around Lars' shoulders and together they staggered out into the street.

The night air was cool and damp. Tyrin shivered. From now on he had to stay very close to Lars. I hope Nik gets his timing right, he thought. I hope the car doesn't break down. And then: I hope to Christ Lars doesn't get killed.

He began talking, asking questions about Lars' home and family. He kept the two of them a few yards behind the main group of sailors.

They passed a blonde woman in a microskirt. She touched her left breast. 'Hello, boys, fancy a cuddle?'

Not tonight, sweetheart, Tyrin thought, and kept walking. He must not let Lars stop and chat. Timing, it was the timing. Nik, where are you?

There. They approached a dark blue Ford Capri 2000 parked at the roadside with its lights out. As the interior light flashed on and off Tyrin glimpsed the face of the man at the wheel: it was Nik Bunin. Tyrin took a flat white cap from his pocket and put it on, the signal that Bunin was to go ahead. When the sailors had passed on the car started up and moved away in the opposite direction.

Not long now.

Lars said, 'I have a fiancée.'

Oh, no, don't start that.

Lars giggled. 'She has . . . hot pants.'

'Are you going to marry her?' Tyrin was peering ahead intently, listening, talking only to keep Lars close.

Lars leered. 'What for?'

'Is she faithful?'

'Better be or I slit her throat.'

'I thought Swedish people believed in free love.' Tyrin was saying anything that came into his head.

'Free love, yes. But she better be faithful.'

'I see.'

'I can explain . . .'

Come on, Nik. Get it over with . . .

One of the sailors in the group stopped to urinate in the gutter. The others stood around making ribald remarks and laughing. Tyrin wished the man would hurry up – the timing, the timing – but he seemed as if he would go on for ever.

At last he finished, and they all walked on.

Tyrin heard a car.

He tensed. Lars said, 'What's matter?'

'Nothing.' Tyrin saw the headlights. The car was moving steadily toward them in the middle of the road. The sailors moved on to the pavement to get out of its way. It wasn't right, it shouldn't be like this, it wouldn't work this way! Suddenly Tyrin was confused and panic-stricken – then he saw the outline of the car more clearly as it passed beneath a street light, and he realized it was not the one he was waiting for, it was a patrolling police car. It went harmlessly by.

The end of the street opened into a wide, empty square, badly paved. There was no traffic about. The sailors headed straight across the middle of the square.

Now.

Come on.

They were halfway across.

Come *on*!

A car came tearing around a corner and into the square, headlights blazing. Tyrin tightened his grip on Lars' shoulder. The car was veering wildly.

'Drunk driver,' Lars said thickly.

It was a Ford Capri. It swung toward the bunch of sailors in front. They stopped laughing and scattered out of its way, shouting curses. The car turned away, then screeched around and accelerated straight for Tyrin and Lars.

'Look out!' Tyrin yelled.

When the car was almost on top of them he pulled Lars to one side, jerking the man off balance, and threw himself sideways. There was a stomach-turning thud, followed by a scream and crash of breaking glass. The car went by.

It's done, Tyrin thought.

He scrambled to his feet and looked for Lars.

The sailor lay on the road a few feet away. Blood glistened in the lamplight.

Lars groaned.

He's alive, Tyrin thought; thank God.

The car braked. One of its headlights had gone out – the one that had hit Lars, he presumed. It coasted, as if the driver were hesitating. Then it gathered speed and, one-eyed, it disappeared into the night.

Tyrin bent over Lars. The other sailors gathered around, speaking Swedish. Tyrin touched Lars' leg. He yelled out in pain.

'I think his leg is broken,' Tyrin said. *Thank God that's all.*

Lights were going on in some of the buildings around the square. One of the officers said something, and a rating ran off toward a house presumably to call for an ambulance. There was more rapid dialogue and another went off in the direction of the dock.

Lars was bleeding, but not too heavily. The officer bent over him. He would not allow anyone to touch his leg.

The ambulance arrived within minutes, but it seemed forever to Tyrin: he had never killed a man, and he did not want to.

They put Lars on a stretcher. The officer got into the ambulance, and turned to speak to Tyrin. 'You had better come.'

'Yes.'

'You saved his life, I think.'

'Oh.'

He got into the ambulance with the officer.

They sped through the wet streets. the flashing blue light on the roof casting an unpleasant glow over the buildings. Tyrin sat in the back, unable to look at Lars or the officer, unwilling to look out of the windows like a tourist, not knowing where to direct his eyes. He had done many unkind things in the service of his country and Colonel Rostov – he had taped the conversations of lovers for blackmail, he had shown terrorists how to make bombs, he had helped capture people who would later be tortured – but he had never been forced to ride in the ambulance with his victim. He did not like it.

They arrived at the hospital. The ambulance men carried the stretcher inside. Tyrin and the officer were shown where to wait. And, suddenly, the rush was over. They had nothing to do but worry. Tyrin was astonished to look at the plain electric clock on the hospital wall and see that it was not yet midnight. It seemed hours since they had left the pub.

After a long wait a doctor came out. 'He's broken his leg and lost some blood,' he said. He seemed very tired. 'He's got a lot of alcohol in him, which doesn't help. But he's young, strong and healthy. His leg will mend and he should be fit again in a few weeks.'

Relief flooded Tyrin. He realized he was shaking.

The officer said, 'Our ship sails in the morning.'

'He won't be on it,' the doctor said. 'Is your captain on his way here?'

'I sent for him.'

'Fine.' The doctor turned and left.

The captain arrived at the same time as the police. He spoke to the officer in Swedish while a young sergeant took down Tyrin's vague description of the car.

Afterwards the captain approached Tyrin. 'I believe you saved Lars from a much worse accident.'

Tyrin wished people would stop saying that. 'I tried to pull him out of the way, but he fell. He was very drunk.'

'Horst here says you are between ships.'

'Yes, sir.'

'You are a fully qualified radio operator?'

'Yes, sir.'

'I need a replacement for poor Lars. Would you like to sail with us in the morning?'

Pierre Borg said, 'I'm pulling you out.'

Dickstein whitened. He stared at his boss.

Borg said, 'I want you to come back to Tel Aviv and run the operation from the office.'

Dickstein said, 'You go and fuck yourself.'

They stood beside the lake at Zurich. It was crowded with boats, their multicoloured sails flapping prettily in the Swiss sunshine. Borg said, 'No arguments, Nat.'

'No arguments, *Pierre*. I won't be pulled out. Finish.'

'I'm ordering you.'

'And I'm telling you to fuck yourself.'

'Look.' Borg took a deep breath. 'Your plan is complete. The only flaw in it is that you've been compromised: the opposition knows you're working, and they're trying to find you and screw up whatever it is you're doing. You can still run the project – all you have to do is hide your face.'

'No,' Dickstein said. 'This isn't the kind of project where you can sit in an office and push all the buttons to make it go. It's too complex, there are too many variables. I have to be in the field myself to make instant decisions.' Dickstein stopped himself talking and began to think: *Why* do I want to do it myself? Am I really the only man in Israel who can pull this off? Is it just that I want the glory?

Borg voiced his thoughts. 'Don't try to be a hero, Nat. You're too smart for that. You're a professional: you follow orders.'

Dickstein shook his head. 'You should know better than to take that line with me. Remember how Jews feel about people who always follow orders?'

'All right, so you were in a concentration camp – that doesn't give you the right to do whatever the hell you like for the rest of your life!'

Dickstein made a deprecatory gesture. 'You can stop me. You can withdraw support. But you also won't get your uranium, because I'm not going to tell anyone else how it can be done.'

Borg stared at him. 'You bastard, you mean it.'

Dickstein watched Borg's expression. He had once had the embarrassing experience of seeing Borg have a row with his teenage son Dan. The boy had stood there, sullenly confident, while Borg tried to explain that going on peace marches was disloyal to father, mother, country and God, until Borg had strangled himself with his own inarticulate rage. Dan, like Dickstein, had learned how to refuse to be bullied, and Borg would never quite know how to handle people who could not be bullied.

The script now called for Borg to go red in the face and begin to yell. Suddenly Dickstein realized that this was not going to happen. Borg was remaining calm.

Borg smiled slyly and said, 'I believe you're fucking one of the other side's agents.'

Dickstein stopped breathing. He felt as if he had been hit from behind with a sledgehammer. This was the last thing he had been expecting. He was filled with irrational guilt, like a boy caught masturbating: shame, embarrassment, and the sense of something spoiled. Suza was private, in a compartment separate from the rest of his life, and now Borg was dragging her out and holding her up to public view: Just *look* at what Nat was doing!

'No,' Dickstein said tonelessly.

'I'll give you the headlines,' Borg said. 'She's Arab, her father's politics are pro-Arab, she travels all over the world in her cover job to have opportunity for contacts, and the agent Yasif Hassan, who spotted you in Luxembourg, is a friend of the family.'

Dickstein turned to face Borg, standing too close, gazing fiercely into Borg's eyes, his guilt turning to resentment. 'That's all?'

'All? What the fuck do you mean, *all*? You'd shoot people on that much evidence!'

'Not people I know.'

'Has she got any information out of you?'

Dickstein shouted, 'No!'

'You're getting angry because you know you've made a mistake.'

Dickstein turned away and looked across the lake, struggling to make himself calm: rage was Borg's act, not his. After a long pause he said, 'Yes, I'm angry because I've made a mistake. I should have told you about her; not the other way around. I understand how it must seem to you—'

'Seem? You mean you don't believe she's an agent?'

'Have you checked through Cairo?'

Borg gave a false little laugh. 'You talk as if Cairo was my intelligence service. I can't just call and ask them to look her up in their files while I hold the line.'

'But you've got a very good double agent in Egyptian Intelligence.'

'How can he be good? Everybody seems to know about him.'

'Stop playing games. Since the Six-Day War even the newspapers say you have good doubles in Egypt. The point is, you haven't checked her.'

Borg held up both hands, palms outward, in a

gesture of appeasement. 'Okay, I'm going to check her with Cairo. It will take a little time. Meanwhile, you're going to write a report giving all details of your scheme and I'm going to put other agents on the job.'

Dickstein thought of Al Cortone and Andre Papago-polous: neither of them would do what he had agreed to do for anyone other than Dickstein. 'It won't work, Pierre,' he said quietly. 'You've got to have the uranium, and I'm the only one who can get it for you.'

'And if Cairo confirms her to be an agent?'

'I'm confident the answer will be negative.'

'But if it's not?'

'You'll kill her, I suppose.'

'Oh, no.' Borg pointed a finger at Dickstein's nose, and when he spoke there was real, deep-down malice in his voice. 'Oh, no, I won't, Dickstein. If she's an agent, *you* will kill her.'

With deliberate slowness, Dickstein took hold of Borg's wrist and removed the pointing finger from in front of his face. There was only the faintest perceptible tremor in his voice as he said, 'Yes, Pierre. I will kill her.'

CHAPTER ELEVEN

I N T H E bar at Heathrow Airport David Rostov ordered another round of drinks and decided to take a gamble on Yasif Hassan. The problem, still, was how to stop Hassan telling all he knew to an Israeli double agent in Cairo. Rostov and Hassan were both going back for interim debriefing so a decision had to be made now. Rostov was going to let Hassan know everything, then appeal to his professionalism – such as it was. The alternative was to provoke him, and just now he needed him as an ally, not a suspicious antagonist.

'Look at this,' Rostov said, and he showed Hassan a decoded message.

To: Colonel David Rostov *via* London Residency
From: Moscow Centre
Date: 3 September 1968

Comrade Colonel:
   We refer to your signal g/35–21a, requesting further information concerning each of four ships named in our signal r/35–21.
   The motor vessel *Stromberg*, 2500 tons, Dutch

ownership and registration, has recently changed
hands. She was purchased for DM 1,500,000 by one
Andre Papagopolous, a ship broker, on behalf of
the Savile Shipping Corporation of Liberia.

Savile Shipping was incorporated on 6 August
this year at the New York office of Liberian
Corporation Services Inc., with a share capital of
five hundred dollars. The shareholders are Mr Lee
Chung, a New York lawyer, and a Mr Robert
Roberts, whose address is care of Mr Chung's office.
The three directors were provided in the usual way
by Liberian Corporation Services, and they resigned
the day after the company was set up, again in the
usual way. The aforementioned Papagopolous took
over as president and chief executive.

Savile Shipping has also bought the motor vessel
Gil Hamilton, 1500 tons, for £80,000.

Our people in New York have interviewed
Chung. He says that 'Mr Roberts' came into his
office from the street, gave no address and paid his
fee in cash. He appeared to be an Englishman. The
detailed description is on file here, but it is not very
helpful.

Papagopolous is known to us. He is a wealthy
international businessman of indeterminate
nationality. Shipbroking is his principal activity. He
is believed to operate close to the fringes of the law.
We have no address for him. There is considerable
material in his file, but much of it is speculative. He
is believed to have done business with Israeli

Intelligence in 1948. Nevertheless, he has no known political affiliation.

We continue to gather information on all the ships in the list.

– Moscow Centre.

Hassan gave the sheet of paper back to Rostov. 'How do they get hold of all this stuff?'

Rostov began tearing the signal into shreds. 'It's all on file somewhere or other. The sale of the *Stromberg* would have been notified to Lloyd's of London. Someone from our consulate in Liberia would have got the details on Savile Shipping from public records in Monrovia. Our New York people got Chung's address out of the phone book, and Papagopolous was on file in Moscow. None of it is secret, except the Papagopolous file. The trick is knowing where to go to ask the questions. The squirrels specialize in that trick. It's all they do.'

Rostov put the shreds of paper into a large glass ashtray and set fire to them. 'Your people should have squirrels,' he added.

'I expect we're working on it.'

'Suggest it yourself. It won't do you any harm. You might even get the job of setting it up. That could help your career.'

Hassan nodded. 'Perhaps I will.'

Fresh drinks arrived: vodka for Rostov, gin for Hassan. Rostov was pleased that Hassan was responding well to his friendly overtures. He examined the cinders in the ashtray to make sure the signal had burned completely.

Hassan said, 'You're assuming Dickstein is behind the Savile Shipping Corporation.'

'Yes.'

'So what will we do about the *Stromberg*?'

'Well . . .' Rostov emptied his glass and set it on the table. 'My guess is he wants the *Stromberg* so he can get an exact layout of the sister ship *Coparelli*.'

'It will be an expensive blueprint.'

'He can sell the ship again. However, he may also use the *Stromberg* in the hijack of the *Coparelli* – I don't quite see how, just yet.'

'Will you put a man aboard the *Stromberg*, like Tyrin on the *Coparelli*?'

'No point. Dickstein is sure to get rid of the old crew and fill the ship with Israeli sailors. I'll have to think of something else.'

'Do we know where the *Stromberg* is now?'

'I've asked the squirrels. They'll have an answer by the time I get to Moscow.'

Hassan's flight was called. He stood up. 'We meet in Luxembourg?'

'I'm not sure. I'll let you know. Listen, there's something I've got to say. Sit down again.'

Hassan sat down.

'When we started to work together on Dickstein I was very hostile to you. I regret that now, I'm apologizing; but I must tell you there was a reason for it. You see, Cairo isn't secure. It's certain there are double agents in the Egyptian Intelligence apparatus. What I was concerned about – and still am – is that everything you report to your superiors will get back, via a double agent, to Tel Aviv; and then Dickstein will know how close we are and will take evasive action.'

'I appreciate your frankness.'

Appreciate, Rostov thought: He loves it. 'However, you are now completely in the picture, and what we must discuss is how to prevent the information you have in your possession getting back to Tel Aviv.'

Hassan nodded. 'What do you suggest?'

'Well. You'll have to tell what we've found out, of course, but I want you to be as vague as possible about the details. Don't give names, times, places. When you're pushed, complain about me, say I've refused to let you share all the information. Don't talk to anyone except the people you're obliged to report to. In particular, tell nobody about Savile Shipping, the *Stromberg*, or the *Coparelli*. As for Pyotr Tyrin being aboard the *Coparelli* – try to forget it.'

Hassan looked worried. 'What's left to tell?'

'Plenty. Dickstein, Euratom, uranium, the meeting with Pierre Borg . . . you'll be a hero in Cairo if you tell half the story.'

Hassan was not convinced. 'I'll be as frank as you. If I do this your way, my report will not be as impressive as yours.'

Rostov gave a wry smile. 'Is that unfair?'

'No,' Hassan conceded, 'you deserve most of the credit.'

'Besides, nobody but the two of us will know how different the reports are. And you're going to get all the credit you need in the end.'

'All right,' Hassan said. 'I'll be vague.'

'Good.' Rostov waved his hand for a waiter. 'You've got a little time, have a quick one before you go.' He settled back in his chair and crossed his legs. He was satisfied: Hassan would do as he had been told. 'I'm looking forward to getting home.'

'Any plans?'

'I'll try to take a few days on the coast with Mariya and the boys. We've a dacha in the Riga Bay.'

'Sounds nice.'

'It's pleasant there – but not as warm as where you're going, of course. Where will you head for – Alexandria?'

The last call for Hassan's flight came over the public address system, and the Arab stood up. 'No such luck,' he said. 'I expect to spend the whole time stuck in filthy Cairo.'

And Rostov had the peculiar feeling that Yasif Hassan was lying.

Franz Albrecht Pedler's life was ruined when Germany lost the war. At the age of fifty, a career officer in the Wehrmacht, he was suddenly homeless, penniless and unemployed. And, like millions of other Germans, he started again.

He became a salesman for a French dye manufacturer: small commission, no salary. In 1946 there were few customers, but by 1951 German industry was rebuilding and when at last things began to look up Pedler was in a good position to take advantage of the new opportunities. He opened an office in Wiesbaden, a rail junction on the right bank of the Rhine that promised to develop into an industrial centre. His product list grew, and so did his tally of customers: soon he was selling soaps as well as dyes, and he gained entry to the U.S. bases, which at the time administered that part of occupied Germany. He had learned, during the hard years, to be an opportunist: if a U.S. Army procurement officer wanted disinfectant in pint bottles, Pedler would buy disinfectant in ten-gallon drums, pour the stuff from the drums into secondhand bottles in a rented barn, put on a label saying 'F. A. Pedler's Special Disinfectant' and resell at a fat profit.

From buying in bulk and repackaging it was not a very big step to buying ingredients and manufacturing. The first barrel of F. A. Pedler's Special Industrial Cleanser – never called simply 'soap' – was mixed in the same rented barn and sold to the U.S. Air Force for use by aircraft maintenance engineers. The company never looked back.

In the late Fifties Pedler read a book about chemical warfare and went on to win a big defence contract to supply a range of solutions designed to neutralize various kinds of chemical weapon.

F. A. Pedler had become a military supplier, small but secure and profitable. The rented barn had grown into a small complex of single-storey buildings. Franz married again – his first wife had been killed in the

1944 bombing – and fathered a child. But he was still an opportunist at heart, and when he heard about a small mountain of uranium ore going cheap, he smelled a profit.

The uranium belonged to a Belgian company called Société Générale de la Chimie. Chimie was one of the corporations which ran Belgium's African colony, the Belgian Congo, a country rich in minerals. After the 1960 pullout Chimie stayed on; but, knowing that those who did not walk out would eventually be thrown out, the company expended all its efforts to ship home as much raw material as it could before the gates slammed shut. Between 1960 and 1965 it accumulated a large stockpile of yellowcake at its refinery near the Dutch border. Sadly for Chimie, a nuclear test ban treaty was ratified in the meantime, and when Chimie was finally thrown out of the Congo there were few buyers for uranium. The yellowcake sat in a silo, tying up scarce capital.

F. A. Pedler did not actually use very much uranium in the manufacture of their dyes. However, Franz loved a gamble of this sort: the price was low, he could make a little money by having the stuff refined, and if the uranium market improved – as it was likely to sooner or later – he would make a big capital profit. So he bought some.

Nat Dickstein liked Pedler right away. The German was a sprightly seventy-three-year-old who still had all his hair and the twinkle in his eye. They met on a Saturday. Pedler wore a loud sports jacket and fawn trousers, spoke good English with an American accent and gave Dickstein a glass of Sekt, the local champagne.

They were wary of each other at first. After all, they had fought on opposite sides in a war which had been cruel to them both. But Dickstein had always believed that the enemy was not Germany but Fascism, and he was nervous only that Pedler might be uneasy. It seemed the same was true of Pedler.

Dickstein had called from his hotel in Wiesbaden to make an appointment. His call had been awaited eagerly. The local Israeli consul had alerted Pedler that Mr Dickstein, a senior army procurement officer with a large shopping list, was on his way. Pedler had suggested a short tour of the factory on Saturday morning, when it would be empty, followed by lunch at his home.

If Dickstein had been genuine he would have been put off by the tour: the factory was no gleaming model of German efficiency, but a straggling collection of old huts and cluttered yards with a pervasive bad smell.

After sitting up half the night with a textbook on chemical engineering Dickstein was ready with a handful of intelligent questions about agitators and baffles, materials-handling and quality-control and packaging. He relied upon the language problem to camouflage any errors. It seemed to be working.

The situation was peculiar. Dickstein had to play the role of a buyer and be dubious and noncommittal while the seller wooed him, whereas in reality he was hoping to seduce Pedler into a relationship the German would be unable or unwilling to sever. It was Pedler's uranium he wanted, but he was not going to ask for it, now or ever. Instead he would try to manoeuvre Pedler into a position where he was dependent upon Dickstein for his livelihood.

After the factory tour Pedler drove him in a new Mercedes from the works to a wide chalet-style house on a hillside. They sat in front of a big window and sipped their Sekt while Frau Pedler – a pretty, cheerful woman in her forties – busied herself in the kitchen. Bringing a potential customer home to lunch on the weekend was a somewhat Jewish way of doing business, Dickstein mused, and he wondered if Pedler had thought of that.

The window overlooked the valley. Down below, the river was wide and slow, with a narrow road running alongside it. Small grey houses with white shutters clustered in small groups along the banks, and the vineyards sloped upward to the Pedlers' house and beyond it to the treeline. If I were going to live in a cold country, Dickstein thought, this would do nicely.

'Well, what do you think?' said Pedler.

'About the view, or the factory?''

Pedler smiled and shrugged. 'Both.'

'The view is magnificent. The factory is smaller than I expected.'

Pedler lit a cigarette. He was a heavy smoker – he was lucky to have lived so long. 'Small?'

'Perhaps I should explain what I'm looking for.'

'Please.'

Dickstein launched into his story. 'Right now the Army buys cleaning materials from a variety of suppliers: detergents from one, ordinary soap from another, solvents for machinery from someone else and so on. We're trying to cut costs, and perhaps we can do this by taking our entire business in this area to one manufacturer.'

Pedler's eyes widened. 'That is . . .' He fumbled for a phrase '. . . a tall order.'

'I'm afraid it may be too tall for you,' Dickstein said, thinking: Don't say yes!

'Not necessarily. The only reason we haven't got that kind of bulk manufacturing capacity is simply that we've never had this scale of business. We certainly have the managerial and technical knowhow, and with a large firm order we could get finance to expand . . . it all depends on the figures, really.'

Dickstein picked up his briefcase from beside his chair and opened it. 'Here are the specifications for the products,' he said, handing Pedler a list. 'Plus the quantities required and the time scale. You'll want time to consult with your directors and do your sums—'

'I'm the boss,' Pedler said with a smile. 'I don't have to consult anybody. Give me tomorrow to work on the figures, and Monday to see the bank. On Tuesday I'll call and give you prices.'

'I was told you were a good man to work with,' Dickstein said.

'There are some advantages to being a small company.'

Frau Pedler came in from the kitchen and said, 'Lunch is ready.'

My darling Suza.

I have never written a love letter before. I don't think I ever called anyone darling until now. I must tell you, it feels very good.

I am alone in a strange town on a cold Sunday afternoon. The town is quite pretty, with lots of parks, in fact I'm sitting in one of them now, writing to you with a leaky ballpoint pen and some vile green stationery, the only kind I could get. My bench is beneath a curious kind of pagoda with a circular dome and Greek columns all around in a circle – like a folly, or the kind of summer house you might find in an English country garden designed by a Victorian eccentric. In front of me is a flat lawn dotted with poplar trees, and in the distance I can hear a brass band playing something by Edward Elgar. The park is full of people with children and footballs and dogs.

I don't know why I'm telling you all this. What I really want to say is I love you and I want to spend the rest of my life with you. I knew that a couple of days after we met. I hesitated to tell you, not because I wasn't sure, but . . .

Well, if you want to know the truth, I thought it might scare you off. I know you love me, but I also know that you are twenty-five, that love comes easily to you (I'm the opposite way), and that love which comes easily may go easily. So I thought: Softly,

softly, give her a chance to get to like you before
you ask her to say 'For ever.' Now that we've been
apart for so many weeks I'm no longer capable of
such deviousness, I just have to tell you how it is
with me. For ever is what I want, and you might as
well know it now.

I'm a changed man. I know that sounds trite, but
when it happens to you it isn't trite at all, it's just
the opposite. Life looks different to me now, in
several ways – some of which you know about,
others I'll tell you one day. Even this is different,
this being alone in a strange place with nothing to
do until Monday. Not that I mind it, particularly.
But before, I wouldn't even have thought of it as
something I might like or dislike. Before, there was
nothing I'd prefer to do. Now there is always
something I'd rather do, and you're the person I'd
rather do it to. I mean *with*, not to. Well, either, or
both. I'm going to have to get off that subject, it's
making me fidget.

I'll be gone from here in a couple of days, don't
know where I'm going next, don't know – and this
is the worst part – don't even know when I'll see you
again. But when I do, believe me, I'm not going to
let you out of my sight for ten or fifteen years.

None of this sounds how it's supposed to sound.
I want to tell you how I feel, and I can't put it into
words. I want you to know what it's like for me to
picture your face many times every day, to see a
slender girl with black hair and hope, against all
reason, that somehow she might be you, to imagine

all the time what you might say about a view, a
newspaper article, a small man with a large dog, a
pretty dress; I want you to know how, when I get
into bed alone, I just ache with the need to touch
you.

I love you so much.

N.

Franz Pedler's secretary phoned Nat Dickstein at his
hotel on Tuesday morning and made a date for lunch.

They went to a modest restaurant in the Wilhelm-
strasse and ordered beer instead of wine: this was to be
a working session. Dickstein controlled his impatience
– Pedler, not he, was supposed to do the wooing.

Pedler said, 'Well, I think we can accommodate you.'

Dickstein wanted to shout 'Hooray!' but he kept his
face impassive.

Pedler continued: 'The prices, which I'll give you in
a moment, are conditional. We need a five-year contract. We will guarantee prices for the first twelve
months; after that they may be varied in accordance
with an index of world prices of certain raw materials.
And there's a cancellation penalty amounting to ten
per cent of the value of one year's supply.'

Dickstein wanted to say, 'Done!' and shake hands on
the deal, but he reminded himself to continue to play
his part. 'Ten per cent is stiff.'

'It's not excessive,' Pedler argued. 'It certainly would
not recompense us for our losses if you did cancel. But
it must be large enough to deter you from cancelling
except under very compelling circumstances.'

'I see that. But we may suggest a smaller percentage.'

Pedler shrugged. 'Everything is negotiable. Here are the prices.'

Dickstein studied the list, then said, 'This is close to what we're looking for.'

'Does that mean we have a deal?'

Dickstein thought: Yes, yes! But he said, 'No, it means that I think we can do business.'

Pedler beamed. 'In that case,' he said, 'let's have a real drink. Waiter!'

When the drinks came Pedler raised his glass in a toast. 'To many years of business together.'

'I'll drink to that,' Dickstein said. As he raised his glass he was thinking: How about that – I did it again!

Life at sea was uncomfortable, but it was not as bad as Pyotr Tyrin had expected. In the Soviet Navy, ships had been run on the principles of unremitting hard work, harsh discipline and bad food. The *Coparelli* was very different. The captain, Eriksen, asked only for safety and good seamanship, and even there his standards were not remarkably high. The deck was swabbed occasionally, but nothing was ever polished or painted. The food was quite good, and Tyrin had the advantage of sharing a cabin with the cook. In theory Tyrin could be called upon at any hour of the day or night to send radio signals, but in practice all the traffic occurred during the normal working day so he even got his eight hours sleep every night. It was a comfortable regimen, and Pyotr Tyrin was concerned about comfort.

Sadly, the ship was the opposite of comfortable. She was a bitch. As soon as they rounded Cape Wrath and left The Minch and the North Sea she began to pitch and roll like a toy yacht in a gale. Tyrin felt terribly seasick, and had to conceal it since he was supposed to be a sailor. Fortunately this occurred while the cook was busy in the galley and Tyrin was not needed in the radio room, so he was able to lie flat on his back in his bunk until the worst was over.

The quarters were poorly ventilated and inadequately heated, so immediately it got a little damp above, the mess decks were full of wet clothing hanging up to dry and making the atmosphere worse.

Tyrin's radio gear was in his sea-bag, well protected by polythene and canvas and some sweaters. However, he could not set it up and operate it in his cabin, where the cook or anyone else might walk in. He had already made routine radio contact with Moscow on the ship's radio, during a quiet – but nonetheless tense – moment when nobody was listening; but he needed something safer and more reliable.

Tyrin was a nest-building man. Whereas Rostov would move from embassy to hotel room to safe house without noticing his environment, Tyrin liked to have a base, a place where he could feel comfortable and familiar and secure. On static surveillance, the kind of assignment he preferred, he would always find a large easy chair to place in front of the window, and would sit at the telescope for hours, perfectly content with his bag of sandwiches, his bottle of soda and his thoughts. Here on the *Coparelli*, he had found a place to nest.

Exploring the ship in daylight, he had discovered a little labyrinth of stores up in the bow beyond the for'ard hatch. The naval architect had put them there merely to fill a space between the hold and the prow. The main store was entered by a semiconcealed door down a flight of steps. It contained some tools, several drums of grease for the cranes and – inexplicably – a rusty old lawnmower. Several smaller rooms opened off the main one: some containing ropes, bits of machinery and decaying cardboard boxes of nuts and bolts; others empty but for insects. Tyrin had never seen anyone enter the area – stuff that was used was stored aft, where it was needed.

He chose a moment when darkness was falling and most of the crew and officers were at supper. He went to his cabin, picked up his sea-bag and climbed the companionway to the deck. He took a flashlight from a locker below the bridge but did not yet switch it on.

The almanac said there was a moon, but it did not show through the thick clouds. Tyrin made his way stealthily for'ard holding on to the gunwale, where his silhouette would be less likely to show against the off-white deck. There was some light from the bridge and the wheelhouse, but the duty officers would be watching the surrounding sea, not the deck.

Cold spray fell on him, and as the *Coparelli* executed her notorious roll he had to grab the rail with both hands to avoid being swept overboard. At times she shipped water – not much, but enough to soak into Tyrin's sea boots and freeze his feet. He hoped fervently that he would never find out what she was like in a real gale.

He was miserably wet and shivering when he reached the bow and entered the little disused store. He closed the door behind him, switched on his flashlight and made his way through the assorted junk to one of the small rooms off the main store. He closed that door behind him too. He took off his oilskin, rubbed his hands on his sweater to dry and warm them some, then opened his bag. He put the transmitter in a corner, lashed it to the bulkhead with a wire tied through rings in the deck, and wedged it with a cardboard box.

He was wearing rubber soles, but he put on rubber gloves as an additional precaution for the next task. The cables to the ship's radio mast ran through a pipe along the deckhead above him. With a small hacksaw pilfered from the engine room Tyrin cut away a six-inch section of the pipe, exposing the cables. He took a tap from the power cable to the power input of the transmitter, then connected the aerial socket of his radio with the signal wire from the mast.

He switched on the radio and called Moscow.

His outgoing signals would not interfere with the ship's radio because he was the radio operator and it was unlikely that anyone else would attempt to send on the ship's equipment. However, while he was using his own radio, incoming signals would not reach the ship's radio room; and he would not hear them either since his set would be tuned to another frequency. He could have wired everything so that both radios would receive at the same time, but then Moscow's replies to him would be received by the ship's radio, and somebody might notice . . . Well, there was nothing very suspicious about a small ship taking a few minutes to pick up signals. Tyrin would take care to use his radio only at times when no traffic was expected for the ship.

When he reached Moscow he made: *Checking secondary transmitter.*

They acknowledged, then made: *Stand by for signal from Rostov.* All this was in a standard KGB code.

Tyrin made: *Standing by, but hurry.*

The message came: *Keep your head down until something happens. Rostov.*

Tyrin made: *Understood. Over and out.* Without waiting for their sign-off he disconnected his wires and restored the ship's cables to normal. The business of twisting and untwisting bare wires, even with insulated pliers, was time-consuming and not very safe. He had some quick-release connectors amongst his equipment in the ship's radio room: he would pocket a few and bring them here next time to speed up the process.

He was well satisfied with his evening's work. He had made his nest, he had opened his lines of communication, and he had remained undiscovered. All he had to do now was sit tight: and sitting tight was what he liked to do.

He decided to drag in another cardboard box to put in front of the radio and conceal it from a casual glance. He opened the door and shone his flashlight into the main store – and got a shock.

He had company.

The overhead light was on, casting restless shadows

with its yellow glow. In the centre of the storeroom, sitting against a grease drum with his legs stretched out before him, was a young sailor. He looked up, just as startled as Tyrin and – Tyrin realized from his face – just as guilty.

Tyrin recognized him. His name was Ravlo. He was about nineteen years old, with pale blond hair and a thin white face. He had not joined in the pub-crawls in Cardiff, yet he often looked hung over, with dark discs under his eyes and a distracted air.

Tyrin said, 'What are you doing here?' And then he saw.

Ravlo had rolled up his left sleeve past the elbow. On the deck between his legs was a phial, a watch-glass and a small waterproof bag. In his right hand was a hypodermic syringe, with which he was about to inject himself.

Tyrin frowned. 'Are you diabetic?'

Ravlo's face twisted and he gave a dry, humourless laugh.

'An addict,' Tyrin said, understanding. He did not know much about drugs, but he knew that what Ravlo was doing could get him discharged at the next port of call. He began to relax a little. This could be handled.

Ravlo was looking past him, into the smaller store. Tyrin looked back and saw that the radio was clearly visible. The two men stared at one another, each understanding that the other was doing something he needed to hide.

Tyrin said, 'I will keep your secret, and you will keep mine.'

Ravlo gave the twisted smile and the dry, humourless laugh again: then he looked away from Tyrin, down at his arm, and he stuck the needle into his flesh.

The exchange between the *Coparelli* and Moscow was picked up and recorded by a U.S. Naval Intelligence listening station. Since it was in standard KGB code, they were able to decipher it. But all it told them was that someone aboard a ship – they did not know which ship – was checking his secondary transmitter, and somebody called Rostov – the name was not on any of their files – wanted him to keep his head down. Nobody could make any sense of it, so they opened a file titled 'Rostov' and put the signal in the file and forgot about it.

CHAPTER TWELVE

W HEN HE had finished his interim debriefing in Cairo, Hassan asked permission to go to Syria to visit his parents in the refugee camp. He was given four days. He took a plane to Damascus and a taxi to the camp.

He did not visit his parents.

He made certain inquiries at the camp, and one of the refugees took him, by means of a series of buses, to Dara, across the Jordanian border, and all the way to Amman. From there another man took him on another bus to the Jordan River.

On the night of the second day he crossed the river, guided by two men who carried submachine guns. By now Hassan was wearing Arab robes and a headdress like them, but he did not ask for a gun. They were young men, their soft adolescent faces just taking on lines of weariness and cruelty, like recruits in a new army. They moved across the Jordan valley in confident silence, directing Hassan with a touch or a whisper: they seemed to have made the journey many times. At one point all three of them lay flat behind a stand of cactus while lights and soldiers' voices passed a quarter of a mile away.

Hassan felt helpless – and something more. At first he thought that the feeling was due to his being so completely in the hands of these boys, his life dependent on their knowledge and courage. But later, when they had left him and he was alone on a country road trying to get a lift, he realized that this journey was a kind of regression. For years now he had been a European banker, living in Luxembourg with his car and his refrigerator and his television set. Now, suddenly, he was walking in sandals along the dusty Palestine roads of his youth: no car, no jet; an Arab again, a peasant, a second-class citizen in the country of his birth. None of his reflexes would work here – it was not possible to solve a problem by picking up a phone or pulling out a credit card or calling a cab. He felt like a child, a pauper and a fugitive all at the same time.

He walked five miles without seeing a vehicle, then a fruit truck passed him, its engine coughing unhealthily and pouring smoke, and pulled up a few yards ahead. Hassan ran after it.

'To Nablus?' he shouted.

'Jump in.'

The driver was a heavy man whose forearms bulged with muscle as he heaved the truck around bends at top speed. He smoked all the time. He must have been certain there would not be another vehicle in the way all night, driving as he did on the crown of the road and never using the brake. Hassan could have used some sleep, but the driver wanted to talk. He told Hassan that the Jews were good rulers, business had prospered since they occupied Jordan, but of course the land must be free one day. Half of what he said was insincere, no doubt; but Hassan could not tell which half.

They entered Nablus in the cool Samaritan dawn, with a red sun rising behind the hillside and the town still asleep. The truck roared into the market square and stopped. Hassan said goodbye to the driver.

He walked slowly through the empty streets as the sun began to take away the chill of the night. He savoured the clean air and the low white buildings, enjoying every detail, basking in the glow of nostalgia for his boyhood: he was in Palestine, he was home.

He had precise directions to a house with no number in a street with no name. It was in a poor quarter, where the little stone houses were crowded too close together and nobody swept the streets. A goat was tethered outside, and he wondered briefly what it ate, for there was no grass. The door was unlocked.

He hesitated a moment outside, fighting down the excitement in his belly. He had been away too long – now he was back in the Land. He had waited too many years for this opportunity to strike a blow in revenge for what they had done to his father. He had suffered exile, he had endured with patience, he had nursed his hatred enough, perhaps too much.

He went in.

There were four or five people asleep on the floor. One of them, a woman, opened her eyes, saw him and sat up instantly, her hand under the pillow reaching for what might have been a gun.

'What do you want?'

Hassan spoke the name of the man who commanded the Fedayeen.

Mahmoud had lived not far from Yasif Hassan when they were both boys in the late Thirties, but they had never met, or if they had neither remembered it. After the European war, when Yasif went to England to study, Mahmoud tended sheep with his brothers, his father, his uncles and his grandfather. Their lives would have continued to go in quite different directions but for the 1948 war. Mahmoud's father, like Yasif's, made the decision to pack up and flee. The two sons – Yasif was a few years older than Mahmoud – met at the refugee camp. Mahmoud's reaction to the ceasefire was even stronger than Yasif's, which was paradoxical, for Yasif had lost more. But Mahmoud was possessed by a great rage that would allow him to do nothing other than fight for the liberation of his homeland. Until then he had been oblivious of politics, thinking it had nothing to do with shepherds; now he set out to understand it. Before he could do that, he had to teach himself to read.

They met again in the Fifties, in Gaza. By then Mahmoud had blossomed, if that was the right word for something so fierce. He had read Clausewitz on war and Plato's *Republic*, *Das Kapital* and *Mein Kampf*, Keynes and Mao and Galbraith and Gandhi, history and biography, classical novels and modern plays. He spoke good English and bad Russian and a smattering of Cantonese. He was directing a small cadre of terrorists

on forays into Israel, bombing and shooting and stealing and then returning to disappear into the Gaza
camps like rats into a garbage dump. The terrorists
were getting money, weapons and intelligence from
Cairo: Hassan was, briefly, part of the intelligence
backup, and when they met again Yasif told Mahmoud
where his ultimate loyalty lay – not with Cairo, not even
with the pan-Arab cause, but with Palestine.

Yasif had been ready to abandon everything there
and then – his job at the bank, his home in Luxembourg, his role in Egyptian Intelligence – and join the
freedom fighters. But Mahmoud had said no, and the
habit of command was already fitting him like a tailored
coat. In a few years, he said – for he took a long view –
they would have all the guerrillas they wanted, but they
would still need friends in high places, European
connections, and secret intelligence.

They had met once more, in Cairo, and set up lines
of communication which bypassed the Egyptians. With
the Intelligence Establishment Hassan had cultivated a
deceptive image: he pretended to be a little less percep-
tive than he was. At first Yasif sent over much the same
kind of stuff he was giving to Cairo, principally the
names of loyal Arabs who were stashing away fortunes
in Europe and could therefore be touched for funds.
Recently he had been of more immediate practical
value as the Palestinian movement began to operate
in Europe. He had booked hotels and flights, rented
cars and houses, stockpiled weapons and transferred
funds.

He was not the kind of man to use a gun. He knew this and was faintly ashamed of it, so he was all the more proud to be so useful in other, non-violent but nonetheless practical, ways.

The results of his work had begun to explode in Rome that year. Yasif believed in Mahmoud's programme of European terrorism. He was convinced that the Arab armies, even with Russian support, could never defeat the Jews, for this allowed the Jews to think of themselves as a beleaguered people defending their homes against foreign soldiers, and that gave them strength. The truth was, in Yasif's view, that the Palestine Arabs were defending their home against invading Zionists. There were still more Arab Palestinians than Jewish Israelis. counting the exiles in the camps; and it was *they*, not a rabble of soldiers from Cairo and Damascus, who would liberate the homeland. But first they had to believe in the Fedayeen. Acts such as the Rome airport affair would convince them that the Fedayeen had international resources. And when the people believed in the Fedayeen, the people would be the Fedayeen, and then they would be unstoppable.

The Rome airport affair was trivial, a peccadillo, by comparison with what Hassan had in mind.

It was an outrageous, mind-boggling scheme that would put the Fedayeen on the front pages of the world's newspapers for weeks and prove that they were a powerful international force, not a bunch of ragged refugees. Hassan hoped desperately that Mahmoud would accept it.

Yasif Hassan had come to propose that the Fedayeen should hijack a holocaust.

They embraced like brothers, kissing cheeks, then stood back to look at one another.

'You smell like a whore,' said Mahmoud.

'You smell like a goatherd,' said Hassan. They laughed and embraced again.

Mahmoud was a big man, a fraction taller than Hassan and much broader; and he *looked* big, the way he held his head and walked and spoke. He did smell, too: a sour familiar smell that came from living very close to many people in a place that lacked the modern inventions of hot baths and sanitation and garbage disposal. It was three days since Hassan had used after-shave and talcum powder, but he still smelled like a scented woman to Mahmoud.

The house had two rooms: the one Hassan had entered, and behind that another, where Mahmoud slept on the floor with two other men. There was no upper storey. Cooking was done in a yard at the back, and the nearest water supply was one hundred yards away. The woman lit a fire and began to make a porridge of crushed beans. While they waited for it, Hassan told Mahmoud his story.

'Three months ago in Luxembourg I met a man I had known at Oxford, a Jew called Dickstein. It turns out he is a big Mossad operative. Since then I have been watching him, with the help of the Russians, in particular a KGB man named Rostov. We have discovered that Dickstein plans to steal a shipload of uranium so the Zionists will be able to make atom bombs.'

At first Mahmoud refused to believe this. He cross-questioned Hassan: how good was the information, what exactly was the evidence, who might be lying, what mistakes might have been made? Then, as Hassan's answers made more and more sense, the truth began to sink in, and Mahmoud became very grave.

'This is not only a threat to the Palestinian cause. These bombs could ravage the whole of the Middle East.'

It was like him, Hassan thought, to see the big picture.

'What do you and this Russian propose to do?' Mahmoud asked.

'The plan is to stop Dickstein and expose the Israeli plot, showing the Zionists to be lawless adventurers. We haven't worked out the details yet. But I have an alternative proposal.' He paused, trying to form the right phrases, then blurted it out. 'I think the Fedayeen should hijack the ship before Dickstein gets there.'

Mahmoud stared blankly at him for a long moment.

Hassan thought: Say something, for God's sake! Mahmoud began to shake his head from side to side slowly, then his mouth widened in a smile, and at last he began to laugh, beginning with a small chuckle and finishing up giving a huge, body-shaking bellow that brought the rest of the household around to see what was happening.

Hassan ventured, 'But what do you think?'

Mahmoud sighed. 'It's wonderful,' he said. 'I don't see how we can do it, but it's a wonderful idea.'

Then he started asking questions.

He asked questions all through breakfast and for most of the morning: the quantity of uranium, the names of the ships involved, how the yellowcake was converted into nuclear explosive, places and dates and people. They talked in the back room, just the two of them for most of the time, but occasionally Mahmoud would call someone in and tell him to listen while Hassan repeated some particular point.

About midday he summoned two men who seemed to be his lieutenants. With them listening, he again went over the points he thought crucial.

'The *Coparelli* is an ordinary merchant ship with a regular crew?'

'Yes.'

'She will be sailing through the Mediterranean to Genoa.'

'Yes.'

'What does this yellowcake weigh?'

'Two hundred tons.'

'And it is packed in drums.'

'Five hundred and sixty of them.'

'Its market price?'

'Two million American dollars.'

'And it is used to make nuclear bombs.'

'Yes. Well, it is the raw material.'

'Is the conversion to the explosive form an expensive or difficult process?'

'Not if you've got a nuclear reactor. Otherwise, yes.'

Mahmoud nodded to the two lieutenants. 'Go and tell this to the others.'

In the afternoon, when the sun was past its zenith and it was cool enough to go out, Mahmoud and Yasif walked over the hills outside the town. Yasif was desperate to know what Mahmoud really thought of his plan, but Mahmoud refused to talk about uranium. So Yasif spoke about David Rostov and said that he admired the Russian's professionalism despite the difficulties he had made for him.

'It is well to admire the Russians,' Mahmoud said, 'so long as we do not trust them. Their heart is not in our cause. There are three reasons why they take our side. The least important is that we cause trouble for the West, and anything that is bad for the West is good for the Russians. Then there is their image. The underdeveloped nations identify with us rather than with the Zionists, so by supporting us the Russians gain credit with the Third World – and remember, in the contest between the United States and the Soviet Union the Third World has all the floating voters. But the most important reason – the only *really* important reason – is oil. The Arabs have oil.'

They passed a boy tending a small flock of bony sheep. The boy was playing a flute. Yasif remembered that Mahmoud had once been a shepherd boy who could neither read nor write.

'Do you understand how important oil is?' Mahmoud said. 'Hitler lost the European war because of oil.'

'No.'

'Listen. The Russians defeated Hitler. They were bound to. Hitler knew this: he knew about Napoleon, he knew nobody could conquer Russia. So why did he try? He was running out of oil. There is oil in Georgia, in the Caucasian oilfields. Hitler had to have the Caucasus. But you cannot hold the Caucasus secure unless you have Volgograd, which was then called Stalingrad, the place where the tide turned against Hitler. Oil. That's what our struggle is about, whether we like it or not, do you realize that? If it were not for oil, nobody but us would care about a few Arabs and Jews fighting over a dusty little country like ours.'

Mahmoud was magnetic when he talked. His strong, clear voice rolled out short phrases, simple explanations, statements that sounded like devastating basic truths: Hassan suspected he said these same things often to his troops. In the back of his mind he remembered the sophisticated ways in which politics were discussed in places like Luxembourg and Oxford, and it seemed to him now that for all their mountains of information those people knew less than Mahmoud. He knew, too, that international politics were complicated: that there was more than oil behind these things, yet at bottom he believed Mahmoud was right.

They sat in the shade of a fig tree. The smooth, dun-coloured landscape stretched all around them, empty. The sky glared hot and blue, cloudless from one horizon to the other. Mahmoud uncorked a water bottle and gave it to Hassan, who drank the tepid liquid and handed it back. Then he asked Mahmoud whether he wanted to rule Palestine after the Zionists were beaten back.

'I have killed many people,' Mahmoud said. 'At first I did it with my own hands, with a knife or a gun or a bomb. Now I kill by devising plans and giving orders, but I kill them still. We know this is a sin, but I cannot repent. I have no remorse, Yasif. Even if we make a mistake, and we kill children and Arabs instead of soldiers and Zionists, still I think only, "This is bad for our reputation," not, "This is bad for my soul." There is blood on my hands, and I will not wash it off. I will not try. There is a story called *The Picture of Dorian Gray*. It is about a man who leads an evil and debilitating life, the kind of life that should make him look old, give him lines on his face and bags under his eyes, a destroyed liver and venereal disease. Still, he does not suffer. Indeed, as the years go by he seems to stay young, as if he had found the elixir of life. But in a locked room in his house there is a painting of him, and it is the picture that ages, and takes on the ravages of evil living and terrible disease. Do you know the story? It is English.'

'I saw the movie,' said Yasif.

'I read it when I was in Moscow. I would like to see that film. Do you remember how it ended?'

'Oh, yes. Dorian Gray destroyed the painting, and then all the disease and damage fell on him in an instant, and he died.'

'Yes.' Mahmoud put the stopper back in the bottle,

and looked out over the brown hillsides with unseeing eyes. Then he said, 'When Palestine is free, my picture will be destroyed.'

After that they sat in silence for a while. Eventually, without speaking, they stood up and began to walk back to the town.

Several men came to the little house in Nablus that evening at dusk, just before curfew. Hassan did not know who they were exactly: they might have been the local leaders of the movement, or an assorted group of people whose judgment Mahmoud respected, or a permanent council of war that stayed close to Mahmoud but did not actually live with him. Hassan could see the logic in the last alternative, for if they all lived together, they could all be destroyed together.

The woman gave them bread and fish and watery wine, and Mahmoud told them of Hassan's scheme. Mahmoud had thought it through more thoroughly than Hassan. He proposed that they hijack the *Coparelli* before Dickstein got there, then ambush the Israelis as they came aboard. Expecting only an ordinary crew and halfhearted resistance, Dickstein's group would be wiped out. Then the Fedayeen would take the *Coparelli* to a North African port and invite the world to come aboard and see the bodies of the Zionist criminals. The cargo would be offered to its owners for a ransom of half its market price – one million U.S. dollars.

There was a long debate. Clearly a faction of the

movement was already nervous about Mahmoud's
policy of taking the war into Europe, and saw the
proposed hijack as a further extension of the same
strategy. They suggested that the Fedayeen could
achieve most of what they wanted simply by calling a
press conference in Beirut or Damascus and revealing
the Israeli plot to the international press. Hassan was
convinced that was not enough: accusations were
cheap, and it was not the lawlessness of Israel that had
to be demonstrated, it was the power of the Fedayeen.

They spoke as equals, and Mahmoud seemed to
listen to each with the same attention. Hassan sat
quietly, hearing the low, calm voices of these people
who looked like peasants and spoke like senators. He
was at once hopeful and fearful that they would adopt
his plan: hopeful because it would be the fulfilment of
twenty years of vengeful dreams; fearful because it
would mean he would have to do things more difficult,
violent and risky than the work he had been involved
in so far.

In the end he could not stand it any longer and he
went outside and squatted in the mean yard, smelling
the night and the dying fire. A little later there was a
chorus of quiet voices from inside, like voting.

Mahmoud came out and sat beside Hassan. 'I have
sent for a car.'

'Oh?'

'We must go to Damascus. Tonight. There is a lot to
do. It will be our biggest operation. We must start work
immediately.'

'It is decided, then.'

'Yes. The Fedayeen will hijack the ship and steal the uranium.'

'So be it,' said Yasif Hassan.

David Rostov had always liked his family in small doses, and as he got older the doses got smaller. The first day of his holiday was fine. He made breakfast, they walked along the beach, and in the afternoon Vladimir, the young genius, played chess against Rostov, Mariya, and Yuri simultaneously, and won all three games. They took hours over supper, catching up on all the news and drinking a little wine. The second day was similar, but they enjoyed it less; and by the third day the novelty of each other's company had worn off. Vladimir remembered he was supposed to be a prodigy and stuck his nose back into his books; Yuri began to play degenerate Western music on the record player and argued with his father about dissident poets; and Mariya fled into the kitchen of the dacha and stopped putting make-up on her face.

So when the message came to say that Nik Bunin was back from Rotterdam and had successfully bugged the *Stromberg*, Rostov used that as an excuse to return to Moscow.

Nik reported that the *Stromberg* had been in dry dock for the usual inspection prior to completion of the sale to Savile Shipping. A number of small repairs were in progress, and without difficulty Nik had got on board, posing as an electrician, and planted a powerful radio beacon in the prow of the ship. On leaving he had been questioned by the dock foreman, who did not have any electrical work on his schedule for that day; and Nik had pointed out that if the work had not been requested, no doubt it would not have to be paid for.

From that moment, whenever the ship's power was on – which was all the time she was at sea and most of the time she was in dock – the beacon would send out a signal every thirty minutes until the ship sank or was broken up for scrap. For the rest of her life, wherever in the world she was, Moscow would be able to locate her within an hour.

Rostov listened to Nik, then sent him home. He had plans for the evening. It was a long time since he had seen Olga, and he was impatient to see what she would do with the battery-operated vibrator he had brought her as a present from London.

In Israeli Naval Intelligence there was a young captain named Dieter Koch who had trained as a ship's engineer. When the *Coparelli* sailed from Antwerp with her cargo of yellowcake Koch had to be aboard.

Nat Dickstein reached Antwerp with only the vaguest idea of how this was to be achieved. From his hotel room he phoned the local representative of the company that owned the *Coparelli*.

When I die, he thought as he waited for the connection, they will bury me from a hotel room.

A girl answered the phone. Dickstein said briskly, 'This is Pierre Beaudaire, give me the director.'

'Hold on, please.'

A man's voice, 'Yes?'

'Good morning, this is Pierre Beaudaire from the Beaudaire Crew List.' Dickstein was making it up as he went along.

'Never heard of you.'

'That's why I'm calling you. You see, we're contemplating opening an office in Antwerp, and I'm wondering whether you would be willing to try us.'

'I doubt it, but you can write to me and—'

'Are you completely satisfied with your present crew agency?'

'They could be worse. Look here—'

'One more question and I won't trouble you further. May I ask whom you use at the moment?'

'Cohen's. Now, I haven't any more time—'

'I understand. Thank you for your patience. Goodbye.'

Cohen's! That was a piece of luck. Perhaps I will be able to do this bit without brutality, Dickstein thought as he put down the phone. Cohen! It was unexpected – docks and shipping were not typical Jewish business. Well, sometimes you got lucky.

He looked up Cohen's crew agency in the phone book, memorized the address, put on his coat, left the hotel and hailed a cab. Cohen had a little two-room office above a sailor's bar in the red-light district of the city. It was not yet midday, and the night people were still asleep – the whores and thieves, musicians and strippers and waiters and bouncers, the people who made the place come to life in the evening. Now it might have been any run-down business district, grey and cold in the morning, and none too clean.

Dickstein went up a staircase to a first-floor door, knocked and went in. A middle-aged secretary presided over a small reception room furnished with filing cabinets and orange plastic chairs.

'I'd like to see Mr Cohen,' Dickstein told her.

She looked him over and seemed to think he did not appear to be a sailor. 'Are you wanting a ship?' she said doubtfully.

'No,' he said. 'I'm from Israel.'

'Oh.' She hesitated. She had dark hair and deep-set, shadowed eyes, and she wore a wedding ring. Dickstein wondered if she might be Mrs Cohen. She got up and went through a door behind her desk into the inner office. She was wearing a pants suit, and from behind she looked her age.

A minute later she reappeared and ushered him into Cohen's office. Cohen stood up, shook hands and said without preamble, 'I give to the cause every year. In the war I gave twenty thousand guilders, I can show you the cheque. This is some new appeal? There is another war?'

'I'm not here to raise money, Mr Cohen,' Dickstein said with a smile. Mrs Cohen had left the door open: Dickstein closed it. 'Can I sit down?'

'If you don't want money, sit down, have some coffee, stay all day,' said Cohen, and he laughed.

Dickstein sat. Cohen was a short man in spectacles, bald and clean-shaven, and looked to be about fifty years old. He wore a brown check suit that was not very new. He had a good little business here, Dickstein guessed, but he was no millionaire.

Dickstein said, 'Were you here in World War II?'

Cohen nodded. 'I was a young man. I went into the country and worked on a farm where nobody knew me, nobody knew I was Jewish. I was lucky.'

'Do you think it will happen again?'

'Yes. It's happened all through history, why should it stop now? It will happen again – but not in my lifetime. It's all right here. I don't want to go to Israel.'

'Okay. I work for the government of Israel. We would like you to do something for us.'

Cohen shrugged. 'So?'

'In a few weeks' time, one of your clients will call you with an urgent request. They will want an engineer officer for a ship called *Coparelli*. We would like you to send them a man supplied by us. His name is Koch, and he is an Israeli, but he will be using a different name and false papers. However, he *is* a ship's engineer – your clients will not be dissatisfied.'

Dickstein waited for Cohen to say something. You're a nice man, he thought; a decent Jewish businessman, smart and hardworking and a little frayed at the edges; don't make me get tough with you.

Cohen said, 'You're not going to tell me why the government of Israel wants this man Koch aboard the *Coparelli*?'

'No.'

There was a silence.

'You carry any identification?'

'No.'

The secretary came in without knocking and gave them coffee. Dickstein got hostile vibrations from her. Cohen used the interruption to gather his thoughts. When she had gone out he said, 'I would have to be *meshugenah* to do this.'

'Why?'

'You come in off the street saying you represent the government of Israel, yet you have no identification, you don't even tell me your name. You ask me to take part in something that is obviously underhanded and probably criminal; you will not tell me what it is that you're trying to do. Even if I believe your story, I don't know that I would approve of the Israelis doing what you want to do.'

Dickstein sighed, thinking of the alternatives: blackmail him, kidnap his wife, take over his office on the crucial day . . . He said, 'Is there anything I can do to convince you?'

'I would need a personal request from the Prime Minister of Israel before I would do this thing.'

Dickstein stood up to leave, then he thought: Why not? Why the hell not? It was a wild idea, they would think he was crazy . . . but it would work, it would serve the purpose . . . He grinned as he thought it through. Pierre Borg would have apoplexy.

He said to Cohen, 'All right.'

'What do you mean, "all right"?'

'Put on your coat. We'll go to Jerusalem.'

'Now?'

'Are you busy?'

'Are you serious?'

'I told you it's important.' Dickstein pointed to the phone on the desk. 'Call your wife.'

'She's just outside.'

Dickstein went to the door and opened it. 'Mrs Cohen?'

'Yes.'

'Would you come in here, please?'

She hurried in, looking worried. 'What is it, Josef?' she asked her husband.

'This man wants me to go to Jerusalem with him.'

'When?'

'Now.'

'You mean this week?'

Dickstein said, 'I mean this morning, Mrs Cohen. I must tell you that all this is highly confidential. I've asked your husband to do something for the Israeli government. Naturally he wants to be certain that it is the government that is asking this favour and not some criminal. So I'm going to take him there to convince him.'

She said, 'Don't get involved, Josef—'

Cohen shrugged. 'I'm Jewish, I'm involved already. Mind the shop.'

'You don't know anything about this man!'

'So I'm going to find out.'

'I don't like it.'

'There's no danger,' Cohen told her. 'We'll take a scheduled flight, we'll go to Jerusalem. I'll see the Prime Minister and we'll come back.'

'The Prime Minister!' Dickstein realized how proud

she would be if her husband met the Prime Minister of Israel. He said, 'This has to be secret. Mrs Cohen. Please tell people your husband has gone to Rotterdam on business. He will be back tomorrow.'

She stared at the two of them. 'My Josef meets the Prime Minister, and I can't tell Rachel Rothstein?'

Then Dickstein knew it was going to be all right.

Cohen took his coat from a hook and put it on. Mrs Cohen kissed him, then put her arms around him.

'It's all right,' he told her. 'This is very sudden and strange, but it's all right.'

She nodded dumbly and let him go.

They took a cab to the airport. Dickstein's sense of delight grew as they travelled. The scheme had an air of mischief about it, he felt a bit like a schoolboy, this was a terrific prank. He kept grinning, and had to turn his face away so that Cohen would not see.

Pierre Borg would go through the *roof.*

Dickstein bought two round-trip tickets to Tel Aviv, paying with his credit card. They had to take a connecting flight to Paris. Before they took off he called the embassy in Paris and arranged for someone to meet them in the transit lounge.

In Paris he gave the man from the embassy a message to send to Borg, explaining what was required. The diplomat was a Mossad man, and treated Dickstein with deference. Cohen was allowed to listen to the conversation, and when the man had gone back to the embassy he said, 'We could go back. I'm convinced already.'

'Oh, no,' Dickstein said. 'Now that we've come this far I want to be sure of you.'

On the plane Cohen said, 'You must be an important man in Israel.'

'No. But what I'm doing is important.'

Cohen wanted to know how to behave, how to address the Prime Minister. Dickstein told him, 'I don't know, I've never met him. Shake hands and call him by his name.'

Cohen smiled. He was beginning to share Dickstein's feeling of mischievousness.

Pierre Borg met them at Lod Airport with a car to take them to Jerusalem. He smiled and shook hands with Cohen, but he was seething underneath. As they walked to the car he muttered to Dickstein, 'You better have a fucking good reason for all this.'

'I have.'

They were with Cohen all the while, so Borg did not have an opportunity to cross-examine Dickstein. They went straight to the Prime Minister's residence in Jerusalem. Dickstein and Cohen waited in an anteroom while Borg explained to the Prime Minister what was required and why.

A couple of minutes later they were admitted. 'This is Nat Dickstein, sir,' Borg said.

They shook hands, and the Prime Minister said, 'We haven't met before, but I've heard of you, Mr Dickstein.'

Borg said, 'And this is Mr Josef Cohen of Antwerp.'

'Mr Cohen.' The Prime Minister smiled. 'You're a very cautious man. You should be a politician. Well, now . . . please do this thing for us. It is very important, and you will come to no harm from it.'

Cohen was bedazzled. 'Yes, sir, of course I will do this, I'm sorry to have caused so much trouble . . .'

'Not at all. You did the right thing.' He shook Cohen's hand again. 'Thank you for coming. Goodbye.'

Borg was less polite on the way back to the airport. He sat silent in the front seat of the car, smoking a cigar and fidgeting. At the airport he managed to get Dickstein alone for a minute. 'If you ever pull a stunt like this again . . .'

'It was necessary,' Dickstein said. 'It took less than a minute. Why not?'

'Why not, is because half my fucking department has been working all day to fix that minute. Why didn't you just point a gun at the man's head or something?'

'Because we're not barbarians,' Dickstein said.

'So people keep telling me.'

'They do? That's a bad sign.'

'Why?'

'Because you shouldn't need to be told.'

Then their flight was called. Boarding the plane with Cohen, Dickstein reflected that his relationship with Borg was in ruins. They had always talked like this, with bantering insults, but until now there had been an undertone of . . . perhaps not affection, but at least respect. Now that had vanished. Borg was genuinely hostile. Dickstein's refusal to be pulled out was a piece of basic defiance which could not be tolerated. If Dickstein had wanted to continue in the Mossad, he would have had to fight Borg for the job of director –

there was no longer sufficient room for both men in the organization. But there would be no contest now, for Dickstein was going to resign.

Flying back to Europe through the night, Cohen drank some gin and went to sleep. Dickstein ran over in his mind the work he had done in the past five months. Back in May he had started out with no real idea of how he was going to steal the uranium Israel needed. He had taken the problems as they came up, and found a solution to each one: how to locate uranium, which uranium to steal, how to hijack a ship, how to camouflage the Israeli involvement in the theft, how to prevent the disappearance of the uranium being reported to the authorities, how to placate the owners of the stuff. If he had sat down at the beginning and tried to dream up the whole scheme he could never have foreseen all the complications.

He had had some good luck and some bad. The fact that the owners of the *Coparelli* used a Jewish crew agency in Antwerp was a piece of luck; so was the existence of a consignment of uranium for non-nuclear purposes, and one going by sea. The bad luck mainly consisted of the accidental meeting with Yasif Hassan.

Hassan, the fly in the ointment. Dickstein was reasonably certain he had shaken off the opposition when he flew to Buffalo to see Cortone, and that they had not picked up his trail again since. But that did not mean they had dropped the case.

It would be useful to know how much they had found out before they lost him.

Dickstein could not see Suza again until the whole

affair was over, and Hassan was to blame for that too. If he were to go to Oxford, Hassan was sure to pick up the trail somehow.

The plane began its descent. Dickstein fastened his seat belt. It was all done now, the scheme in place, the preparations made. The cards had been dealt. He knew what was in his hand, and he knew some of his opponents' cards, and they knew some of his. All that remained was to play out the game, and no one could foretell the outcome. He wished he could see the future more clearly, he wished his plan were less complicated, he wished he did not have to risk his life once more, and he wished the game would start so that he could stop wishing and start doing things.

Cohen was awake. 'Did I dream all that?' he said.

'No.' Dickstein smiled. There was one more unpleasant duty he had to perform: he had to scare Cohen half to death. 'I told you this was important, and secret.'

'Of course, I understand.'

'You don't understand. If you talk about this to anyone other than your wife, we will take drastic action.'

'Is that a threat? What are you saying?'

'I'm saying, if you don't keep your mouth shut, we will kill your wife.'

Cohen stared, and went pale. After a moment he turned away and looked out of the window at the airport coming up to meet them.

CHAPTER THIRTEEN

Moscow's Hotel Rossiya was the largest hotel in Europe. It had 5,738 beds, ten miles of corridors, and no air-conditioning.

Yasif Hassan slept very badly there.

It was simple to say, 'The Fedayeen should hijack the ship before Dickstein gets there,' but the more he thought about it, the more terrified he was.

The Palestine Liberation Organization in 1968 was not the tightly-knit political entity it pretended to be. It was not even a loose federation of individual groups working together. It was more like a club for people with a common interest: it represented its members, but it did not control them. The individual guerrilla groups could speak with one voice through the PLO, but they did not and could not act as one. So when Mahmoud said the Fedayeen would do something, he spoke only for his own group. Furthermore, in this case it would be unwise even to ask for PLO cooperation. The organization was given money, facilities and a home by the Egyptians, but it had also been infiltrated by them: if you wanted to keep something secret from the Arab establishment, you had to keep it secret from the PLO. Of course, after the coup, when the world's press came to look over the captured ship with its atomic cargo, the Egyptians would know and would probably suspect that the Fedayeen had deliberately thwarted them, but Mahmoud would play innocent and the Egyptians would be obliged to join in the general acclamation of the Fedayeen for frustrating an Israeli act of aggression.

Anyway, Mahmoud believed he did not need the help of the others. His group had the best connections outside Palestine, the best European set-up, and plenty of money. He was now in Benghazi arranging to borrow a ship while his international team was gathered up from various parts of the world.

But the most crucial task devolved on Hassan: if the Fedayeen were to get to the *Coparelli* before the Israelis, he would have to establish exactly when and where Dickstein's hijack was to take place. For that, he needed the KGB.

He felt terribly uneasy around Rostov now. Until his visit to Mahmoud he had been able to tell himself he was working for two organizations with a common objective. Now he was indisputably a double agent, merely pretending to work with the Egyptians and the KGB while he sabotaged their plans. He felt different – he felt a traitor, in a way – and he was afraid that Rostov would observe the difference in him.

When Hassan had flown in to Moscow Rostov himself had been uneasy. He had said there was not enough room in his apartment for Hassan to stay, although Hassan knew the rest of the family were away on holiday. It seemed Rostov was hiding something.

Hassan suspected he was seeing some woman and did not want his colleague getting in the way.

After his restless night at the Hotel Rossiya, Hassan met Rostov at the KGB building on the Moscow ring road, in the office of Rostov's boss, Feliks Vorontsov. There were undercurrents there too. The two men were having an argument when Hassan entered the room, and although they broke it off immediately the air was stiff with unspoken hostility. Hassan, however, was too busy with his own clandestine moves to pay much attention to theirs.

He sat down. 'Have there been any developments?'

Rostov and Vorontsov looked at one another. Rostov shrugged. Vorontsov said, 'The *Stromberg* has been fitted with a very powerful radio beacon. She's out of dry dock now and heading south across the Bay of Biscay. The assumption would be that she is going to Haifa to take on a crew of Mossad agents. I think we can all be quite satisfied with our intelligence-gathering work. The project now falls into the sphere of positive action. Our task becomes prescriptive rather than descriptive, as it were.'

'They all talk like this in Moscow Centre,' Rostov said irreverently. Vorontsov glared at him.

Hassan said, 'What action?'

'Rostov here is going to Odessa to board a Polish merchant ship called the *Karla*,' Vorontsov said. 'She's an ordinary cargo vessel superficially, but she's very fast and has certain extra equipment – we use her quite often.'

Rostov was staring up at the ceiling, an expression of

mild distaste on his face. Hassan guessed that Rostov wanted to keep some of these details from the Egyptians: perhaps that was what he and Vorontsov had been arguing about.

Vorontsov went on, 'Your job is to get an Egyptian vessel and make contact with the *Karla* in the Mediterranean.'

'And then?' Hassan said.

'We wait for Tyrin, aboard the *Coparelli*, to tell us when the Israeli hijack takes place. He will also tell us whether the uranium is transferred from the *Coparelli* to the *Stromberg*, or simply left aboard the *Coparelli* to be taken to Haifa and unloaded.'

'And then?' Hassan persisted.

Vorontsov began to speak, but Rostov forestalled him. 'I want you to tell Cairo a cover story,' he said to Hassan. 'I want your people to think that we don't know about the *Coparelli*, we just know the Israelis are planning something in the Mediterranean and we are still trying to discover what.'

Hassan nodded, keeping his face impassive. He had to know what the plan was, and Rostov did not want to tell him! He said, 'Yes, I'll tell them that – if you tell me the actual plan.'

Rostov looked at Voronstov and shrugged. Vorontsov said, 'After the hijack the *Karla* will set a course for Dickstein's ship, whichever one carries the uranium. The *Karla* will collide with that ship.'

'Collide!'

'Your ship will witness the collision, report it, and observe that the crew of the vessel are Israelis and their cargo is uranium. You will report these facts too. There will be an international inquiry into the collision. The presence of both Israelis and stolen uranium on the ship will be established beyond doubt. Meanwhile the uranium will be returned to its rightful owners and the Israelis will be covered with opprobrium.'

'The Israelis will fight,' Hassan said.

Rostov said, 'So much the better, with your ship there to see them attack us and help us beat them off.'

'It's a good plan,' said Vorontsov. 'It's simple. All they have to do is crash – the rest follows automatically.'

'Yes, it's a good plan,' Hassan said. It fitted in perfectly with the Fedayeen plan. Unlike Dickstein, Hassan knew that Tyrin was aboard the *Coparelli*. After the Fedayeen had hijacked the *Coparelli* and ambushed the Israelis, they could throw Tyrin and his radio into the sea, then Rostov would have no way of locating them.

But Hassan needed to know when and where Dickstein intended to carry out his hijack so that the Fedayeen could be sure of getting there first.

Vorontsov's office was hot. Hassan went to the window and looked down at the traffic on the Moscow ring road. 'We need to know exactly when and where Dickstein will hijack the *Coparelli*,' he said.

'Why?' Rostov asked, making a gesture with both arms spread, palms upward. 'We have Tyrin aboard the *Coparelli* and a beacon on the *Stromberg*. We know where both of them are at all times. We need only to stay close and move in when the time comes.'

'My ship has to be in the right area at the crucial time.'

'Then follow the *Stromberg*, staying just over the horizon – you can pick up her radio signal. Or keep in touch with me on the *Karla*. Or both.'

'Suppose the beacon fails, or Tyrin is discovered?'

Rostov said, 'The risk of that must be weighed against the danger of tipping our hand if we start following Dickstein around again – assuming we could find him.'

'He has a point, though,' Vorontsov said.

It was Rostov's turn to glare.

Hassan unbuttoned his collar. 'May I open a window?'

'They don't open,' said Vorontsov.

'Haven't you people heard of air-conditioning?'

'In Moscow?'

Hassan turned and spoke to Rostov. 'Think about it. I want to be perfectly sure we nail these people.'

'I've thought about it,' Rostov said. 'We're as sure as we can be. Go back to Cairo, organize that ship and stay in touch with me.'

You patronizing bastard, Hassan thought. He turned to Vorontsov. 'I cannot, in all honesty, tell my people I'm happy with the plan unless we can eliminate that remaining uncertainty.'

Vorontsov said, 'I agree with Hassan.'

'Well, I don't,' said Rostov. 'And the plan as it stands has already been approved by Andropov.'

Until now Hassan had thought he was going to have his way, since Vorontsov was on his side and Vorontsov was Rostov's boss. But the mention of the Chairman of the KGB seemed to constitute a winning move in this game: Vorontsov was almost cowed by it, and once again Hassan had to conceal his desperation.

Vorontsov said, 'The plan can be changed.'

'Only with Andropov's approval,' Rostov said. 'And you won't get my support for the change.'

Vorontsov's lips were compressed into a thin line. He hates Rostov, thought Hassan; and so do I.

Vorontsov said, 'Very well, then.'

In all his time in the intelligence business Hassan had been part of a professional team – Egyptian Intelligence, the KGB, even the Fedayeen. There had been other people, experienced and decisive people, to give him orders and guidance and to take ultimate responsibility. Now, as he left the KGB building to return to his hotel, he realized he was on his own.

Alone, he had to find a remarkably elusive and clever man and discover his most closely guarded secret.

For several days he was in a panic. He returned to Cairo, told them Rostov's cover story, and organized the Egyptian ship Rostov had requested. The problem stayed in front of his mind like a sheer cliff he could not begin to climb until he saw at least part of the route to the top. Unconsciously he searched back in his personal history for attitudes and approaches which would enable him to tackle such a task, to act independently.

He had to go a long way back.

Once upon a time Yasif Hassan had been a different

kind of man. He had been a wealthy, almost aristocratic young Arab with the world at his feet. He had gone about with the attitude that he could do more or less anything – and thinking had made it so. He had gone to study in England, an alien country, without a qualm; and he had entered its society without caring or even wondering what people thought of him.

There had been times, even then, when he had to learn; but he did that easily too. Once a fellow undergraduate, a Viscount something-or-other, had invited him down to the country to play polo. Hassan had never played polo. He had asked the rules and watched the others play for a while, noticing how they held the mallets, how they hit the ball, how they passed it and why; then he had joined in. He was clumsy with the mallet but he could ride like the wind: he played passably well, he thoroughly enjoyed the game, and his team won.

Now, in 1968, he said to himself: I can do anything, but whom shall I emulate?

The answer, of course, was David Rostov.

Rostov was independent, confident, capable, brilliant. He could find Dickstein, even when it seemed he was stumped, clueless, up a blind alley. He had done it twice. Hassan recalled:

Question: Why is Dickstein in Luxembourg?

Well, what do we know about Luxembourg? What is there here?

There is the stock exchange, the banks, the Council of Europe, Euratom –

Euratom!

Question: Dickstein has disappeared – where might he have gone?

Don't know.

But who do we know that he knows?

Only Professor Ashford in Oxford—

Oxford!

Rostov's approach was to search out bits of information – *any* information, no matter how trivial – in order to get on the target. The trouble was, they seemed to have used all the bits of information they had.

So I'll get some more, Hassan thought; I can do anything.

He racked his brains for all that he could remember from the time they had been at Oxford together. Dickstein had been in the war, he played chess, his clothes were shabby –

He had a mother.

But she had died.

Hassan had never met any brothers or sisters, no relatives of any sort. It was all such a long time ago, and they had not been very close even then.

There was, however, someone else who might know a little more about Dickstein: Professor Ashford.

So, in desperation, Yasif Hassan went back to Oxford.

All the way – in the plane from Cairo, the taxi from London airport to Paddington Station, the train to Oxford and the taxi to the little green-and-white house by the river – he wondered about Ashford. The truth was, he despised the professor. In his youth perhaps he had been an adventurer, but he had become a weak old man, a political dilettante, an academic who could not even hold his wife. One could not respect an old cuckold – and the fact that the English did not think like that only increased Hassan's contempt.

He worried that Ashford's weakness, together with some kind of loyalty to Dickstein as one who had been a friend and a student, might make him balk at getting involved.

He wondered whether to play up to the fact that Dickstein was Jewish. He knew from his time at Oxford that the most enduring anti-Semitism in England was that of the upper classes: the London clubs that still blackballed Jews were in the West End, not the East End. But Ashford was an exception there. He loved the Middle East, and his pro-Arab stance was ethical, not racial, in motivation. No: that approach would be a mistake.

In the end he decided to play it straight; to tell Ashford why he wanted to find Dickstein, and hope that Ashford would agree to help for the same reasons.

When they had shaken hands and poured sherry, they sat down in the garden and Ashford said, 'What brings you back to England so soon?'

Hassan told the truth. 'I'm chasing Nat Dickstein.'

They were sitting by the river in the little corner of the garden that was cut off by the hedge, where Hassan had kissed the beautiful Eila so many years ago. The corner was sheltered from the October wind, and there was a little autumn sunshine to warm them.

Ashford was guarded, wary, his face expressionless. 'I think you'd better tell me what's going on.'

Hassan observed that during the summer the professor had actually yielded a little to fashion. He had cultivated side-whiskers and allowed his monkish fringe of hair to grow long, and was wearing denim jeans with a wide leather belt beneath his old tweed jacket.

'I'll tell you,' Hassan said, with an awful feeling that Rostov would have been more subtle than this, 'but I must have your word that it will go no farther.'

'Agreed.'

'Dickstein is an Israeli spy.'

Ashford's eyes narrowed, but he said nothing.

Hassan plunged on. 'The Zionists are planning to make nuclear bombs but they have no plutonium. They need a secret supply of uranium to feed to their reactor to make plutonium. Dickstein's job is to steal that uranium – and my job is to find him and stop him. I want you to help me.'

Ashford stared into his sherry, then drained the glass at a gulp. 'There are two questions at issue here,' he said, and Hassan realized that Ashford was going to treat this as an intellectual problem, the characteristic defence of the frightened academic. 'One is whether or not I *can* help; the other, whether or not I *should.* The latter is prior, I think; morally, anyway.'

Hassan thought: I'd like to pick you up by the scruff

of the neck and shake you. Maybe I can do that, at least figuratively. He said, 'Of course you *should*. You believe in our cause.'

'It's not so simple. I'm asked to interfere in a contest between two people, both of whom are my friends.'

'But only one of them is in the right.'

'So I should help the one who is in the right – and betray the one who is in the wrong?'

'Of course.'

'There isn't any "of course" about it . . . What will you do, if and when you find Dickstein?'

'I'm with Egyptian Intelligence, professor. But my loyalty – and, I believe, yours – lies with Palestine.'

Ashford refused to take the bait. 'Go on,' he said noncommittally.

'I have to find out exactly when and where Dickstein plans to steal this uranium.' Hassan hesitated. 'The Fedayeen will get there before Dickstein and steal it for themselves.'

Ashford's eyes glittered. 'My God,' he said. 'How marvellous.'

He's almost there, Hassan thought. He's frightened, but he's excited too. 'It's easy for you to be loyal to Palestine, here in Oxford, giving lectures, going to meetings. Things are a little more difficult for those of us who are out there fighting for the country. I'm here to ask you to do something concrete about your politics, to decide whether your ideals mean anything or not. This is where you and I find out whether the Arab cause is anything more to you than a romantic concept. This is the test, professor.'

Ashford said, 'Perhaps you're right.'
And Hassan thought: I've got you.

Suza had decided to tell her father that she was in love
with Nat Dickstein.

At first she had not been sure of it herself, not really.
The few days they had spent together in London had
been wild and happy and loving, but afterwards she
had realized that those feelings could be transient. She
had resolved to make no resolutions. She would carry
on normally and see how things turned out.

Something had happened in Singapore to change
her mind. Two of the cabin stewards on the trip were
gay, and used only one of the two hotel rooms allotted
to them; so the crew could use the other room for a
party. At the party the pilot had made a pass at Suza.
He was a quiet, smiling blond man with delicate bones
and a delightfully wacky sense of humour. The steward-
esses all agreed he was a piece of ass. Normally Suza
would have got into bed with him without thinking
twice. But she had said no, astonishing the whole crew.
Thinking about it later, she decided that she no longer
wanted to get laid. She had just gone off the whole
idea. All she wanted was Nathaniel. It was like . . . it was
a bit like five years ago when the second Beatles album
came out, and she had gone through her pile of records
by Elvis and Roy Orbison and the Everly Brothers and
realized that she did not want to play them, they held
no more enchantment for her, the old familiar tunes
had been heard once too often, and now she wanted

music of a higher order. Well, it was a bit like that, but more so.

Dickstein's letter had been the clincher. It had been written God knew where and posted at Orly Airport, Paris. In his small neat handwriting with its incongruously curly loops on the *g* and *y* he had poured out his heart in a manner that was all the more devastating because it came from a normally taciturn man. She had cried over that letter.

She wished she could think of a way to explain all that to her father.

She knew that he disapproved of Israelis. Dickstein was an old student, and her father had been genuinely pleased to see him and prepared to overlook the fact that the old student was on the enemy side. But now she planned to make Dickstein a permanent part of her life, a member of the family. His letter said, 'For ever is what I want,' and Suza could hardly wait to tell him, 'Oh, yes; me, too.'

She thought both sides were in the wrong in the Middle East. The plight of the refugees was unjust and pitiful, but she thought they ought to set about making themselves new homes – it was not easy, but it was easier than war, and she despised the theatrical heroics which so many Arab men found irresistible. On the other hand, it was clear that the whole damn mess was originally the fault of the Zionists, who had taken over a country that belonged to other people. Such a cynical view had no appeal for her father, who saw Right on one side and Wrong on the other, and the beautiful ghost of his wife on the side of Right.

It would be hard for him. She had long ago scotched his dreams of walking up the aisle with his daughter beside him in a white wedding dress; but he still talked occasionally of her settling down and giving him a granddaughter. The idea that this grandchild might be Israeli would come as a terrible blow.

Still, that was the price of being a parent, Suza thought as she entered the house. She called, 'Daddy, I'm home,' as she took off her coat and put down her airline bag. There was no reply, but his briefcase was in the hall: he must be in the garden. She put the kettle on and walked out of the kitchen and down toward the river, still searching in her mind for the right words with which to tell him her news. Maybe she should begin by talking about her trip, and gradually work around—

She heard voices as she approached the hedge.

'And what will you do with him?' It was her father's voice.

Suza stopped, wondering whether she ought to interrupt or not.

'Just follow him,' said another voice, a strange one. 'Dickstein must not be killed until afterwards, of course.'

She put her hand over her mouth to stifle a gasp of horror. Then, terrified, she turned around and ran, soft-footed, back to the house.

'Well, now,' said Professor Ashford, 'following what we might call the Rostov Method, let us recall everything we know about Nat Dickstein.'

Do it any way you want, Hassan thought, but for God's sake come up with *something*.

Ashford went on: 'He was born in the East End of London. His father died when he was a boy. What about the mother?'

'She's dead, too, according to our files.'

'Ah. Well, he went into the army midway through the war – 1943, I think it was. Anyway he was in time to be part of the attack on Sicily. He was taken prisoner soon afterwards, about halfway up the leg of Italy, I can't remember the place. It was rumoured – you'll remember this, I'm sure – that he had a particularly bad time in the concentration camps, being Jewish. After the war he came here. He—'

'Sicily,' Hassan interrupted.

'Yes?'

'Sicily is mentioned in his file. He is supposed to have been involved in the theft of a boatload of guns. Our people had bought the guns from a gang of criminals in Sicily.'

'If we are to believe what we read in the newspapers,' said Ashford, 'there is only one gang of criminals in Sicily.'

Hassan added, 'Our people suspected that the hijackers had bribed the Sicilians for a tip-off.'

'Wasn't it Sicily where he saved that man's life?'

Hassan wondered what Ashford was talking about. He controlled his impatience, thinking: Let him ramble – that's the whole idea. 'He saved someone's life?'

'The American. Don't you remember? I've never forgotten it. Dickstein brought the man here. A rather brutish G.I. He told me the whole story, right here at this house. Now we're getting somewhere. You must have met the man, you were here that day, don't you remember?'

'I can't say I do,' Hassan muttered. He was embarrassed . . . he had probably been in the kitchen feeling Eila up.

'It was . . . unsettling,' Ashford said. He stared at the slowly moving water as his mind went back twenty years, and his face was shadowed by sadness for a moment, as if he were remembering his wife. Then he said, 'Here we all were, a gathering of academics and students, probably discussing atonal music or existentialism while we sipped our sherry, when in came a big soldier and started talking about snipers and tanks and blood and death. It cast a real chill: that's why I recall it so clearly. He said his family originated in Sicily, and his cousins had fêted Dickstein after the life-saving incident. Did you say a Sicilian gang had tipped off Dickstein about the boatload of guns?'

'It's possible, that's all.'

'Perhaps he didn't have to bribe them.'

Hassan shook his head. This was information, the kind of trivial information Rostov always seemed to make something of – but how was he going to use it? 'I don't see what use all this is going to be to us,' he said. 'How could Dickstein's ancient hijack be connected with the Mafia?'

'The Mafia,' said Ashford. 'That's the word I was looking for. And the man's name was Cortone – Tony Cortone – no, Al Cortone, from Buffalo. I told you, I remember every detail.'

'But the connection?' Hassan said impatiently.

Ashford shrugged. 'Simply this. Once before Dickstein used his connection with Cortone to call on the Sicilian Mafia for help with an act of piracy in the Mediterranean. People repeat their youth, you know: he may do the same thing again.'

Hassan began to see: and, as enlightenment dawned, so did hope. It was a long shot, a guess, but it made sense, the chance was real, maybe he could catch up with Dickstein again.

Ashford looked pleased with himself. 'It's a nice piece of speculative reasoning – I wish I could publish it, with footnotes.'

'I wonder,' said Hassan longingly. 'I wonder.'

'It's getting cool, let's go into the house.'

As they walked up the garden Hassan thought fleetingly that he had not learned to be like Rostov; he had merely found in Ashford a substitute. Perhaps his former proud independence had gone for ever. There was something unmanly about it. He wondered if the other Fedayeen felt the same way, and if that was why they were so bloodthirsty.

Ashford said, 'The trouble is, I don't suppose Cortone will tell you anything, whatever he knows.'

'Would he tell you?'

'Why should he? He'll hardly remember me. Now, if Eila were alive, she could have gone to see him and told him some story . . .'

'Well . . .' Hassan wished Eila would stay out of the conversation. 'I'll have to try myself.'

They entered the house. Stepping into the kitchen,

they saw Suza; and then they looked at each other and knew they had found the answer.

By the time the two men came into the house Suza had almost convinced herself that she had been mistaken when, in the garden, she thought she heard them talk about killing Nat Dickstein. It was simply unreal: the garden, the river, the autumn sunshine, a professor and his guest . . . murder had no place there, the whole idea was fantastic, like a polar bear in the Sahara Desert. Besides, there was a very good psychological explanation for her mistake: she had been planning to tell her father that she loved Dickstein, and she had been afraid of his reaction – Freud could probably have predicted that at that point she might well imagine her father plotting to kill her lover.

Because she nearly believed this reasoning, she was able to smile brightly at them and say, 'Who wants coffee? I've just made some.'

Her father kissed her cheek. 'I didn't realize you were back, my dear.'

'I just arrived, I was thinking of coming out to look for you.' Why am I telling these lies?

'You don't know Yasif Hassan – he was one of my students when you were very small.'

Hassan kissed her hand and stared at her the way people always did when they had known Eila. 'You're every bit as beautiful as your mother,' he said, and his voice was not flirtatious at all, not even flattering: it sounded amazed.

Her father said, 'Yasif was here a few months ago, shortly after a contemporary of his visited us – Nat Dickstein. You met Dickstein, I think, but you were away by the time Yasif came.'

'Was there any connec-connection?' she asked, and silently cursed her voice for cracking on the last word.

The two men looked at one another, and her father said, 'Matter of fact, there was.'

And then she knew it was true, she had not misheard, they really were going to kill the only man she had ever loved. She felt dangerously close to tears, and turned away from them to fiddle with cups and saucers.

'I want to ask you to do something, my dear,' said her father. 'Something very important, for the sake of your mother's memory. Sit down.'

No more, she thought; this can't get worse, please.

She took a deep breath, turned around, and sat down facing him.

He said, 'I want you to help Yasif here to find Nat Dickstein.'

From that moment she hated her father. She knew then suddenly, instantly, that his love for her was fraudulent, that he had never seen her as a person, that he used her as he had used her mother. Never again would she take care of him, serve him; never again would she worry about how he felt, whether he was lonely, what he needed . . . She realized, in the same flash of insight and hatred, that her mother had reached this same point with him, at some time; and that she would now do what Eila had done, and despise him.

Ashford continued, 'There is a man in America who may know where Dickstein is. I want you to go there with Yasif and ask this man.'

She said nothing. Hassan took her blankness for incomprehension, and began to explain. 'You see, this Dickstein is an Israeli agent, working against our people. We must stop him. Cortone – the man in Buffalo – may be helping him, and if he is he will not help us. But he will remember your mother, and so he may cooperate with you. You could tell him that you and Dickstein are lovers.'

'Ha-hah!' Suza's laugh was faintly hysterical, and she hoped they would assume the wrong reasons for it. She controlled herself, and managed to become numb, to keep her body still and her face expressionless, while they told her about the yellowcake, and the man aboard the *Coparelli*, and the radio beacon on the *Stromberg*, and about Mahmoud and his hijack plan, and how much it would all mean for the Palestine liberation movement; and at the end she was numb, she no longer had to pretend.

Finally her father said, 'So, my dear, will you help? Will you do it?'

With an effort of self-control that astonished her, she gave them a bright air-hostess smile, got up from her stool, and said, 'It's a lot to take in in one go, isn't it? I'll think about it while I'm in the bath.'

And she went out.

*

It all sank in, gradually, as she lay in the hot water with a locked door between her and them.

So this was the thing that Nathaniel had to do before he could see her again: steal a ship. And then, he had said, he would not let her out of his sight for ten or fifteen years . . . Perhaps that meant he could give up this work.

But, of course, none of his plans was going to succeed, because his enemies knew all about them. This Russian planned to ram Nat's ship, and Hassan planned to steal the ship first and ambush Nat. Either way Dickstein was in danger; either way they wanted to destroy him. Suza could warn him.

If only she knew where he was.

How little those men downstairs knew about her! Hassan simply assumed, just like an Arab male chauvinist pig, that she would do as she was told. Her father assumed she would take the Palestinian side, because he did and he was the brains of the family. He had never known what was in his daughter's mind: for that matter, he had been the same with his wife. Eila had always been able to deceive him: he never suspected that she might not be what she seemed.

When Suza realized what she had to do, she was terrified all over again.

There was, after all, a way she might find Nathaniel and warn him.

'Find Nat' was what *they* wanted her to do.

She knew she could deceive them, for they already assumed she was on their side, when she was not.

So she could do what they wanted. She could find Nat – and then she could warn him.

Would she be making things worse? To find him herself, she had to lead them to him.

But even if Hassan did not find him, Nat was in danger from the Russian.

And if he was forewarned, he could escape both dangers.

Perhaps, too, she could get rid of Hassan somehow, before she actually reached Nat.

What was the alternative? To wait, to go on as if nothing had happened, to hope for a phone call that might never come . . . It was, she realized, partly her need to see Dickstein again that made her think like this, partly the thought that after the hijack he might be dead, that this might be her last chance. But there were good reasons, too: by doing nothing she might help frustrate Hassan's scheme, but that still left the Russians and their scheme.

Her decision was made. She would pretend to work with Hassan so that she could find Nathaniel.

She was peculiarly happy. She was trapped, but she felt free; she was obeying her father, yet she felt that at last she was defying him; for better or worse, she was committed to Nathaniel.

She was also very, very frightened.

She got out of the bath, dried herself, dressed, and went downstairs to tell them the good news.

*

At four A.M. on November 16, 1968, the *Coparelli* hove to at Vlissingen, on the Dutch coast, and took on board a port pilot to guide her through the channel of the Westerschelde to Antwerp. Four hours later, at the entrance to the harbour, she took on another pilot to negotiate her passage through the docks. From the main harbour she went through Royers Lock, along the Suez Canal, under the Siberia Bridge and into Kattendijk Dock, where she tied up at her berth.

Nat Dickstein was watching.

When he saw her sweep slowly in, and read the name *Coparelli* on her side, and thought of the drums of yellowcake that would soon fill her belly, he was overcome by a most peculiar feeling, like the one he had when he looked at Suza's naked body . . . yes, almost like lust.

He looked away from berth No. 42 to the railway line, which ran almost to the edge of the quay. There was a train on the line now, consisting of eleven cars and an engine. Ten of the cars carried fifty-one 200-litre drums with sealed lids and the word PLUMBAT stencilled on the side; the eleventh car had only fifty drums. He was so close to those drums, to that uranium; he could stroll over and touch the railway cars – he already had done this once, earlier in the morning, and had thought: Wouldn't it be terrific just to raid this place with choppers and a bunch of Israeli commandos and simply *steal* the stuff.

The *Coparelli* was scheduled for a fast turnaround. The port authorities had been convinced that the yellowcake could be handled safely, but all the same they did not want the stuff hanging about their harbour one minute longer than necessary. There was a crane standing by ready to load the drums on to the ship.

Nevertheless, there were formalities to be completed before loading could begin.

The first person Dickstein saw boarding the ship was an official from the shipping company. He had to give the pilots their *pourboire* and secure from the captain a crew list for the harbour police.

The second person aboard was Josef Cohen. He was here for the sake of customer relations: he would give the captain a bottle of whisky and sit down for a drink with him and the shipping company official. He also had a wad of tickets for free entry and one drink at the best nightclub in town, which he would give to the captain for the officers. And he would discover the name of the ship's engineer. Dickstein had suggested he do this by asking to see the crew list, then counting out one ticket for each officer on the list.

Whatever way he had decided to do it, he had been successful: as he left the ship and crossed the quay to return to his office he passed Dickstein and muttered, 'The engineer's name is Sarne,' without breaking stride.

It was not until afternoon that the crane went into action and the dockers began loading the drums into the three holds of the *Coparelli*. The drums had to be moved one at a time, and inside the ship each drum had to be secured with wedges of wood. As expected, the loading was not completed that day.

In the evening Dickstein went to the best nightclub in town. Sitting at the bar, close to the telephone, was a quite astonishing woman of about thirty, with black hair and a long, aristocratic face possessed of a faintly haughty expression. She wore an elegant black dress which made the most of her sensational legs and her high, round breasts. Dickstein gave her an almost imperceptible nod but did not speak to her.

He sat in a corner, nursing a glass of beer, hoping the sailors would come. Surely they would. Did sailors ever refuse a free drink?

Yes.

The club began to fill up. The woman in the black dress was propositioned a couple of times but refused both men, thereby establishing that she was not a hooker. At nine o'clock Dickstein went out to the lobby and phoned Cohen. By previous arrangement, Cohen had called the captain of the *Coparelli* on a pretext. He now told Dickstein what he had discovered: that all but two of the officers were using their free tickets. The exceptions were the captain himself, who was busy with paperwork, and the radio operator – a new man they had taken on in Cardiff after Lars broke his leg – who had a head cold.

Dickstein then dialled the number of the club he was in. He asked to speak to Mr Sarne, who, he understood, would be found in the bar. While he waited he could hear a barman calling out Sarne's name: it came to him two ways, one directly from the bar, the other through several miles of telephone cable. Eventually he heard, over the phone, a voice say, 'Yes? Hello? This is Sarne. Is anybody there? Hello?'

Dickstein hung up and walked quickly back into the bar. He looked over to where the bar phone was. The woman in the black dress was speaking to a tall, suntanned blond man in his thirties whom Dickstein had seen on the quay earlier that day. So this was Sarne.

The woman smiled at Sarne. It was a nice smile, a smile to make any man look twice: it was warm and red-lipped, showing even, white teeth, and it was accompanied by a certain languid half-closing of the eyes, which was very sexy and looked not at all as though it had been rehearsed a thousand times in front of a mirror.

Dickstein watched, spellbound. He had very little idea how this sort of thing worked, how men picked up women and women picked up men, and he understood even less how a woman could pick up a man while letting the man believe *he* was doing the picking up.

Sarne had his own charm, it seemed. He gave her his smile, a grin with something wickedly boyish in it that made him look ten years younger. He said something to her, and she smiled again. He hesitated, like a man who wants to talk some more but cannot think of anything to say; then, to Dickstein's horror, he turned away to go.

The woman was equal to this: Dickstein need not have worried. She touched the sleeve of Sarne's blazer, and he turned back to her. A cigarette had suddenly appeared in her hand. Sarne slapped his pockets for matches. Apparently he did not smoke. Dickstein groaned inwardly. The woman took a lighter from the evening bag on the bar in front of her and handed it to him. He lit her cigarette.

Dickstein could not go away, or watch from a distance; he would have a nervous breakdown. He had to listen. He pushed his way through the bar and stood behind Sarne, who was facing the woman. Dickstein ordered another beer.

The woman's voice was warm and inviting, Dickstein knew already, but now she was really using it. Some women had bedroom eyes, she had a bedroom voice.

Sarne was saying, 'This kind of thing is always happening to me.'

'The phone call?' the woman said.

Sarne nodded. 'Woman trouble. I hate women. All my life, women have caused me pain and suffering. I wish I were a homosexual.'

Dickstein was astonished. What was he saying? Did he mean it? Was he trying to give her the brush-off?

She said, 'Why don't you become one?'

'I don't fancy men.'

'Be a monk.'

'Well, you see, I have this other problem, this insatiable sexual appetite. I have to get laid, all the time, often several times a night. It's a great problem to me. Would you like a fresh drink?'

Ah. It was a line of chat. How did he think it up? Dickstein supposed that sailors did this sort of thing all the time, they had it down to a fine art.

It went on that way. Dickstein had to admire the way the woman led Sarne by the nose while letting him think he was making the running. She told him she was stopping over in Antwerp just for the night, and let him know she had a room in a good hotel. Before long he said they should have champagne, but the champagne sold in the club was very poor stuff, not like they might be able to get somewhere else; at a hotel, say; her hotel, for example.

They left when the floor show started. Dickstein was pleased: so far, so good. He watched a line of girls kicking their legs for ten minutes, then he went out.

He took a cab to the hotel and went up to the room. He stood close to the communicating door which led through to the next room. He heard the woman giggle and Sarne say something in a low voice.

Dickstein sat on the bed and checked the cylinder of gas. He turned the tap on and off quickly, and got a sharp whiff of sweetness from the face mask. It had no effect on him. He wondered how much you had to breathe before it worked. He had not had time to try out the stuff properly.

The noises from the next room became louder, and Dickstein began to feel embarrassed. He wondered how conscientious Sarne was. Would he want to go back to his ship as soon as he had finished with the woman? That would be awkward. It would mean a fight in the hotel corridor – unprofessional, risky.

Dickstein waited – tense, embarrassed. anxious. The woman was good at her trade. She knew Dickstein wanted Sarne to sleep afterwards, and she was trying to tire him. It seemed to take for ever.

It was past two A.M. when she knocked on the

communicating door. The code was three slow knocks to say he was asleep, six fast knocks to say he was leaving.

She knocked three times, slowly.

Dickstein opened the door. Carrying the gas cylinder in one hand and the face mask in the other, he walked softly into the next room.

Sarne lay flat on his back, naked, his blond hair mussed, his mouth wide open, his eyes closed. His body looked fit and strong. Dickstein went close and listened to his breathing. He breathed in, then all the way out – then, just as he began to inhale again, Dickstein turned on the tap and clapped the mask over the sleeping man's nose and mouth.

Sarne's eyes opened wide. Dickstein held the mask on more firmly. Half a breath: incomprehension in Sarne's eyes. The breath turned into a gasp, and Sarne moved his head, failed to weaken Dickstein's grip, and began to thrash about. Dickstein leaned on the sailor's chest with an elbow, thinking: For God's sake, this is too slow!

Sarne breathed out. The confusion in his eyes had turned to fear and panic. He gasped again, about to increase his struggles. Dickstein thought of calling the woman to help hold him down. But the second inhalation defeated its purpose: the struggles were perceptibly weaker; the eyelids fluttered and closed; and by the time he exhaled the second breath, he was asleep.

It had taken about three seconds. Dickstein relaxed. Sarne would probably never remember it. He gave him a little more of the gas to make sure, then he stood up.

He looked at the woman. She was wearing shoes.

stockings, and garters; nothing else. She looked ravishing. She caught his gaze, and opened her arms, offering herself: at your service, sir. Dickstein shook his head with a regretful smile that was only partly disingenuous.

He sat in the chair beside the bed and watched her dress: skimpy panties, soft brassiere, jewellery, dress, coat, bag. She came to him, and he gave her eight thousand Dutch guilders. She kissed his cheek, then she kissed the banknotes. She went out without speaking.

Dickstein went to the window. A few minutes later he saw the headlights of her sports car as it went past the front of the hotel, heading back to Amsterdam.

He sat down to wait, again. After a while he began to feel sleepy. He went into the next room and ordered coffee from room service.

In the morning Cohen phoned to say the first officer of the *Coparelli* was searching the bars, brothels and flophouses of Antwerp for his engineer.

At twelve-thirty Cohen phoned again. The captain had called him to say that all the cargo was now loaded and he was without an engineer officer. Cohen had said, 'Captain, it's your lucky day.'

At two-thirty Cohen called to say he had seen Dieter Koch aboard the *Coparelli* with his kitbag over his shoulder.

Dickstein gave Sarne a little more gas each time he showed signs of waking. He administered the last dose at six A.M. the following day, then he paid the bill for the two rooms and left.

*

When Sarne finally woke up he found that the woman he had slept with had gone without saying goodbye. He also found he was massively, ravenously hungry.

During the course of the morning he discovered that he had been asleep not for one night, as he had imagined, but for two nights and the day in between.

He had an insistent feeling in the back of his mind that there was something remarkable he had forgotten, but he never found out what had happened to him during that lost twenty-four hours.

Meanwhile, on Sunday, November 17, 1968, the *Coparelli* had sailed.

CHAPTER FOURTEEN

WHAT SUZA should have done was phone any Israeli embassy and give them a message for Nat Dickstein.

This thought occurred to her an hour after she had told her father that she would help Hassan. She was packing a case at the time, and she immediately picked up the phone in her bedroom to call Inquiries for the number. But her father came in and asked her whom she was calling. She said the airport, and he said he would take care of that.

Thereafter she constantly looked for an opportunity to make a clandestine call, but there was none. Hassan was with her every minute. They drove to the airport, caught the plane, changed at Kennedy for a flight to Buffalo, and went straight to Cortone's house.

During the journey she came to loathe Yasif Hassan. He made endless vague boasts about his work for the Fedayeen; he smiled oilily and put his hand on her knee; he hinted that he and Eila had been more than friends, and that he would like to be more than friends with Suza. She told him that Palestine would not be free until its women were free; and that Arab men had to learn the difference between being manly and being porcine. That shut him up.

They had some trouble discovering Cortone's address – Suza half hoped they would fail – but in the end they found a taxi driver who knew the house. Suza was dropped off; Hassan would wait for her half a mile down the road.

The house was large, surrounded by a high wall, with guards at the gate. Suza said she wanted to see Cortone, that she was a friend of Nat Dickstein.

She had given a lot of thought to what she should say to Cortone: should she tell him all or only part of the truth? Suppose he knew, or could find out, where Dickstein was: why should he tell her? She would say Dickstein was in danger, she had to find him and warn him. What reason did Cortone have to believe her? She would charm him – she knew how to do that with men his age – but he would still be suspicious.

She wanted to explain to Cortone the complete picture: that she was looking for Nat to warn him, but she was also being used by his enemies to lead them to him, that Hassan was half a mile down the road in a taxi waiting for her. But then he would certainly never tell her anything.

She found it very difficult to think clearly about all this. There were so many deceits and double deceits involved. And she wanted so badly to see Nathaniel's face and speak to him herself.

She still had not decided what to say when the guard opened the gate for her, then led her up the gravel drive to the house. It was a beautiful place, but rather overripe, as if a decorator had furnished it lavishly then the owners had added a lot of expensive junk of their own choosing. There seemed to be a lot of servants. One of them led Suza upstairs, telling her that Mr Cortone was having late breakfast in his bedroom.

When she walked in Cortone was sitting at a small table, digging into eggs and homefries. He was a fat man, completely bald. Suza had no memory of him from the time he had visited Oxford, but he must have looked very different then.

He glanced at her, then stood upright with a look of terror on his face and shouted: 'You should be old!' and then his breakfast went down the wrong way and he began to cough and splutter.

The servant grabbed Suza from behind, pinning her arms in a painful grip; then let her go and went to pound Cortone on the back. 'What did you do?' he yelled at her. 'What did you do, for Christ's sake?'

In a peculiar way this farce helped calm her a little. She could not be terrified of a man who had been so terrified of her. She rode the wave of confidence, sat down at his table and poured herself coffee. When Cortone stopped coughing she said, 'She was my mother.'

'My God,' Cortone said. He gave a last cough, then waved the servant away and sat down again 'You're so like her, hell, you scared me half to death.' He screwed up his eyes, remembering. 'Would you have been about four or five years old, back in, um, 1947?'

'That's right.'

'Hell, I remember you, you had a ribbon in your hair. And now you and Nat are an item.'

She said, 'So he has been here.' Her heart leaped with joy.

'Maybe,' Cortone said. His friendliness vanished. She realized he would not be easy to manipulate.

She said, 'I want to know where he is.'

'And I want to know who sent you here.'

'Nobody sent me.' Suza collected her thoughts, struggling to hide her tension. 'I guessed he might have come to you for help with this . . . project he's working on. The thing is, the Arabs know about it, and they'll kill him, and I have to warn him . . . Please, if you know where he is, please help me.'

She was suddenly close to tears, but Cortone was unmoved. 'Helping you is easy,' he said. 'Trusting you is the hard part.' He unwrapped a cigar and lit it, taking his time. Suza watched in an agony of impatience. He looked away from her and spoke almost to himself. 'You know, there was a time when I'd just see something I wanted and I'd grab it. It's not so simple any more. Now I've got all these complications. I got to make choices, and none of them are what I really want. I don't know whether it's the way things are now or if it's me.'

He turned again and faced her. 'I owe Dickstein my life. Now I have a chance to save his, if you're telling the truth. This is a debt of honour. I have to pay it myself, in person. So what do I do?' He paused.

Suza held her breath.

'Dickstein is in a wreck of a house somewhere on the Mediterranean. It's a ruin, hasn't been lived in for years, so there's no phone there. I could send a message, but I couldn't be sure it would get there, and like I said, I have to do this myself, in person.'

He drew on the cigar. 'I could tell you where to go look for him, but you just might pass the information on to the wrong people. I won't take that risk.'

'What, then?' Suza said in a high-pitched voice. 'We have to help him!'

'I know that,' Cortone said imperturbably. 'So I'm going there myself.'

'Oh!' Suza was taken by surprise: it was a possibility she had never considered.

'And what about you?' he went on. 'I'm not going to tell you where I'm headed, but you could still have people follow me. I need to keep you real close from now on. Let's face it, you could be playing it both ways. So I'm taking you with me.'

She stared at him. Tension drained out of her in a flood, she slumped in her chair. 'Oh, thank you,' she said. Then, at last, she cried.

They flew first class. Cortone always did. After the meal Suza left him to go to the toilet. She looked through the curtain into economy, hoping against hope, but she was disappointed: there was Hassan's wary brown face staring at her over the rows of headrests.

She looked into the galley and spoke to the chief

steward in a confiding voice. She had a problem, she said. She needed to contact her boyfriend but she couldn't get away from her Italian father, who wanted her to wear iron knickers until she was twenty-one. Would he phone the Israeli consulate in Rome and leave a message for a Nathaniel Dickstein? Just say, Hassan has told me everything, and he and I are coming to see you. She gave him money for the phone call, far too much, it was a way of tipping him. He wrote the message down and promised.

She went back to Cortone. Bad news, she said. One of the Arabs was back there in economy. He must be following us.

Cortone cursed, then told her never mind, the man would just have to be taken care of later.

Suza thought: Oh, God, what have I done?

From the big house on the clifftop Dickstein went down a long zigzag flight of steps cut into the rock to the beach. He splashed through the shallows to a waiting motorboat, jumped in and nodded to the man at the wheel.

The engine roared and the boat surged through the waves out to sea. The sun had just set. In the last faint light the clouds were massing above, obscuring the stars as soon as they appeared. Dickstein was deep in thought, racking his brains for things he had not done, precautions he might yet take, loopholes he still had time to close. He went over his plan again and again in his mind, like a man who has learned by heart an important speech he must make but still wishes it were better.

The high shadow of the *Stromberg* loomed ahead, and the boatman brought the little vessel around in a foamy arc to stop alongside, where a rope ladder dangled in the water. Dickstein scrambled up the ladder and on to the deck.

The ship's master shook his hand and introduced himself. Like all the officers aboard the *Stromberg*, he was borrowed from the Israeli Navy.

They took a turn around the deck. Dickstein said, 'Any problems, captain?'

'She's not a good ship,' the captain said. 'She's slow, clumsy and old. But we've got her in good shape.'

From what Dickstein could see in the twilight the *Stromberg* was in better condition than her sister ship the *Coparelli* had been in Antwerp. She was clean, and everything on deck looked squared away, shipshape.

They went up to the bridge, looked over the powerful equipment in the radio room, then went down to the mess, where the crew were finishing dinner. Unlike the officers, the ordinary seamen were all Mossad agents, most with a little experience of the sea. Dickstein had worked with some of them before. They were all, he observed, at least ten years younger than he. They were bright-eyed, well-built, dressed in a peculiar assortment of denims and homemade sweaters: all tough, humorous, well-trained men.

Dickstein took a cup of coffee and sat at one of the tables. He outranked all these men by a long way, but there was not much bull in the Israeli armed forces, and even less in the Mossad. The four men at the table nodded and said hello. Ish, a gloomy Palestine-born Israeli with a dark complexion, said, 'The weather's changing.'

'Don't say that. I was planning to get a tan on this cruise.' The speaker was a lanky ash-blond New Yorker named Feinberg, a deceptively pretty-faced man with eyelashes women envied. Calling this assignment a 'cruise' was already a standing joke. In his briefing earlier in the day Dickstein had said the *Coparelli* would be almost deserted when they hijacked it. 'Soon after she passes through the Strait of Gibraltar,' he had told them, 'her engines will break down. The damage will be such that it can't be repaired at sea. The captain cables the owners to that effect – and we are now the owners. By an apparently lucky coincidence, another of our ships will be close by. She's the *Gil Hamilton*, now moored across the bay here. She will go to the *Coparelli* and take off the whole crew except for the engineer. Then she's out of the picture: she'll go to her next port of call, where the crew of the *Coparelli* will be let off and given their train fares home.'

They had had the day to think about the briefing, and Dickstein was expecting questions. Now Levi Abbas, a short, solid man 'built like a tank and about as handsome,' Feinberg had said, asked Dickstein, 'You didn't tell us how come you're so sure the *Coparelli* will break down when you want her to.'

'Ah.' Dickstein sipped his coffee. 'Do you know Dieter Koch, in naval intelligence?'

Feinberg knew him.

'He's the *Coparelli*'s engineer.'

Abbas nodded. 'Which is also how come we know we'll be able to repair the *Coparelli*. We know what's going to go wrong.'

'Right.'

Abbas went on. 'We paint out the name *Coparelli*, rename her *Stromberg*, switch log books, scuttle the old *Stromberg* and sail the *Coparelli*, now called the *Stromberg*, to Haifa with the cargo. But why not transfer the cargo from one ship to the other at sea? We have cranes.'

'That was my original idea,' Dickstein said. 'It was too risky. I couldn't guarantee it would be possible, especially in bad weather.'

'We could still do it if the good weather holds.'

'Yes, but now that we have identical sister ships it will be easier to switch names than cargoes.'

Ish said lugubriously, 'Anyway, the good weather won't hold.'

The fourth man at the table was Porush, a crewcut youngster with a chest like a barrel of ale, who happened to be married to Abbas's sister. He said, 'If it's going to be so easy, what are all of us tough guys doing here?'

Dickstein said, 'I've been running around the world for the past six months setting up this thing. Once or twice I've bumped into people from the other side – inevitably. I don't *think* they know what we're about to do . . . but if they do, we may find out just how tough we are.'

One of the officers came in with a piece of paper

and approached Dickstein. 'Signal from Tel Aviv, sir. The *Coparelli* just passed Gibraltar.'

'That's it,' said Dickstein, standing up. 'We sail in the morning.'

Suza Ashford and Al Cortone changed planes in Rome and arrived in Sicily early in the morning. Two of Cortone's cousins were at the airport to meet him. There was a long argument between them: not acrimonious, but nevertheless loudly excitable. Suza could not follow the rapid dialect properly, but she gathered the cousins wanted to accompany Cortone and he was insisting that this was something he had to do alone because it was a debt of honour.

Cortone seemed to win the argument. They left the airport, without the cousins, in a big white Fiat. Suza drove. Cortone directed her on to the coast road. For the hundredth time she played over in her mind the reunion scene with Nathaniel: she saw his slight, angular body; he looked up; he recognized her and his face split in a smile of joy; she ran to him; they threw their arms around each other; he squeezed her so hard it hurt; she said, 'Oh, I love you,' and kissed his cheek, his nose, his mouth. But she was guilty and frightened too, and there was another scene she played less often in which he stared at her stony-faced and said, 'What the hell do you think you're doing here?'

It was a little like the time she had behaved badly on Christmas Eve, and her mother got angry and told her Santa Claus would put stones in her Christmas stocking instead of toys and candy. She had not known whether to believe this or not, and she had lain awake, alternately wishing for and dreading the morning.

She glanced across at Cortone in the seat beside her. The transatlantic journey tired him. Suza found it difficult to think of him as being the same age as Nat, he was so fat and bald and . . . well, he had an air of weary depravity that might have been amusing but in fact was merely elderly.

The island was pretty when the sun came out. Suza looked at the scenery, trying to distract herself so that the time would pass more quickly. The road twisted along the edge of the sea from town to town, and on her right-hand side there were views of rocky beaches and the sparkling Mediterranean.

Cortone lit a cigar. 'I used to do this kind of thing a lot when I was young,' he said. 'Get on a plane, go somewhere with a pretty girl, drive around, see places. Not any more. I've been stuck in Buffalo for years, it seems like. That's the thing with business – you get rich, but there's always something to worry about. So you never go places, you have people come to you, bring you stuff. You get too lazy to have fun.'

'You chose it,' Suza said. She felt more sympathy for Cortone than she showed: he was a man who had worked hard for all the wrong things.

'I chose it,' Cortone admitted. 'Young people have no mercy.' He gave a rare half smile and puffed on his cigar.

For the third time Suza saw the same blue car in her

rearview mirror. 'We're being followed,' she said, trying to keep her voice calm and normal.

'The Arab?'

'Must be.' She could not see the face behind the windshield. 'What will we do? You said you'd handle it.'

'I will.'

He was silent. Expecting him to say more, Suza glanced across at him. He was loading a pistol with ugly brown-black bullets. She gasped: she had never seen a real-life gun.

Cortone looked up at her, then ahead. 'Christ, watch the goddamn road!'

She looked ahead, and braked hard for a sharp bend. 'Where did you get that thing?' she said.

'From my cousin.'

Suza felt more and more as if she were in a nightmare. She had not slept in a bed for four days. From the moment when she had heard her father talking so calmly about killing Nathaniel she had been running: fleeing from the awful truth about Hassan and her father, to the safety of Dickstein's wiry arms; and, as in a nightmare, the destination seemed to recede as fast as she ran.

'Why don't you tell me where we're going?' she asked Cortone.

'I guess I can, now. Nat asked me for the loan of a house with a mooring and protection from snooping police. We're going to that house.'

Suza's heart beat faster. 'How far?'

'Couple of miles.'

A minute later Cortone said, 'We'll get there, don't rush, we don't want to die on the way.'

She realized she had unconsciously put her foot down. She eased off the accelerator but she could not slow her thoughts. Any minute now, to see him and touch his face, to kiss him hello, to feel his hands on her shoulders—

'Turn in there, on the right.'

She drove through an open gateway and along a short gravel drive overgrown with weeds to a large ruined villa of white stone. When she pulled up in front of the pillared portico she expected Nathaniel to come running out to greet her.

There were no signs of life on this side of the house.

They got out of the car and climbed the broken stone staircase to the front entrance. The great wooden door was closed but not locked. Suza opened it and they went in.

There was a great hall with a floor of smashed marble. The ceiling sagged and the walls were blotched with damp. In the centre of the hall was a great fallen chandelier sprawled on the floor like a dead eagle.

Cortone called out, 'Hello, anybody here?'

There was no reply.

Suza thought: It's a big place, he must be here, it's just that he can't hear, maybe he's out in the garden.

They crossed the hall, skirting the chandelier. They entered a cavernous bare drawing room, their footsteps echoing loudly, and went out through the glassless french doors at the back of the building.

A short garden ran down to the edge of the cliff. They walked that far and saw a long stairway cut into the rock zigzagging down to the sea.

There was no one in sight.

He's not here, Suza thought; this time, Santa really did leave me stones.

'Look.' Cortone was pointing out to sea with one fat hand. Suza looked, and saw two vessels: a ship and a motorboat. The motorboat was coming toward them fast, jumping the waves and slicing the water with its sharp prow: there was one man in it. The ship was sailing out of the bay, leaving a broad wake.

'Looks like we just missed them,' Cortone said.

Suza ran down the steps, shouting and waving insanely, trying to attract the attention of the people on the ship, knowing it was impossible, they were too far away. She slipped on the stones and fell heavily on her bottom. She began to cry.

Cortone ran down after her, his heavy body jerking on the steps. 'It's no good,' he said. He pulled her to her feet.

'The motorboat,' she said desperately. 'Maybe we can take the motorboat and catch up with the ship—'

'No way. By the time the boat gets here the ship will be too far away, much too far, and going faster than the boat can.'

He led her back up the steps. She had run a long way down, and the climb back taxed him heavily. Suza hardly noticed: she was full of misery.

Her mind was a blank as they walked up the slope of the garden and back into the house.

'Have to sit down,' Cortone said as they crossed the drawing room.

Suza looked at him. He was breathing hard, and his face was grey and covered with perspiration. Suddenly she realized it had all been too much for his overweight body. For a moment she forgot her own awful disappointment. 'The stairs,' she said.

They went into the ruined hall. She led Cortone to the wide curving staircase and sat him on the second step. He went down heavily. He closed his eyes and rested his head on the wall beside him.

'Listen,' he said, 'you can call ships . . . or send them a wire . . . we can still reach him . . .'

'Sit quietly for a minute,' she said. 'Don't talk.'

'Ask my cousins – who's there?'

Suza spun around. There had been a clink of chandelier shards, and now she saw what had caused it.

Yasif Hassan walked toward them across the hall.

Suddenly, with a massive effort, Cortone stood up.

Hassan stopped.

Cortone's breath was coming in ragged gulps. He fumbled in his pocket.

Suza said, 'No—'

Cortone pulled out the gun.

Hassan was rooted to the spot, frozen.

Suza screamed. Cortone staggered, the gun in his hand weaving about in the air.

Cortone pulled the trigger. The gun went off twice, with a huge, deafening double bang. The shots went wild. Cortone sank to the ground, his face as dark as death. The gun fell from his fingers and hit the cracked marble floor.

Yasif Hassan threw up.

Suza knelt beside Cortone.

He opened his eyes. 'Listen,' he said hoarsely.

Hassan said, 'Leave him, let's go.'

Suza turned her head to face him. At the top of her voice she shouted, 'Just fuck *off.*' Then she turned back to Cortone.

'I've killed a lot of men,' Cortone said. Suza bent closer to hear. 'Eleven men. I killed myself . . . I fornicated with a lot of women . . .' His voice trailed off, his eyes closed, and then he made a huge effort to speak again. 'All my goddamn life I been a thief and a bully. But I died for my friend, right? This counts for something, it has to, doesn't it?'

'Yes,' she said. 'This really counts for something.'

'Okay,' he said.

Then he died.

Suza had never seen a man die. It was awful. Suddenly there was nothing there, nothing but a body; the person had vanished. She thought: No wonder death makes us cry. She realized her own face was streaked with tears. I didn't even like him, she thought, until just now.

Hassan said, 'You did very well, now let's get out of here.'

Suza did not understand. I did well? she thought. And then she understood. Hassan did not know she had told Cortone an Arab had been following them. As far as Hassan was concerned she had done just what he wanted her to: she had led him here. Now she must try to keep up the pretence that she was on his side until she could find a way to contact Nat.

I can't lie and cheat any more, I can't, it's too much, I'm tired, she thought.

Then: You can phone a ship, or at least send a cable, Cortone said.

She could still warn Nat.

Oh, God, when can I sleep?

She stood up. 'What are we waiting for?'

They went out through the high derelict entrance. 'We'll take my car,' Hassan told her.

She thought of trying to run away from him then, but it was a foolish idea. He would let her go soon. She had done what he'd asked, hadn't she? Now he would send her home.

She got into the car.

'Wait,' Hassan said. He ran to Cortone's car, took out the keys, and threw them into the bushes. He got into his own car. 'So the man in the motorboat can't follow,' he explained.

As they drove off he said, 'I'm disappointed in your attitude. That man was helping our enemies. You should rejoice, not weep, when an enemy dies.'

She covered her eyes with her hand. 'He was helping his friend.'

Hassan patted her knee. 'You've done well, I shouldn't criticize you. You got the information I wanted.'

She looked at him. 'Did I?'

'Sure. That big ship we saw leaving the bay – that

was the *Stromberg*. I know her time of departure and her maximum speed, so now I can figure out the earliest possible moment at which she could meet up with the *Coparelli*. And I can have my men there a day earlier.' He patted her knee again, this time letting his hand rest on her thigh.

'Don't touch me,' she said.

He took his hand away.

She closed her eyes and tried to think. She had achieved the worst possible outcome by what she had done: she had led Hassan to Sicily but she'd failed to warn Nat. She must find out how to send a telegram to a ship, and do it as soon as she and Hassan parted company. There was only one other chance – the airplane steward who had promised to call the Israeli consulate in Rome.

She said, 'Oh, God, I'll be glad to get back to Oxford.'

'Oxford?' Hassan laughed. 'Not yet. You'll have to stay with me until the operation is over.'

She thought: Dear God, I can't stand it. 'But I'm so tired,' she said.

'We'll rest soon. I couldn't let you go. Security, you know. Anyway, you wouldn't want to miss seeing the dead body of Nat Dickstein.'

At the Alitalia desk in the airport three men approached Yasif Hassan. Two of them were young and thuggish, the third was a tall sharp-faced man in his fifties.

The older man said to Hassan, 'You damn fool, you deserve to be shot.'

Hassan looked up at him, and Suza saw naked fear in his eyes as he said, 'Rostov!'

Suza thought: Oh God, what now?

Rostov took hold of Hassan's arm. It seemed for a moment that Hassan would resist, and jerk his arm away. The two young thugs moved closer. Suza and Hassan were enclosed. Rostov led Hassan away from the ticket desk. One of the thugs took Suza's arm and they followed.

They went into a quiet corner. Rostov was obviously blazing with fury but kept his voice low. 'You might have blown the whole thing if you hadn't been a few minutes late.'

'I don't know what you mean,' Hassan said desperately.

'You think I don't know you've been running around the world looking for Dickstein? You think I can't have you followed just like any other bloody imbecile? I've been getting hourly reports on your movements ever since you left Cairo. And what made you think you could trust her?' He jerked a thumb at Suza.

'She led me here.'

'Yes, but you didn't know that then.'

Suza stood still, silent and frightened. She was hopelessly confused. The multiple shocks of the morning – missing Nat, watching Cortone die, now this – had paralyzed her ability to think. Keeping the lies straight had been difficult enough when she had been deceiving Hassan and telling Cortone a truth that Hassan thought was a lie. Now there was this Rostov, to whom Hassan was lying, and she could not even begin to think about whether what she said to Rostov should be the truth or another, different lie.

Hassan was saying, 'How did you get here?'

'On the *Karla*, of course. We were only forty or fifty miles off Sicily when I got the report that you had landed here. I also obtained permission from Cairo to order you to return there immediately and directly.'

'I still think I did the right thing,' said Hassan.

'Get out of my sight.'

Hassan walked away. Suza began to follow him but Rostov said, 'Not you.' He took her arm and began to walk.

She went with him, thinking: What do I do now?

'I know you've proved your loyalty to us, Miss Ashford, but in the middle of a project like this we can't allow newly recruited people simply to go home. On the other hand I have no people here in Sicily other than those I need with me on the ship, so I can't have you escorted somewhere else. I'm afraid you're going to have to come aboard the *Karla* with me until this business is over. I hope you don't mind. Do you know, you look exactly like your mother.'

They had walked out of the airport to a waiting car. Rostov opened the door for her. Now was the time she should run: after this it might be too late. She hesitated. One of the thugs stood beside her. His jacket fell open slightly and she saw the butt of his gun. She remembered the awful bang Cortone's gun had made in the ruined villa, and how she had screamed; and suddenly she was afraid to die, to become a lump of clay like poor fat Cortone; she was terrified of that gun and that bang and the bullet entering her body, and she began to shake.

'What is it?' Rostov said.

'Al Cortone died.'

'We know,' Rostov said. 'Get in the car.'

Suza got in the car.

Pierre Borg drove out of Athens and parked his car at one end of a stretch of beach where occasional lovers strolled. He got out and walked along the shoreline until he met Kawash coming the other way. They stood side by side, looking out to sea, wavelets lapping sleepily at their feet. Borg could see the handsome face of the tall Arab double agent by starlight. Kawash was not his usual confident self.

'Thank you for coming,' Kawash said.

Borg did not know why he was being thanked. If anyone should say thank you, it was he. And then he realized that Kawash had been making precisely that point. The man did everything with subtlety, including insults.

'The Russians suspect there is a leak out of Cairo,' Kawash said. 'They are playing their cards very close to their collective Communist chest, so to speak.' Kawash smiled thinly. Borg did not see the joke. 'Even when Yasif Hassan came back to Cairo for debriefing we didn't learn much – and *I* didn't get all the information Hassan gave.'

Borg belched loudly: he had eaten a big Greek dinner. 'Don't waste time with excuses, please. Just tell me what you do know.'

'All right,' Kawash said mildly. 'They know that Dickstein is to steal some uranium.'

'You told me that last time.'

'I don't think they know any of the details. Their intention is to let it happen, then expose it afterwards. They've put a couple of ships into the Mediterranean, but they don't know where to send them.'

A plastic bottle floated in on the tide and landed at Borg's feet. He kicked it back into the water. 'What about Suza Ashford?'

'Definitely working for the Arab side. Listen. There was an argument between Rostov and Hassan. Hassan wanted to find out exactly where Dickstein was, and Rostov thought it was unnecessary.'

'Bad news. Go on.'

'Afterwards Hassan went out on a limb. He got the Ashford girl to help him look for Dickstein. They went to a place called Buffalo, in the U.S., and met a gangster called Cortone who took them to Sicily. They missed Dickstein, but only just: they saw the *Stromberg* leave. Hassan is in considerable trouble over this. He has been ordered back to Cairo but he hasn't turned up yet.'

'But the girl led them to where Dickstein had been?'

'Exactly.'

'Jesus Christ, this is bad.' Borg thought of the message that had arrived in the Rome consulate for Nat Dickstein from his 'girl friend'. He told Kawash about it. 'Hassan has told me everything and he and I are coming to see you.' What the hell did it mean? Was it intended to warn Dickstein, or to delay him, or to confuse him? Or was it a double bluff – an attempt to make him think she was being coerced into leading Hassan to him?

'A double bluff, I should say,' Kawash said. 'She knew her role in this would eventually be exposed, so she tried for a longer lease on Dickstein's trust. You won't pass the message on . . . '

'Of course not.' Borg's mind turned to another tack. 'If they went to Sicily they know about the *Stromberg*. What conclusions can they draw from that?'

'That the *Stromberg* will be used in the uranium theft?'

'Exactly. Now, if I were Rostov, I'd follow the *Stromberg*, let the hijack take place, then attack. Damn, damn, damn. I think this will have to be called off.' He dug the toe of his shoe into the soft sand. 'What's the situation at Qattara?'

'I was saving the worst news until last. All tests have been completed satisfactorily. The Russians are supplying uranium. The reactor goes on stream three weeks from today.'

Borg stared out to sea, and he was more wretched, pessimistic and depressed than he had ever been in the whole of his unhappy life. 'You know what this fucking means don't you? It means we can't call it off. It means I can't stop Dickstein. It means that Dickstein is Israel's last chance.'

Kawash was silent. After a moment Borg looked at

him. The Arab's eyes were closed. 'What are you doing?' Borg said.

The silence went on for a few moments. Finally Kawash opened his eyes, looked at Borg, and gave his polite little half smile. 'Praying,' he said.

TEL AVIV TO MV STROMBERG
PERSONAL BORG TO DICKSTEIN EYES ONLY
MUST BE DECODED BY THE ADDRESSEE
BEGINS SUZA ASHFORD CONFIRMED ARAB AGENT
STOP SHE PERSUADED CORTONE TO TAKE HER AND
HASSAN TO SICILY STOP THEY ARRIVED AFTER YOU
LEFT STOP CORTONE NOW DEAD STOP THIS AND
OTHER DATA INDICATES STRONG POSSIBILITY YOU
WILL BE ATTACKED AT SEA STOP NO FURTHER
ACTION WE CAN TAKE AT THIS END STOP YOU
FUCKED IT UP ALL ON YOUR OWN NOW GET OUT OF
IT ALONE ENDS

The clouds which had been massing over the western Mediterranean for the previous few days finally burst that night, drenching the *Stromberg* with rain. A brisk wind blew up, and the shortcomings of the ship's design became apparent as she began to roll and yaw in the burgeoning waves.

Nat Dickstein did not notice the weather.

He sat alone in his little cabin, at the table which was screwed to the bulkhead, a pencil in hand and a pad, a codebook and a signal in front of him, transcribing Borg's message word by crucifying word.

He read it over and over again, and finally sat staring at the blank steel wall in front of him.

It was pointless to speculate about why she might have done this, to invent far-fetched hypotheses that Hassan had coerced or blackmailed her, to imagine that she had acted from mistaken beliefs or confused motives: Borg had said she was a spy, and he had been right. She had been a spy all along. That was why she had made love to him.

She had a big future in the intelligence business, that girl.

Dickstein put his face in his hands and pressed his eyeballs with his fingertips, but still he could see her, naked except for her high-heeled shoes, leaning against the cupboard in the kitchen of that little flat, reading the morning paper while she waited for a kettle to boil.

The worst of it was, he loved her still. Before he met her he had been a cripple, an emotional amputee with an empty sleeve hanging where he should have had love; and she had performed a miracle, making him whole again. Now she had betrayed him, taking away what she had given, and he would be more handicapped than ever. He had written her a love letter. Dear God, he thought, what did she do when she read that letter? Did she laugh? Did she show it to Yasif Hassan and say, 'See how I've got him hooked?'

If you took a blind man, and gave him back his sight, and then, after a day made him blind again during the night while he was sleeping, this was how he would feel when he woke up.

He had told Borg he would kill Suza if she were an

agent, but now he knew that he had been lying. He could never hurt her, no matter what she did.

It was late. Most of the crew were asleep except for those taking watches. He left the cabin and went up on deck without seeing anyone. Walking from the hatch to the gunwale he got soaked to the skin, but he did not notice. He stood at the rail, looking into the darkness, unable to see where the black sea ended and the black sky began, letting the rain stream across his face like tears.

He would never kill Suza, but Yasif Hassan was a different matter.

If ever a man had an enemy, he had one in Hassan. He had loved Eila, only to see her in a sensual embrace with Hassan. Now he had fallen in love with Suza, only to find that she had already been seduced by the same old rival. And Hassan had also used Suza in his campaign to take away Dickstein's homeland.

Oh, yes, he would kill Yasif Hassan, and he would do it with his bare hands if he could. And the others. The thought brought him up out of the depths of despair in a fury: he wanted to hear bones snap, he wanted to see bodies crumple, he wanted the smell of fear and gunfire, he wanted death all around him.

Borg thought they would be attacked at sea. Dickstein stood gripping the rail as the ship sawed through the unquiet sea; the wind rose momentarily and lashed his face with cold, hard rain; and he thought, So be it; and then he opened his mouth and shouted into the wind: 'Let them come – let the bastards come!'

CHAPTER FIFTEEN

H ASSAN DID not go back to Cairo, then or ever.

Exultation filled him as his plane took off from Palermo. It had been close, but he had outwitted Rostov again! He could hardly believe it when Rostov had said, 'Get out of my sight.' He had felt sure he would be forced to board the *Karla* and consequently miss the hijack by the Fedayeen. But Rostov completely believed that Hassan was merely over-enthusiastic, impulsive, and inexperienced. It had never occurred to him that Hassan might be a traitor. But then, why should it? Hassan was the representative of Egyptian Intelligence on the team and he was an Arab. If Rostov had toyed with suspicions about his loyalty, he might have considered whether he was working for the Israelis, for they were the opposition – the Palestinians, if they entered the picture at all, could be assumed to be on the Arab side.

It was wonderful. Clever, arrogant, patronizing Colonel Rostov and the might of the notorious KGB had been fooled by a lousy Palestinian refugee, a man they thought was a nobody.

But it was not over yet. He still had to join forces with the Fedayeen.

The flight from Palermo took him to Rome, where he tried to get a plane to Annaba or Constantine, both near the Algerian coast. The nearest the airlines could offer was Algiers or Tunis. He went to Tunis.

There he found a young taxi driver with a newish Renault and thrust in front of the man's face more money in American dollars than he normally earned in a year. The taxi took him across the hundred-mile breadth of Tunisia, over the border into Algeria, and dropped him off at a fishing village with a small natural harbour. One of the Fedayeen was waiting for him. Hassan found him on the beach, sitting under a propped-up dinghy, sheltering from the rain and playing backgammon with a fisherman. The three men got into the fisherman's boat and cast off.

The sea was rough as they headed out in the last of the day. Hassan, no seaman, worried that the little motorboat would capsize, but the fisherman grinned cheerfully through it all.

The trip took them less than a half hour. As they approached the looming hulk of the ship, Hassan felt again the rising sense of triumph. A ship . . . they had a *ship*.

He clambered up on to the deck while the man who had met him paid off the fisherman. Mahmoud was waiting for him on deck. They embraced, and Hassan said, 'We should weigh anchor immediately – things are moving very fast now.'

'Come to the bridge with me.'

Hassan followed Mahmoud forward. The ship was a small coaster of about one thousand tons, quite new and in good condition. She was sleek, with most of her accommodations below deck. There was a hatch for one hold. She had been designed to carry small loads quickly and to manoeuvre in local North African ports.

They stood on the foredeck for a moment, looking about.

'She's just what we need,' Hassan said joyfully.

'I have renamed her the *Nablus*,' Mahmoud told him. 'She is the first ship of the Palestine Navy.'

Hassan felt tears start to his eyes.

They climbed the ladder. Mahmoud said, 'I got her from a Libyan businessman who wanted to save his soul.'

The bridge was compact and tidy. There was only one serious lack: radar. Many of these small coastal vessels still managed without it, and there had been no time to buy the equipment and fit it.

Mahmoud introduced the captain, also a Libyan – the businessman had provided a crew as well as a ship; none of the Fedayeen were sailors. The captain gave orders to weigh anchor and start engines.

The three men bent over a chart as Hassan told what he had learned in Sicily. 'The *Stromberg* left the south coast of Sicily at midday today. The *Coparelli* was due to pass through the Strait of Gibraltar late last night, heading for Genoa. They are sister ships, with the same top speed, so the earliest they can meet is twelve hours east of the midpoint between Sicily and Gibraltar.'

The captain made some calculations and looked at

another chart. 'They will meet south-east of the island of Minorca.'

'We should intercept the *Coparelli* no less than eight hours earlier.'

The captain ran his finger back along the trade route. 'That would put her just south of the island of Ibiza at dusk tomorrow.'

'Can we make it?'

'Yes, with a little time to spare, unless there is a storm.'

'Will there be a storm?'

'Sometime in the next few days, yes. But not tomorrow, I think.'

'Good. Where is the radio operator?'

'Here. This is Yaacov.'

Hassan turned to see a small, smiling man with tobacco-stained teeth and told him, 'There is a Russian aboard the *Coparelli*, a man called Tyrin, who will be sending signals to a Polish ship, the *Karla*. You must listen on this wavelength.' He wrote it down. 'Also, there is a radio beacon on the *Stromberg* that sends a simple thirty-second tone every half hour. If we listen for that every time we will be sure the *Stromberg* is not outrunning us.'

The captain was giving a course. Down on the deck the first officer had the hands making ready. Mahmoud was speaking to one of the Fedayeen about an arms inspection. The radio operator began to question Hassan about the *Stromberg*'s beacon. Hassan was not really listening. He was thinking: Whatever happens, it will be glorious.

The ship's engines roared, the deck tilted, the prow broke water and they were on their way.

Dieter Koch, the new engineer officer of the *Coparelli*, lay in his bunk in the middle of the night thinking: but what do I say if somebody sees me?

What he had to do now was simple. He had to get up, go to the aft engineering store, take out the spare oil pump and get rid of it. It was almost certain he could do this without being seen, for his cabin was close to the store, most of the crew were asleep, and those that were awake were on the bridge and in the engine room and likely to stay there. But 'almost certain' was not enough in an operation of this importance. If anyone should suspect, now or later, what he was really up to . . .

He put on a sweater, trousers, sea boots and an oilskin. The thing had to be done, and it had to be done now. He pocketed the key to the store, opened his cabin door and went out. As he made his way along the gangway he thought: I'll say I couldn't sleep so I'm checking the stores.

He unlocked the door to the store, turned on the light, went in and closed it behind him. Engineering spares were racked and shelved all around him – gaskets, valves, plugs, cable, bolts, filters . . . given a cylinder block, you could build a whole engine out of these parts.

He found the spare oil pump in a box on a high shelf. He lifted it down – it was not bulky but it was heavy – and then spent five minutes double-checking that there was not a second spare oil pump.

Now for the difficult part.

. . . I couldn't sleep, sir, so I was checking the spares. Very good, everything in order? Yes, sir. And what's that you've got under your arm? A bottle of whisky, sir. A cake my mother sent me. The spare oil pump, sir, I'm going to throw it overboard . . .

He opened the storeroom door and looked out.

Nobody.

He killed the light, went out, closed the door behind him and locked it. He walked along the gangway and out on deck.

Nobody.

It was still raining. He could see only a few yards, which was good, because it meant others could see only that far.

He crossed the deck to the gunwale, leaned over the rail, dropped the oil pump into the sea, turned, and bumped into someone.

A cake my mother sent me, it was so dry . . .

'Who's that?' a voice said in accented English.

'Engineer. You?' As Koch spoke, the other man turned so that his profile was visible in the deck light, and Koch recognized the rotund figure and big-nosed face of the radio operator.

'I couldn't sleep,' the radio operator said. 'I was . . . getting some air.'

He's as embarrassed as I am, Koch thought. I wonder why?

'Lousy night,' Koch said. 'I'm going in.'

'Goodnight.'

Koch went inside and made his way to his cabin. Strange fellow, that radio operator. He was not one of the regular crew. He had been taken on in Cardiff after the original radioman broke his leg. Like Koch, he was something of an outsider here. A good thing he had bumped into him rather than one of the others.

Inside his cabin he took off his wet outer clothes and lay on his bunk. He knew he would not sleep. His plan for tomorrow was all worked out, there was no point in going over it again, so he tried to think of other things: of his mother, who made the best potato kugel in the world; of his fiancée, who gave the best head in the world; of his mad father now in an institution in Tel Aviv; of the magnificent tapedeck he would buy with his back pay after this assignment; of his fine apartment in Haifa; of the children he would have, and how they would grow up in an Israel safe from war.

He got up two hours later. He went aft to the galley for some coffee. The cook's apprentice was there, standing in a couple of inches of water, frying bacon for the crew.

'Lousy weather,' Koch said.

'It will get worse.'

Koch drank his coffee, then refilled the mug and a second one and took them up to the bridge. The first officer was there. 'Good morning,' Koch said.

'Not really,' said the first officer, looking out into a curtain of rain.

'Coffee?'

'Good of you. Thank you.'

Koch handed him the mug. 'Where are we?'

'Here.' The officer showed him their position on a chart. 'Dead on schedule, in spite of the weather.'

Koch nodded. That meant he had to stop the ship in fifteen minutes. 'See you later,' he said. He left the bridge and went below to the engine room.

His number two was there, looking quite fresh, as if he had taken a good long nap during his night's duty. 'How's the oil pressure?' Koch asked him.

'Steady.'

'It was going up and down a bit yesterday.'

'Well, there was no sign of trouble in the night,' the number two said. He was a little too firm about it, as if he was afraid of being accused of sleeping while the gauge oscillated.

'Good,' Koch said. 'Perhaps it's repaired itself.' He put his mug down on a level cowling, then picked it up quickly as the ship rolled. 'Wake Larsen on your way to bed.'

'Right.'

'Sleep well.'

The number two left, and Koch drank down his coffee and went to work.

The oil pressure gauge was located in a bank of dials aft of the engine. The dials were set into a thin metal casing, painted matt black and secured by four self-tapping screws. Using a large screwdriver, Koch removed the four screws and pulled the casing away. Behind it was a mass of many-coloured wires leading to the different gauges. Koch swapped his large screwdriver for a small electrical one with an insulated handle. With a few turns he disconnected one of the wires to the oil pressure gauge. He wrapped a couple of inches of insulating tape around the bare end of the wire, then taped it to the back of the dial so that only a close inspection would reveal that it was not connected to the terminal. Then he replaced the casing and secured it with the four screws.

When Larsen came in he was topping up the transmission fluid.

'Can I do that, sir?' Larsen said. He was a donkeyman greaser, and lubrication was his province.

'I've done it now,' Koch said. He replaced the filler cap and stowed the can in a locker.

Larsen rubbed his eyes and lit a cigarette. He looked over the dials, did a double take and said, 'Sir! Oil pressure zero!'

'Zero?'

'Yes!'

'Stop engines!'

'Aye, aye, sir.'

Without oil, friction between the engine's metal parts would cause a very rapid build-up of heat until the metal melted, the parts fused and the engines stopped, never to go again. So dangerous was the sudden absence of oil pressure that Larsen might well have stopped the engines on his own initiative, without asking Koch.

Everyone on the ship heard the engine die and felt the *Coparelli* lose way; even those dayworkers who were still asleep in their bunks heard it through their dreams and woke up. Before the engine was completely still the first officer's voice came down the pipe. 'Bridge! What's going on below?'

Koch spoke into the voice-pipe. 'Sudden loss of oil pressure.'

'Any idea why?'

'Not yet.'

'Keep me posted.'

'Aye, aye, sir.'

Koch turned to Larsen. 'We're going to drop the sump,' he said. Larsen picked up a toolbox and followed Koch down a half deck to where they could get at the engine from underneath. Koch told him, 'If the main bearings or the big end bearings were worn the drop in oil pressure would have been gradual. A sudden drop means a failure in the oil supply. There's plenty of oil in the system – I checked earlier – and there are no signs of leaks. So there's probably a blockage.'

Koch released the sump with a power spanner and the two of them lowered it to the deck. They checked the sump strainer, the full flow filter, the filter relief valve and the main relief valve without finding any obstructions.

'If there's no blockage, the fault must be in the pump,' Koch said. 'Break out the spare oil pump.'

'That will be in the store on the main deck,' Larsen said.

Koch handed him the key, and Larsen went above.

Now Koch had to work very quickly. He took the casing off the oil pump, exposing two broad-toothed meshing gear wheels. He took the spanner off the power drill and fitted a bit, then attacked the cogs of the gear wheels with the drill, chipping and breaking them until they were all but useless. He put down the drill, picked up a crowbar and a hammer, and forced the bar in between the two wheels, prising them apart until he heard something give with a loud, dull crack. Finally he took out of his pocket a small nut made of toughened steel, battered and chipped. He had brought it with him when he had boarded the ship. He dropped the nut into the sump.

Done.

Larsen came back.

Koch realized he had not taken the bit off the power drill: when Larsen left there had been a spanner attachment on the tool. Don't look at the drill! he thought.

Larsen said, 'The pump isn't there, sir.'

Koch fished the nut out of the sump. 'Look at this,' he said, distracting Larsen's eye from the incriminating power drill. 'This is the cause of the trouble.' He showed Larsen the ruined gear wheels of the oil pump. 'The nut must have been dropped in the last time the filters were changed. It got into the pump and it's been going round and round in those gear wheels ever since. I'm surprised we didn't hear the noise, even over the sound of the engine. Anyway, the oil pump is beyond repair, so you'll have to find that spare. Get a few hands to help you look for it.'

Larsen went out. Koch took the bit off the power drill and put back the spanner attachment. He ran up the steps to the main engine room to remove the other piece of incriminating evidence. Working at top speed in case someone else should come in, he removed the casing on the gauges and reconnected the oil pressure gauge. Now it would genuinely read zero. He replaced the casing and threw away the insulating tape.

It was finished. Now to pull the wool over the captain's eyes.

As soon as the search party admitted defeat Koch went up to the bridge. He told the captain, 'A mechanic must have dropped a nut into the oil sump last time the engine was serviced, sir.' He showed the captain the nut. 'At some point – maybe while the ship was pitching so steeply – the nut got into the oil pump. After that it was just a matter of time. The nut went around in the gear wheels until it had totally ruined them. I'm afraid we can't make gear wheels like that on board. The ship should carry a spare oil pump, but it doesn't.'

The captain was furious. 'There will be hell to pay when I find out who's responsible for this.'

'It's the engineer's job to check the spares, but as you know, sir, I came on board at the last minute.'

'That means it's Sarne's fault.'

'There may be an explanation—'

'Indeed. Such as he spent too much time chasing Belgian whores to look after his engine. Can we limp along?'

'Absolutely not, sir. We wouldn't move half a cable before she seized.'

'Damnation. Where's that radio operator?'

The first officer said, 'I'll find him, sir,' and went out.

'You're certain you can't put something together?' the captain asked Koch.

'I'm afraid you can't make an oil pump out of spare parts and string. That's why we have to carry a spare pump.'

The first officer came back with the radio operator. The captain said, 'Where the devil have you been?'

The radio operator was the rotund, big-nosed man Koch had bumped into on the deck during the night. He looked hurt. 'I was helping to search the for'ard store for the oil pump, sir, then I went to wash my hands.' He glanced at Koch, but there was no hint of suspicion in his look: Koch was not sure how much he had seen during that little confrontation on the deck, but if he had made any connection between a missing spare and a package thrown overboard by the engineer, he wasn't saying.

'All right,' the captain said. 'Make a signal to the owners: Report engine breakdown at . . . What's our exact position, number one?'

The first officer gave the radio operator the position.

The captain continued: 'Require new oil pump or tow to port. Please instruct.'

Koch's shoulders slumped a little. He had done it.

Eventually the reply came from the owners: COPA-RELLI SOLD TO SAVILE SHIPPING OF ZURICH. YOUR MESSAGED PASSED TO NEW OWNERS. STAND BY FOR THEIR INSTRUCTIONS.

Almost immediately afterward there was a signal from Savile Shipping: OUR VESSEL GIL HAMILTON IN YOUR WATERS. SHE WILL COME ALONGSIDE AT APPROXI-

MATELY NOON. PREPARE TO DISEMBARK ALL CREW
EXCEPT ENGINEER. GIL HAMILTON WILL TAKE CREW TO
MARSEILLES. ENGINEER WILL AWAIT NEW OIL PUMP.
PAPAGOPOLOUS.

The exchange of signals was heard sixty miles away by
Solly Weinberg, the master of the *Gil Hamilton* and a
commander in the Israeli Navy. He muttered, 'Right on
schedule. Well done, Koch.' He set a course for the
Coparelli and ordered full speed ahead.

It was *not* heard by Yasif Hassan and Mahmoud aboard
the *Nablus* 150 miles away. They were in the captain's
cabin, bent over a sketch plan Hassan had drawn of the
Coparelli, and they were deciding exactly how they
would board her and take over. Hassan had instructed
the *Nablus*'s radio operator to listen out on two wave-
lengths: the one on which the *Stromberg*'s radio beacon
broadcast and the one Tyrin was using for his clandestine signals from the *Coparelli* to Rostov aboard
the *Karla*. Because the messages were sent on the
Coparelli's regular wavelength, the *Nablus* did not
pick them up. It would be some time before the
Fedayeen realized they were hijacking an almost abandoned ship.

The exchange was heard 200 miles away on the bridge
of the *Stromberg*. When the *Coparelli* acknowledged the

signal from Papagopolous, the officers on the bridge cheered and clapped. Nat Dickstein, leaning against a bulkhead with a mug of black coffee in his hand, staring ahead at the rain and the heaving sea, did not cheer. His body was hunched and tense, his face stiff, his brown eyes slitted behind the plastic spectacles. One of the others noticed his silence and made a remark about getting over the first big hurdle. Dickstein's muttered reply was uncharacteristically peppered with the strongest of obscenities. The cheerful officer turned away, and later in the mess observed that Dickstein looked like the kind of man who would stick a knife in you if you stepped on his toe.

And it was heard by David Rostov and Suza Ashford 300 miles away aboard the *Karla*.

Suza had been in a daze as she walked across the gangplank from the Sicilian quayside on to the Polish vessel. She had hardly noticed what was happening as Rostov showed her to her cabin – an officer's room with its own head – and said he hoped she would be comfortable. She sat on the bed. She was still there, in the same position, an hour later when a sailor brought some cold food on a tray and set it down on her table without speaking. She did not eat it. When it got dark she began to shiver, so she got into the bed and lay there with her eyes wide open, staring at nothing, still shivering.

Eventually she had slept – fitfully at first, with strange

meaningless nightmares, but in the end deeply. Dawn woke her.

She lay still, feeling the motion of the ship and looking blankly at the cabin around her; and then she realized where she was. It was like waking up and remembering the blind terror of a nightmare, except that instead of thinking: Oh, thank God it was a dream, she realized it was all true and it was still going on.

She felt horribly guilty. She had been fooling herself, she could see that now. She had convinced herself that she had to find Nat to warn him, no matter the risk: but the truth was she would have reached for any excuse to go and see him. The disastrous consequences of what she had done followed naturally from the confusion of her motives. It was true that Nat had been in danger; but he was in worse danger now, and it was Suza's fault.

She thought of that, and she thought of how she was at sea in a Polish ship commanded by Nat's enemies and surrounded by Russian thugs, and she closed her eyes tightly and pushed her head under the pillow and fought the hysteria that bubbled up in her throat.

And then she began to feel angry, and that was what saved her sanity.

She thought of her father, and how he wanted to use her to further his political ideas, and she felt angry with him. She thought of Hassan, manipulating her father, putting his hand on her knee, and she wished she had slapped his face while she had the chance. Finally she thought of Rostov, with his hard, intelligent face and his cold smile, and how he intended to ram Nat's ship and kill him, and she got mad as hell.

Dickstein was her man. He was funny, and he was strong, and he was oddly vulnerable, and he wrote love letters and stole ships, and he was the only man she had ever loved like *this*; and she was not going to lose him.

She was in the enemy camp, a prisoner, but only from *her* point of view. They thought she was on their side; they trusted her. Perhaps she would have a chance to throw a wrench in their works. She must look for it. She would move about the ship, concealing her fear, talking to her enemies, consolidating her position in their confidence, pretending to share their ambitions and concerns, until she saw her opportunity.

The thought made her tremble. Then she told herself: If I don't do this, I lose him; and if I lose him I don't want to live.

She got out of bed. She took off the clothes she had slept in, washed and put on clean sweater and pants from her suitcase. She sat at the small nailed-down table and ate some of the sausage and cheese that had been left there the day before. She brushed her hair and, just to boost her morale a little, put on a trace of make-up.

She tried her cabin door. It was not locked.

She went out.

She walked along a gangway and followed the smell of food to the galley. She went in and looked swiftly about.

Rostov sat alone, eating eggs slowly with a fork. He

looked up and saw her. Suddenly his face seemed icily
evil, his narrow mouth hard, his eyes without emotion.
Suza hesitated, then forced herself to walk toward him.
Reaching his table, she leaned briefly on a chair, for
her legs felt weak.

Rostov said, 'Sit down.'

She dropped into the chair.

'How did you sleep?'

She was breathing too quickly, as if she had been
walking very fast. 'Fine,' she said. Her voice shook.

His sharp, sceptical eyes seemed to bore into her
brain. 'You seem upset.' He spoke evenly, without
sympathy or hostility.

'I . . .' Words seemed to stick in her throat, choking
her. 'Yesterday . . . was confusing.' It was true, anyway:
it was easy to say this. 'I never saw someone die.'

'Ah.' At last a hint of human feeling showed in
Rostov's expression: perhaps he remembered the first
time he watched a man die. He reached for a coffee
pot and poured her a cup. 'You're very young,' he said.
'You can't be much older than my first son.'

Suza sipped at the hot coffee gratefully, hoping he
would go on talking in this fashion – it would help her
to calm down.

'Your son?' she said.

'Yuri Davidovitch, he's twenty.'

'What does he do?'

Rostov's smile was not as chilly as before. 'Unfortu-
nately he spends most of his time listening to decadent
music. He doesn't study as hard as he should. Not like
his brother.'

Suza's breathing was slowing to normal, and her hand no longer shook when she picked up her cup. She knew that this man was no less dangerous just because he had a family; but he *seemed* less frightening when he talked like this. 'And your other son?' she asked. 'The younger one?'

Rostov nodded. 'Vladimir.' Now he was not frightening at all: he was staring over Suza's shoulder with a fond, indulgent expression on his face. 'He's very gifted. He will be a great mathematician if he gets the right schooling.'

'That shouldn't be a problem,' she said, watching him. 'Soviet education is the best in the world.'

It seemed like a safe thing to say, but must have had some special significance for him, because the faraway look disappeared and his face turned hard and cold again. 'No,' he said. 'It shouldn't be a problem.' He continued eating his eggs.

Suza thought urgently: He was becoming friendly, I mustn't lose him now. She cast about desperately for something to say. What did they have in common, what could they talk about? Then she was inspired. 'I wish I could remember you from when you were at Oxford.'

'You were very small.' He poured himself some coffee. 'Everyone remembers your mother. She was easily the most beautiful woman around. And you're exactly like her.'

That's better, Suza thought. She asked him, 'What did you study?'

'Economics.'

'Not an exact science in those days, I imagine.'

'And not much better today.'

Suza put on a faintly solemn expression. 'We speak of bourgeois economics, of course.'

'Of course.' Rostov looked at her as if he could not tell whether she were serious or not. He seemed to decide she was.

An officer came into the galley and spoke to him in Russian. Rostov looked at Suza regretfully. 'I must go up to the bridge.'

She had to go with him. She forced herself to speak calmly. 'May I come?'

He hesitated. Suza thought: He *should* let me. He's enjoyed talking to me, he believes I'm on his side, and if I learn any secrets how could he imagine I could use them, stuck here on a KGB ship?

Rostov said: 'Why not?'

He walked away. Suza followed.

Up in the radio room Rostov smiled as he read through the messages and translated them for Suza's benefit. He seemed delighted with Dickstein's ingenuity. 'The man is smart as hell,' he said.

'What's Savile Shipping?' Suza asked.

'A front for Israeli Intelligence. Dickstein is eliminating all the people who have reason to be interested in what happens to the uranium. The shipping company isn't interested because they no longer own the ship. Now he's taking off the captain and crew. No doubt he has some kind of hold over the people who actually own the uranium. It's a beautiful scheme.'

This was what Suza wanted. Rostov was talking to her like a colleague, she was at the centre of events; she must be able to find a way to foul things up for him. She said, 'I suppose the breakdown was rigged?'

'Yes. Now Dickstein can take over the ship without firing a shot.'

Suza thought fast. When she 'betrayed' Dickstein she had proved her loyalty to the Arab side. Now the Arab side had split into two camps: in one were Rostov, the KGB and Egyptian Intelligence; in the other Hassan and the Fedayeen. Now Suza could prove her loyalty to Rostov's side by betraying Hassan.

She said, as casually as she possibly could, 'And so can Yasif Hassan, of course.'

'What?'

'Hassan can also take over the *Coparelli* without firing a shot.'

Rostov stared at her. The blood seemed to drain from his thin face. Suza was shocked to see him suddenly lose all his poise and confidence. He said, 'Hassan intends to hijack the *Coparelli*?'

Suza pretended to be shocked. 'Are you telling me that you didn't *know*?'

'But who? Not the Egyptians, surely!'

'The Fedayeen. Hassan said this was *your* plan.'

Rostov banged the bulkhead with his fist, looking very uncool and Russian for a moment. 'Hassan is a liar and a traitor!'

This was Suza's chance, she knew. She thought: Give me strength. She said: 'Maybe we can stop him . . .'

Rostov looked at her. 'What's his plan?'

'To hijack the *Coparelli* before Dickstein gets there, then ambush the Israeli team, and sail to . . . he didn't tell me exactly, somewhere in North Africa. What was your plan?'

'To ram the ship after Dickstein had stolen the uranium—'

'Can't we still do that?'

'No. We're too far away, we'd never catch them.'

Suza knew that if she did not do the next bit exactly right, both she and Dickstein would die. She crossed her arms to stop the shaking. She said, 'Then there is only one thing we can do.'

Rostov looked up at her. 'There is?'

'We must warn Dickstein of the Fedayeen ambush so that he can take back the *Coparelli*.'

There. She had said it. She watched Rostov's face. He must swallow it, it was logical, it was the right thing for him to do!

Rostov was thinking hard. He said, 'Warn Dickstein so that he can take the *Coparelli* back from the Fedayeen. Then he can proceed according to his plan and we can proceed according to ours.'

'Yes!' said Suza. 'That's the only way! Isn't it? Isn't it?'

FROM: SAVILE SHIPPING, ZURICH
TO: ANGELUZZI E BIANCO, GENOA
YOUR YELLOWCAKE CONSIGNMENT FROM F.A. PEDLER INDEFINITELY DELAYED DUE TO ENGINE TROUBLE AT SEA. WILL ADVISE SOONEST OF NEW DELIVERY DATES. PAPAGOPOLOUS.

*

As the *Gil Hamilton* came into view, Pyotr Tyrin cornered Ravlo, the addict, in the 'tweendecks of the *Coparelli*. Tyrin acted with a confidence he did not feel. He adopted a bullying manner and grabbed hold of Ravlo's sweater. Tyrin was a bulky man, and Ravlo was somewhat wasted. Tyrin said, 'Listen, you're going to do something for me.'

'Sure, anything you say.'

Tyrin hesitated. It would be risky. Still, there was no alternative. 'I need to stay on board ship when the rest of you go on the *Gil Hamilton*. If I'm missed, you will say that you have seen me go over.'

'Right, okay, sure.'

'If I'm discovered, and I have to board the *Gil Hamilton*, you can be sure I'll tell them your secret.'

'I'll do everything I can.'

'You'd better.'

Tyrin let him go. He was not reassured: a man like that would promise you anything, but when it came to the crunch he might fall to pieces.

All hands were summoned on deck for the changeover. The sea was too rough for the *Gil Hamilton* to come alongside, so she sent a launch. Everyone had to wear lifebelts for the crossing. The officers and crew of the *Coparelli* stood quietly in the pouring rain while they were counted, then the first sailor went over the side and down the ladder, jumped into the well of the launch.

The boat would be too small to take the whole crew – they would have to go over in two or three detachments, Tyrin realized. While everyone's attention was on the first men to go over the rail, Tyrin whispered to Ravlo, 'Try and be last to go.'

'All right.'

The two of them edged out to the back of the crowd on deck. The officers were peering over the side at the launch. The men were standing, waiting, facing toward the *Gil Hamilton.*

Tyrin slipped back behind a bulkhead.

He was two steps from a lifeboat whose cover he had loosened earlier. The stem of the boat could be seen from the deck amidships, where the sailors were standing, but the stern could not. Tyrin moved to the stern, lifted the cover, got in and from inside put the cover back in place.

He thought: If I'm discovered now I've had it.

He was a big man, and the life jacket made him bigger. With some difficulty he crawled the length of the boat to a position from which he could see the deck through an eyelet in the tarpaulin. Now it was up to Ravlo.

He watched as a second detachment of men went down the ladder to the launch, then heard the first officer say, 'Where's that radio operator?'

Tyrin looked for Ravlo and located him. Speak. damn you!

Ravlo hesitated. 'He went over with the first lot, sir.'

Good boy!

'Are you sure?'

'Yes, sir. I saw him.'

The officer nodded and said something about not being able to tell one from another in this filthy rain.

The captain called to Koch, and the two men stood talking in the lee of a bulkhead, close to Tyrin's hiding place. The captain said, 'I've never heard of Savile Shipping, have you?'

'No, sir.'

'This is all wrong, selling a ship while she's at sea, then leaving the engineer in charge of her and taking the captain off.'

'Yes, sir. I imagine they're not seafaring people, these new owners.'

'They're surely not, or they'd know better. Probably accountants.' There was a pause. 'You could refuse to stay alone, of course, then I would have to stay with you. I'd back you up afterwards.'

'I'm afraid I'd lose my ticket.'

'Right, I shouldn't have suggested it. Well, good luck.'

'Thank you, sir.'

The third group of seamen had boarded the launch. The first officer was at the top of the ladder waiting for the captain, who was still muttering about accountants as he turned around, crossed the deck and followed the first officer over the side.

Tyrin turned his attention to Koch, who now thought he was the only man aboard the *Coparelli*. The engineer watched the launch go across to the *Gil Hamilton*, then climbed the ladder to the bridge.

Tyrin cursed aloud. He wanted Koch to go below so

that he could get to the for'ard store and radio to the *Karla*. He watched the bridge, and saw Koch's face appear from time to time behind the glass. If Koch stayed there, Tyrin would have to wait until dark before he could contact Rostov and report.

It looked very much as if Koch planned to remain on the bridge all day.

Tyrin settled down for a long wait.

When the *Nablus* reached the point south of Ibiza where Hassan expected to encounter the *Coparelli*, there was not a single ship in sight.

They circled the point in a widening spiral while Hassan scanned the desolate rainswept horizon through binoculars.

Mahmoud said, 'You have made a mistake.'

'Not necessarily.' Hassan was determined he would not appear panicked. 'This was just the earliest point at which we could meet her. She doesn't have to travel at top speed.'

'Why should she be delayed?'

Hassan shrugged, seeming less worried than he was. 'Perhaps the engine isn't running well. Perhaps they've had worse weather than we have. A lot of reasons.'

'What do you suggest, then?'

Mahmoud was also very uneasy, Hassan realized. On this ship he was not in control, only Hassan could make the decisions. 'We travel south-west, backing along the *Coparelli*'s route. We must meet her sooner or later.'

'Give the order to the captain,' Mahmoud said, and

went below to his troops, leaving Hassan on the bridge with the captain.

Mahmoud burned with the irrational anger of tension. So did his troops, Hassan had observed. They had been expecting a fight at midday, and now they had to wait, dawdling about in the crew quarters and the galley, cleaning weapons, playing cards, and bragging about past battles. They were hyped up for combat, and inclined to play dangerous knife-throwing games to prove their courage to each other and to themselves. One of them had quarrelled with two seamen over an imaginary insult, and had cut them both about the face with a broken glass before the fight was broken up. Now the crew were staying well away from the Fedayeen.

Hassan wondered how he would handle them if he were Mahmoud. He had thought along these lines a lot recently. Mahmoud was still the commander, but he was the one who had done all the important work: discovered Dickstein, brought the news of his plan, conceived the counter-hijack, and established the *Stromberg*'s whereabouts. He was beginning to wonder what would be his position in the movement when all this was over.

Clearly, Mahmoud was wondering the same thing.

Well. If there was to be a power struggle between the two of them, it would have to wait. First they had to hijack the *Coparelli* and ambush Dickstein. Hassan felt a little nauseous when he thought about that. It was all very well for the battle-hardened men below to convince themselves they looked forward to a fight, but

Hassan had never been in war, never even had a gun pointed at him except by Cortone in the ruined villa. He was afraid, and he was even more afraid of disgracing himself by showing his fear, by turning and running away, by throwing up as he had done in the villa. But he also felt excited, for if they won – if they won!

There was a false alarm at four-thirty in the afternoon when they sighted another ship coming toward them, but after examining her through binoculars Hassan announced she was not the *Coparelli*, and as she passed they were able to read the name on her side: *Gil Hamilton*.

As daylight began to fade Hassan became worried. In this weather, even with navigation lights, two ships could pass within half a mile of one another at night without seeing each other. And there had been not a sound out of the *Coparelli*'s secret radio all afternoon, although Yaacov had reported that Rostov was trying to raise Tyrin. To be certain that the *Coparelli* did not pass the *Nablus* in the night they would have to go about and spend the night travelling toward Genoa at the *Coparelli*'s speed, then resume searching in the morning. But by that time the *Stromberg* would be close by and the Fedayeen might lose the chance of springing a trap on Dickstein.

Hassan was about to explain this to Mahmoud – who had just returned to the bridge – when a single white light winked on in the distance.

'She's at anchor,' said the captain.

'How can you tell?' Mahmoud asked.

'That's what a single white light means.'

Hassan said, 'That would explain why she wasn't off Ibiza when we expected her. If that's the *Coparelli*, you should prepare to board.'

'I agree,' said Mahmoud, and went off to tell his men.

'Turn out your navigation lights,' Hassan told the captain.

As the *Nablus* closed with the other ship, night fell.

'I'm almost certain that's the *Coparelli*,' Hassan said.

The captain lowered his binoculars. 'She has three cranes on deck, and all her upperworks are aft of the hatches.'

'Your eyesight is better than mine,' Hassan said. 'She's the *Coparelli*.'

He went below to the galley, where Mahmoud was addressing his troops. Mahmoud looked at him as he stepped inside. Hassan nodded. 'This is it.'

Mahmoud turned back to his men. 'We do not expect much resistance. The ship is crewed by ordinary seamen, and there is no reason for them to be armed. We go in two boats, one to attack the port side and one the starboard. On board our first task is to take the bridge and prevent the crew from using the radio. Next we round up the crew on deck.' He paused and turned to Hassan. 'Tell the captain to get as close as possible to the *Coparelli* and then stop engines.'

Hassan turned. Suddenly he was errand boy again: Mahmoud was demonstrating that he was still the battle leader. Hassan felt the humiliation bring a rush of blood to his cheeks.

'Yasif.'

He turned back.

'Your weapon.' Mahmoud threw him a gun. Hassan caught it. It was a small pistol, almost a toy, the kind of gun a woman might carry in her handbag. The Fedayeen roared with laughter.

Hassan thought: I can play these games too. He found what looked like the safety catch and released it. He pointed the gun at the floor and pulled the trigger. The report was very loud. He emptied the gun into the deck.

There was a silence.

Hassan said, 'I thought I saw a mouse.' He threw the gun back to Mahmoud.

The Fedayeen laughed even louder.

Hassan went out. He went back up to the bridge, passed the message to the captain, and returned to the deck. It was very dark now. For a time all that could be seen of the *Coparelli* was its light. Then, as he strained his eyes, a silhouette of solid black became distinguishable against the wash of dark grey.

The Fedayeen, quiet now, had emerged from the galley and stood on deck with the crew. The *Nablus*'s engines died. The crew lowered the boats.

Hassan and his Fedayeen went over the side.

Hassan was in the same boat as Mahmoud. The little launch bobbed on the waves, which now seemed immense. They approached the sheer side of the *Coparelli*. There was no sign of activity on the ship. Surely, Hassan thought, the officer on watch must hear the sound of two engines approaching? But no alarms sounded, no lights flooded the deck, no one shouted orders or came to the rail.

Mahmoud was first up the ladder.

By the time Hassan reached the *Coparelli*'s deck the other team was swarming over the starboard gunwale.

Men poured down the companionways and up the ladders. Still there was no sign of the *Coparelli*'s crew. Hassan had a dreadful premonition that something had gone terribly wrong.

He followed Mahmoud up to the bridge. Two of the men were already there. Hassan asked, 'Did they have time to use the radio?'

'Who?' Mahmoud said.

They went back down to the deck. Slowly the men were emerging from the bowels of the boat, looking puzzled, their cold guns in their hands.

Mahmoud said: 'The wreck of the *Marie Celeste*.'

Two men came across the deck with a frightened looking sailor between them.

Hassan spoke to the sailor in English. 'What's happened here?'

The sailor replied in some other language.

Hassan had a sudden terrifying thought. 'Let's check the hold,' he said to Mahmoud.

They found a companionway leading below and went down into the hold. Hassan found a light switch and turned it on.

The hold was full of large oil drums, sealed and secured with wooden wedges. The drums had the word PLUMBAT stencilled on their sides.

'That's it,' said Hassan. 'That's the uranium.'

They looked at the drums, then at each other. For a moment all rivalry was forgotten.

'We did it,' said Hassan. 'By God, we did it.'

As darkness fell Tyrin had watched the engineer go forward to switch on the white light. Coming back, he had not gone up to the bridge but had walked farther aft and entered the galley. He was going to get something to eat. Tyrin was hungry too. He would give his arm for a plate of salted herring and a loaf of brown bread. Sitting cramped in his lifeboat all afternoon, waiting for Koch to move, he had had nothing to think about but his hunger, and he had tortured himself with thoughts of caviar, smoked salmon, marinated mushrooms and most of all brown bread.

Not yet, Pyotr, he told himself.

As soon as Koch had disappeared from sight, Tyrin got out of the lifeboat, his muscles protesting as he stretched, and hurried along the deck to the for'ard store.

He had shifted the boxes and junk in the main store so that they concealed the entrance to his small radio room. Now he had to get down on hands and knees, pull away one box, and crawl through a little tunnel to get in.

The set was repeating a short two-letter signal. Tyrin checked the code book and found it meant he was to switch to another wavelength before acknowledging. He set the radio to transmit and followed his instructions.

Rostov immediately replied. CHANGE OF PLAN. HASSAN WILL ATTACK COPARELLI.

Tyrin frowned in puzzlement, and made: REPEAT PLEASE.

HASSAN IS A TRAITOR, FEDAYEEN WILL ATTACK COPARELLI.

Tyrin said aloud: 'Jesus, what's going on?' The *Coparelli* was *here*, he was on it . . . Why would Hassan . . . for the uranium, of course.

Rostov was still signalling. HASSAN PLANS TO AMBUSH DICKSTEIN. FOR OUR PLAN TO PROCEED WE MUST WARN DICKSTEIN OF THE AMBUSH.

Tyrin frowned as he decoded this, then his face cleared as he understood. 'Then we'll be back to square one,' he said to himself. 'That's clever. But what do I do?'

He made: HOW?

YOU WILL CALL STROMBERG ON COPARELLI'S REGU-LAR WAVELENGTH AND SEND FOLLOWING MESSAGE PRE-CISELY REPEAT PRECISELY. QUOTE COPARELLI TO STROMBERG I AM BOARDED ARABS I THINK. WATCH UNQUOTE.

Tyrin nodded. Dickstein would think that Koch had time to get a few words off before the Arabs killed him. Forewarned, Dickstein should be able to take the *Coparelli*. Then Rostov's *Karla* could collide with Dick-stein's ship as planned. Tyrin thought: But what about me?

He made: UNDERSTOOD. He heard a distant bump, as if something had hit the ship's hull. At first he ignored it, then he remembered there was nobody aboard but him and Koch. He went to the door of the for'ard store and looked out.

The Fedayeen had arrived.

He closed the door and hurried back to his transmitter. He made: HASSAN IS HERE.

Rostov replied, SIGNAL DICKSTEIN NOW.

WHAT DO I DO THEN?

HIDE.

Thanks very much, Tyrin thought. He signed off and tuned to the regular wavelength to signal the *Stromberg*.

The morbid thought occurred to him that he might never eat salted herring again.

'I've heard of being armed to the teeth, but this is ridiculous,' said Nat Dickstein, and they all laughed.

The message from the *Coparelli* had altered his mood. At first he had been shocked. How had the opposition managed to learn so much of his plan that they had been able to hijack the *Coparelli* first? Somewhere he must have made terrible errors of judgment. Suza . . .? But there was no point now in castigating himself. There was a fight ahead. His black depression vanished. The tension was still there, coiled tight inside him like a steel spring, but now he could ride it and use it, now he had something to do with it.

The twelve men in the mess room of the *Stromberg* sensed the change in Dickstein and they caught his eagerness for the battle, although they knew some of them would die soon.

Armed to the teeth they were. Each had an Uzi 9-mm

submachine gun, a reliable, compact firearm weighing nine pounds when loaded with the 25-round magazine and only an inch over two feet long with its metal stock extended. They had three spare magazines each. Each man had a 9-mm Luger in a belt holster – the pistol would take the same cartridges as the machine gun – and a clip of four grenades on the opposite side of his belt. Almost certainly, they all had extra weapons of their own choice: knives, blackjacks, bayonets, knuckle-dusters and others more exotic, carried superstitiously, more like lucky charms than fighting implements.

Dickstein knew their mood, knew they had caught it from him. He had felt it before with men before a fight. They were afraid, and – paradoxically – the fear made them eager to get started, for the waiting was the worst part, the battle itself was anaesthetic, and afterwards you had either survived or you were dead and did not care any more.

Dickstein had figured his battle plan in detail and briefed them. The *Coparelli* was designed like a miniature tanker, with holds forward and amidships, the main superstructure on the afterdeck, and a secondary superstructure in the stern. The main superstructure contained the bridge, the officers' quarters and the mess; below it were crew's quarters. The stern superstructure contained the galley, below that stores, and below these the engine room. The two superstructures were separate above deck, but below deck they were connected by gangways.

They were to go over in three teams. Abbas's would

attack the bows. The other two, led by Bader and Gibli, would go up the port and starboard ladders at the stern.

The two stern teams were detailed to go below and work forward, flushing out the enemy amidships where they could be mown down by Abbas and his men from the prow. The strategy was likely to leave a pocket of resistance at the bridge, so Dickstein planned to take the bridge himself.

The attack would be by night; otherwise they would never get aboard – they would be picked off as they came over the rails. That left the problem of how to avoid shooting at one another as well as the enemy. For this he provided a recognition signal, the word *Aliyah*, and the attack plan was designed so that they were not expected to confront one another until the very end.

Now they were waiting.

They sat in a loose circle in the galley of the *Stromberg*, identical to the galley of the *Coparelli* where they would soon be fighting and dying. Dickstein was speaking to Abbas: 'From the bows you'll control the foredeck, an open field of fire. Deploy your men behind cover and stay there. When the enemy on deck reveal their positions, pick them off. Your main problem is going to be hailing fire from the bridge.'

Slumped in his chair, Abbas looked even more like a tank than usual. Dickstein was glad Abbas was on his side. 'And we hold our fire at first.'

Dickstein nodded. 'Yes. You've a good chance of getting aboard unseen. No point in shooting until you know the rest of us have arrived.'

Abbas nodded. 'I see Porush is on my team. You know he's my brother-in-law.'

'Yes. I also know he's the only married man here. I thought you might want to take care of him.'

'Thanks.'

Feinberg looked up from the knife he was cleaning. The lanky New Yorker was not grinning for once. 'How do you figure these Arabs?'

Dickstein shook his head. 'They could be regular army or Fedayeen.'

Feinberg grinned. 'Let's hope they're regular army – we make faces, they surrender.'

It was a lousy joke, but they all laughed anyway.

Ish, always pessimistic, sitting with his feet on a table and his eyes closed, said, 'Going over the rail will be the worst part. We'll be naked as babes.'

Dickstein said, 'Remember that they believe we're expecting to take over a deserted boat. Their ambush is supposed to be a big surprise for us. They're looking for an easy victory – but we're prepared. And it will be dark—'

The door opened and the captain came in. 'We've sighted the *Coparelli*.'

Dickstein stood up. 'Let's go. Good luck, and don't take any prisoners.'

CHAPTER SIXTEEN

THE THREE boats pulled away from the *Stromberg* in the last few minutes before dawn.

Within seconds the ship behind them was invisible. She had no navigation lights, and deck lights and cabin lamps had been extinguished, even below the water-line, to ensure that no light escaped to warn the *Coparelli*.

The weather had worsened during the night. The captain of the *Stromberg* said it was still not bad enough to be called a storm, but the rain was torrential, the wind strong enough to blow a steel bucket clattering along the deck, the waves so high that now Dickstein was obliged to cling tightly to his bench seat in the well of the motorboat.

For a while they were in limbo, with nothing visible ahead or behind. Dickstein could not even see the faces of the four men in the boat with him. Feinberg broke the silence: 'I still say we should have postponed this fishing trip until tomorrow.'

Whistling past the graveyard.

Dickstein was as superstitious as the rest: underneath his oilskin and his life jacket he wore his father's old striped waistcoat with a smashed fob watch in the pocket over his heart. The watch had once stopped a German bullet.

Dickstein was thinking logically, but in a way he knew he had gone a little crazy. His affair with Suza, and her betrayal, had turned him upside down: his old values and motivations had been jolted, and the new ones he had acquired with her had turned to dust in his hands. He still cared for some things: he wanted to win this battle, he wanted Israel to have the uranium, and he wanted to kill Yasif Hassan; the one thing he did not care about was himself. He had no fear, suddenly, of bullets and pain and death. Suza had betrayed him, and he had no burning desire to live a long life with that in his past. So long as Israel got its bomb, Esther would die peacefully, Mottie would finish *Treasure Island*, and Yigael would look after the grapes.

He gripped the barrel of the machine gun beneath his oilskin.

They crested a wave and suddenly, there in the next trough, was the *Coparelli*.

Switching from forward to reverse several times in rapid succession, Levi Abbas edged his boat closer to the bows of the *Coparelli*. The white light above them enabled him to see quite clearly, while the outward-curving hull shielded his boat from the sight of anyone on deck or on the bridge. When the boat was close enough to the ladder Abbas took a rope and tied it around his waist under the oilskin. He hesitated a moment, then shucked off the oilskin, unwrapped his gun and slung the gun over his neck. He stood with one foot in the boat and one on the gunwale, waited for his moment, and jumped.

He hit the ladder with both feet and both hands. He untied the rope around his waist and secured it to a rung of the ladder. He went up the ladder almost to the top, then stopped. They should go over the rail as close together as possible.

He looked back down. Sharrett and Sapir were already on the ladder below him. As he looked, Porush made his jump, landed awkwardly and missed his grip, and for a moment Abbas's breath caught in his throat; but Porush slipped down only one rung before he manged to hook an arm around the side of the ladder and arrest his descent.

Abbas waited for Porush to come up close behind Sapir, then he went over the rail. He landed softly on all fours and crouched low beside the gunwale. The others followed swiftly: one, two, three. The white light was above them and they were very exposed.

Abbas looked about. Sharrett was the smallest and he could wriggle like a snake. Abbas touched his shoulder and pointed across the deck. 'Take cover on the port side.'

Sharret bellied across two yards of open deck, then he was partly concealed by the raised edge of the for'ard hatch. He inched forward.

Abbas looked up and down the deck. At any moment they could be spotted; they would know nothing until a hail of bullets tore into them. Quick, quick! Up in the stem was the winding gear for the anchor, with a large pile of slack chain. 'Sapir.' Abbas pointed, and Sapir crawled along the deck to the position.

'I like the crane,' Porush said.

Abbas looked at the derrick towering over them, dominating the whole of the foredeck. The control cabin was some ten feet above deck level. It would be a dangerous position, but it made good tactical sense. 'Go,' he said.

Porush crawled forward, following Sharrett's route. Watching, Abbas thought: He's got a fat ass – my sister feeds him too well. Porush gained the foot of the crane and began to climb the ladder. Abbas held his breath – if one of the enemy should happen to look this way now, while Porush was on the ladder – then he reached the cabin.

Behind Abbas, in the prow, was a companion head over a short flight of steps leading down to a door. The area was not big enough to be called a fo'c'sle, and there was almost certainly no proper accommodation in there – it was simply a for'ard store. He crawled to it, crouched at the foot of the steps in the little well, and gently cracked the door. It was dark inside. He closed the door and turned around, resting his gun on the head of the steps, satisfied that he was alone.

There was very little light at the stern end, and Dickstein's boat had to get very close to the *Coparelli*'s starboard ladder. Gibli, the team leader, found it difficult to keep the boat in position. Dickstein found a boathook in the well of the launch and used it to hold the boat steady, pulling toward the *Coparelli* when the sea tried to part them and pushing away when the boat and the ship threatened to collide broadside.

Gibli, who was ex-army, insisted on adhering to the Israeli tradition that the officers lead their men from in front, not from behind: he had to go first. He always wore a hat to conceal his receding hairline, and now he sported a beret. He crouched at the edge of the boat while it slid down a wave: then, in the trough when boat and ship moved closer together, he jumped. He landed well and moved upward.

On the edge, waiting for his moment, Feinberg said, 'Now, then – I count to three, then open my parachute, right?' Then he jumped.

Katzen went next, then Raoul Dovrat. Dickstein dropped the boathook and followed. On the ladder, he leaned back and looked up through the streaming rain to see Gibli reach the level of the gunwale then swing one leg over the rail.

Dickstein looked back over his shoulder and saw a faint band of lighter grey in the distant sky, the first sign of dawn.

Then there was a sudden shocking burst of machine-gun fire and a shout.

Dickstein looked up again to see Gibli falling slowly backward off the top of the ladder. His beret came off and was whipped away by the wind, disappearing into the darkness. Gibli fell down, down past Dickstein and into the sea.

Dickstein shouted, 'Go, go, go!'

Feinberg flew over the rail. He would hit the deck

rolling, Dickstein knew, then – yes, there was the sound of his gun as he gave covering fire for the others—

And Katzen was over and there were four, five, many guns crackling, and Dickstein was scampering up the ladder and pulling the pin from a grenade with his teeth and hurling it up and over the rail some thirty yards forward, where it would cause a diversion without injuring any of his men already on deck, and then Dovrat was over the rail and Dickstein saw him hit the deck rolling, gain his feet, dive for cover behind the stern superstructure and Dickstein yelled, 'Here I come you fuckers' and went over in a high-jumper's roll, landed on hands and knees, bent double under a sheet of covering fire and scampered to the stern.

'Where are they?' he yelled.

Feinberg stopped shooting to answer him. 'In the galley,' he said, jerking a thumb toward the bulkhead beside them. 'In the lifeboats, and in the doorways amidships.'

'All right.' Dickstein got to his feet. 'We hold this position until Bader's group makes the deck. When you hear them open fire, move. Dovrat and Katzen, hit the galley door and head below. Feinberg, cover them, then work your way forward along this edge of the deck. I'll make for the first lifeboat. Meantime give them something to distract their attention from the port stern ladder and Bader's team. Fire at will.'

Hassan and Mahmoud were interrogating the sailor when the shooting started. They were in the chartroom, aft of the bridge. The sailor would speak only German, but Hassan spoke German. His story was that the *Coparelli* had broken down and the crew had been taken off, leaving him to wait in the ship until a spare part arrived. He knew nothing of uranium or hijacks or Dickstein. Hassan did not believe him, for – as he pointed out to Mahmoud – if Dickstein could arrange for the ship to break down, he could surely arrange for one of his own men to be left aboard it. The sailor was tied to a chair, and now Mahmoud was cutting off his fingers one by one in an attempt to make him tell a different story.

They heard one quick burst of firing, then a silence, then a second burst followed by a barrage. Mahmoud sheathed his knife and went down the stairs which led from the chartroom to the officers' quarters.

Hassan tried to assess the situation. The Fedayeen were grouped in three places – the lifeboats, the galley and the main amidships superstructure. From where he was Hassan could see both port and starboard sides of the deck, and if he went forward from the chartroom to the bridge he could see the foredeck. Most of the Israelis seemed to have boarded the ship at the stern. The Fedayeen, both those immediately below Hassan and those in the lifeboats at either side, were firing toward the stern. There was no firing from the galley, which must mean the Israelis had taken it. They must have gone below, but they had left two men on deck, one on either side, to guard their rear.

Mahmoud's ambush had failed, then. The Israelis were supposed to be mown down as they came over the rail. In fact they had succeeded in reaching cover, and now the battle was even.

The fighting on deck was stalemated, with both sides shooting at each other from good cover. That was the Israelis' intention, Hassan assumed: to keep the opposition busy on deck while they made their progress below. They would attack the Fedayeen stronghold, the amidships superstructure, from below, after making their way the length of the 'tweendecks gangways.

Where was the best place to be? Right where he was, Hassan decided. To reach him the Israelis had to fight their way along the 'tweendecks, then up through the officers' quarters, then up again to the bridge and chartroom. It was a tough position to take.

There was a huge explosion from the bridge. The heavy door separating bridge and chartroom rattled, sagged on its hinges and fell slowly inward. Hassan looked through.

A grenade had landed in the bridge. The bodies of three Fedayeen were spread across the bulkheads. All the glass of the bridge was smashed. The grenade must have come from the foredeck, which meant that there was another group of Israelis in the prow. As if to confirm his supposition, a burst of gunfire came from the for'ard crane.

Hassan picked up a submachine gun from the floor, rested it on the window frame, and began to shoot back.

*

Levi Abbas watched Porush's grenade sail through the air and into the bridge, then saw the explosion shatter what remained of the glass. The guns from that quarter were briefly silenced, and then a new one started up. For a minute Abbas could not figure out what the new gun was shooting at, for none of the bullets landed near him. He looked at either side. Sapir and Sharrett were both shooting at the bridge, and neither seemed to be under fire. Abbas looked up at the crane. Porush – it was Porush who was under fire. There was a burst from the cabin of the crane as Porush fired back.

The shooting from the bridge was amateurish, wild and inaccurate – the man was just spraying bullets. But he had a good position. He was high, and well protected by the walls of the bridge. He would hit something sooner or later. Abbas took out a grenade and lobbed it, but it fell short. Only Porush was close enough to throw into the bridge, and he had used all his grenades – only the fourth had landed on target.

Abbas fired again, then looked up at the control cabin of the crane. As he looked, he saw Porush come toppling backward out of the control cabin, turn over in the air, and fall like a dead weight to the deck.

Abbas thought: And how will I tell my sister?

The gunman in the bridge stopped firing, then resumed with a burst in Sharrett's direction. Unlike Abbas and Sapir, Sharrett had very little cover: he was squeezed between a capstan and the gunwale. Abbas and Sapir both shot at the bridge. The unseen sniper was improving: bullets stitched a seam in the deck toward Sharrett's capstan; then Sharrett screamed, jumped sideways, and jerked as if electrocuted while more bullets thudded into his body, until at last he lay still and the screaming stopped.

The situation was bad. Abbas's team was supposed to command the foredeck, but at the moment the man on the bridge was doing that. Abbas had to take him out.

He threw another grenade. It landed short of the bridge and exploded; the flash might dazzle the sniper for a second or two. When the bang came Abbas was on his feet and running for the crane, the crash of Sapir's covering fire in his ears. He made the foot of the ladder and started firing before the sniper on the bridge saw him. Then bullets were clanging on the girders all around him. It seemed to take him an age to climb each step. Some lunatic part of his mind began to count the steps: seven-eight-nine-ten—

He was hit by a ricochet. The bullet entered his thigh just below the hip bone. It did not kill him, but the shock of it seemed to paralyze the muscles in the lower half of his body. His feet slipped from the rungs of the ladder. He had a moment of confused panic as he discovered that his legs would not work. Instinctively he grabbed for the ladder with his hands, but he missed and fell. He turned partly over and landed awkwardly, breaking his neck; and he died.

The door to the for'ard store opened slightly and a wide-eyed, frightened Russian face looked out; but nobody saw it, and it went back inside; and the door closed.

As Katzen and Dovrat rushed the galley, Dickstein took advantage of Feinberg's covering fire to move forward. He ran, bent double, past the point at which they had boarded the ship and past the galley door, to throw himself behind the first of the lifeboats, one that had already been grenaded. From there, in the faint but increasing light, he could make out the lines of the amidships superstructure, shaped like a flight of three steps rising forward. At the main deck level was the officers' mess, the officers' dayroom, the sick bay and a passenger cabin used as a dry store. On the next level up were officers' cabins, heads, and the captain's quarters. On the top deck was the bridge with adjoining chartroom and radio booth.

Most of the enemy would now be at deck level in the mess and the dayroom. He could bypass them by climbing a ladder alongside the funnel to the walkway around the second deck, but the only way to the bridge was through the second deck. He would have to take out any soldiers in the cabins on his own.

He looked back. Feinberg had retreated behind the galley, perhaps to reload. He waited until Feinberg started shooting again, then got to his feet. Firing wildly from the hip, he broke from behind the lifeboat and dashed across the afterdeck to the ladder. Without breaking stride, he jumped on to the fourth rung and scrambled up, conscious that for a few seconds he made an easy target, hearing a clutch of bullets rattle on the funnel beside him, until he reached the level of the upper deck and flung himself across the walkway to fetch up, breathing hard and shaking with effort, lying against the door to the officers' quarters.

'Stone the bloody crows,' he muttered.

He reloaded his gun. He put his back to the door and slowly slid upright to a porthole in the door at eye level. He risked a look. He saw a passage with three doors on either side and, at the far end, ladders going down to the mess and up to the chartroom. He knew that the bridge could be reached by either of two outside ladders leading up from the main deck as well as by way of the chartroom. However, the Arabs still controlled that part of the deck and could cover the outside ladders; therefore the only way to the bridge was this way.

He opened the door and stepped in. He crept along the passage to the first cabin door, opened it, and threw in a grenade. He saw one of the enemy begin to turn around, and closed the door. He heard the grenade explode in the small space. He ran to the next door on the same side, opened it, and threw in another grenade. It exploded into empty space.

There was one more door on this side, and he had no more grenades.

He ran to the door, threw it open, and went in firing. There was one man here. He had been firing through the porthole, but now he was easing his gun

out of the hole and turning around. Dickstein's burst
of bullets sliced him in half.

Dickstein turned and faced the open door, waiting.
The door of the opposite cabin flew open and Dickstein
shot down the man behind it.

Dickstein stepped into the gangway, firing blind.
There were two more cabins to account for. The door
of the nearer one opened as Dickstein was spraying it,
and a body fell out.

One to go. Dickstein watched. The door opened a
crack, then closed again. Dickstein ran down the gangway, and kicked open the door, sprayed the cabin.
There was no return fire. He stepped inside: the
occupant had been hit by a ricochet and lay bleeding
on the bunk.

Dickstein was seized with a kind of mad exultation:
he had taken the entire deck on his own.

Next, the bridge. He ran forward along the gangway.
At the far end the companionway led up to the chartroom and down to the officers' mess. He stepped on to
the ladder, looked up, and threw himself down and
away as the snout of a gun poked down at him and
began to fire.

His grenades were gone. The man in the chartroom
was impregnable to gunfire. He could stay behind the
edge of the companionhead and fire blind down the
ladder. Dickstein had to get on the ladder, for he
wanted to go up.

He went into one of the forward cabins to overlook
the deck and try to assess the situation. He was appalled

when he saw what had happened on the foredeck: only one of the four men of Abbas's team was still firing, and Dickstein could just make out three bodies. Two or three guns seemed to be firing from the bridge at the remaining Israeli, trapping him behind a stack of anchor chain.

Dickstein looked to the side. Feinberg was still well aft – he had not managed to progress forward. And there was still no sign of the men who had gone below.

The Fedayeen were well entrenched in the mess below him. From their superior position they were able to keep at bay the men on deck and the men in the 'tweendecks below them. The only way to take the mess would be to attack it from all sides at once – including from above. But that meant taking the bridge first. And the bridge was impregnable.

Dickstein ran back along the gangway and out of the aft door. It was still pouring with rain, but there was a dim cold light in the sky. He could make out Feinberg on one side and Dovrat on the other. He called out their names until he caught their attention, then pointed at the galley. He jumped from the walkway to the afterdeck, raced across it, and dived into the galley.

They had got his meaning. A moment later they followed him in. Dickstein said, 'We have to take the mess.'

'I don't see how,' said Feinberg.

'Shut up and I'll tell you. We rush it from all sides at once: port, starboard, below and above. First we have to take the bridge. I'm going to do that. When I get there I'll sound the foghorn. That will be the signal. I want you both to go below and tell the men there.'

'How will you reach the bridge?' Feinberg said.

Dickstein said, 'Over the roof.'

On the bridge, Yasif Hassan had been joined by Mahmoud and two more of his Fedayeen, who took up firing positions while the leaders sat on the floor and conferred.

'They can't win,' Mahmoud said. 'From here we control too much deck. They can't attack the mess from below, because the companionway is easy to dominate from above. They can't attack from the sides or the front because we can fire down on them from here. They can't attack from above because we control the down companion. We just keep shooting until they surrender.'

Hassan said, 'One of them tried to take this companion a few minutes ago. I stopped him.'

'You were on your own up here?'

'Yes.'

He put his hands on Hassan's shoulders. 'You are now one of the Fedayeen,' he said.

Hassan voiced the thought that was on both their minds. 'After this?'

Mahmoud nodded. 'Equal partners.'

They clasped hands.

Hassan repeated, 'Equal partners.'

Mahmoud said, 'And now, I think they will try for that companionway again – it's their only hope.'

'I'll cover it from the chartroom,' Hassan said.

They both stood up; then a stray bullet from the

foredeck came in through the glassless windows and entered Mahmoud's brain, and he died instantly.

And Hassan was the leader of the Fedayeen.

Lying on his belly, arms and legs spread wide for traction, Dickstein inched his way across the roof. It was curved, and totally without handholds, and it was slick with rain. As the *Coparelli* heaved and shifted in the waves, the roof tilted forward, backward, and from side to side. All Dickstein could do was press himself to the metal and try to slow his slide.

At the forward end of the roof was a navigation light. When he reached that he would be safe, for he could hold on to it. His progress toward it was painfully slow. He got within a foot of it, then the ship rolled to port and he slid away. It was a long roll, and it took him all the way to the edge of the roof. For a moment he hung with one arm and a leg over a thirty-foot drop to the deck. The ship rolled a little more, the rest of his leg went over and he tried to dig the fingernails of his right hand into the painted metal of the roof.

There was an agonizing pause.

The *Coparelli* rolled back.

Dickstein let himself go with the roll, sliding faster and faster toward the navigation light.

But the ship pitched up, the roof tilted backward, and he slid in a long curve, missing the light by a yard. Once again he pressed his hands and feet into the metal, trying to slow himself down; once again he went all the way to the edge; once again he hung over the drop to the deck; but this time it was his right arm which dangled over the edge, and his machine gun slipped off his right shoulder and fell into a lifeboat.

She rolled back and pitched forward, and Dickstein found himself sliding with increasing speed toward the navigation light. This time he reached it. He grabbed with both hands. The light was about a foot from the forward edge of the roof. Immediately below the edge were the front windows of the bridge. their glass smashed out long ago, and two gun barrels poking out through them.

Dickstein held on to the light, but he could not stop his slide. His body swung about in a wide sweep, heading for the edge. He saw that the front of the roof, unlike the sides, had a narrow steel gutter to take away the rain from the glass below. As his body swung over the edge he released his grip on the navigation light, let himself slide forward with the pitch of the ship, grabbed the steel gutter with his fingertips, and swung his legs down and in. He came flying through the broken windows feet first to land in the middle of the bridge. He bent his knees to take the shock of landing, then straightened up. His submachine gun had been lost and he had no time to draw his pistol or his knife. There were two Arabs on the bridge, one on either side of him, both holding machine guns and firing down on to the deck. As Dickstein straightened up they began to turn toward him, their faces a picture of amazement.

Dickstein was fractionally nearer the one on the port side. He lashed out with a kick which, more by luck than by judgment, landed on the point of the man's elbow, momentarily paralyzing his gun arm. Then Dickstein jumped for the other man. His machine gun was swinging toward Dickstein just a split second too late: Dickstein got inside its swing. He brought up his right hand in the most vicious two-stroke blow he knew: the heel of his hand hit the point of the Arab's chin, snapping his head back for the second stroke as Dickstein's hand, fingers stiffened for a karate chop, came down hard into the exposed flesh of the soft throat.

Before the man could fall Dickstein grabbed him by the jacket and swung him around between himself and the other Arab. The other man was bringing up his gun. Dickstein lifted the dead man and hurled him across the bridge as the machine gun opened up. The dead body took the bullets and crashed into the other Arab, who lost his balance, went backward out through the open doorway and fell to the deck below.

There was a third man in the chartroom, guarding the companionway leading down. In the three seconds during which Dickstein had been on the bridge the man had stood up and turned around; and now Dickstein recognized Yasif Hassan.

Dickstein dropped to a crouch, stuck out a leg, kicked at the broken door which lay on the floor between himself and Hassan. The door slid along the deck, striking Hassan's feet. It was only enough to throw him off balance, but as he spread his arms to recover his equilibrium Dickstein moved.

Until this moment Dickstein had been like a machine, reacting reflexively to everything that confronted him, letting his nervous system plan every move without conscious thought, allowing training and instinct to guide him; but now it was more than that. Now, faced with the enemy of all he had ever loved, he was possessed by blind hatred and mad rage.

It gave him added speed and power.

He took hold of Hassan's gun arm by the wrist and shoulder, and with a downward pull broke the arm over his knee. Hassan screamed and the gun dropped from his useless hand. Turning slightly, Dickstein brought his elbow back in a blow which caught Hassan just under the ear. Hassan turned away, falling. Dickstein grabbed his hair from behind, pulling the head backward; and as Hassan sagged away from him he lifted his foot high and kicked. His heel struck the back of Hassan's neck at the moment he jerked the head. There was a snap as all the tension went out of the man's muscles and his head lolled, unsupported, on his shoulders.

Dickstein let go and the body crumpled.

He stared at the harmless body with exultation ringing in his ears.

Then he saw Koch.

The engineer was tied to a chair, slumped over, pale as death but conscious. There was blood on his clothes. Dickstein drew his knife and cut the ropes that bound Koch. Then saw the man's hands.

He said, 'Christ.'

'I'll live,' Koch muttered. He did not get up from the chair.

Dickstein picked up Hassan's machine gun and

checked the magazine. It was almost full. He moved out on to the bridge and located the foghorn.

'Koch,' he said, 'can you get out of that chair?'

Koch got up, swaying unsteadily until Dickstein stepped across and supported him, leading him through to the bridge. 'See this button? I want you to count slowly to ten, then lean on it.'

Koch shook his head to clear it. 'I think I can handle it.'

'Start. Now.'

'One,' Koch said. 'Two.'

Dickstein went down the companionway and came out on the second deck, the one he had cleared himself. It was still empty, He went on down, and stopped just before the ladder emerged into the mess. He figured all the remaining Fedayeen must be here, lined against the walls, shooting out through portholes and doorways; one or two perhaps watching the companionway. There was no safe, careful way to take such a strong defensive position.

Come on, Koch!

Dickstein had intended to spend a second or two hiding in the companionway. At any moment one of the Arabs might look up it to check. If Koch had collapsed he would have to go back up there and—

The foghorn sounded.

Dickstein jumped. He was firing before he landed. There were two men close to the foot of the ladder. He shot them first. The firing from outside went into a crescendo. Dickstein turned in a rapid half circle, dropped to one knee to make a smaller target, and sprayed the Fedayeen along the walls. Suddenly there was another gun as Ish came up from below; then Feinberg was at one door, shooting; and Dovrat, wounded, came in through another door. And then, as if by signal, they all stopped shooting, and the silence was like thunder.

All the Fedayeen were dead.

Dickstein, still kneeling, bowed his head in exhaustion. After a moment he stood up and looked at his men. 'Where are the others?' he said.

Feinberg gave him a peculiar look. 'There's someone on the foredeck, Sapir I think.'

'And the rest?'

'That's it,' Feinberg said. 'All the others are dead.'

Dickstein slumped against a bulkhead. 'What a price,' he said quietly.

Looking out through the smashed porthole he saw that it was day.

CHAPTER SEVENTEEN

A YEAR earlier the BOAC jet in which Suza Ashford was serving dinner had abruptly begun to lose height for no apparent reason over the Atlantic Ocean. The pilot had switched on the seat-belt lights. Suza had walked up and down the aisle, saying, 'Just a little turbulence,' and helping people fasten their seat belts, all the time thinking: We're going to die, we're all going to die.

She felt like that now.

There had been a short message from Tyrin: *Israel is attacking* – then silence. At this moment Nathaniel was being shot at. He might be wounded, he might have been captured, he might be dead; and while Suza seethed with nervous tension she had to give the radio operator the BOAC Big Smile and say. 'It's quite a setup you've got here.'

The *Karla*'s radio operator was a big grey-haired man from Odessa. His name was Aleksandr, and he spoke passable English. 'It cost one hundred thousand dollar,' he said proudly. 'You know about radio?'

'A little . . . I used to be an air hostess.' She had said 'used to be' without forethought, and now she wondered whether that life really was gone. 'I've seen the air crew using their radios. I know the basics.'

'Really, this is four radios,' Aleksandr explained. 'One picks up the *Stromberg* beacon. One listens to Tyrin on *Coparelli*. One listens to *Coparelli*'s regular wave-length. And this one wanders. Look.'

He showed her a dial whose pointer moved around slowly. 'It seeks a transmitter, stops when it finds one,' Aleksandr said.

'That's incredible. Did you invent that?'

'1 am an operator, not inventor, sadly.'

'And you can broadcast on any of the sets, just by switching to TRANSMIT?'

'Yes, Morse code or speech. But of course, on this operation nobody uses speech.'

'Did you have to go through long training to become a radio operator?'

'Not long. Learning Morse is easy. But to be a ship's radioman you must know how to repair the set.' He lowered his voice. 'And to be a KGB operator, you must go to spy school.' He laughed, and Suza laughed with him, thinking: come on, Tyrin; and then her wish was granted.

The message began, Aleksandr started writing and at the same time said to Suza, 'Tyrin. Get Rostov, please.'

Suza left the bridge reluctantly; she wanted to know what was in the message. She hurried to the mess, expecting to find Rostov there drinking strong black coffee, but the room was empty. She went down another deck and made her way to his cabin. She knocked on the door.

His voice in Russian said something which might have meant come in.

She opened the door. Rostov stood there in his shorts, washing in a bowl.

'Tyrin's coming through,' Suza said. She turned to leave.

'Suza.'

She turned back. 'What would you say if I surprised you in your underwear?'

'I'd say piss off,' she said.

'Wait for me outside.'

She closed the door, thinking: That's done it.

When he came out she said, 'I'm sorry.'

He gave a tight smile. 'I should not have been so unprofessional. Let's go.'

She followed him up to the radio room, which was immediately below the bridge in what should have been the captain's cabin. Because of the mass of extra equipment, Aleksandr had explained, it was not possible to put the radio operator adjacent to the bridge, as was customary. Suza had figured out for herself that this arrangement had the additional advantage of segregating the radio from the crew when the ship carried a mixture of ordinary seamen and KGB agents.

Aleksandr had transcribed Tyrin's signal. He handed it to Rostov, who read it in English. 'Israelis have taken *Coparelli. Stromberg* alongside. Dickstein alive.'

Suza went limp with relief. She had to sit down. She slumped into a chair.

No one noticed. Rostov was already composing his reply to Tyrin: 'We will hit at six A.M. tomorrow.'

The tide of relief went out for Suza and she thought: Oh, God, what do I do now?

Nat Dickstein stood in silence, wearing a borrowed seaman's cap, as the captain of the *Stromberg* read the words of the service for the dead, raising his voice against the noise of wind, rain and sea. One by one the canvas-wrapped bodies were tipped over the rail into the black water: Abbas, Sharrett, Porush, Gibli, Bader, Rcmez, and Jabotinsky. Seven of the twelve had died. Uranium was the most costly metal in the world.

There had been another funeral earlier. Four Fedayeen had been left alive – three wounded, one who had lost his nerve and hidden – and after they had been disarmed Dickstein had allowed them to bury their dead. Theirs had been a bigger funeral – they had dropped twenty-five bodies into the sea. They had hurried through their ceremony under the watchful eyes – and guns – of three surviving Israelis, who understood that this courtesy should be extended to the enemy but did not have to like it.

Meanwhile, the *Stromberg*'s captain had brought aboard all his ship's papers. The team of fitters and joiners, which had come along in case it was necessary to alter the *Coparelli* to match the *Stromberg*, was set to work repairing the battle damage. Dickstein told them to concentrate on what was visible from the deck: the rest would have to wait until they reached port. They set about filling holes, repairing furniture, and replacing panes of glass and metal fittings with spares cannibalized from the doomed *Stromberg*. A painter went down a ladder to remove the name *Coparelli* from the hull and replace it with the stencilled letters s-t-r-o-m-b-e-r-g. When he had finished he set about painting over the repaired bulkheads and woodwork on deck. All the *Coparelli*'s lifeboats, damaged beyond repair, were chopped up and thrown over the side, and the *Stromberg*'s boats were brought over to replace them. The new oil pump, which the *Stromberg* had carried on Koch's instructions, was installed in the *Coparelli*'s engine.

Work had stopped for the burial. Now, as soon as the captain had uttered the final words, it began again. Towards the end of the afternoon the engine rumbled to life. Dickstein stood on the bridge with the captain while the anchor was raised. The crew of the *Stromberg* quickly found their way round the new ship, which was identical to their old one. The captain set a course and ordered full speed ahead.

It was almost over, Dickstein thought. The *Coparelli* had disappeared: for all intents and purposes the ship in which he now sailed was the *Stromberg*, and the *Stromberg* was legally owned by Savile Shipping. Israel had her uranium, and nobody knew how she had got it. Everyone in the chain of operation was now taken care of – except Pedler, still the legal owner of the yellowcake. He was the one man who could ruin the whole scheme if he should become either curious or hostile. Papagopolous would be handling him right now: Dickstein silently wished him luck.

'We're clear,' the captain said.

The explosives expert in the chartroom pulled a lever on his radio detonator, then everybody watched the empty *Stromberg*, now more than a mile away.

There was a loud, dull thud, like thunder, and the *Stromberg* seemed to sag in the middle. Her fuel tanks caught fire and the stormy evening was lit by a gout of flame reaching for the sky. Dickstein felt elation and faint anxiety at the sight of such great destruction. The *Stromberg* began to sink, slowly at first and then faster. Her stern went under; seconds later her bows followed; her funnel poked up above the water for a moment like the raised arm of a drowning man, and then she was gone.

Dickstein smiled faintly and turned away.

He heard a noise. The captain heard it too. They went to the side of the bridge and looked out, and then they understood.

Down on the deck, the men were cheering.

Franz Albrecht Pedler sat in his office on the outskirts of Wiesbaden and scratched his snowy-white head. The telegram from Angeluzzi e Bianco in Genoa, translated from the Italian by Pedler's multilingual secretary, was perfectly plain and at the same time totally incomprehensible. It said: PLEASE ADVISE SOONEST OF NEW EXPECTED DELIVERY DATE OF YELLOWCAKE.

As far as Pedler knew there was nothing wrong with the old expected delivery date, which was a couple of days away. Clearly Angeluzzi e Bianco knew something he did not. He had already wired the shippers: IS

YELLOWCAKE DELAYED? He felt a little annoyed with them. Surely they should have informed him as well as the receiving company if there was a delay. But maybe the Italians had their wires crossed. Pedler had formed the opinion during the war that you could never trust Italians to do what they were told. He had thought they might be different nowadays, but perhaps they were the same.

He stood at his window, watching the evening gather over his little cluster of factory buildings. He could almost wish he had not bought the uranium. The deal with the Israeli Army, all signed, sealed and delivered, would keep his company in profit for the rest of his life, and he no longer needed to speculate.

His secretary came in with the reply from the shippers, already translated: COPARELLI SOLD TO SAVILE SHIPPING OF ZURICH WHO NOW HAVE RESPONSIBILITY FOR YOUR CARGO. WE ASSURE YOU OF COMPLETE RELIABILITY OF PURCHASERS. There followed the phone number of Savile Shipping and the words SPEAK TO PAPAGOPOLOUS.

Pedler gave the telegram back to the secretary. 'Would you call that number in Zurich and get this Papagopolous on the line please?'

She came back a few minutes later. 'Papagopolous will call you back.'

Pedler looked at his watch. 'I suppose I'd better wait for his call. I might as well get to the bottom of this now that I've started.'

Papagopolous came through ten minutes later. Pedler said to him, 'I'm told you are now responsible for my cargo on board the *Coparelli*. I've had a cable from the Italians asking for a new delivery date – is there some delay?'

'Yes, there is,' Papagopolous said. 'You should have been informed – I'm terribly sorry.' The man spoke excellent German but it was still clear he was not a German. It was also clear he was not really terribly sorry. He went on, 'The *Coparelli*'s oil pump broke down at sea and she is becalmed. We're making arrangements to have your cargo delivered as early as possible.'

'Well, what am I to say to Angeluzzi e Bianco?'

'I have told them that I will let them know the new date just as soon as I know it myself,' Papagopolous said. 'Please leave it to me. I will keep you both informed.'

'Very well. Goodbye.'

Odd, Pedler thought as he hung up the phone. Looking out of the window, he saw that all the workers had left. The staff car parking lot was empty except for his Mercedes and his secretary's Volkswagen. What the hell, time to go home. He put on his coat. The uranium was insured. If it was lost he would get his money back. He turned out the office lights and helped his secretary on with her coat, then he got into his car and drove home to his wife.

Suza Ashford did not close her eyes all night.

Once again, Nat Dickstein's life was in danger. Once again, she was the only one who could warn him. And this time she could not deceive others into helping her.

She had to do it alone.

It was simple. She had to go to the *Karla*'s radio room, get rid of Aleksandr, and call the *Coparelli*.

I'll never do it, she thought. The ship is full of KGB. Aleksandr is a big man. I want to go to sleep. For ever. It's impossible. I can't do it.

Oh, Nathaniel.

At four A.M. she put on jeans, a sweater, boots and an oilskin. The full bottle of vodka she had taken from the mess − 'to help me sleep' − went in the inside pocket of the oilskin.

She had to know the *Karla*'s position.

She went up to the bridge. The first officer smiled at her. 'Can't sleep?' he said in English.

'The suspense is too much,' she told him. The BOAC Big Smile. Is your seat belt fastened, sir? Just a little turbulence, nothing to worry about. She asked the first officer, 'Where are we?'

He showed her their position on the map, and the estimated position of the *Coparelli*.

'What's that in numbers?' she said.

He told her the coordinates, the course, and the speed of the *Karla*. She repeated the numbers once aloud and twice more in her head, trying to burn them into her brain. 'It's fascinating,' she said brightly. 'Everyone on a ship has a special skill . . . Will we reach the *Coparelli* on time, do you think?'

'Oh, yes,' he said. 'Then − boom.'

She looked outside. It was completely black − there

were no stars and no ships' lights in sight. The weather was getting worse.

'You're shivering,' the first officer said. 'Are you cold?'

'Yes,' she said, though it was not the weather making her shiver. 'When is Colonel Rostov getting up?'

'He's to be called at five.'

'I think I'll try to get another hour's sleep.'

She went down to the radio room. Aleksandr was there. 'Couldn't you sleep, either?' she asked him.

'No. I've sent my number two to bed.'

She looked over the radio equipment. 'Aren't you listening to the *Stromberg* any more?'

'The signal stopped. Either they found the beacon, or they sank the ship. We think they sank her.'

Suza sat down and took out the bottle of vodka. She unscrewed the cap. 'Have a drink.' She handed him the bottle.

'Are you cold?'

'A little.'

'Your hand is shaking.' He took the bottle and put it to his lips, taking a long swallow. 'Ah, thank you.' He handed it back to her.

Suza drank a mouthful for courage. It was rough Russian vodka, and it burned her throat, but it had the desired effect. She screwed down the cap and waited for Aleksandr to turn his back on her.

'Tell me about life in England,' he said conversationally. 'Is it true that the poor starve while the rich get fat?'

'Not many people starve,' she said. Turn around,

469

damn it, turn *around*. I can't do this facing you. 'But there is great inequality.'

'Are there different laws for rich and poor?'

'There's a saying: "The law forbids rich and poor alike to steal bread and sleep under bridges."'

Aleksandr laughed. 'In the Soviet Union people are equal, but some have privileges. Will you live in Russia now?'

'I don't know.' Suza opened the bottle and passed it to him again.

He took a long swallow and gave it back. 'In Russia you won't have such clothes.'

The time was passing too quickly, she had to do it now. She stood up to take the bottle. Her oilskin was open down the front. Standing before him, she tilted her head back to drink from the bottle, knowing he would stare at her breasts as they jutted out. She allowed him a good look, then shifted her grip on the bottle and brought it down as hard as she could on top of his head.

There was a sickening thud as it hit him. He stared at her dazedly. She thought: You're supposed to be knocked out! His eyes would not shut. What do I do? She hesitated, then she gritted her teeth and hit him again.

His eyes closed and he slumped in the chair. Suza got hold of his feet and pulled. As he came off the chair his head hit the deck, making Suza wince, but then she thought: It's just as well, he'll stay out longer.

She dragged him to a cupboard. She was breathing fast, from fear as well as exertion. From her jeans pocket she took a long piece of baling twine she had picked up in the stern. She tied Aleksandr's feet, then turned him over and bound his hands behind his back.

She had to get him into the cupboard. She glanced at the door. Oh, God, don't let anyone come in now! She put his feet in, then straddled his unconscious body and tried to lift him. He was a heavy man. She got him half upright, but when she tried to shift him into the cupboard he slipped from her grasp. She got behind him to try again. She grasped him beneath the armpits and lifted. This way was better: she could lean his weight against her chest while she shifted her grip. She got him half upright again, then wrapped her arms around his chest and inched sideways. She had to go into the cupboard with him, let him go, then wriggle out from underneath him.

He was in a sitting position now, his feet against one side of the cupboard, his knees bent, and his back against the opposite side. She checked his bonds: still tight. But he could still shout! She looked about for something to stuff in his mouth to gag him. She could see nothing. She could not leave the room to search for something because he might come round in the meantime. The only thing that she could think of was her pantyhose.

It seemed to take her for ever to do it. She had to pull off her borrowed sea boots, take off her jeans, pull her pantyhose off, put her jeans on, get into her boots, then crumple the nylon cloth into a ball and stuff it between his slack jaws.

She could not close the cupboard door. 'Oh, God!'

she said out loud. It was Aleksandr's elbow that was in the way. His bound hands rested on the floor of the cupboard, and because of his slumped position his arms were bent outward. No matter how she pushed and shoved at the door that elbow stopped it from closing. Finally she had to get back into the cupboard with him and turn him slightly sideways so that he leaned into the corner. Now his elbow was out of the way.

She looked at him a moment longer. How long did people stay knocked out? She had no idea. She knew she should hit him again, but she was afraid of killing him. She went and got the bottle, and even lifted it over her head; but at the last moment she lost her nerve, put the bottle down, and slammed the cupboard door.

She looked at her wristwatch and gave a cry of dismay: it was ten minutes to five. The *Coparelli* would soon appear on the *Karla*'s radar screen, and Rostov would be here, and she would have lost her chance.

She sat down at the radio desk, switched the lever to TRANSMIT, selected the set that was already tuned to the *Coparelli*'s wavelength and leaned over the microphone.

'Calling *Coparelli*, come in please.'

She waited.

Nothing.

'Damn you to hell, Nat Dickstein, *speak* to me. Nathaniel!'

Nat Dickstein stood in the amidships hold of the *Coparelli*, staring at the drums of sandy metallic ore that had cost so much. They looked nothing special – just large black oil drums with the word PLUMBAT stencilled on their sides. He would have liked to open one and feel the stuff, just to know what it was like, but the lids were heavily sealed.

He felt suicidal. Instead of the elation of victory, he had only bereavement. He could not rejoice over the terrorists he had killed, he could only mourn for his own dead.

He went over the battle again, as he had been doing throughout a sleepless night. If he had told Abbas to open fire as soon as he got aboard it might have distracted the Fedayeen long enough for Gibli to get over the rail without being shot. If he had gone with three men to take out the bridge with grenades at the very start of the fight the mess might have been taken earlier and lives would have been saved. If . . . but there were a hundred things he would have done differently if he had been able to see into the future, or if he were just a wiser man.

Well, Israel would now have atom bombs to protect her for ever.

Even that thought gave him no joy. A year ago it would have thrilled him. But a year ago he had not met Suza Ashford.

He heard a noise and looked up. It sounded as if people were running around on deck. Some nautical crisis, no doubt.

Suza had changed him. She had taught him to expect more out of life than victory in battle. When he had anticipated this day, when he had thought about what it would feel like to have pulled off this tremendous coup, she had always been in his daydream, waiting for him somewhere, ready to share his triumph. But she would not be there. Nobody else would do. And there was no joy in a solitary celebration.

He had stared long enough. He climbed the ladder out of the hold, wondering what to do with the rest of his life. He emerged on deck. A rating peered at him. 'Mr Dickstein?'

'Yes. What do you want?'

'We've been searching the ship for you, sir . . . It's the radio, someone is calling the *Coparelli*. We haven't answered, sir, because we're not supposed to be the *Coparelli*, are we? But she says—'

'She?'

'Yes, sir. She's coming over clear – speech, not Morse code. She sounds close. And she's upset. "Speak to me, Nathaniel," she says, stuff like that, sir.'

Dickstein grabbed the rating by his peajacket. 'Nathaniel?' he shouted. 'Did she say Nathaniel?'

'Yes, sir, I'm sorry, if—'

But Dickstein was heading for the bridge at a run.

The voice of Nat Dickstein came over the radio: 'Who is calling *Coparelli*?'

She found her voice. 'Oh, Nat, at last.'

'Suza? Is that Suza?'

'Yes, yes.'

'Where are you?'

She gathered her thoughts. 'I'm with David Rostov

474

on a Russian ship called the *Karla*. Make a note of this.'
She gave him the position, course and speed just as the
first officer had told them to her. 'That was at four-ten
this morning. Nat, this ship is going to ram yours at six
A.M.'

'Ram? Why? Oh, I see . . .'

'Nat, they'll catch me at the radio any minute, what
are we going to do, quickly—'

'Can you create a diversion of some kind at precisely
five-thirty?'

'Diversion?'

'Start a fire, shout "man overboard", anything to
keep them all very busy for a few minutes.'

'Well – I'll try—'

'Do your best. I want them all running around,
nobody quite sure what's going on or what to do – are
they all KGB?'

'Yes.'

'Okay, now—'

The door of the radio room opened – Suza flipped
the switch to TRANSMIT and Dickstein's voice was
silenced and David Rostov walked in. He said, 'Where's
Aleksandr?'

Suza tried to smile. 'He went for coffee. I'm minding
the shop.'

'The damn fool . . .' His curses switched into Russian
as he stormed out.

Suza moved the lever to RECEIVE.

Nat said, 'I heard that. You'd better make yourself
scarce until five-thirty—'

'Wait,' she shouted. 'What are you going to do?'

'Do?' he said. 'I'm coming to get you.'

'Oh,' she said. 'Oh, thank you.'

'I love you.'

As she switched off, Morse began to come through on another set. Tyrin would have heard every word of her conversation, and now he would be trying to warn Rostov. She had forgotten to tell Nat about Tyrin.

She could try to contact Nat again, but it would be very risky, and Tyrin would get his message through to Rostov in the time it took Nat's men to search the *Coparelli*, locate Tyrin and destroy his equipment. And when Tyrin's message got to Rostov, he would know Nat was coming, and he would be prepared.

She had to block that message.

She also had to get away.

She decided to wreck the radio.

How? All the wiring must be behind the panels. She would have to take a panel off. She needed a screwdriver. Quickly, quickly before Rostov gives up looking for Aleksandr! She found Aleksandr's tools in a corner and picked out a small screwdriver. She undid the screws on two corners of the panel. Impatient, she pocketed the screwdriver and forced the panel out with her hands. Inside was a mass of wires like psychedelic spaghetti. She grabbed a fistful and pulled. Nothing happened: she had pulled too many at once. She selected one, and tugged: it came out. Furiously she pulled wires until fifteen or twenty were hanging loose. Still the Morse code chattered. She poured the remains of the vodka into the innards of the radio. The Morse stopped, and every light on the panel went out.

There was a thump from inside the cupboard. Aleksandr must be coming round. Well, they would know everything as soon as they saw the radio now anyway.

She went out, closing the door behind her.

She went down the ladder and out on to the deck, trying to figure out where she could hide and what kind of diversion she could create. No point now in shouting 'man overboard' – they certainly would not believe her after what she had done to their radio and their radio operator. Let down the anchor? She would not know where to begin.

What was Rostov likely to do now? He would look for Aleksandr in the galley, the mess, and his cabin. Not finding him, he would return to the radio room, and then would start a shipwide search for her.

He was a methodical man. He would start at the prow and work backwards along the main deck, then send one party to search the upperworks and another to sweep below, deck by deck, starting at the top and working down.

What was the lowest part of the ship? The engine room. That would have to be her hiding place. She went inside and found her way to a downward companionway. She had her foot on the top rung of the ladder when she saw Rostov.

And he saw her.

She had no idea where her next words came from. 'Aleksandr's come back to the radio room. I'll be back in a moment.'

Rostov nodded grimly, and went off in the direction of the radio room.

She headed straight down through two decks and emerged into the engine room. The second engineer was on duty at night. He stared at her as she came in and approached him.

'This is the only warm place on the ship,' she said cheerfully. 'Mind if I keep you company?'

He looked mystified, and said slowly, 'I cannot . . . speak English . . . please.'

'You don't speak English?'

He shook his head.

'I'm cold,' she said, and mimed a shiver. She held her hands out toward the throbbing engine. 'Okay?'

He was more than happy to have this beautiful girl for company in his engine room. 'Okay,' he said, nodding vigorously.

He continued to stare at her, with a pleased look on his face, until it occurred to him that he should perhaps show some hospitality. He looked about, then pulled a pack of cigarettes from his pocket and offered her one.

'I don't usually, but I think I will,' she said, and took a cigarette. It had a small cardboard tube for a filter. The engineer lit it for her. She looked up at the hatch, half expecting to see Rostov. She looked at her watch. It could not be five-twenty-five already! She had no time to think. Diversion, start a diversion. Shout 'man overboard', drop the anchor, light a fire—

Light a fire.

With what?

Petrol, there must be petrol, or diesel fuel, or something, right here in the engine room.

She looked over the engine. Where did the petrol

come in? The thing was a mass of tubes and pipes. Concentrate, concentrate! She wished she had learned more about the engine of her car. Were boat engines the same? No, sometimes they used truck fuel. Which kind was this? It was supposed to be a fast ship, so perhaps it used petrol, she remembered vaguely that petrol engines were more expensive to run but faster. If it was a petrol engine it would be similar to the engine of her car. Were there cables leading to spark plugs? She had changed a spark plug once.

She stared. Yes, it was like her car. There were six plugs, with leads from them to a round cap like a distributor. Somewhere there had to be a carburettor. The petrol went through the carburettor. It was a small thing that sometimes got blocked—

The voice-pipe barked in Russian, and the engineer walked toward it to answer. His back was to Suza.

She had to do it now.

There was something about the size of a coffee tin with a lid held on by a central nut. It could be the carburettor. She stretched herself across the engine and tried to undo the nut with her fingers. It would not budge. A heavy plastic pipe led into it. She grabbed it and tugged. She could not pull it out. She remembered she had put Aleksandr's screwdriver into her oilskin pocket. She took it out and jabbed at the pipe with the sharp end. The plastic was thick and tough. She stabbed the screwdriver into it with all her might. It made a small cut in the surface of the pipe. She stuck the point of the screwdriver into the cut and worked it.

The engineer reached the voice-pipe and spoke into it in Russian.

Suza felt the screwdriver break through the plastic. She tugged it out. A spray of clear liquid jetted out of the little hole, and the air was filled with the unmistakable smell of petrol. She dropped the screwdriver and ran toward the ladder.

She heard the engineer answer yes in Russian and nod his head to a question from the voice-pipe. An order followed. The voice was angry. As she reached the foot of the ladder she looked back. The engineer's smiling face had been transformed into a mask of malice. She went up the ladder as he ran across the engine-room deck after her.

At the top of the ladder she turned around. She saw a pool of petrol spreading over the deck, and the engineer stepping on the bottom rung of the ladder. In her hand she still held the cigarette he had given her. She threw it toward the engine, aiming at the place where the petrol was squirting out of the pipe.

She did not wait to see it land. She carried on up the ladder. Her head and shoulders were emerging on to the next deck when there was a loud *whooosh*, a bright red light from below, and a wave of scorching heat. Suza screamed as her trousers caught fire and the skin of her legs burned. She jumped the last few inches of the ladder and rolled. She beat at her trousers, then struggled out of her oilskin and managed to wrap it around her legs. The fire was killed, but the pain got worse.

She wanted to collapse. She knew if she lay down she

would pass out and the pain would go, but she had to get away from the fire, and she had to be somewhere where Nat could find her. She forced herself to stand up. Her legs felt as if they were still burning. She looked down to see bits like burned paper falling off, and she wondered if they were bits of trouser or bits of leg.

She took a step.

She could walk.

She staggered along the gangway. The fire alarm began to sound all over the ship. She reached the end of the gangway and leaned on the ladder.

Up, she had to go up.

She raised one foot, placed it on the bottom rung, and began the longest climb of her life.

CHAPTER EIGHTEEN

F OR THE second time in twenty-four hours Nat
Dickstein was crossing huge seas in a small boat
to board a ship held by the enemy. He was dressed as
before, with life jacket, oilskin, and sea boots; and
armed as before with submachine gun, pistol and
grenades; but this time he was alone, and he was
terrified.

There had been an argument aboard the *Coparelli*
about what to do after Suza's radio message. Her
dialogue with Dickstein had been listened to by the
captain, Feinberg, and Ish. They had seen the jubilation
in Nat's face, and they had felt entitled to argue that
his judgment was now distorted by personal
involvement.

'It's a trap,' argued Feinberg. 'They can't catch us,
so they want us to turn and fight.'

'I know Rostov,' Dickstein said hotly. 'This is exactly
how his mind works: he waits for you to make a break,
then he pounces. This ramming idea has his name
written all over it.'

Feinberg got angry. 'This isn't a game, Dickstein.'

'Listen, Nat,' Ish said more reasonably, 'let's us
carry on and be ready to fight if and when they catch

us. What have we got to gain by sending a boarding party?'

'I'm not suggesting a boarding party. I'm going alone.'

'Don't be a damn fool,' Ish said. 'If you go, so do we – you can't take a ship alone.'

'Look,' Dickstein said, trying to pacify them. 'If I make it, the *Karla* will never catch this ship. If I don't, the rest of you can still fight when the *Karla* gets to you. And if the *Karla* really can't catch you, and it's a trap, then I'm the only one who falls into it. It's the best way.'

'I don't think it's the best way,' Feinberg said.

'Nor do I,' Ish said.

Dickstein smiled. 'Well, I do, and it's my life, and besides, I'm the senior officer here and it's my decision, so to hell with all of you.'

So he had dressed and armed himself, and the captain had shown him how to operate the launch's radio and how to maintain an interception course with the *Karla*, and they had lowered the launch, and he had climbed down into it and pulled away.

And he was terrified.

It was impossible for him to overcome a whole boat-load of KGB all on his own. However, he was not planning that. He would not fight with any of them if he could help it. He would get aboard, hide himself until Suza's diversion began, and then look for her; and when he had found her, he would get off the *Karla* with her and flee. He had a small magnetic mine with him that he would fix to the *Karla*'s side before boarding. Then,

483

whether he managed to escape or not, whether the whole thing was a trap or genuine, the *Karla* would have a hole blown in her side big enough to keep her from catching the *Coparelli*.

He was sure it was not a trap. He knew she was there, he knew that somehow she had been in their power and had been forced to help them, he knew she had risked her life to save his. He knew that she loved him.

And *that* was why he was terrified.

Suddenly he wanted to live. The blood-lust was gone: he was no longer interested in killing his enemies, defeating Rostov, frustrating the schemes of the Fedayeen or outwitting Egyptian Intelligence. He wanted to find Suza, and take her home, and spend the rest of his life with her. He was afraid to die.

He concentrated on steering his boat. Finding the *Karla* at night was not easy. He could keep a steady course but he had to estimate and make allowance for how much the wind and the waves were carrying him sideways. After fifteen minutes he knew he should have reached her, but she was nowhere to be seen. He began to zigzag in a search pattern, wondering desperately how far off course he was.

He was contemplating radioing the *Coparelli* for a new fix when suddenly the *Karla* appeared out of the night alongside him. She was moving fast, faster than his launch could go, and he had to reach the ladder at her bows before she was past, and at the same time avoid a collision. He gunned the launch forward, swerved away as the *Karla* rolled toward him, then turned back, homing in, while she rolled the other way.

He had the rope tied around his waist ready. The ladder came within reach. He flipped the engine of his launch into idle, stepped on the gunwale, and jumped. The *Karla* began to pitch forward as he landed on the ladder. He clung on while her prow went down into the waves. The sea came up to his waist, up to his shoulders. He took a deep breath as his head went under. He seemed to be under water for ever. The *Karla* just kept on going down. When he felt his lungs would burst she hesitated, and at last began to come up; and that seemed to take even longer. At last he broke surface and gulped lungfuls of air. He went up the ladder a few steps, untied the rope around his waist and made it fast to the ladder, securing the boat to the *Karla* for his escape. The magnetic mine was hanging from a rope across his shoulders. He took it off and slapped it on to the *Karla*'s hull.

The uranium was safe.

He shed his oilskin and climbed up the ladder.

The sound of the launch engine was inaudible in the noise of the wind, the sea, and the *Karla*'s own engines, but something must have attracted the attention of the man who looked over the rail just as Dickstein came up level with the deck. For a moment the man stared at Dickstein, his face registering amazement. Then Dickstein reached out his hand for a pull as he climbed over the rail. Automatically, with a natural instinct to help someone trying to get aboard out of the raging sea, the other man grabbed his arm. Dickstein got one leg over the rail, used his other hand to grab the outstretched arm, and threw the other man overboard and into the sea. His cry was lost in the wind. Dickstein brought the other leg over the rail and crouched down on the deck.

It seemed nobody had seen the incident.

The *Karla* was a small ship, much smaller than the *Coparelli*. There was only one superstructure, located amidships, two decks high. There were no cranes. The foredeck had a big hatch over the for'ard hold, but there was no aft hold: the crew accommodations and the engine room must occupy all the below-deck space aft, Dickstein concluded.

He looked at his watch. It was five-twenty-five. Suza's diversion should begin any moment, if she could do it.

He began to walk along the deck. There was some light from the ship's lamps, but one of the crew would have to look twice at him before being sure he was not one of them. He took his knife out of the sheath at his belt: he did not want to use his gun unless he had to, for the noise would start a hue and cry.

As he drew level with the superstructure a door opened, throwing a wedge of yellow light on to the rain-spattered deck. He dodged around the corner, flattening himself against the for'ard bulkhead. He heard two voices speaking Russian. The door slammed, and the voices receded as the men walked aft in the rain.

In the lee of the superstructure he crossed to the port side and continued toward the stern. He stopped at the corner and, looking cautiously around it, saw the two men cross the afterdeck and speak to a third man in the stern. He was tempted to take all three out with a burst from his submachine gun – three men was probably one fifth of the opposition – but decided not to: it was too early, Suza's diversion had not yet started and he had no idea where she was.

The two men came back along the starboard deck and went inside. Dickstein walked up to the remaining man in the stern, who seemed to be on guard. The man spoke to him in Russian. Dickstein grunted something unintelligible, the man replied with a question, then Dickstein was close enough and he jumped forward and cut the man's throat.

He threw the body overboard and retraced his steps. Two dead, and still they did not know he was on board. He looked at his watch. The luminous hands showed five-thirty. It was time to go inside.

He opened a door and saw an empty gangway and a companionway leading up, presumably to the bridge. He climbed the ladder. Loud voices came from the bridge. As he emerged through the companionhead he saw three men – the captain, the first officer and the second sublieutenant, he guessed. The first officer was shouting into the voice-pipe. A strange noise was coming back. As Dickstein brought his gun level, the captain pulled a lever and an alarm began to sound all over the ship. Dickstein pulled the trigger. The loud chatter of the gun was partly smothered by the wailing klaxon of the fire alarm. The three men were killed where they stood.

Dickstein hurried back down the ladder. The alarm must mean that Suza's diversion had started. Now all he had to do was stay alive until he found her.

The companionway from the bridge met the deck at

a junction of two gangways – a lateral one, which Dickstein had used, and another running the length of the superstructure. In response to the alarm doors were opening and men emerging all down both gangways. None of them seemed to be armed: this was a fire alarm, not a call to battle stations. Dickstein decided to run a bluff, and shoot only if it failed. He proceeded briskly along the central gangway, pushing his way through the milling men, shouting, 'Get out of the way' in German. They stared at him, not knowing who he was or what he was doing, except that he seemed to be in authority and there was a fire. One or two spoke to him. He ignored them. There was a rasping order from somewhere, and the men began to move purposefully. Dickstein reached the end of the gangway and was about to go down the ladder when the officer who had given the order came into sight and pointed at him, shouting a question.

Dickstein dropped down.

On the lower deck things were better organized. The men were running in one direction, toward the stern, and a group of three hands under the supervision of an officer was breaking out fire-fighting gear. There, in a place where the gangway widened for access to hoses, Dickstein saw something which made him temporarily unhinged, and brought a red mist of hatred to his eyes.

Suza was on the floor, her back to the bulkhead. Her legs were stretched out in front of her, her trousers torn. He could see her scorched and blackened skin through the tatters. He heard Rostov's voice, shouting

at her over the sound of the alarm: 'What did you tell
Dickstein?'

Dickstein jumped from the ladder onto the deck.
One of the hands moved in front of him. Dickstein
knocked him to the deck with an elbow blow to the
face, and jumped on Rostov.

Even in his rage, he realized that he could not use
the gun in this confined space while Rostov was so close
to Suza. Besides, he wanted to kill the man with his
hands.

He grabbed Rostov's shoulder and spun him around.
Rostov saw his face. 'You!' Dickstein hit him in the
stomach first, a pile-driving blow that buckled him at
the waist and made him gasp for air. As his head came
down Dickstein brought a knee up fast and hard,
snapping Rostov's chin up and breaking his jaw; then,
continuing the motion, he put all his strength behind a
kick into the throat that smashed Rostov's neck and
drove him backward into the bulkhead.

Before Rostov had completed his fall Dickstein
turned quickly around, went down on one knee to
bring his machine gun off his shoulder, and with Suza
behind him and to one side opened fire on three hands
who appeared in the gangway.

He turned again, picking Suza up in a fireman's lift,
trying not to touch her charred flesh. He had a moment
to think, now. Clearly the fire was in the stern, the
direction in which all the men had been running. If he
went forward now he was less likely to be seen.

He ran the length of the gangway, then carried her
up the ladder. He could tell by the feel of her body on

his shoulder that she was still conscious. He came off the top of the ladder to the main deck level, found a door and stepped out.

There was some confusion out on deck. A man ran past him, heading for the stern; another ran off in the opposite direction. Somebody was in the prow. Down in the stern a man lay on the deck with two others bending over him; presumably he had been injured in the fire.

Dickstein ran forward to the ladder that he had used to board. He eased his gun on to his shoulder, shifted Suza a little on the other shoulder, and stepped over the rail.

Looking about the deck as he started to go down, he knew that they had seen him.

It was one thing to see a strange face on board ship, wonder who he was, and delay asking questions until later because there was a fire alarm; but it was quite another to see someone leaving the ship with a body over his shoulder.

He was not quite halfway down the ladder when they began to shoot at him.

A bullet pinged off the hull beside his head. He looked up to see three men leaning over the rail, two of them with pistols. Holding on to the ladder with his left hand, he put his right hand to his gun, pointed up and fired. His aim was hopeless but the men pulled back.

And he lost his balance.

As the prow of the ship pitched up, he swayed to the left, dropped his gun into the sea and grabbed hold of the ladder with his right hand. His right foot slipped off the rung – and then, to his horror, Suza began to slip from his left shoulder.

'Hold on to me,' he yelled at her, no longer sure whether she was conscious or not. He felt her hands clutch at his sweater, but she continued to slip away, and now her unbalanced weight was pulling him even more to the left.

'No!' he yelled.

She slipped off his shoulder and went plunging into the sea.

Dickstein turned, saw the launch, and jumped, landing with a jarring shock in the well of the boat.

He called her name into the black sea all around him, swinging from one side of the boat to the other, his desperation increasing with every second she failed to surface. And then he heard, over the noise of the wind, a scream. Turning toward the sound he saw her head just above the surface, between the side of the boat and the hull of the *Karla*.

She was out of his reach.

She screamed again.

The launch was tied to the *Karla* by the rope, most of which was piled on the deck of the boat. Dickstein cut the rope with his knife, letting go of the end that was tied to the *Karla*'s ladder and throwing the other end toward Suza.

As she reached for the rope the sea rose again and engulfed her.

Up on the deck of the *Karla* they started shooting over the rail again.

He ignored the gunfire.

Dickstein's eyes swept the sea. With the ship and the boat pitching and rolling in different directions the chances of a hit were relatively slim.

After a few seconds that seemed hours, Suza surfaced again. Dickstein threw her the rope. This time she was able to grab it. Swiftly he pulled it, bringing her closer and closer until he was able to lean over the gunwale of the launch perilously and take hold of her wrists.

He had her now, and he would never let her go.

He pulled her into the well of the launch. Up above a machine gun opened fire. Dickstein threw the launch into gear, then fell on top of Suza, covering her body with his own. The launch moved away from the *Karla*, undirected, riding the waves like a lost surfboard.

The shooting stopped. Dickstein looked back. The *Karla* was out of sight.

Gently he turned Suza over, fearing for her life. Her eyes were closed. He took the wheel of the launch, looked at the compass, and set an approximate course. He turned on the boat's radio and called the *Coparelli*. Waiting for them to come in, he lifted Suza toward him and cradled her in his arms.

A muffled thud came across the water like a distant explosion: the magnetic mine.

The *Coparelli* replied. Dickstein said, 'The *Karla* is on fire. Turn back and pick me up. Have the sick bay ready for the girl – she's badly burned.' He waited for their acknowledgment, then switched off and stared at Suza's expressionless face. 'Don't die,' he said. 'Please don't die.'

She opened her eyes and looked up at him. She opened her mouth, struggling to speak. He bent his head to her. She said, 'Is it really you?'

'It's me,' he said.

The corners of her mouth lifted in a faint smile. 'I'll make it.'

There was the sound of a tremendous explosion. The fire had reached the fuel tanks of the *Karla*. The sky was lit up for several moments by a sheet of flame, the air was filled with a roaring noise, and the rain stopped. The noise and the light died, and so did the *Karla*.

'She's gone down,' Dickstein said to Suza. He looked at her. Her eyes were closed, she was unconscious again, but she was still smiling.

EPILOGUE

NATHANIEL DICKSTEIN resigned from the Mossad, and his name passed into legend. He married Suza and took her back to the kibbutz, where they tended grapes by day and made love half the night. In his spare time he organized a political campaign to have the laws changed so that his children could be classified Jewish; or, better still, to abolish classification.

They did not have children for a while. They were prepared to wait: Suza was young, and he was in no hurry. Her burns never healed completely. Sometimes, in bed, she would say, 'My legs are horrible,' and he would kiss her knees and tell her, 'They're beautiful, they saved my life.'

When the opening of the Yom Kippur War took the Israeli armed forces by surprise, Pierre Borg was blamed for the lack of advance intelligence, and he resigned. The truth was more complicated. The fault lay with a Russian intelligence officer called David Rostov – an elderly-looking man who had to wear a neck brace every moment of his life. He had gone to Cairo and, beginning with the interrogation and death of an Israeli agent called Towfik early in 1968, he had investigated all the events of that year and concluded that Kawash was a double agent. Instead of having Kawash tried and hanged for espionage, Rostov had told the Egyptians how to feed him disinformation, which Kawash, in all innocence, duly passed on to Pierre Borg.

The result was that Nat Dickstein came out of retirement to take over Pierre Borg's job for the duration of the war. On Monday, October 8, 1973, he attended a crisis meeting of the Cabinet. After three days of war the Israelis were in deep trouble. The Egyptians had crossed the Suez Canal and pushed the Israelis back into Sinai with heavy casualties. On the other front, the Golan Heights, the Syrians were pushing forward, again with heavy losses to the Israeli side. The proposal before the Cabinet was to drop atom bombs on Cairo and Damascus. Not even the most hawkish ministers actually relished the idea; but the situation was desperate and the Americans were dragging their heels over the arms airlift which might save the day.

The meeting was coming around to accepting the idea of using nuclear weapons when Nat Dickstein made his only contribution to the discussion: 'Of course, we could *tell* the Americans that we plan to drop these bombs – on Wednesday, say – unless they start the airlift immediately . . .'

And that is exactly what they did.

The airlift turned the tide of the war, and later a similar crisis meeting took place in Cairo. Once again, nobody was in favour of nuclear war in the Middle East; once again, the politicians gathered around the table began to persuade one another that there was no alternative; and once again, the proposal was stopped by an unexpected contribution.

This time it was the military that stepped in. Knowing of the proposal that would be before the assembled presidents, they had run checks on their nuclear strike force in readiness for a positive decision; and they had found that all the plutonium in the bombs had been taken out and replaced with iron filings. It was assumed that the Russians had done this, as they had mysteriously rendered unworkable the nuclear reactor in Qattara, before being expelled from Egypt in 1972.

That night, one of the presidents talked to his wife for five minutes before falling asleep in his chair. 'It's all over,' he told her. 'Israel has won – permanently. They have the bomb, and we do not, and that single fact will determine the course of history in our region for the rest of the century.'

'What about the Palestine refugees?' his wife said.

The president shrugged and began to light his last pipe of the day. 'I remember reading a story in the London *Times* . . . this must be five years ago, I suppose. It said that the Free Wales Army had put a bomb in the police station in Cardiff.'

'Wales?' said his wife. 'Where is Wales?'

'It is a part of England, more or less.'

'I remember,' she said. 'They have coal mines and choirs.'

'That's right. Have you any idea how long ago the Anglo-Saxons conquered the Welsh?'

'None at all.'

'Nor have I, but it must be more than a thousand years ago, because the Norman French conquered the Anglo-Saxons nine hundred years ago. You see? A thousand years, and they are still bombing police stations! The Palestinians will be like the Welsh . . . They can bomb Israel for a thousand years, but they will always be the losers.'

His wife looked up at him. All these years they had been together, and still he was capable of surprising her. She had thought she would never hear words like this from him.

'I will tell you something else,' he went on. 'There will have to be peace. We cannot possibly win, now, so we will have to make peace. Not now; perhaps not for five or ten years. But the time will come, and then I will have to go to Jerusalem and say, "No more war." I may even get some credit for it, when the dust settles. It is not how I planned to go down in history, but it's not such a bad way, for all that. "The man who brought peace to the Middle East." What would you say to that?'

His wife got up from her chair and came across to hold his hands. There were tears in her eyes. 'I would give thanks to God,' she said.

Franz Albrecht Pedler died in 1974. He died content. His life had seen some ups and downs – he had, after all, lived through the most ignominious period in the history of his nation – but he had survived and ended his days happily.

He had guessed what had happened to the uranium. One day early in 1969 his company had received a cheque for two million dollars, signed by A. Papagopolous, with a statement from Savile Shipping which read: 'To lost cargo.' The next day a representative of the Israeli Army had called, bringing the payment for the first shipment of cleaning materials. As he left, the army man had said, 'On the matter of your lost cargo, we would be happy if you were not to pursue any further inquiries.'

Pedler began to understand then. 'But what if Euratom asks me questions?'

'Tell them the truth,' the man said. 'The cargo was lost, and when you tried to discover what had happened to it, you found that Savile Shipping had gone out of business.'

'Have they?'

'They have.'

And that was what Pedler told Euratom. They sent an investigator to see him, and he repeated his story, which was completely true, if not truly complete. He said to the investigator, 'I suppose there will be publicity about all this soon.'

'I doubt it,' the investigator told him. 'It reflects badly on us. I don't suppose we'll broadcast the story unless we get more information.'

They did not get more information, of course; at least, not in Pedler's lifetime.

On Yom Kippur in 1974 Suza Dickstein went into labour.

In accordance with the custom of this particular

kibbutz, the baby was delivered by its father, with a midwife standing by to give advice and encouragement.

The baby was small, like both parents. As soon as its head emerged it opened its mouth and cried. Dickstein's vision became watery and blurred. He held the baby's head, checked that the cord was not around its neck, and said, 'Almost there, Suza.'

Suza gave one more heave, and the baby's shoulders were born, and after that it was all downhill. Dickstein tied the cord in two places and cut it, then again in accordance with the local custom he put the baby in the mother's arms.

'Is it all right?' she said.

'Perfect,' said the midwife.

'What is it?'

Dickstein said, 'Oh, God, I didn't even look . . . it's a boy.'

A little later Suza said, 'What shall we call him? Nathaniel?'

'I'd like to call him Towfik,' Dickstein said.

'Towfik? Isn't that an Arab name?'

'Yes.'

'Why? Why Towfik?'

'Well,' he said, 'that's a long story.'

POSTSCRIPT

From the London *Daily Telegraph* of May 7, 1977:

ISRAEL SUSPECTED OF HIJACKING SHIP WITH URANIUM
by Henry Miller in New York

Israel is believed to have been behind the disappearance from the high seas nine years ago of a uranium shipment large enough to build 30 nuclear weapons, it was disclosed yesterday.

Officials say that the incident was 'a real James Bond affair' and that although intelligence agencies in four countries investigated the mystery, it was never determined what had actually happened to the 200 tons of uranium ore that vanished . . .

– Quoted by permission of The Daily Telegraph, Ltd.